GOAL LINE

By
Bianca Sommerland
Copyright © 2015, Bianca Sommerland

ALL RIGHTS RESERVED

Edited by Lisa A. Hollett
Cover art by Reese Dante

Copyright © 2015, Bianca Sommerland

ALL RIGHTS RESERVED

Edited by Lisa A. Hollett
Cover art by Reese Dante

Photo credit to:
Jenn LeBlanc/Illustrated Romance

License Notes

This e-book is licensed for your personal enjoyment only. This e-book may not be resold or given away to other people. If you would like to share this book with another person, please purchase an additional copy for each recipient. If you're reading this book and did not purchase it, or it was not purchased for your use only, then please return it to the vendor and purchase your own copy. Thank you for respecting the hard work of this author.

This book is a work of fiction and any resemblance to persons, living or dead, or actual events is purely coincidental. The characters are products of the author's imagination and used fictitiously.

Licensed material is being used for illustrative purposes only and any person depicted in the licensed material is a model.

Warning

This book contains material not suitable for readers under 18. Besides the usual combination of loving in all different forms, there is edgeplay that may go beyond what some readers are used to. There are also confrontations with a past abuser and flashbacks that may trigger those who've been in this terrible situation. I'd like to add that if you ever find yourself the victim of physical, emotional, or mental abuse, please reach out to friends or family or one of the many organizations that can give you a safe way out. While this is fiction, some situations happen in real life. Everyone deserves to be treated with love and respect.

Author's Note: The Cobras series has a continuing arc about the franchise, players, and previous relationships. Some plots continue through the series and may involve more than the main relationship. The series is best read in order.

Also by Bianca Sommerland

The Dartmouth Cobras

Game Misconduct (The Dartmouth Cobras #1)
Defensive Zone (The Dartmouth Cobras #2)
Breakaway (The Dartmouth Cobras #3)
Offside (The Dartmouth Cobras #4)
Delayed Penalty (The Dartmouth Cobras #5)
Iron Cross (The Dartmouth Cobras #6)
Goal Line (The Dartmouth Cobras #7)
Line Brawl (The Dartmouth Cobras #8) – Coming 2016

Also
Deadly Captive
Deadly Captive (Collateral Damage)
The End – Coming 2015

Celestial Pets-Evil's Embrace

Rosemary Entwined
Rosemary & Mistletoe

The Trip

Dedication

Oh captain... Mon capitaine
1931-2014

Acknowledgements

This could be a really long list of people, but I'm going to keep it as short and sweet as possible. ;)

I have a massive support group consisting of readers, authors, and people in the business who have been there for me at every turn, whether I'm streaming down life's highway or stuck on a muddy dirt road. You all know who you are. You're the beautiful people that make living my dream still feel like a dream even when it looks more like a nightmare.

During one of the most horrible times of my life, I had a few people who were always willing to hold me while I fell apart, even when they couldn't be there physically. Stacey and Doug Price, I have never had truer friends in my life and I'm grateful for you every day. I'm also happy I haven't driven you both nuts yet!

Reese Dante, who does all the beautiful Cobra covers, you are such an amazing person and I'm so grateful to have you in my life. Jennifer Zapata, we've shared so much insanity while keeping one another sane and you know just when I need to laugh and forget and how to bring me to a better place. Stella Price, I don't care what anyone says, you are such a warm, loving person and I feel damn blessed to have you in my life.

As always, Cherise, your honesty in critting my work has made Goal Line a much better book. Your faith that I can always 'Do better' has made for stronger characters. And has made ME stronger time and time again.

To all those who helped with the language and facts in the books, I would name each and every one of you, but I've kept you all waiting long enough for this book! <3 So what I will say is it's here, now, because you were willing to share your stories, to give advice, and talk over different concepts. Thank you from the bottom of my crazy little heart!

Dartmouth Cobra Roster

Centers

No	Name	Age	Ht	Wt	Shot	Birth Place
27	Scott Demyan	29	6'3"	198	L	Anaheim, California, USA
45	Keaton Manning	32	5'11"	187	R	Ulster, Ireland
18	Ctirad Jelinek	28	6'0"	204	L	Rakovnik, Czech Republic
3	Erik Hjalmar	25	6'3"	219	R	Stockolm, Sweden
4	Heath Ladd	19	6'1"	198	R	Bourke, Australia

Left Wings

No	Name	Age	Ht	Wt	Shot	Birth Place
16	Luke Carter	24	5'11"	190	L	Warroad, Minnesota, USA
53	Shawn Pischlar	30	6'0"	200	L	Villach, Austria
71	Dexter Tousignant	25	6'2"	208	L	Matane, Quebec, Canada
5	Ian White	26	6'1"	212	L	Winnipeg, Manitoba, Canada
42	Braxton Richards	19	5'11	196	L	Edmonton, Alberta, Canada

Right Wings

No	Name	Age	Ht	Wt	Shot	Birth Place
22	Tyler Vanek	23	5'8"	174	R	Greenville, North Carolina, USA
72	Dante Palladino	36	6'2"	215	L	Fossano, Italy
21	Bobby Williams	35	5'10"	190	R	Sheffield, England
46	Vadim Zetsev	28	6'0"	203	R	Yaroslavl, Russia
66	Zachary Pearce	33	6'0"	210	L	Ottawa, Ontario, Canada

Defense

No	Name	Age	Ht	Wt	Shot	Birth Place
6	Dominik Mason	33	6'4"	235	R	Chicago, Illinois, USA
17	Einar Olsson	29	6'0"	200	L	Örnsköldsvik, Sweden
74	Beau Mischlue	27	6'2"	223	L	Gaspe, Quebec, Canada
26	Peter Kral	29	6'1"	200	L	Hannover, Germany
2	Mirek Brends	35	6'1"	214	L	Malmö, Sweden
11	Sebastian Ramos	30	6'5"	227	R	Arlanza, Burgos, Spain
40	Max Perron	32	6'2"	228	L	Alamo, Texas, USA

Goalies

No	Name	Age	Ht	Wt	Shot	Birth Place
20	Landon Bower	27	6'3"	215		Gaspe, Quebec, Canada
29	Dave Hunt	21	6'2"	217		Hamilton, Ontario, Canada

Chapter One

Mid April

Ugly and threadbare, the patchwork sofa had never really gone with anything in the apartment, but Sahara Dionne still missed the big old thing. Funny, because she'd once playfully complained about the comfy eyesore to one of her roommates, but she'd found a new love for the sofa when she'd learned about the sentiment attached to it. The new, pale blue loveseat taking its place didn't have the same character.

Actually, the whole apartment felt empty.

You're the last woman standing, Sahara.

She laughed at her own dry humor, but it was close enough to the truth. Akira had moved out months ago, but Jami had still considered this her home until yesterday. She was engaged, and there was no point to her staying here any longer.

Not that she'd been here often, but now the move was official. All her things were gone.

And Sahara was alone.

She walked around the apartment, all the rooms bright with their big windows, but one room was completely empty. She could set up an exercise room or something, but she simply closed the door so she wouldn't have to think that far ahead yet. The kitchen looked the same; the girls hadn't taken any dishes or furniture from there, so Sahara curled up on the window seat Scott Demyan, her closest male friend and one of the players for the Dartmouth Cobras, had made for them. The teddy bear he'd gotten her for Valentine's day—because, as he pointed out, guys could get gifts for their fake girlfriends—sat on the gold cushion by the window. She hugged the bear and opened Facebook on her phone.

Putting up a status report that was all depressing wouldn't be good; she had too many followers since she was the alternate captain for the Cobras' Ice Girls, but people liked her being real. So she typed in a little happy face, choosing her words carefully.

Got the place all to myself! So happy for Akira and Jami, they deserve the best—I better get invites to the weddings! Lol! Being single is cool though. So many hot boys to play with. How does a girl decide...not that I'm in a rush! <g> Did you see Pischlar's new tattoo? She added the picture he'd let her take the last time she saw him at the Delgado Forum. A phoenix that looked like it was rising from melting flesh over his ribs. She could almost feel the heat of the fire even from the picture. In person the tattoo was...breathtaking.

She could say more, but she decided just to post the update. The likes came fast—her followers *loved* her posting stuff about the players. And making them happy gave her something to do. She grinned at the comments and replied as fast as she could. Chin resting on the head of the teddy bear, she read a longer post from a woman who was absolutely in love with Shawn Pischlar, one of the Cobras' forwards. Apparently she'd gotten him to sign her arm and now the ink was permanent. She gave all the reasons why Pischlar was the ultimate fantasy boyfriend—and then suggested Sahara find someone else because Pischlar was *hers*.

I so have to get Pisch to look at this. He'll find it funny. Sahara smiled as she checked her messages. Some from her cousins who wanted to know if she'd be in New York since the Cobras were playing the Islanders in the first round of the playoffs. Sahara told them she'd try, but the reminder of who the Cobras would be facing made it hard to keep up the happy front. Grant Higgins, her ex-boyfriend, played for the Islanders. The first game was tomorrow. In Dartmouth.

And there was a message from him. She clicked on it and held her breath as she read.

Grant: You doing okay, babe? You seem sad.

Sahara frowned and checked her status again. How had she seemed sad?

She shook her head and replied. *I'm fine.*

Grant: *You're not. I know things ended bad, and it's my fault, but I still consider you a friend. Did you hear about my mom?*

Sahara had liked Grant's mother. The poor woman had died while volunteering overseas in Haiti as a teacher. When Sahara had first heard about her death, she'd been tempted to call Grant. But she was afraid. They were over, and she needed to make that clear.

She was careful as she typed her reply: *I heard and I'm so sorry. She was a wonderful woman. But the team putting up a memorial for her was nice. It's good that you have them.*

No reply for a long time. She looked out the window, enjoying the view. This part of Nova Scotia, smack dab in the middle of Dartmouth, was nice. Not close to the ocean, but even looking out at the backyards with pools and freshly planted gardens was pleasant.

A ding and she glanced at her phone.

Grant: *I miss you.*

How to answer that without encouraging him? She bit the tip of her tongue. And wrote a quick response. *We're both doing better now, Grant.*

Grant: *I need to see you. Can I? I'm at the door, but I'll go away if you want me to.*

The knock at the door tripped up her heart. Her phone rang. Akira. She didn't move and kept her voice low as she answered. "Hello?"

"*Pischlar?* Hell, your 'fans' might buy that, but we both know you're not moving on with him. And if you're even considering it, I'm going to kick your ass!"

Sahara let out a strained laugh. "I've had great scenes with him." Another knock. She pressed her eyes shut. "Damn it, I don't know what to do."

"About what?" Akira let out a sharp "*Hush!*" to whoever was talking to her. "If the house is too quiet, come over here."

"I have to get used to this. I'll be okay, but…I think Grant's at the door."

"*What?* Grant—as in your *ex?* Damn it, Sahara, don't you dare answer. I'm calling the cops—Cort, relax. I—"

"I'm *fine*, Akira!" Sahara rose off the window seat. Grant wasn't banging hard or anything. She heard him speaking softly on the other side of the door, but she couldn't make out what he was saying yet. "His mother just died. I can't ignore him."

"Yes, you can! Sahara, he hurt you!"

"I know that, but we had a messed-up relationship. You only know my side. And it's not like I'm going to take him back." Standing by the door, Sahara stared at the lock. She didn't have to open the door. She really *could* ignore him. But she didn't want to. She wasn't that cruel. "Maybe we can be friends. Would be good since the Cobras are playing the Islanders. I can ask him to stop getting the boys riled up. Make it a clean game."

"Fuck no. Sahara, listen to me." Akira's tone was soft. Gentle. Her words…not so much. "A man who hits a woman can never be a friend. Call the cops, or I will."

"Don't be dramatic. You don't know why…" Sahara scowled as she put her hand on the lock. Her friends loved her, and she appreciated their concern, but she hated how easily they dismissed her responsibility for how the relationship had failed. "I have to let you go. I love you. And I'll talk to you tomorrow."

Hanging up, Sahara made up her mind and unlocked the door. Grant stood there, and… She wasn't sure what she'd expected, but he looked exactly the same as he had the day they'd met. That charming, boyish face, dirty blond hair badly in need of a trim only complementing his laid-back manner. He had a way of giving off the impression that he didn't give a damn about anything, but you only had to check out his perfectly maintained body to know that wasn't true. He was rugged and buff and so damn hot. He'd turned her head even though she'd grown up around enough hockey players for her to be used to big, muscular guys.

A dull ache in her chest made speaking difficult as he met her eyes with his dreamy, deep blue ones. How damn easy would it be to forget the horrible end of the relationship and just focus on the wonderful times they'd had? To forgive him for turning mean, then violent.

Don't even fucking think about it, Sahara. Maybe she could forgive him, but she'd never forget what he'd done to her. She held the door just wide enough to talk to him, leaving no doubt that he wasn't being welcomed inside.

"What are you doing here, Grant?" She bit down hard on her bottom lip, a lip he'd left swollen and bloody one too many times, and refused to feel bad as he shuffled his feet and dropped his gaze. "How did you find me?"

"Facebook." He shoved his hands into the pockets of his faded blue jeans. "Your location was on the message, so I figured you weren't trying to hide. I saw your car out back… One of your neighbors told me which door was yours."

"Yeah, because that's not creepy or stalkerish." Sahara frowned when he shrugged. "This is a bad idea. You have a game tomorrow and you should focus on that. I don't want any trouble—"

Grant shook his head and brought his hands up, fast enough that she almost jumped back and slammed the door in his face, but he simply held them up in an "I'm harmless" gesture. "No trouble—and damn it, Sahara, I hate that you're afraid of me. I have a horrible temper and I've been working on controlling it. I love you, and I understand that you can't love me back, but my mother would want me to make things right with you. She'd be so ashamed of me if she knew…"

Well, he was right about that. Mrs. Higgins was—*had* been—the gentlest, most caring person Sahara had ever met. Losing her must have forced Grant to face all the mistakes he'd made, because he hadn't accepted any blame before. Sure, he'd said he was sorry when he hurt her, but he'd always accused her of pissing him off to get a reaction.

And she'd been so blinded by love for him that she'd taken responsibility for each and every time he'd lifted a hand to her.

Never again.

But she'd give him a chance to make things right. To prove he was the man she'd fallen in love with, rather than the monster he became. "Is that all you want, Grant? Seriously? You're fine just being friends?"

"That's all I want." Grant backed away from the door. "You're right, coming here was…creepy. I just wasn't sure if you'd meet me anywhere, but maybe we can have coffee sometime before the teams head to New York for the third round?"

"I guess so…" She pursed her lips, knowing if she waited too long, one of her friends would talk her out of giving him so much as the time of day. He'd clearly made progress, and she didn't want to ruin that by turning him down. "What are you doing now?"

He ducked his head. "Trying to convince myself this is for real? I imagined all the things I would say to you, but every time your only reply was 'fuck off.'"

She laughed and rolled her eyes. "Would probably be the smartest response. Wait here, let me grab my shoes."

"You won't regret this, babe. I promise."

Those words were hauntingly familiar, but she shook off her misgivings as she grabbed her running shoes from beside the door. She pulled them on, wondering for a second if she should change out of her black yoga pants and baggy white sweater, but decided, if he wanted to hang out, he'd take her as she was.

Grabbing her keys from the entry table, she joined him in the hall, locked her door, then led the way out to the parking lot behind the apartment. "We're taking separate cars. And I'm warning you, any funny business—"

His fingers were suddenly at her ribs, tickling her as he laughed. "Like this?"

"Grant!" She squealed and smacked his hands away. "Stop!"

A huge body shoved between her and Grant, knocking Grant onto the pavement while tugging Sahara back. Cortland Nash, Akira's boyfriend and the head of the Cobras' security team, pulled off his leather jacket and handed it to Sahara as he held Grant down with a boot on his throat. "Go wait in my car, Sahara. I'll make sure this bastard never comes near you again."

Eyes wide, Sahara dropped the jacket and quickly latched on to Cort's arm as he jerked Grant to his knees by the front of his shirt. "Cort, don't! You don't understand—"

"You were screaming for him to stop." Cort glanced over at her, speaking like he thought she was a little slow. "What's to understand?"

"He was tickling me. We're going for coffee. I'm fine!" She slapped Cort's arm when he hauled back like he was going to hit Grant no matter what she said. "Let him go! Damn it, Cort, he's playing tomorrow."

This time Cort released Grant. And turned to her, drawing her aside and keeping his voice low. "I get that he's with your old team, but they have other players. There's no need to protect him. Go inside if you won't get in my car. I won't give you details."

The man was insane. She grabbed his arm again before he could resume his attack on Grant—who, for some reason, hadn't moved. "I'm not going inside. You are going to leave him alone."

"And why is that, exactly?" He glared at Grant, which got Grant out of his stupor and scrambling to his feet, closer to his car. "Did he threaten you?"

"No. And I think you should go home before someone calls the cops. My house is not on the list of places you're supposed to be with that ankle monitor."

"I don't give a fuck." Cort groaned as his phone went off. He held up a finger, then answered. "Yeah, I know. Like I give a shit? One minute." He looked at Grant. "I'll give you ten fucking seconds to get the hell out of here. After that, the only question is where you want me to send your body."

Someone was shouting on the phone. Cort lifted his hand and started folding fingers down as he stared down at Grant.

And continued his conversation with the caller, sounding much calmer. "No, ma'am. I think you heard wrong."

He continued counting down with his fingers. Started on the last five.

Grant shot her an apologetic look and got in his car, swerving out of the parking lot before Cort reached one.

After ending the call, Cort faced Sahara with his hands on her shoulders. "Give me one good reason not to make sure the man can't walk, never mind play."

Sahara planted her hands in the center of Cort's chest and shoved him away from her, so angry she couldn't find words at first. Then she found plenty. "His mother just died and he needs a friend! I can't believe you just did that! You're nothing but a...a thug! You're protecting me from him with violence? Do you really think you're better than him?"

Cort blinked, jerking back like she'd slapped him. "I've never hurt a woman, Sahara. Akira told me not to come, but she was crying—she's afraid for you. The man left bruises on you. I thought you were smarter than this."

"I'm smart enough to handle my own affairs. I'll explain things to Akira, but I don't have to explain myself to you!" Tears blurred her vision as she spun away from him and ran back into the apartment. Grant had reached out to her and now he probably thought he couldn't come near her if he wanted to live. She slammed her door and checked her phone. He hadn't called. Not that she blamed him. Apparently being around her wasn't safe.

Groaning, she slumped onto her stiff new loveseat and buried her face in her hands. The one chance she'd had to tear out a dark page of her past was ruined.

Her phone rang. She snatched it up and let out a sob of relief when she saw Grant's number. She answered. "I'm so sorry about that. Are you okay?"

"I'm all right." Grant laughed nervously. "That dude was nuts! Who is he?"

"One of my best friends' boyfriends. I talked to her just before I answered the door."

"Ah...well, then I can't really blame her for sending him."

Sahara blinked. "What?"

"Sweetie, all she knows is who I was. She's right to worry, and I'm happy you have people who care about you." He sighed. "Maybe, one day, I'll earn their trust. And yours. But that won't happen overnight."

She rubbed her eyes and smiled. If Akira could hear Grant now, she'd understand why Sahara couldn't turn her back on him. He needed someone to believe in him. She could be that person.

Reclining on the sofa, she let out a rough exhale. "Well, you're off to an awesome start."

* * * *

With the first playoff game starting tomorrow, Dominik Mason knew he should rest. Instead, he ditched his white tank top, pulled on boxing gloves, and prepared to face off against the Dartmouth Cobras' assistant coach. A man he'd once considered a good friend. Maybe would again someday.

Today wasn't about being friendly. Assistant Coach Sloan Callahan had invited the players for optional physical training in the semiprivate boxing club the Cobras' owner had recently drawn up a contract with. Other hockey teams had their players take boxing for conditioning and discipline, and the owner had decided the Cobras were badly in need of both. With professionals carefully supervising, any risk was negligible. A fight on the ice would do more damage, but most of the players weren't brawlers anyway. They'd pull their punches and each match would be short. Not a single man wanted to do real harm.

As the team's captain, Dominik was expected to set a good example. But he was more than willing to get into the ring with Sloan and work off some steam. He let the trainer put in his mouthguard and glanced around the large, dimly lit room. All the men were dressed similarly to him and Sloan, in white tank tops or T-shirts and black and gold Cobra gym shorts. Several players had teamed up at the hanging punching bags. Scott Demyan, reformed playboy and one of their team's top snipers, secured a bag for their rookie backup goalie, Dave Hunt. The youngster was a large mammal with a shorter fuse than Dominik had on his worst day. The way he hit the bag, with precise jabs and powerful swings, made it clear he'd done this before.

Doesn't look like training helped the kid control his temper much. Dominik grinned when Demyan released the bag and stumbled backward when it swung and hit him. Demyan's lack of experience was pretty obvious, but with hands like his, the last thing they wanted was for him to be fighting on the ice.

Sloan was the prime example of why. He'd had a hell of a shot when he'd played for them, but he'd broken his hand on a helmet during a fight, trying to prove himself an asset when the old team management had attempted to turn the Cobras into a more "physical" team. His bones hadn't set right, and after surgery, his stickhandling and shot had never returned to his former elite level, so he'd retired young. But he was still a damn good leader and he'd be a decent match for Dominik in a fight.

Bouncing in place to warm up, Dominik glanced over at the boxing trainer who gestured for him and Sloan to meet in the center of the ring. A feminine cheer drew his attention to the side, and he had to bite down on his mouthpiece to keep from groaning when he saw the Delgado girls. Or, more specifically, Oriana.

He'd been in love with Oriana once, had shared her with Sloan and Max Perron, a man the team and fans called The Catalyst. Oriana was married to Max and collared by Sloan. She'd once been collared by Dominik, but he knew now he'd never really meshed with the other two men. They were Oriana's future. Together, they made her happy. He'd only stood in their way.

Enough time had passed for him to make peace with letting her go, but he wasn't comfortable with her cheering on Sloan from the sidelines. Not that he could tell her to go away. Her family might not own the team anymore, but they were still deeply involved in management. With Silver here and... Yeah, there he was, their brother, Ford, standing near the door observing all the players with detached interest. The siblings had a right to see how well prepared the players were for tomorrow's game. Maybe, if he could just be professional about the whole thing, her being here wouldn't matter.

Her being here doesn't *matter, Mason.* Dominik nodded to himself and bumped his gloves against Sloan's. The other man didn't seem at all affected by his woman's presence. Dominik tensed and relaxed his muscles. Rolled his neck and backed a few paces, giving Sloan the opening to make the first move. He didn't *really* want to hurt the other man, but the sadistic fuck would get off on hurting him. Best to end this as quickly as possible.

Sloan's dark green eyes fixed on Dominik's face and his lips quirked at the edges. He inched forward, fists raised.

A whistle blew and they both looked over to the left where the head coach, Roger Shero, was climbing into the ring. Gray and white streaked his dark auburn hair and the beard he'd started to grow. He reminded Dominik of someone's grandfather, soft enough for a kid to sit in his lap for story-time. But he was a damn good coach, tailoring his approach to each player, not missing so much as a dirty look or a grumble in the locker room. No doubt he knew every detail of Dominik and Sloan's past conflict.

The older man took off his black suit jacket and handed it to the trainer before waving him away. He straightened his black-and-white striped tie, his brown eyes twinkling with amusement as he looked from Dominik to Sloan.

"I'd hoped the two of you would get us started." Shero patted Sloan's bare shoulder. "New whiteboard rule proposed by Callahan. You boys have a problem, it gets resolved in the ring. No more fighting in the locker room." He laughed and shook his head. "For the two of you, perhaps I should add the hallway as well."

Not much fazed Sloan, but his cheeks reddened slightly at the reminder of their scuffle weeks ago. The fight hadn't started with them, but it had escalated with their lingering animosity. He jerked his chin in a sharp nod. "You got it, Coach."

Dominik inclined his head. "I'm good with that, Coach Shero."

"Excellent. Keep it clean and don't forget we've got a game tomorrow. You get five minutes to knock each other around." Shero stepped back and motioned them toward one another. "You may begin."

Cheers from the players that gathered around Oriana and Silver distracted Sloan for a split second. Dominik swung his fist, clipping Sloan in the jaw just hard enough to get his attention. Dark eyes narrowed, Sloan brought his fist up to protect his face and shifted sideways, snapping out a right hook at Dominik's ribs.

Smoothly blocking, Dominik drove an uppercut into Sloan's chin. Sloan stumbled a few steps, then returned in full force, each punch solid, but none landing anywhere that could slow Dominik in the least. The man didn't have the technique to catch Dominik off guard. He blocked fairly well, but he was tiring himself out with each ineffective swing.

Maybe Dominik had misjudged him. He snapped a jab into Sloan's sternum, then a left hook to Sloan's face. Kept swinging until Sloan's back hit the ropes. A sharp command from Shero and Dominik retreated to let Sloan catch his breath. The satisfaction in overpowering the other man was shallow. Without the rules of the ring, Sloan might have had a chance, but he was playing Dominik's game now.

Blood pumping, his whole body vibrating with energy, Dominik watched Sloan recover and turned as Sloan circled him. He braced when Sloan lunged forward, absorbing the impact and slamming both his fists into Sloan's sides. He shoved Sloan off and cracked him in the jaw hard enough to end the fight. Sloan fell to the mat, snarled, and bounded to his feet.

Shero blew the whistle. Time was up. He grabbed Dominik's arm. "Good match! The enforcer takes this round." He glanced over at Sloan. "Gloves off and shake hands. Show the men how it's done."

After removing his gloves, Dominik pulled out his mouthpiece. He met Sloan's eyes, not sure how he'd take the loss. He held out his hand.

Grinning, Sloan took Dominik's hand. His grip was solid, not a display of strength, but a genuine handshake. He even laughed as Dominik's brow furrowed and pulled him in for a rough, backslapping hug. "If I'd wanted to win, I wouldn't have gotten in the ring with you."

Dominik snorted. "Fair enough."

Sloan lowered his voice. "This isn't the end. We'll pretend for the guys though. If they think we've gotten over our shit, they'll do the same."

Jaw hardening, Dominik released Sloan's hand. He forced a smile as he got out of the ring, but he couldn't shake the impact of Sloan's words. There was no reason for them to hang on to the past. He'd moved on. Oriana was Sloan's now. What more did the man want?

But as Sloan moved over to the refreshment table with Oriana at his side, Dominik hesitated. His mouth was dry and he wanted to grab a bottle of Gatorade, but seeing Oriana touch Sloan's cheek with concern in her eyes brought a bitter taste to his mouth. He inhaled slowly and went to the pile of white towels on a bench against the wall at the other side of the room.

Something cold touched his back. He cursed and spun around, almost knocking Tyler Vanek, the team's golden boy, right on his ass.

Vanek held out the bottle of water like a peace offering. Behind him, Raif Zovko, the team's newest star acquisition, steadied Vanek with a hand on the young man's shoulder. Zovko was Vanek's Dom, and one of the few players Dominik considered a friend.

So Dominik took the bottle and grinned at Vanek. "Sorry, kid. Adrenaline has me all edgy." He uncapped the bottle, gulped half, and then wiped his lips with the back of his hand. "You're not here to fight, are you?"

"Hell no! No one I hate enough to try and punch them, and Chicklet would get pissed if I came home with my face all messed up. And Raif would do bad things to me that would be no fun before I even got home to her, so…" Vanek shrugged, then looked over at Sloan. "Did that really work for you guys? If Callahan hadn't been there for me in the hospital, I might have considered getting in the ring with him."

Zovko's expression shifted from amusement to interest. "If you truly want to be beaten by Callahan, I'm sure it could be arranged, Ty."

"Umm…no thanks." Vanek chewed on his bottom lip. "Besides, Chicklet wouldn't let you—"

"Would you care to make a wager on that?" Zovko smirked when Vanek quickly shook his head, then turned to Dominik. "We are here because Demyan has asked to meet me in the ring."

"Awesome." Dominik shook his head and looked over to where Scott Demyan, one of the trio—which included Vanek—that players, and now fans, referred to as the "trouble triplets." Zovko had dated Demyan's partner, Zachary Pearce, in the minors. When Zovko joined the team, many had believed he and Pearce were having an affair. The issue was resolved, but apparently Demyan wanted his pound of flesh for his troubles.

Done with his own match, Dominik had planned to go home and chill for the night, but he decided to stay and offer Zovko his support since the man had few friends on the team. Besides, several of the other pairings were worth watching. The reasons for the fights were laughable. Everything from hogging the puck to not paying the fair share on a dinner bill. But unlike Sloan and Dominik, most of the players seemed to be having fun in the ring. Men came out laughing and arranging to go out for a couple of beers.

The last fight was supposed to be Demyan and Zovko, but raised voices on the other side of the crowd cut off Coach Shero's call to the ring. Ian White, who usually handled the fights on the ice when Dominik wasn't out there, was staring down Hunt. Both appeared to be growling like two junkyard dogs off their chains. Hell, Dominik must have missed whatever drama had come between the two, but Shero didn't seem surprised.

Hunt headed for the ring. "Come on, *Bruiser*. You think you can take me?"

White laughed and followed him. "I know it, kid. Let's go."

Climbing out of the ring, Shero cut them off and shook his head. "No. Matches are planned in advance. Yours wasn't approved."

"Come on, Coach. We've got shi—stuff to work out." White looked past Hunt, a taunting smile on his lips. "If not, I'm out of here. Wanna go for a beer, Richards?"

Braxton Richards, the youngest player on the team, quickly shook his head. Hunt had taken to looking after the kid, so maybe he thought White was a bad influence? White's interest in Richards seemed slightly off, though Dominik couldn't quite put his finger on why. Either way, Richards clearly didn't like the position he'd found himself in. His eyes were wide and he was pale. Poor boy.

Thankfully, Shawn Pischlar, a solid player and easygoing Dom, was right by his side. Speaking low as he flung his arm around Richards's shoulders. Whatever he said had Richards ducking his head and laughing.

"Back off, Pisch." Hunt changed direction and strode up to Richards's side, looking ready to yank the rookie away from Pischlar. He didn't seem at all comforted by the way Pischlar moved his arm and stepped back. But he appeared to have forgotten about fighting White.

The two young men walked out. White grunted something at Pischlar before trailing after them.

Pischlar went to the refreshment table to grab an apple.

"Consider this experiment a failure, Callahan." Shero retrieved his suit jacket from a bench by the ring and shot Zovko and Demyan an apologetic look. "This may have worked for minor issues, but I am beginning to see how easily it could be taken advantage of. Boxing is excellent for conditioning, but I hope the two of you can find a peaceful resolution."

"I see no reason why not." Zovko turned to Demyan, holding out his hand. After a brief hesitation, Demyan shook it.

But he didn't say anything. Simply joined the crowd leaving.

Dominik's lips thinned as he took in the unease that had been left behind. He hated the idea that the "experiment" had been a complete waste of time. But maybe Sloan was right. Maybe, once the men saw them getting along, they'd be motivated to do the same. With the playoffs on the line, personal shit wasn't all that important.

He approached the table where Sloan stood with Oriana, Silver, and Ford. Sloan had taken a peach from the fruit bowl. He pulled the large knife from the watermelon platter and used it to slice a small sliver of the peach.

Oriana pressed her teeth into her lush bottom lip, half her attention on her siblings, most on Sloan who licked the peach juice off the knife.

Silver didn't appear to notice. "Landon will be between the pipes tomorrow. His leg is fine. He had a nasty bruise but no serious damage."

"That's good." Oriana pressed her hand to her cheek, blushing as Sloan slid the blade carefully over the flesh of the peach.

"Oh, get a room. Damn it, Sloan, I think you're getting Ford off." Silver tossed her long blond hair over one shoulder and shoved her brother. "Gross."

"Fuck off, Silver." Ford folded his arms over his chest, but he was watching the knife as though hypnotized. "Sloan trains Cort. I'm…interested."

"Mmm. Knife play involves a certain…finesse." Sloan turned the peach, drawing the blade over it in a way that barely broke the skin. He'd obviously been practicing.

When he and Dominik had played with Oriana together, Sloan had kept to the mental aspect of knives in the bedroom. Dominik shouldn't be surprised that he'd taken the play to the next level, but he hadn't let himself think on the kinds of scenes Sloan would be doing with Oriana.

And he didn't want to start now. Without drawing attention to himself, he moved out the door, prepared to leave. A small, soft hand touched his arm and he took a deep breath. He looked at the hand, long fingers tipped in perfect French-manicured nails, so pale against his dark skin. A large diamond in the engagement ring, not the small diamond in Oriana's wedding ring.

He met Silver's eyes.

She studied his face. "Maybe this should wait. Are you—?"

"I'm fine. What is it, Silver?"

"Hanes Brands and Champion have asked you to do a series of commercials. I don't know if your manager spoke to you, since he told me he wasn't interested because he thinks they just want a 'token black man.' His words." Her pink-glossed lips thinned and she was all business. "I disagree. You're the captain of a team about to make the playoffs. And you're a good-looking man. I don't appreciate your manager making issues where there are none and—"

"I'll do it. And I'll deal with him, don't worry, sweetheart." Dominik grinned and gave Silver a hug. He kissed her forehead before letting her go. He still considered her family even though he wasn't with her sister. "He feeds on drama. Don't let him get to you."

"Ford told me to let him handle the man, but fuck that." She wrinkled her nose. "Sorry, Dean's asked me to practice speaking in a more 'professional manner,' but between dealing with your manager and my brother, I'm at my wits' end."

"I'll let you know if I'm offended. You're fine, Silver." Dominik held the door open, pausing in the hall when Silver put her hand on his arm again. "Was there something else?"

"Are you okay? Really?" Silver eased the door shut. The hall was empty, which seemed to encourage her to drop the business persona and talk to him as the young woman who'd know him for years. "You won the fight, but what was the point? There's no prize and nothing's changed."

"I think *that* was the point, little one. Not for the others, but for me and Sloan." There was no use holding back and pretending with Silver. So he spoke plainly. "We will get through each and every game, deal with every situation in a way that's best for the team, but at the end of the day, we aren't friends. He will go home with your sister, and I've accepted that."

"Have you?"

"Yes."

"Okay, that's good, I guess. But…" She sighed and looked down at her hand on his arm. "Where does that leave you? You aren't training anyone at the club. You're not moving on."

"I've moved on. Don't worry—just because I'm single doesn't mean I'm pining over your sister. I'm focused on the game." Not the full truth, but he didn't need to bare his soul to Silver. "Enough meddling now, pet. How's Amia doing?"

Silver's eyes brightened at the mention of her daughter. She smiled, practically glowing with pride. "She's taken her first steps, but she still crawls more than anything. She talks nonstop, but I have no idea what she's saying most of the time. Dean said that's normal. You should see her."

"I'd like that."

"Sahara offered to babysit while we go to Casey's spring concert next Thursday. You could always—"

He chuckled and put his finger over Silver's lips. "I don't need you setting me up with Sahara. We are good friends. I'm not sure why people think there's more going on."

She snorted and folded her arms over her small breasts. "You're full of shit. When you're together, it's obvious—"

"Careful, Silver." Dominik didn't bother lowering his voice as he spotted the team's starting goalie, Landon Bower, ambling down the hall. Silver was his fiancée and the mother of his child, but Bower was a proficient Master who expected his sub to behave herself when addressing other Doms. Letting him handle Silver was the quickest way out of the conversation. Her smirk proved she hadn't noticed Bower's approach. There was some satisfaction in wiping it off her face with his next words. "I have no tolerance for rudeness. Your

Masters are creative with their punishments. Don't force me to request they give you one on my behalf."

Her eyes widened and the color faded from her cheeks. "You wouldn't—"

"He won't have to." Bower slid his hand under Silver's hair and took a firm hold on the back of her neck. "Apologize and come with me. Dean had a special night planned for us, but I have a feeling we'll have to address your behavior first."

"But I…" Silver cut herself off at a dark look from Bower. She dropped her gaze to the tip of her pink high-heeled shoes as she did what she'd been told. "I'm sorry, Sir."

"You're forgiven, sweetheart." Dominik met Bower's eyes and inclined his head. The man wouldn't be too hard on Silver, but she'd likely think twice before playing matchmaker again. He watched the couple walk down the hall, then headed in the other direction toward the gym's locker room. After a quick shower, he changed into blue jeans and a plain white T-shirt. Pulled on his wool, khaki-colored jacket, and grabbed his sports bag. In the parking lot, he hesitated beside his pickup truck and pulled out his phone.

Despite her improper approach, Silver had a point. There'd been the potential of a relationship between him and Sahara. He wasn't sure who'd decided to draw the line at friendship. She'd stopped approaching him at the club—actually, he couldn't recall the last time she'd *been* at the BDSM club where he served as a Dungeon Monitor every weekend. Maybe she'd gotten over her attempts at being a sub to draw the attention of the team's owner, Lorenzo Keane. Dominik found her beautiful and alluring, but he had no interest in a woman playing at being submissive.

But there was chemistry between them that he couldn't deny. He'd pushed the possibilities aside to focus on the game, but there was more to life. He could tell everyone who asked that he was moving on from his failed relationship with Oriana, yet he hadn't done a thing to prove it. Maybe he should.

He dialed Sahara's number. No answer. So he left a message. "Hey, sweet lady. Been a while, so I thought we could catch up over dinner. My treat."

Straightforward and simple, but as he hung up, he couldn't decide whether or not he wanted her to call back. Training subs, putting his all out there on the ice, were things he knew how to do. But taking that first step into a future that didn't involve Oriana was different.

He was fine with it. For the most part. But when he closed his eyes, he could still see himself growing old with her. Still remember how often he'd seen his children with her eyes. Her smile.

In his mind, he knew that would never happen. But he couldn't lie to himself as easily as he lied to everyone else.

Oriana still had his heart. And he had a feeling she always would.

Chapter Two

Sahara picked up her phone. Put it down. Then brought her hands up to tug her hair and groaned really loud when Jami laughed. Today was not her day.

Jami had shown up at her door about twenty minutes ago, acting like she just wanted to visit. Except, Luke Carter was with her. Sahara had no problem with her friend's fiancé, but Jami wasn't in the habit of bringing him along when they hung out. What the hell was he going to do while they chatted about the insanity of Sahara's life? And discussed how *Dominik* had left her a message asking her out like it was the most normal thing in the world?

She'd let Jami hear the message, and they'd sat on the couch and discussed how she should respond, but Luke sitting in the kitchen playing Angry Birds on his phone was still weird.

Jami and Akira had probably talked about what had gone down with Cort. After all Jami had been through in the past, right down to having her very own demented stalker, her men were understandably protective. But it wasn't like Sahara would invite Grant over while Jami was here and let him—damn it, he wasn't some kind of animal! He'd never hurt anyone without reason.

So he had a reason to hurt you?

Yes. No. Hell, she didn't want to think about him now. She wanted to think about what to say to Dominik. And she needed her best friend's help.

She wouldn't ask Akira. At this point, she'd be lucky if Akira ever spoke to her again. But she needed Jami *not* to be laughing at her. This was serious. And messed up. And damn confusing.

"Stop it!" Sahara tossed her phone on the sofa beside Jami and sat on the coffee table. "You may have done great throwing yourself at Seb, but I—"

"Whoa, Sahara. You really want to go there?" Jami's eyes narrowed and she leaned forward, her hands on her knees. "If you want to do bitch-chick mode, I'm up for it, but that's fucking low. Yes, I went after Sebastian, but I don't judge you for being scared of starting a new relationship. It's a fucking date—"

"Jami, boo, please retract the claws." Luke came into the room and Sahara groaned again. There was no way he could improve the situation. And he only had to open his mouth to prove it. "You're friends. Sahara needs to get back in the game. How about telling her *why* she should go out with Mason? He's big and sexy and has a nice ass—"

"You are taking Sebastian's suggestion of embracing who you are *way* too seriously, Luke." Jami cocked her head as Luke sat on the arm of the sofa. "You do know Mason would dismember you if you hit on him, right?"

"Naw, he'd just laugh at me. Seb, however..." Luke smiled and closed his eyes as though picturing their Dom's reaction. "He might beat me within an inch of my life. He's so possessive lately."

"Umm, yeah. You are a freak." Jami patted Luke's knee fondly before returning her attention to Sahara. "Look, here's the deal. Neither you nor Dominik are looking for anything serious right now. He'll treat you great, you'll have fun, and I insist you make it perfectly clear to Grant that going back to him is *not* an option."

"*Annnnnd* we're back on that." Sahara sighed. So much for not thinking about him. "Jami, I'm not an idiot. Grant is...a friend."

Jami covered her face with her hands. "And you're *not* an idiot?"

Luke grabbed Jami's ponytail and tugged, frowning at her. "Jami—"

"Luke." Jami made a face at him. "In the kitchen, man of mine, before I beat you to death myself."

Hopping off the arm of the sofa, Luke turned, leaning down to take Jami's head between his hands and kiss her long and hard. He rose, winked at Sahara, and then disappeared into the kitchen.

"Don't mind him. He keeps telling me I should be nice, but with how cold he is to his sister…"

Yes! Sahara sat forward, motioning for Jami to go on. Talking about Luke's sister was a much safer topic.

"Oh, fine, I'll change the subject, but only because I love you." Jami gave Sahara a crooked smile and sat back against the sofa. "She's a hot mess, but she's such a sweetie once you get past the attitude. We had another ultrasound just the other day. She's really starting to show, and our baby boy is getting so big! Sebastian is helping me set up a nursery. Luke helps too, but only when Sam's at work."

"She's working? I thought she got fired." Sahara could remember at least two jobs Sam had gotten and held for no more than a day. The girl insisted she wanted to support herself, but she'd stolen from both her employers. It was almost like she couldn't help herself.

Jami shrugged, hunching her shoulders and staring at her hands. "Silver pulled some strings and got her working at one of the concession stands at the Forum. I hated asking because Silver wants me to talk to my dad and I can't, so it's weird. But…anyway, Sam doesn't work at the cash register, so all she can steal is pretzels. She's doing all right."

"That's good." Sahara rolled her eyes as Jami picked up her phone and handed it to her. The temporary reprieve was over. Either she called Dominik or Jami would force her to explain why she was avoiding him. Not that she was, exactly. She clasped her hands around her phone and chewed on her bottom lip.

"Do you want me to stay here or give you some privacy?" Jami's tone was soft, like she finally understood how hard this was. She knew about Sahara's casual lovers, knew that Sahara had been crushing on the Cobras' owner for way too long, but she couldn't seem to let go of her concern over Sahara not moving on.

And maybe she was right to. Grant coming over was messed up. Sahara wouldn't deny that, and she wouldn't deny that dating would be healthy and liberating, and it would close and lock the door to Grant in a way that saying "We're just friends" couldn't do.

Besides, she liked being around Dominik. Liked the way he smiled at her, the way he watched out for her at the club, the way she'd felt ready to go along with whatever he suggested.

If only he'd taken the lead with all the chances she'd given him. Then again, they'd either been around other players, or her friends, or at the club. They'd never truly been alone. And now they would be.

"Go keep your fiancé busy. I don't care if you make out, but if you fuck on my table—"

Jami snickered as she stood. "That was my table too until this morning. And I always washed it after—"

"No! I didn't need to know that!" Sahara shoved Jami toward the kitchen, laughing. Her friends were out of their minds, but she loved them anyway. She searched for Dominik's name on her phone and dialed before she could think about it too much. She was in a good mood and she wasn't scared anymore. Nothing would happen unless she let it.

Which was one of the most wonderful things about the man. He always gave her a choice, and maybe one day, the choice would be she didn't want the option to run away anymore.

"Hello, sunshine." Dominik's voice sent a dark thrill right through her. Deep and rich, like a mouthful of Black Forest cake so delicious she'd never forget the way it tasted even after she licked her plate clean. "I wasn't sure you'd call me back."

"I wasn't sure if I should." Sahara moved to the sofa, tucking her feet under her as she toyed with her hair. "What made you decide to call?"

"I missed you."

"Did you?" Inhaling, Sahara shifted, bringing her knees to her chest and hugging them with one arm. "You were the one who told me not to come to the club until I knew why I wanted to be there."

"This is true. But that doesn't mean I don't want to see you."

"You're a Dom. You should be looking for girls at—"

"I'm a man, Sahara. Let's not make this complicated." His gentle chiding reminded her so much of how he'd treated her at the club. As a Dom who cared for her, but would never push her to submit. "We can have dinner as friends if you'd like. No pressure."

Saying yes would be so easy, but she didn't want "just friends" with him. Not today, not after putting that wall up between herself and Grant. She didn't need a wall between her and Dominik. "I thought it was a date. I…I wanted to know when you were coming to pick me up."

Silence, and then a soft laugh. "I'd braced myself for a polite no. I need time to get ready, so let's say around five thirty?"

Less than an hour. She giggled, feeling unexpectedly giddy. A deep breath and she was able to give him a coherent answer. "That works. If you need time to get ready, I'm guessing I should dress nice?"

"Don't tempt me, girl." The low growl in Dominik's tone had Sahara pressing her thighs together and holding her breath. "If you give me the opening, I will tell you exactly what to wear."

"What if that's *exactly* what I want?" Sahara was playing with fire, but she didn't care. With Dominik's control wrapping around her like the sleekest silk ropes, she'd never felt more freedom. "Tell me what will please you, Sir."

A chuckle that made all the hairs on the back of her neck rise and Dominik replied. "So naughty. Wear a red dress and leave your hair loose. I'm warning you now, Sahara. No matter how much you beg, you will get no more than a kiss from me tonight."

Sahara's lips parted. She swallowed hard. "Why would I beg?"

He let out a soft, amused sound. "I'll see you in a bit."

The call ended. Sahara brought the phone to her chest and fell back on the sofa, squealing so loud Jami rushed into the room, leaning over her and staring at her like she'd gone nuts.

"Are you okay?"

"I'm wonderful. He's…he's amazing. And he wants to go on a date with me." Clearly, but Jami couldn't possibly understand what that meant. "A *real* date!"

That didn't make anything clear, but Sahara shot off the sofa and ran to her room to find her sexiest red dress. She had tears in her eyes and she wasn't even sure why. Except…well, she'd avoided relationships because she couldn't trust a single man who lusted after her. Going to the club, she knew she was safe. And that was because Dominik was always there. And he was the only one she needed with her tonight.

She wasn't damaged. Wasn't broken. A wonderful, caring man wanted to take her out and...

It's just a date, Sahara. Her hands shook as she pulled the dress from her closet and laid it on her bed. She was making *way* too much of this. She needed to relax or he'd think she was a head case. Not that he didn't already know, with how often she'd had to safeword during a scene and crawl away in shame.

He understands.

She didn't doubt that at all. He would probably give her good advice about Grant if she told him about this morning, but she didn't even want to bring up her ex. Tonight was for her and Dominik. No past, no fear. Nothing but him and her and so many possibilities.

"No more than a kiss."

The idea of him kissing her made her heart flutter. She threw herself on her bed and laughed into her hands. After the morning she'd had, the evening couldn't have turned out more wonderful. She heard someone come into her room and peeked through her fingers at Jami.

Who sat on the edge of her bed and took her hand away from her face. "So...you're happy?"

"I am." Sahara sniffed and swiped away her silly tears. "And I think I really will be. I don't want to get too excited, but..."

Jami waited for her to continue, and when she didn't, simply lay down beside her and grinned. "It's about fucking time. You deserve this."

Okay, that was going a little far. Sahara didn't think she deserved happiness more than anyone else. But she wanted it.

And for the first time, she really believed it was possible.

* * * *

Dressed in charcoal slacks and jacket, with a white shirt and black tie and a warm, dark gray wool coat because it was still damn cold out, Dominik stepped up to Sahara's door and knocked softly. He was well aware that he looked like he was going somewhere fancy. He wanted Sahara to see she deserved the best. Her uncertainty had him reassessing their every encounter, and he was determined to make this one different.

Behind the door, he heard rapid footsteps. Shouting—yes, that was Jami. He grinned, recalling the girl as a shy young teen before she'd gone through her rebellious phase. Now she'd grown into an intelligent, feisty young woman who'd enveloped Sahara in her close-knit group of friends. Friends she was quite protective of.

He wondered if she would have a few things to say to him before he left with Sahara. The door opened and he snorted as Carter let out a heavy sigh and gestured for him to come in.

"If it helps any, she looks really hot." Carter shut the door behind them and led the way to the small kitchen. He reached into the fridge for a beer, shutting it after Dominik turned down his offer for one. "There's some lipstick drama going on. They might be a while."

Nothing new, Dominik had waited on women before dates in the past. He'd never seen Sahara out and about without the extra polish she honestly didn't need. But he wouldn't rush her. If putting on just the right lipstick made her more comfortable, all the better.

He sat with Carter in the living room with one ankle propped on his knee, only half listening to the young man until an unexpected subject came up. He dropped his foot and leaned forward. "Ramos is letting you and Jami try to have a baby?"

Carter's eyes narrowed. "We're not his damn pets, Mason!" He rolled his eyes when Dominik arched a brow. "Not like that. You know what I mean. It's not so much that we're *trying*. We're just not trying not to anymore. And he's doing his fair share."

"And you're telling me this because…?"

"There could be a little me in nine months!"

Dominik smiled as the situation became clear. "And you're scared to death."

"Fuck yes." Carter kept his tone low as he rubbed his thighs. "It's just a lot, you know? Getting married with her dad hating me so much, making a kid a real possibility. I want to be with her and Seb forever, and everything is awesome, but…I know it won't be easy. I just want everything to be perfect for her."

Well, the boy's growing up after all. Dominik patted Carter's forearm as he met his eyes. "If you weren't a little afraid, I'd say you were a fool. Both you and Jami are very young, but not so young that you're not capable of being great parents. It could take a long time or she could be pregnant already. Despite the situation with her father, you know you're not alone. You, Jami, and Ramos have a strong relationship and so much to offer. And you know the team will be there for you."

Swallowing hard, Carter nodded. "Right. And she's got Silver. And the other girls. But…*wow*. That wasn't what I was expecting from you."

Of course not. Knowing Carter, this wasn't the first time he'd had this conversation. But Dominik was curious. "What were you expecting?"

"Umm, something like we're too young. Wait until we're married. We're not ready and—"

"And I'm not one to waste my time lecturing you on things you already know. I can't tell you if you're ready. But I can tell you to take care of my girl, which you'll probably hear from most of the guys. Jami will always be the little girl we watched grow up, and both you and Ramos will have to answer to all of us if you hurt her." Dominik gave Carter a pleasant, warning smile. "Not sure what else there is to say."

"Got it. And I won't. She's my boo." Carter turned at footsteps coming down the hall, opening his arms as Jami came over to sit on his lap. He held her close and kissed her shoulder. "How you feeling?"

"I heard you talking. And I'm not pregnant, so stop worrying. I'm so telling Sebastian what you were saying, and you're gonna have to bag it again, stud." She planted a kiss on his cheek as he groaned, then hopped up to give Dominik a hug. "You, however, are awesome. I was going to warn you to treat Sahara good, but I'm not worried."

Dominik gave Jami a little squeeze, making an "I'm watching you" gesture with two fingers pointed from his eyes to Carter while she settled back on his thighs. She giggled as Carter fell back against the sofa with his hands over his face.

The discussion turned to less serious topics, but Sahara still hadn't come out. Dominik suspected she was overthinking things and decided to put a stop to that.

Jami grabbed his arm when he stood. "She's coming."

"I find that hard to believe." Dominik glanced down at Jami's hand, pleased when she moved it without having to be told. He might not even consider being dominant toward the girl, but she knew better than to lay her hands on men who weren't hers.

Or perhaps he'd grown too accustomed to club protocol. Regardless, he'd come here for Sahara and he didn't need Carter and Jami as chaperones. The whole setup was mildly amusing, but enough was enough.

He headed down the hall quietly, listening to the shuffling just beyond the last door. And the frustrated groan. He cleared his throat. "Please tell me you're not worried about looking perfect for me, Sahara. That takes no effort at all."

Another groan and a strained laugh. "Great, now I feel silly."

"Which is adorable." He leaned against the wall by the door. "But either way, I don't want the fact that this is an 'official date' to change how comfortable you've been with me in the past. I'm not a new man you're trying to impress. I'm a man who already is."

The doorknob turned and the door opened a crack. He heard her take a deep breath before she came out.

Then it was his turn to take in as much oxygen as possible. Sahara always looked amazing, but in a snug, crimson lace dress, clinging to all her curves and falling to just above her knees, she was sexy and elegant all at once. There was something vulnerable in her eyes, in her stance even though she stood with her shoulders back and head held high. He found it hard to believe that she didn't know how beautiful she was, but maybe that wasn't the issue at all. The way she looked at him was expectant, almost shy. As though she wanted to know she'd pleased him.

She had, but he hadn't asked her out just to have a gorgeous woman on his arm. He could call his agent and have his pick of models to make an appearance. He wanted the woman he'd had easy conversations with. The woman he'd held while she cried after the loss of the coach they'd all loved so much.

He could have made this easier on them both by taking her somewhere simple, to a movie, out bowling or...there were many options, but none that would make his intentions clear. He wasn't taking Sahara out because he had nothing better to do. There was something between them that he wanted to explore. Tonight would be special. Possibly a new beginning.

"Look at me." He tipped her chin up with a finger. "What do you see?"

Her lips parted. Then she bit her lush, glistening, red bottom lip. "I see you. You look...very handsome, but you're still the same man who's been there for me, at the club and...and for a long time."

Inclining his head, he gave her a broad smile. "Good girl. Now, you do know that there may be photos of the two of us online before the end of the night. It will go much better if you don't seem afraid of me."

"I'm not afraid of you, Dominik." She exhaled and laughed. "I have no reason to be."

Well now, he wouldn't go that far. A little fear made things interesting. He pulled her close and brushed her ear with his lips. "That's cute. Shall I give you a reason?"

She went perfectly still, her little gasp hot against the side of his neck. "Umm..."

He chuckled and backed up a pace, offering her his arm. "There's no rush. Are you hungry?"

Red spread across the tops of her cheeks. She clearly wasn't thinking about food. But she nodded. "Did you make reservations somewhere?"

"I did." He checked his watch, relieved that he'd shown up early, because they had just enough time to make the six o'clock seating. "Thank God you're low maintenance. Any longer and we'd have to make new plans for the night."

Her brow rose as though to say he was full of it, but she didn't comment as she led the way down the hall to fetch her jacket from the hooks by the door. Jami and Carter quickly joined them and they all left together, Sahara pausing to lock up.

They parted in the parking lot. Dominik opened the passenger seat of his black Range Rover, offering Sahara a hand and making sure she was comfortably settled before going around to the driver's side.

Before he'd even pulled onto the street, Sahara had the radio on. She flicked through each station, cocking her head to listen to the first few seconds of each song. Then she wrinkled her nose and glanced over at him.

"Do you have any CDs?"

"No, but my iPod's in the glove compartment. See if there's anything you like on my playlists."

She pulled out his iPod, then continued checking the glove compartment. "Is there a wire?"

"No, it's wireless." He grinned when she ducked her head, her cheeks going red again. "Just pick a song and play."

There was silence, then Sahara let out a sound of excitement. "Oh! I love this song!"

"Bottoms Up" by Brantley Gilbert came on, a newer country song with a sultry beat and a naughty, sexual outlaw theme. When he stopped at a red light, Dominik watched Sahara out of the corner of his eye as she swayed to the music, singing softly. He had to admit, he'd expected her to find one of the few Top 40 songs he'd downloaded. Or at least show some surprise at his taste in music.

Instead, she spent the entire drive picking songs she clearly knew, losing her shyness halfway there and singing loud enough for him to enjoy the sweetness of her voice. There was a slight New York edge to her tone, and she didn't hit all the notes right, but he liked listening to her. Seeing how the country tunes had her letting go. They'd have fun on a road trip. On the open highway, in the summer, with the windows rolled down and the music blaring, he had a feeling she'd be right in her element.

Hell, she'd probably love going to his older brother Joshua's place down in West Virginia. When his brother wasn't stationed somewhere overseas, he was on the ranch he owned with two of his college buddies. The place was the complete opposite of where they'd grown up. Miles from the closest town, but it suited him.

It was a bit early to be thinking of taking that kind of trip with Sahara, but after pulling in front of the Halifax Dinner Theatre, he couldn't help meeting her eyes as he lifted her from the seat and lowered her to the sidewalk.

The question just came out. "Have you ever been to a tailgate party?"

She blinked and a smile spread across her lips, so big you'd have thought he'd just told her she'd won tickets to the Super Bowl. Or...well, maybe she wasn't that into football. Maybe a trip to the Caribbean.

He was *definitely* overthinking things now, but whatever excited her, his question was on that list.

"I wish! Jami was telling me Max had a tailgate party for his thirtieth birthday and Oriana showed her pictures, and it looked like so much..." Sahara bit her bottom lip. "Actually, you were probably there."

"I was." Dominik put his hand on the small of her back to guide her inside as she looked up at the sign where a harlequin figurine perched. Then she turned her head from side to side to take in the theatrical décor of the lobby. His mind was no longer on the possible future. He remembered that day, sitting with Oriana in the back of Max's father's truck, believing life couldn't get any more perfect. Even at his brother's ranch, he hadn't felt as at home as he had on the farm where Max grew up. Early mornings, doing chores with Max and Sloan, coming in smelly and sweaty to a hearty breakfast Oriana had prepared with Max's aunts.

That wasn't his life anymore. And dwelling on memories while he was with Sahara wasn't fair.

At the end of the lobby, a man dressed as a pirate greeted them with an exaggerated accent and brought them to the table Dominik had reserved, a few feet from center stage. He and his younger brother, Cam, had brought their mother here last time she'd come to visit and she'd loved it. He couldn't say why he'd decided on this place for his date with Sahara, except for the fact that he wanted to avoid anything stiff and awkward. Hopefully, she'd have as much fun as he and his family had.

They settled in and the waiter—also dressed as a pirate—came with their salad. Sahara took a few bites, chewing thoughtfully. Then she set down her fork.

He knew, just by the expression on her face, that whatever she had to say wouldn't get their night off to a good start.

And he was right.

"Did you see her today? Is that why you asked me out?" She dropped her gaze to her napkin. "Not that it matters, but I want to be prepared. I've seen what you expect from subs and…and Oriana is perfect. I can't compete with her."

"It's not a competition, sunshine." He meant every word, but he could tell she didn't believe him. Which was his own damn fault. It was no secret how things between him and Oriana had ended. His teammates tended to avoid mentioning her at all.

But the point was, the relationship was over. He was here with Sahara, and there was nowhere else he'd rather be.

Putting his hand over Sahara's, he leaned forward, speaking low. "I never brought her here. She wouldn't enjoy the…crude humor in some of the acts. But I think you will."

She wrinkled her nose. "So you think I'm into 'crude humor'?"

He laughed and tapped her nose. "I have no idea. But I'd like to find out." He stroked the back of her hand. "When I considered all the places I could bring you, it occurred to me how much I love the way you laugh."

"So why not a comedy show?"

"Sammy Sugar's the only big act in town. I can't stand him—I had a feeling you wouldn't like him either."

"Ugh, no. I've seen his shows and he kinda pisses me off." She speared a piece of salad with her fork, taking a bite and letting out a soft sound of pleasure. "Mmm, I love this salad dressing. Maybe you made a good choice on coming here after all."

Well, he was happy she approved, but her comment amused him. "Based on the salad?"

Cocking her head in thought, she shrugged. "The service is good too. And, to be honest, this place isn't as formal as I thought it would be based on what you're wearing. I mean, other people are dressed nicely, but there's no snobiness. I don't have to worry about knowing which fork to use."

"I do aim to keep the cutlery simple on first dates." He winked when she rolled her eyes at him. So far, so good. She appeared at ease and the first act was about to start. Better yet, the topic of his ex had been abandoned.

They both focused on the stage as the actors, all decked out as pirates or various members of the crew, put on an original show, complete with singing and dancing and quite a lot of exaggerated gyrating. Maybe not crude, but there was a sexual humor to the whole act and many of the jokes were pretty raunchy.

Dominik glanced over at Sahara and grinned as she giggled when their performing waiter caught her eye in the middle of a joke about fainting maidens. When the act ended, the waiter came over and snatched up Sahara's napkin, folding it and fanning her with it when she pressed her hands to her cheeks, which were red from laughing so much.

The young man gave Dominik a sideways glance before sweeping the napkin over Sahara's lap and moving as though to kiss her on the cheek. Dominik's eyes narrowed and Sahara ducked out of reach, which, strangely enough, pleased him. With a dramatic bow, the waiter shifted away from her and gathered their empty plates.

After the second course was served, the actors prepared for the next act. Sahara smiled at Dominik, looking so happy he couldn't think of a thing to say. He'd rarely seen her this carefree and relaxed.

Actually, he couldn't recall feeling this laid-back himself. There was no pressure. Instead of the tension of a first, awkward date, this felt like spending time with a friend. One he hoped would become more.

Just before the show continued, Sahara returned her hand to his and met his eyes. "Thank you for bringing me here. I was so nervous, but you've proved I don't have to be. Not with you."

He turned his hand, stroking her long, delicate fingers with his thumb, amazed at how comfortable he felt touching her. She didn't come off as the type of woman to play games, and he could tell she wasn't holding back from him. His only regret was not bringing her somewhere where they could talk more. He wanted to know more about her. What she liked. What she wanted.

But that would come. There was no need to rush things; they were off to a good start.

"I'm glad you like it. Cam wasn't crazy about the food, but my brother's spoiled rotten. He goes home a few times a month just so our mother can cook for him and he can complain that nothing else measures up." Dominik took a bite of his steak, thinking about how Cam had mentioned their mother's homemade BBQ sauce was ten times better. He had to agree, and their mother had been flattered, but as someone who didn't have the luxury of home-cooked meals very often, Dominik was more than satisfied.

Sahara chewed slowly, a thoughtful expression on her face. "I'm a decent cook, but I find the best meal is one you don't have to make."

"Very true." The act had begun, but Dominik could tell Sahara wanted to talk, so he gave her his full attention.

"Can I ask you something?"

He inclined his head, about to tell her she already had, but refrained when she hunched her shoulders and dropped her gaze. Whatever she had to say was too serious for him to start teasing her.

"You're playing Grant's team. I know you guys don't like him because of the past, but..." Her brow furrowed. She looked frustrated. "What he did was horrible, but it's in the past. He recently lost his mother and he's trying to change. I don't want him targeted because of me."

Dominik clenched his fist under the table, thinking of all the times Grant Higgins had instigated fights on the ice, calling Sahara names and taunting those who cared for her. She should have pressed charges a long time ago and made the man pay for what he'd done to her. Dominik didn't know the extent of Higgins's abuse, but he did know Sahara had still had bruises when she'd joined the Cobras' Ice Girl team.

The man wouldn't even be playing in the league anymore if charges had been filed. Cases like this were on the news all the time, and no professional sports team would tolerate that kind of behavior. Unfortunately, rumors didn't hold much weight, and Sahara seemed to have decided getting out of reach was enough.

Perhaps Higgins had made some drastic changes after his mother's death. Dominik had a hard time trusting that, but telling Sahara as much would only drive a wedge between them. He had to take her lead, despite his misgivings.

So he schooled his features and nodded. "I'll do my best to keep the games clean, but I take no responsibility for Demyan's reactions. Higgins seems to enjoy pushing his buttons."

"He won't anymore. And don't worry about Scott, I'll talk to him."

"Fair enough." Dominik took another bite of steak as he shifted his attention back to the stage.

He could feel Sahara's gaze locked on the side of his face. "That's it?"

Brow arched, Dominik turned back to Sahara. He wasn't sure why everyone expected him to react badly whenever they told him about their problems. He didn't consider himself a judgmental man, but perhaps he came across that way?

"My turn to ask you a question." Dominik steepled his fingers and regarded Sahara for a moment before continuing. "Did you expect me to be unreasonable? Or tell you how to handle the situation?"

She ducked her head and her cheeks reddened. "I don't mind you telling me what to do."

He tightened his lips and shook his head. "You know that's not what I mean."

"All right, fine." She wrinkled her nose, a habit she had that he found endearing. And distracting. If they were at the club, he'd be tempted to spank her for what edged on brattiness, but they weren't and he couldn't let her lead the conversation in that direction.

Not yet anyway.

Tonguing her bottom lip, she studied his face. "Apparently kink is off the table."

"A fact I'm sure the staff here appreciates. Bending you over the table to punish you for being a brat would make the other patrons uncomfortable." *So much for steering clear of that subject.* Dominik leaned back in his chair and smiled at the way she covered her cheeks to hide her blush. "Will you answer me now?"

Picking up her glass of water, she took a sip, then licked her lips. "I respect your opinion, and I appreciate how you've stuck up for me in the past. I was afraid you'd be disappointed in me for forgiving him."

"Have you?"

"I..." She frowned, as though she wasn't sure. "I feel bad for him, and I'm hoping he's serious about changing. I wouldn't mind being friends with him, but I'm not stupid. I'll be careful about it." Her gaze met Dominik's, and he could tell she was looking for his approval again. He wasn't sure he could give it, but he inclined his head so she'd continue. "I don't expect anyone to understand. I guess... I fell in love with him for a reason. Even though I'll never feel that way about him again, part of me wants to see him as the man I know he can be. I can't forget what he did, but not forgiving him feels like I haven't moved on. And I have."

Her reasoning made a lot of sense. Dominik was still concerned that Higgins would take advantage of Sahara giving him any opening to get close to her.

"What makes you think no one will understand? Everyone's seen the steps you've taken to protect yourself. You've been taking self-defense for quite a while. You're not the same woman who came to us with bruises, shying away from sudden movements." He had to force his tone to stay level as the memories came to him and rage simmered within. The color had left her cheeks and he took her hand, knowing all she needed from him right now was his support. "I won't lie to you. I hope you won't regret offering him your friendship, but you're not walking into this blindly. Forgive, but don't forget. Even if he screws up—which he damn well better not—you've got to do what's right for you."

"Thank you!" Her eyes brightened and she lunged forward to hug him. Her lips brushed his throat as he held her. "Akira's so mad at me, and Cort..."

She slipped out of Dominik's arms and sat back in her chair. Then she went over what had happened with Higgins and Cort earlier that day. Dominik was tempted to call Cort and thank him, but Sahara wouldn't appreciate that if she found out. His only option was to make sure she knew he'd be there for her no matter what.

Thankfully, she was eager to change the subject, so conversation moved to the playoffs and the next show the Cobras' Ice Girls would put on. She brought up the club a couple of times with offhand, teasing remarks, but he refused to take the bait. Their interactions at the club they both went to, had mostly consisted of her acting out and him having to discipline her because he was one of the regular Dungeon Monitors. He missed seeing her there, but neither of them was ready to delve into the lifestyle. He couldn't say for sure he was even interested in being a Dom anymore. To her or anyone else.

"Is it me?" She let out a frustrated sound when he dodged another remark about BDSM by bringing up her music choices for the Ice Girls' next performance. He opened his mouth to assure her it wasn't, but she cut him off. "I know I'm not the perfect sub, but I could learn to—"

"I'm not looking for a sub, Sahara." He took her hand, squeezing gently to soften the impact of his words. He used his other hand to tilt her chin up when she dropped her gaze. "Hey, that's not a bad thing. What that means is what we're doing, right here, is all I want."

She nibbled her bottom lip, her eyes sad. "But you need more."

"No, I don't."

"Really?" She brushed her hand over her chest as though there were crumbs there, a crooked smile on her lips. "So do you like the dress? I'm happy I didn't have to choose my own outfit; we would have missed the first act."

Cheeky little thing, isn't she? Dominik chuckled and tugged her closer, whispering against her lips. "Are you fishing for compliments, pet?"

"No, *Sir.*" She held still as he gently stroked her lips with his. Then sighed when he shifted away. "Dominik—"

"Watch the show, Sahara." He wasn't sure whether he should spank her or bring her home with him, but for the moment, she had a point. He did need to exert some control. Over himself. "You'll like how this ends."

Chapter Three

Meanwhile

Max Perron stood in the shower behind Oriana, loving the dreamy look on his wife's face as she gazed up into his eyes. That was all he needed to see to know tonight would go well. To be perfectly honest, he'd been nervous at first, but there was something erotic about setting up a scene that gave the two most important people in his life exactly what they needed.

He enjoyed watching the scenes between her and Sloan, but sometimes he was torn between his desire to watch and his need to participate in their pleasure. He hadn't been sure he'd be of much use this time, but Sloan insisted that he make sure to get Oriana nice and clean while other preparations were made.

The intense focus in Sloan's expression as he'd pulled out his knife kit was enough to make the hairs rise on the back of Max's neck. And blood to pulse steadily into his cock as he considered how fucking hot the whole scenario would be.

He took a deep breath as he cupped his hand to fill his palm with the coconut- and vanilla-scented shampoo. The sweet aroma rose in the steam as he worked it through Oriana's waist length, burnished gold hair. He massaged her scalp, loving how routine intimate moments like this had become over the years. Sex had never been an issue for them, but his biggest fear in their unconventional relationship had been that the little things he enjoyed doing with her would seem boring.

Instead, it was the little things that she craved when life got rough. Yes, she enjoyed a high level of pain when they played, and she found peace in submitting to him and Sloan. But cuddling on the couch, having her hair washed or brushed, soft kisses, and holding hands while walking down the street, were all she needed to make her smile and laugh when she was on the verge of tears.

Casual affection was a bit harder for Sloan, but he did his best. His efforts were appreciated, but Oriana had told Max once that so long as she had one of her men who showed tenderness easily, she'd never feel like their relationship was lacking.

Which made him happy. And yet...hell, he couldn't even explain why it still bothered him that he had to step in after every edgy scene to ease Oriana back to level ground. Sloan was capable enough in providing aftercare, but there was a jarring disconnect in the way he tended to their girl. Almost as if he'd gone so far into himself that he had trouble coming back.

Max suspected Sloan could use some aftercare himself, even if it was just to snuggle and hear he wasn't fucked up for wanting to hurt the woman he loved. Not when it satisfied them both and he was so goddamn careful with her.

"Max?" Oriana glanced over her shoulder, putting a hand over the one he'd rested on her shoulder while drifting away in thought. "Are you okay? I lost you there for a little bit."

He smiled and grabbed the showerhead to rinse her hair. "I'm fine, love. Just thinking about the scene."

She inhaled roughly, closing her eyes to keep the soap out of them. "In a good way? You're not worried, are you?"

He wasn't worried about the scene itself, but he took his time answering. Sloan had mentored with an experienced knife Top for almost a year. He'd renewed his first aid certificate. He'd done everything a responsible Dom could possibly do to make a potentially dangerous scene safe.

But preparing emotionally for a scene that could hit unexpected triggers for the Dom and the sub? There was no course for that. One could prepare for every imaginable outcome and still be blindsided.

Using a washcloth, he wiped away the suds on Oriana's face so she could open her eyes. "I always worry, but it's not a bad thing.

Nothing pleases me more than you both exploring all your twisted kinks."

"But?"

"But I never know if I'm doing enough. During the scene…and after." He gave her a crooked smile and shrugged as he soaped up the sea sponge to wash her beautiful body. "I hope you'll let me know if I'm not."

"I will. But I don't see it happening." She squirmed as he washed her breasts, then giggled as he scrubbed over her ribs and the luscious swell of her belly and hips. A soft sound of pleasure left her as he moved in closer and pressed the sponge between her thighs. "You never miss anything, Max. Even when you're not touching me, just feeling your eyes on me makes me feel…" She pressed her hand to his cheek and smiled at him. "I've seen the girls you were with in the past. They were skinny and perfect. I used to wonder why you'd even want me, but not anymore. I don't see a chubby woman when I look in the mirror. I see the woman you can't take your eyes off of."

"Good. Because I'll take the whip to you myself if you dare compare yourself to anyone." He wrapped his hand around the back of her neck and kissed her wet lips, putting his misgivings aside so he could lose himself in the moment.

Some might assume sharing his wife with another man would make him jealous, or bitter, but he found that it made him appreciate times like this in a way he might not if he had her all to himself. He could be wrong; he didn't have much experience *not* sharing a woman. And yet, he wouldn't change a single thing.

Helping Oriana step out of the shower, Max drew her close and claimed her lips again, not caring that they were both dripping water all over the floor. He'd take care of the mess later—or perhaps make Oriana do it since Sloan often accused him of being too easy on her. For now though, he simply wanted to drink in her excitement. And hold her one last time before she floated away in ecstasy.

She gave him a playful look as he grabbed a towel to wrap around his waist before opening the door that led into the master bedroom. "Speaking of whipping, I noticed you couldn't take your eyes off Sebastian and Luke at the club. Even *after* Sebastian put the whip away."

Max blinked, thinking back on their last visit to the club and wondering what she was getting at. She knew he got off watching people fuck. He wasn't picky about who he watched, and she'd never complained before.

"Does it bother you?" If it did, he'd stop. He just hadn't considered that giving in to his urges as a voyeur might become an issue.

Standing by the bed, Sloan snapped on a pair of sterile gloves from the large first aid kit on the nightstand and let out a soft chuckle. "I do believe she's noticed you're just as interested in watching the men being fucked as the women."

"I..." Max frowned as he realized his focus *had* shifted. He'd never had a problem with who was getting off, but the soft body of a woman had always been more appealing. Lately there was a greater variety at the club, and he was drawn to the passion laid out before him.

"It's not a big deal, my love." Oriana came up behind him and wrapped her arms around his waist. "I enjoy watching them too. Sometimes I wonder..."

Her voice trailed off and Max looked over his shoulder, eager to know what had her blushing and biting her lip. There was nothing he wouldn't do for her.

She ducked her head and pressed her cheek to his back. "Never mind."

Max frowned. "Pet, you—"

"Does she need to spell it out, Max? She gets nice and wet seeing two guys together. Seems like her sister is living every woman's fantasy." Sloan rolled his eyes as Max's brow furrowed. "She wants to be able to watch more often."

All right, he didn't see a problem with that. Max grinned as he pulled Oriana in front of him so he could go back to kissing her sweet lips. She wouldn't be able to squirm once Sloan started playing with her, so Max would enjoy making her do so now.

And tease her a little with her kinky needs, which meshed well with his own. "The guys who go to the club don't mind an audience. I'll make sure you've got the perfect view next time we go. Carter might like it rough like you, but you should see how Zovko and

Chicklet torment Vanek. It would amuse Chicklet to have your eyes on them while I toy with you."

Sloan snorted as he lifted a dagger from the array of sharp implements he'd sterilized and lined up on a raised tray by the bed. "Probably, but Oriana would much prefer watching me fuck you."

With an involuntary shudder, Max shot Sloan a dirty look. "You're crazier than a shithouse mouse."

"And sometimes you make White look like a rocket scientist. Not sure how many different ways you needed her dirty dream scenario explained to you." Sloan tapped his bottom lip thoughtfully with the tip of the dagger, his lips slanting in a smirk. "From the expression on your face, you were willing to give her whatever her heart desired. Did that change, Romeo?"

What kind of question was that? Max stifled the urge to swallow, fully aware that Sloan was in the dark headspace where any discomfort he caused would satiate him. And Max refused to give the man the upper hand.

So he shrugged. "I don't deny our beautiful wife very much."

"Fuck off." Sloan's eyes narrowed at Max's level gaze. "Are you serious?"

"If I am?"

It was Sloan who swallowed before quickly shaking his head. "I couldn't... Hell, you're like a brother to me. Cutting you when you wanted to see how it would feel was almost too much. I won't judge you if you wanted to try—"

"So it wouldn't bother you if I was with another man?" Max ran his fingers up the underside of Oriana's arm, never taking his eyes off Sloan. "Reckon that would be good enough for our girl."

The muscle in Sloan's jaw ticked. "Guess that would be fine."

Max kissed along Oriana's throat. "We've both agreed she can only be shared between us, so she wouldn't participate."

Oriana let out an irritated sound. "*She* is right here."

Sloan ignored her. "We agreed the three of us were committed to this relationship."

Inclining his head, Max ran his teeth down the curve between Oriana's neck and shoulder, grinning when she shivered. "True. But you wouldn't object if it was what I needed?"

"No." Sloan inhaled roughly. "I'm surprised—I thought you talked to me about everything, but—"

"That's good to know, Sloan. It's not an issue, but I appreciate your support." Max drew away from Oriana and reached out to pat the bed, which had been stripped down and covered with a disposable, sterile sheet. "Are you ready, darlin'?"

Covering her mouth to muffle a giggle, Oriana hopped onto the bed. She schooled her features when Sloan frowned down at her.

The disgruntled look shifted to Max. "You were fucking with me, asshole?"

"Yes." Max had to fight not to laugh as Sloan continued to stare at him. Then something occurred to him that made the situation not so funny anymore. "I done pulled you out of your headspace. Sorry about that." He gently petted Oriana's damp hair as she rolled to her side, facing Sloan. "Did I ruin the scene?"

Eyes dark, but expression relaxed, Sloan seemed more *with* them than he had before. He moved to rake his fingers through his black hair, stopping as though he'd suddenly remembered the gloves.

Then he chuckled. "No, but I will take credit for how good you're getting at playing head games. I'm rubbing off on you."

"Careful, Sloan." Max casually drew his fingers down between Oriana's breasts, deciding to tease her a little more now that he and Sloan were on the same page. "The idea of you rubbing anything on me might make me change my mind."

Sloan held up the dagger, blade down, hands wrapped around the handle with the top one moving up and down slowly. "That so? How about this: you suck my dick and we'll go from there."

"I say we make a wager. I score tomorrow night, you suck *my* dick. I don't, and—"

Oriana thumped her fist on the mattress. "You're both horrible! We all know you're never going to do anything together. Or with any other guy. Why do you have to torture me with the images of what will never be?"

Flipping the dagger in his hand, Sloan bent over Oriana, brushing the tip of the blade down her cheek. The dagger had no edge, so Sloan would have to press hard to even scratch her, but the subtle threat of metal against her flesh had the desired effect. Oriana went still, her lips parted and her eyes holding the delicious kind of fear she craved.

"Why do we torture you, pet?" Sloan's slow smile was filled with danger. In scenes like this, he reminded Max of the onscreen killers women swooned over. Deadly and alluring all at once. Sloan was as skilled using fear as he was with every tool in his arsenal. He wielded words with the same careful edge as the lash of his whip. "Because you love it."

A simple gesture from Sloan had Oriana rolling onto her back. He slapped her thigh and she jumped. Then bent her knees and spread her thighs. The scene was about to begin.

There would be opportunities for Max to touch Oriana, even if only to hold her still. Enough contact for Max to assure her, and himself, that it was just a twisted, erotic game. But for the most part, he would watch them in their balance of pain and pleasure, dancing along the edge. Always a sight to behold.

* * * *

Oriana relaxed into the mattress, taking a moment to watch her infuriating, yet wonderful men prepare for the scene with the same harmony they'd once had on the ice. Sloan still held the dagger, but he acted almost as though he'd forgotten her as he observed Max lighting a few red candles—not for light, the room was bright enough and Sloan wouldn't do a scene like this in the dark. They added some ambiance, but Max put one on the nightstand by the first aid kit, within Sloan's reach, meaning blades wouldn't be the only things on her flesh tonight.

While Max shifted his attention from the candles to the Beatbox on the dresser, putting on a playlist of haunting classical music, Sloan turned his dark gaze to Oriana. In black jeans and a dark blue T-shirt, his black hair mussed up and a slanted smile on his lips, he looked positively evil. His muscles seemed even bigger with him standing over her, and she couldn't dismiss the knowledge that this man could hurt her badly if he chose to.

She wanted him to hurt her. And she craved the slice of fear that she experienced whenever they played like this. From the beginning, she'd thought she'd need more and more pain to reach the exquisite high she felt with every bite of the whip or thud of the paddle. Not many would consider what they did safe, but rarely were there any marks that left her more than a little sore for a few days. She loved each and every bruise. When the whip or the cane drew blood, she would admire the marks as Sloan or Max tended to them. They were beautiful reminders of scenes that satisfied her in every way.

But it ended up being fear that made an excess of pain unnecessary. During a scene, she would let herself believe that this time it might go too far. Her trust in Sloan made doing so feel safe. He'd never harm her in a way she couldn't easily recover from. He was careful and he knew what he was doing.

Which included enough of a mindfuck to keep her guessing what he would do next. She always thought she was prepared for anything.

And she was always wrong.

In a swift motion, Sloan raked his fingers through her hair, tipping her head back as he laid the flat of the dagger against her throat. She hissed in a shocked breath and her eyes went wide. A surge of adrenaline had her shivering though she tried to stay very, very still. Heat pooled in her core even as she whimpered at the pain in her scalp.

"So pretty." Sloan tugged harder at her hair and bent down to lay a gentle kiss on her lips. "I shouldn't want to hurt you as much as I do. I should let you go, shouldn't I?"

She wanted to shake her head, but moving with a blade at her throat and his firm grip on her hair was impossible. So she wet her lips and whispered, "Yes."

A movement behind Sloan caught her attention. Max had shifted closer, and for a second, she was afraid he might have changed his mind about the scene. He'd been in the lifestyle long enough to understand using safewords to stop play rather than "No" or "Don't" or any other words that might be spoken to spice things up. He trusted Sloan as much as she did, but…there had been times in the past when he'd needed more reassurance that she was really all right.

His lips quirked and he moved to sit on the edge of the bed. And she let out a sigh of relief. This wasn't one of those times. If she'd read him right, he was enjoying the show.

"Were you expecting him to help you? Let me tell you something about him." Sloan bent down to whisper in her ear. "He'll take whatever's left of you. He's a very patient man."

"Please…" Oriana wasn't even sure what she was asking for, but she needed more. Sensing Max so close, feeling Sloan's restraint as he slowly laid the groundwork for their erotic role-play, made her want to struggle to push it to the next level. But she wouldn't risk any sudden movements with the blade at her throat. Not even when she knew the blade was dull.

Sloan cocked his head, pulling the dagger away and releasing her hair. "Please? Do you think I'll let you go if you beg?"

Holding her breath and giving no warning, Oriana lurched to the other side of the bed. She screamed as Sloan dragged her back by her hair while Max latched on to her ankles. Her eyes teared, but she almost laughed with nervous excitement as they pinned her down.

Dropping the dagger as she swung at him, Sloan caught her wrists in one hand and pulled them up over her head. "Silly girl. Now I'm going to have to hurt you."

Yes! Oriana twisted as Sloan pulled out the cuffs permanently attached to the bed frame, but Max moved up the bed, straddling her and pressing his hands to her shoulders to hold her down. She tried to bite him and he lightly slapped her cheek.

Not hard enough to even sting, but it shocked her. He didn't usually participate in the edgier aspects of their games, and slapping her face was something even Sloan rarely did. Caught off guard, she stared at him as Sloan secured her wrists with the cuffs. It took a moment to sort out her thoughts, but when she did, she realized she loved that he'd gotten into his role enough to do something unexpected. She wet her lips, hoping he'd take that as a sign that she was fine with what he'd done.

But, as he'd say, bless his heart. He'd caught himself off guard too, and his brow furrowed with concern. "I—"

"Just made her very happy. Don't spoil it, buddy." Sloan patted Max's shoulder as he studied Oriana's face, inclining his head when she gave him a quick, reassuring smile. "This slut is probably dripping wet. Are you wet, girl?"

She shook her head, heat spreading over her cheeks as she felt the sheet under her ass grow damp with her arousal. Sloan didn't miss a beat. He put his hand on her throat and smirked. "Why don't you check, Max?"

As Sloan's grip on her throat tightened, her thighs were spread even farther apart. Max thrust two fingers into her, letting out a soft groan as he lowered his head to flick her clit with his tongue.

Her hips bucked and she gasped. "Oh God!"

Sloan chuckled, running his hand down her body, between her breasts, over her stomach, then back up so he could squeeze her breast. "He's not gonna save you either, little girl. The only thing that will save you is if you make me happy. And I'm not easy to please."

The candles on the nightstand flickered as Sloan reached out, taking one and tilting it to let a few drops fall on the back of his own hand. He shifted to hold it over her chest, upending it to drizzle the hot wax across her breasts, using a circular motion to draw wax spirals from the base of one breast all the way to her nipple.

A slight burning sensation hit her with each droplet, and she moaned as the sweet haze clouded her mind. Her skin felt tight under the wax and sensitive where her flesh waited for the bite of pain. Looking down her body, she watched the red cover her pale golden flesh, meeting Max's eyes when he lifted his head and pulled his fingers from her body to slip them into his mouth. Her cunt clenched against the emptiness, more juices spilling at the erotic visual. Combined with the fresh sting of heat, the sensation brought her to the verge of either floating away in ecstasy or being thrown into a fierce orgasm.

She fought both, needing this to last as long as possible. Sloan had promised to do things to her that he'd never done before. The role-playing, the wax, and the knife were all old favorites, but Sloan had spent the last year training to fulfill one of her edgiest fantasies. There was no way she'd give in to the shallow desires of her body and miss the ultimate experience.

"Where are we, my love?" Sloan's tone was soft, letting her know he was checking on her before he went any further. He usually avoided pulling her out of her headspace, but when they tried something new, he always made sure she was in a good place first.

Inhaling slowly, careful to keep her tone level, she smiled at him. "I feel amazing, Sir. Are we role-playing for the rest of this?"

Sloan's expression grew thoughtful. Then he nodded. "Yes. You're not as far gone as I'd let you get during a milder scene. This won't be...pleasant if it becomes too clinical."

"Then please don't worry. I'll tell you the same thing I did when we planned this." She held his gaze, happy to see he was taking in her every word. "I know what I'm asking for."

"I know you do. If I doubted it, we wouldn't be here." He inhaled and pressed his eyes shut. "I mean—"

"I know what you mean, Sloan." She used his name to bring him back to her. They'd talked enough for her to know he was second-guessing his desires more than hers. And as much as she wanted him to use his new skills on her, she wouldn't push him past his limits if he really wasn't comfortable. "I'm not the only one who can stop this, you know."

"I don't want to stop." Sloan inhaled roughly, then glanced over at Max. Max shrugged one shoulder, then reached out to brush his fingers over the faint scars on Sloan's right forearm. There were four long lines, the first a bit thicker than the others, months old, while the thinnest one had been made a few weeks back.

Max had two thin scars on the same spot on his arm. That he'd been willing to let his best friend cut him—especially when any serious injury could take him out of the game, which was unacceptable during the playoffs—showed there was no limit to his trust. Not that he'd needed to let Sloan cut him to prove anything, but he wasn't standing back and simply watching anymore. This was a scene that could potentially bring them all closer. She wanted the sensation, and the marks to remember it by.

"There might not be a scar at all, Oriana." Sloan grinned as he picked up one of his long, razor-sharp knives. "But I'll try to leave something for us all to admire for days to come."

Without being asked, Max secured her ankles, both with the cuffs permanently fixed to the end of the bed—which they'd discussed ahead of time so she wouldn't make any sudden movements—and his own hands as she'd asked so she'd feel him close. Sloan had a good idea of how she moved with different sensations, so it was unlikely that he'd cut her without meaning to even if she jerked with a prick of the blade. Either way, he seemed to have prepared for any possible outcome.

He started with the wax on her breasts, prying off little pieces, letting the sharp tip of the knife shallowly pierce her flesh. A sting on the side of her breast. Liquid heat. The skin freed from the wax felt cool in contrast.

Another tiny sting, more heat, she closed her eyes to soak in the sensation. Whips and canes could leave bruises, even break the flesh, but it wasn't the same as the delicate kiss of the knife. She was aware of the pain, only, not the way she would be with a paper cut or a burn. The perception was entirely different because Sloan hurting her was so closely linked to pleasure.

When her breasts were free of the wax, she opened her eyes and watched Sloan set down the knife. He pulled off his gloves and put on a pair of fresh ones. Then he used a cotton pad with clear liquid to clean her upper thigh.

"You've impressed me, pretty girl." The tone of the evil kidnapper had returned, but Sloan was softening it with the endearment. The game was a careful balance, one that worked because they'd all been together long enough that not much was needed beyond basic negotiations before a scene. He was still playing the bad guy, but enough of his real self came through for her to feel safe. "I've never found a bitch I wanted to keep, but you're fun to play with. Will you cry if I cut you?"

"No, I'll be quiet." She'd read some amazing books where captives fell in love with their captors. She was already in love with Sloan, but to play her part, she could toy with the idea of doing anything to survive and beginning to...feel something more for the man who might spare her if she pleased him. "I want you to keep me. I won't fight you, I promise."

"Hmm." Sloan pressed his hand to her thigh before picking up a scalpel, the only tool he'd laid out that he hadn't used yet. "Are you sure about that?"

All the trust in the world couldn't dim how frightening the scalpel looked in his practiced hold. She reasoned that this wasn't his first time wielding the exquisitely sharp tool. The blade was taped to control how deep it could cut, and the result would be more like the shallow cuts he'd made on Max's arms than the deeper ones he'd made on his own. She braced for the pain as he touched the knife to her thigh, his stroke as light as it would be if he were painting with a brush. She could feel the blood well up. Then the cool dampness of an alcohol swab gliding over the cut.

Pain, acute and intense; almost like the alcohol had been lit on her flesh and flames seeped under her skin. She tossed her head, fighting to bite back a moan. Her core clenched and her eyes teared, not with pain, but with pure ecstasy. The blade returned, followed by the alcohol, and she lost herself to the fiery bliss. Most wouldn't understand why she'd want this, but she'd given up caring about any who would judge. She was exposed to her men, taking all they could give her, knowing they, at least, accepted her needs.

Max had tightened his grip on her ankles. Sloan gently covered the cuts on her thigh with a sterile gauze bandage and compressed the hot spill. The scalpel hit the tray with a clang. He pulled off the gloves with his teeth, keeping one hand on the bandage as he rose over her and undid his jeans. He drove into her in one smooth thrust, making her back arch as the sensation of being filled mixed with the painful pressure on her thigh. Her lips parted and her gasps came with every slap of his flesh against hers.

Pleasure was violent, but Sloan had clearly lost the flow of their game as he leaned back, gentling his motions as he looked down at their joining. He licked his lips as he watched his dick slide into her. The slow motion was torture, but the expression on his face made the delayed gratification more than worth it. He caught her gaze and smiled, his eyes filled with love.

Then he glanced over at Max, who'd been quiet for too long. His tone thick with lust, Sloan closed his eyes and pulled free of her, dipping back in over and over. "Look at our woman, Max. So warm and wet. Do you want her?"

Shifting to the top of the bed, Max trailed his fingers down Oriana's cheek. He bent down to lay a soft kiss on her lips. "Yes, but don't stop what you're doing. I'll take her mouth while you take her body. Seeing her taking you in like that is fucking hot."

Sloan grinned and tightened his grip on her thigh, rocking his hips even as Max dropped his towel and pressed into her mouth. She let her saliva slick his length, not trying to control anything as he held the back of her head and eased in deeper. He tasted fresh from their shower, with the slightly salty tang of precum as he pulled out almost all the way and she circled the head of his dick with her tongue. His groan coming almost in time with Sloan's brought a warm satisfaction deep into her core. They found a rough rhythm, losing themselves to the pleasure her body could give them.

Knowing she could do this to them, that she could fulfill their every desire while they gave her the world was all the sweetness she needed when they fucked her like this. She felt deliciously used, no need to ask for anything she wanted because they already knew and gave her it all with their whispered words, with their gruff noises that told her how much she pleased them. Her focus was so keyed to what they were taking from her that the pleasure she received became almost secondary.

Until Sloan noticed her watching him and went still. An evil glint in his eyes, he lifted her, changing his grip on her bandaged thigh so the pain came fresh and sharp, slamming into her so she felt every inch of him, the angle stimulating the spot inside her that stole her from her pleasant plateau and tossed her to the summit. The bruising ache, the spike of pleasure, held her high on the razor's edge of climax, and he knew her body well enough to keep her there until she was screaming for release.

He gave it to her, driving in hard and grinding his pelvis against her to stimulate her clit. The coiling tightness within splintered like scalding glass dropped in icy liquid. Her eyes teared as her back bowed, lips parted to gulp in air. Her throat felt raw and the strength left her as she rode the last erotic wave, shuddering as Sloan jerked against her one last time.

That he'd come with her was a relief, because she was so sensitive she wasn't sure she could take any more. But she wasn't done. She had to force her heavy head up to see Max, needing to make sure he wasn't left out.

His hand on his dick, he met her eyes, stroking hard as he came on her breasts. She'd have preferred if she could have gotten him off, but he didn't seem to mind at all as he braced his hands on the edge of the bed and let out a tired laugh.

"Give me a minute and I'll clean that up. Bathroom is too far right now." He smiled as he leaned down to kiss her.

Sloan grunted, dragging himself up the bed on her other side. The sound of the nightstand drawer sliding open, then closed, had both her and Max looking over at him. He grinned and held up a container of wet wipes. "No need to go anywhere."

Max took the wipes and tidied up his mess, grinning when she squirmed as he spent more time than necessary rubbing her nipples with the cool cloth. He tossed the wipes in the small trash can on his side of the bed, then stretched out beside her and undid her cuffs, holding her as Sloan tended to her leg, cleaning the cuts with sterile saline water and spreading an antibiotic cream before covering it again. Oriana watched Sloan, bent over her leg, his jaw hard and his hands shaking just a little.

He was either questioning what he'd done or so wound up from his own high that he was slow to come down. Maybe a little of both. She wanted to reassure him, but her body felt heavy and it was a struggle to keep her eyes open. She touched Max's hand, happy to see he was watching Sloan as well.

He cleared his throat. "Didn't want to ruin the scene by mentioning it, but I like what you did there, tracing out S&M. And your knifemanship is exquisite."

"Thanks." Sloan rubbed his lips with his fist, then took a deep breath. "I need a minute."

He was off the bed and out of the room before either she or Max could react. Max sighed, lying down and wrapping his arm around her, preventing her from getting up. He kissed her shoulder, nuzzling her neck as he whispered to her. "How you feeling, sugar?"

Physically, she felt amazing, but her chest ached as she thought of Sloan, so torn between what they all wanted and his inability to share the aftermath with them. They'd talked about it in the past—even he wasn't sure why he needed to be alone when a scene ended. He'd tried forcing himself to stay, but that seemed to make it harder for him to recover. And Oriana hated seeing his strained smile, his touch always too careful, almost hesitant.

Sloan taking a bit of time to himself didn't bother her, so long as he wasn't beating himself up over something that she'd enjoyed. He promised her he didn't, but she knew his conscience was more of a sadist than he was.

"Oriana?" Max laced his fingers with hers, rising up on his elbow to study her face. He relaxed when she smiled at him. "You're worried about him."

She nodded, wishing she could make Max go check on him, but knowing he wouldn't leave her. "I guess I hoped this time would be different. We've been planning and negotiating for a year. Everything went perfectly, but he still..."

"I don't think he regrets the scene, if that helps any." Max's hand left hers as he lifted it to tuck a strand of hair behind her ear. "Honestly, I think he feels vulnerable, and as much as he loves us, he doesn't like showing weakness."

"That's never going to change, is it?"

Max frowned and dropped his gaze to the bed. "Hard to say. Do you want me to check on him?"

"Yes." She giggled when his frown deepened as though he hadn't expected the answer. He usually wouldn't leave her side for hours after a scene, but they weren't at the club. There was no reason for him to worry. About *her* anyway. "He'll probably be all grumpy, but he needs to be reminded that he's part of us. Even if he tells you to go away, at least he'll know we care."

"He knows that." Max rolled his eyes as she shoved his shoulder. "Fine, my pushy little sub. I'll go make sure our big bad sadist is all right."

"Good boy." She jumped when he playfully swatted her butt. As he slipped out of the room, a hazy sensation of tranquility settled over her. Even after years with both men, she still couldn't believe how lucky she was. She had more than any woman could ever ask for. Two men who loved her and she could be completely honest with. Who were willing to explore her darkest desires and never made her wonder if she was messed up for what she needed or wanted.

The house was quiet, so Sloan couldn't be that upset about Max checking on him. She'd hear them otherwise. Content, she closed her eyes, but the urge to pee had her sitting up and untangling herself from the sheets to hurry to the bathroom.

* * * *

With the curtains drawn in the living room, Sloan had to feel his way to the couch through the darkness. He sat slowly, fisting his hands against his knees to stop them from shaking. Eyes closed, he still saw the blood trailing down Oriana's thigh. Blood he'd drawn.

The blood itself didn't do much for him, except for the fact that the stark red on her golden flesh was beautiful. Her soft whimpers, her struggle to be still as he hurt her, was nothing short of exquisite. His hand had been steady as he'd cut her, knowing just how deep he could go without doing serious damage, but it was how he felt when it was over that he couldn't deal with. He'd tried to explain it to Max and Oriana, and yet, he couldn't seem to find the right words.

They thought he was slammed with regrets after a scene, but it wasn't that at all. He just didn't know how to relax into the high. He felt…too good. The control he held during a scene escaped him once it was over. It reminded him of the one time he'd smoked a joint with friends as a teen. Fun until the drug took over and his brain was fuzzy and he couldn't trust his own thoughts. He'd never touched drugs after that. Or anything else that could affect his judgment. Control of himself wasn't something he cared to jeopardize.

But there were times his iron grip on himself faltered, and being alone was the only way he knew how to regain clarity. Whether it was after a game, with a win or a loss, adrenaline agitating him to the point that he might lash out, or at the end of a scene when he couldn't trust himself to say or do anything right.

His only regret was that people thought he was angry when he took off. Max and Oriana understood him better than most, but he was sure they still wondered sometimes if *they'd* done something wrong. He'd offer reassurance once he felt normal again. Until then, at least they had each other.

The hall light came on and Sloan sighed as he saw Max standing in the doorway. He should have expected the man to come, either on his own or because Oriana wanted him to make sure Sloan was okay.

He cracked his knuckles, happy at least that his hands had stopped shaking. And he didn't want to punch Max as his best friend crossed the room. All good things.

"I know what you're gonna ask." Sloan slouched back into the sofa, giving Max a crooked smile as he sat beside him. "I'm fine. I'm sorry I left like that, I just—"

"When I'm not around, you don't take off." Max braced his hands on his thighs, not looking at Sloan. "And yeah, you don't do edgeplay without me, but it's hard to know what's going on in your head when you shut down like this. If you just need a minute, I'll give it to you. Wish you'd stay with us though—even if that means you can't play big, tough Dom all the time."

"I'm not trying to be tough. I just don't want to..." Sloan rubbed the tense spot between his eyes, getting that they had to be able to discuss any issues, but not sure he could be any clearer. "I never know how I'll react when I'm leaving that headspace. I could hurt you or her without meaning to."

Max nodded slowly, finally meeting his eyes. "I don't think you would. But what I think doesn't matter. You don't believe it, and no one's gonna convince you otherwise."

Sloan closed his eyes and shook his head. If Max were a sub, he could probably just order him to back off. Then again, that wouldn't work with Oriana if she decided there was a problem. But Max saw more than either of them, and he was the reason they'd made it this far. Sloan hadn't been sure if he had what it took to be in a stable relationship, but Max had forced him to see all the little things that made them strong together. A lot of negotiation. More talking than Sloan would have ever considered necessary. But it was worth it because Sloan didn't want to know what a life without Oriana and Max would look like.

"I promised I'd try harder. And I haven't. I didn't mean to do this again." He sighed, pushing away from the sofa to stand. "Is Oriana okay? She knows this has nothing to do with her, right? I'm just...fucked up."

"You're not fucked up, you're just a slow learner." Max slapped his shoulder, a broad smile on his lips. "You'd never be as indulgent with a sub as we've been with you. Rather than worrying if you'll share too much when you're feeling all exposed, how about you consider that maybe you need to share that part of yourself with us?"

Realizing he was clenching his jaw to the point of pain, Sloan forced himself to relax. And scratched the scruff on his jaw. "I left before I could tell you both how much I love you. It felt…sappy. And I don't do—"

"Fuck, man." Max threw his arm over Sloan's shoulder and pressed a noisy kiss to his cheek. "I love you too. And next time, I'm cuffing you to the bed frame and forcing you to be sappy and vulnerable and all the rest. No more hiding from us."

Not fucking happening. Sloan scowled, but he felt the tension ease from his muscles. Seriously, what was the worst that could happen if he stayed after a scene? The two most precious people in his life had seen him at his lowest. And Max would never let him hurt Oriana in a bad way.

A smile crept across his lips as he started up the stairs. He was glad Max had come to tell him he was being stupid. He wanted to hold Oriana as she slept. See that she was feeling good after the scene he'd spent months planning.

He just hoped he hadn't spoiled everything for her by being a distant asshole.

As they reached the top of the steps, he heard a loud thump. A cry. Then silence.

His eyes went wide as Max went still beside him. They moved together, rushing into the bedroom to find the bed empty. Sloan tripped over a pile of clothes on the floor, his knees hitting the carpet as Max strode past him and threw the bathroom door open.

Oriana was there. And there was blood. Not beautiful, but frightening.

And she wasn't moving.

Chapter Four

The last act was almost over, but Sahara wasn't ready for the date to end. She also wasn't about to let Dominik know that because it seemed a little desperate. If he didn't ask her to hang out longer, she'd just go home and hope he'd enjoyed himself enough to ask her out again.

Pretty pathetic, Sahara. You're not fifteen anymore. Just say something!

Instead of watching the stage, Dominik had his eyes on her. And a knowing smile on his lips. Her cheeks heated as he reached out to curve his hand under her chin. Something in his eyes made her feel like she'd just painted a very clear picture for him of all her most private thoughts.

"It's a little cold out, but would you like to go for a walk?" Dominik's request sounded so simple, but his attention on her was so intense it was more like being asked to completely expose herself to him. During the show and the meal, there'd been plenty of distractions, but they'd still gotten to know one another better.

The idea of walking with him shouldn't be such a big deal, but she knew she'd be letting him in all the way. Having sex would be so much simpler, but he'd made his intentions clear. With him, she'd never have to wonder if she was nothing more than a good time.

Which was perfect. She was ready to see if this could actually be a new beginning. A real relationship with someone she could trust.

He didn't seem surprised that she didn't answer right away. He inclined his head, watched the rest of the show, and paid the bill.

Helped her put on her coat, then held out his hand as if that was the only reply he needed.

She took a deep breath, a sweet, heart-racing, head-lightening rush hitting her as she placed her hand in his. Being with him felt damn good. She couldn't remember the last time she was this happy.

The cold air hit her as they stepped out onto the sidewalk, and she laughed when Dominik pulled her tight against his side with his big arm around her shoulders. She grinned up at him as they walked. "Do you like perpetuating the illusion that Masters are mind readers?"

He snorted, rubbing her arm as he kept a steady pace that was easy for her to match. "You assume I'm not holding you to keep myself warm?"

"Yep. You're too big and tough to let a little cold bother you." She leaned into him as they strolled down the quiet streets, already in sight of the pier. There weren't many people out and about at this time of year, but there were boats bobbing in the distance and she never got tired of taking in the sights. New York had its own urban charm, and she never went long before visiting her friends and family to take in the familiar hustle. Still, if she compared the two, she could truly say Nova Scotia had become her home.

Curious, she glanced over at Dominik. "Do you like it here?"

He blinked, looking around as though he weren't sure what she meant. "The area is beautiful, but I suspect you mean something more. And the answer is yes. I could see spending the rest of my life here, which probably means I'll be traded next year." He gave her a little squeeze and chuckled when she bit her bottom lip. "Not really. I have a nice long contract and a no-trade clause. I'll probably retire with the Cobras, but I'm not there yet. I'm exactly where I want to be."

"So no regrets?" She had some the second the words left her mouth and shadows filled his eyes. *Nice going, dumbass.* She stopped walking and faced him before he could answer. "I mean, Cam is here now, but your mom isn't. And your other brother…"

"My mother is fine with my sisters. And Josh…" Dominik began rubbing her arm again, his forehead creasing slightly. "I'm afraid for him every time he's deployed, but so proud of him. He's a soldier and that won't change, no matter where I live. We all grow up and make our own way in life. I can't see making mine anywhere but here."

"But you miss him. You didn't hesitate when you said your mom was fine, but you—"

"Perceptive little thing, aren't you?" He smoothed her hair away from her cheeks with his fingertips, studying her face. "Yes. It's been a long time and I miss him. My sisters make him things to get through it, but I'm not really into knitting or quilting." The edges of his lips quirked. "I write him once a week. Hear back from him least every other month. For some reason, he can't do email or Skype. Not sure I want to know why." He paused. "He always asks if Cam is staying out of trouble. I'm happy our little brother has given him no cause for concern."

Sounded good, but there was still a tension in his eyes and his tone. She reached up to touch his cheek, much like he was touching hers. "How long since you heard from him?"

"Little longer than usual, but I'm sure he's fine."

"You like that word."

"I do." He leaned down, pressing his lips to hers gently, the heat of his lips warming her straight down to her toes. Then he took her hand in his and kissed her palm. "Don't worry so much, sunshine."

"I can't help it. I consider you a friend, and I know how much you love your brother."

"Just a friend?" He kissed her palm again, but it was different with the heat in his eyes. If he wanted to change the subject, he'd found the perfect way to do it. "Is friendship all you want from me, Sahara?"

"You know it's not." She tipped her head back as he drew her arms around his waist. His fingers delved into her hair as he slanted his lips to hers. Her lips parted to let him in, no hesitation, no doubts reaching her with the heat of him all around her and the fresh scent of him, all man and spice mingling with the ocean air taking over her senses.

His kiss was complete possession, narrowing her awareness to the pressure of his lips, the way his tongue touched hers, tasting her, guiding hers in an erotic dance that made doing this out in the open seem naughty. Her knees were weak and she tightened her grip on his arms for support. And to get closer to him. She needed to be closer, but they were outside and there was only so much he could give her.

But...*damn*. If this was how the man kissed, she wasn't sure she liked his limits for tonight.

He backed away first, a smile on his lips and hunger in his eyes. Maybe he'd changed his mind?

"You tempt a man, girl." He swept his thumb over her bottom lip. "If I was younger and stupider, I might..." There was a buzzing from his pocket. Probably his phone. He ignored it, continuing when it stopped. "I want to do this again. Playoff schedule is difficult, but maybe a movie Thursday night when I get back from New York?"

"I'd like that." Actually, she wanted everything *now*, but there was something special about him wanting to take things slow. As if she were worth waiting for. She'd never experienced a gradual buildup in a relationship, but her track record wasn't great. Maybe patience would lead to a better end game. "You should probably get some rest. I don't want to be responsible for you not playing your best tomorrow."

He laughed and pulled her against his chest, kissing her hair. "Could you be any more perfect?"

Before she could answer, his phone buzzed again. She backed away so he could pull it out.

He checked the number, then answered. "What's wrong, Max?"

She frowned as he put more space between them, speaking too low for her to hear. It was probably Max Perron, and she knew they were friends. If he was answering the call, Max had probably called both times. Which he wouldn't do unless it was serious.

Serious with the Cobras could mean a lot of things. She pressed her hand to her throat, hoping that they'd already been through the worst. They couldn't lose anyone else.

"How is she?"

Silence. Dominik paced across the sidewalk, nodding as he rubbed his forehead.

"*She*." *So it's Oriana.* Sahara inhaled slowly, trying not to let petty bitterness take over. It wasn't like Oriana was calling him.

But if it was her, and Max thought Dominik should be involved, that meant he was still involved in their life. It was no secret that he cared about Oriana. That he'd loved her.

Only...Sahara wouldn't have even considered a relationship with him if he was still interested in another woman.

Don't assume anything. Maybe Max just needed to talk to his friend.

"Yeah. All right, I'll be right there."

Maybe not.

Dominik hung up and glanced over at her, clearly distracted. He gave her a stiff smile. "I have to go. I'll call you a cab."

Okay, that stung. Sahara couldn't help feeling like an inconvenience that Dominik needed to deal with as quickly as possible.

Which was a stupid way to think of it. She was being nasty and jealous and she didn't like herself very much right now. So she tried to be understanding. "Is it Oriana? Is she okay?"

"She will be." Dominik fisted his hand by his side, sounding like he'd make sure of it himself. "I'm going to kill that idiot."

Her eyes went wide. "Max?"

"No. Sloan. What the fuck was he thinking?" Dominik shook his head and rubbed a hand over his face. "I should have never left him to...his head's not right. She doesn't need this right now."

"Did Sloan hurt her?" The man was scary, but Sahara had always thought he was a good man. And Oriana loved him. There was a big difference between sadistic play and abuse, and Sahara thought she understood that. But she could be wrong. "What did he—"

"No. This isn't his fault. Well, it is, but only what he did after..." Letting out an irritated groan, Dominik started dialing. "I'm sorry, I can't discuss this with you."

"Of course not. It's private." Her throat tightened as she realized this wasn't about his friendship with Max. It sounded like a scene had gone wrong, and Dominik had trained Max and Sloan. And he'd been Oriana's Dom. So he felt responsible. "She's still...I mean, you're still involved with her."

"What?" Dominik pressed "end call" on his phone and stared at her. "Is that what you think? Sahara, I wouldn't have asked you out if I was in a relationship."

"But you're a Dom. And she was your sub."

"She's not anymore."

"Are you sure about that? Max calls and you drop everything. Which is exactly what a responsible Dom should do." Her eyes burned, but she didn't embarrass herself by crying, which was good at least. She should have expected as much. He'd said "this"—as in dating and not going to the club—was all he wanted. But maybe he meant it was all he wanted from *her*. "I don't know what the arrangement with you and Oriana is, but it would have been nice if you'd let me in on it so I could figure out if I wanted to be your girl on the side."

"You're completely misunderstanding the situation, and I don't have time to explain it to you, even if I wanted to." His tone was level, but it didn't change the finality of his words. Or the fact that he held up a hand, preventing her from saying a word as he spoke to the cab company and gave them directions to pick her up.

This time, the heat she felt was from anger. Her nails dug into her palms as she glared at his back. She wanted to throw something at him, she was that pissed off. And she knew, somehow, she was in the wrong.

She should just leave. He wouldn't want to hear what she had to say anyway.

He's not Grant.

True, but he wasn't exactly being the nice guy she was comfortable talking to either.

"Sahara, please don't look at me like that. I'm sorry I have to cut the date short." He sighed and shoved his hands in his pockets. "You've claimed to 'get' the lifestyle many of the players are involved in, but I don't think you do. There are different kinds of commitments. You're right, as a Dom, I still feel some responsibility for—"

"*Now* you're going to use the 'Dom' excuse? Which is it, Dominik? She's not your sub, you're not all that interested in going to the club anymore, but when it's convenient—"

"You think any of this is *convenient*?"

"Of course not, because that would make me a horrible person. Oriana has Max and Sloan, but for some reason she needs you too.

Please forgive me for saying anything. I hope she's okay." Thankfully, the cab had turned the corner. She could get out of there before she let her emotions take the conversation any further. "Thank you for the wonderful evening. If you're ever at the club when I am, make sure to say hi. I may be willing to play if she's busy."

His eyes narrowed as he reached for the back door of the cab and opened it for her. His tone was sharp as she passed. "I don't think you have any business going to the club, Sahara. I don't believe there's a submissive bone in your body."

"Maybe you're right." She sat and hugged herself, glaring at him. "Or maybe I'm just not her."

The door slammed. Dominik paid the cabbie, then strode off down the street, probably in a hurry to get to his car. She trembled, not sure how to absorb how quickly things had gone bad. Then again, she shouldn't be all that surprised. This was why she wished her friends would give Grant a break. They didn't see how badly she could overreact without even realizing she was doing so until it was too late.

What the hell had she just done?

"Miss, where would you like me to take you?" The cab driver asked. The elderly man didn't seem at all annoyed that she hadn't given him directions yet. Which was nice.

She gave him her address, relieved when he didn't try to start a conversation. She didn't need another opportunity to prove what an idiot she could be.

Once, after the *perfect* date, was plenty.

* * * *

Getting to the hospital took less than ten minutes, but Dominik was pretty damn sure he was too late to stop Sloan from flying completely off the handle. He parked as fast as possible and hustled across the lot, into the Emergency entrance, dodging empty wheelchairs and stretchers in the hall. He came to a stop in front of the reception desk, not sure if Oriana would still be in Emergency or if she'd been transferred to a private room.

He didn't hear any shouting, so she had probably been moved. He quickly asked a nurse to look up Mrs. Perron. She smiled after he gave his name and told him where to find Oriana's room.

An elevator took him to the fifth floor. When the doors opened, he heard raised voices.

Yep, this is the right place. He squared his shoulders, taking long strides to reach Sloan's side. And jerk him back before he took a swing at the cop. Who already had a pair of cuffs out.

Sloan twisted free, not getting any closer to the cop, but still talking in a way that was gonna get him hauled in. "I'm not leaving her. Get out of my fucking way."

"You think she wants you around her, you sadistic bastard?" The officer stabbed his finger in the air in front of Sloan's face. "Keep it up. You're just giving us a stronger case against you."

"Then talk to my goddamn lawyer. Until then, you have no right—"

"Her husband is the only one with any rights here, pal. The doctor considers you a risk to his patient, so you will leave or I'm bringing you in."

Well, that made the situation pretty clear. Max had explained as much as possible on the phone, but Dominik hadn't quite understood why Sloan would flip out in the hospital while Oriana was in bad shape.

Not that it was smart of him to lose it either way, but Dominik could sympathize. For whatever reason, the doctor and the police were treating this like it was a case of domestic abuse. Max could legally stay with Oriana. The cop had a point; Sloan didn't have any rights.

"Look at me, Sloan." Dominik fisted his hand in Sloan's jacket, giving him a little shake to get his attention. When those dark green eyes narrowed at him, he gave Sloan a short nod. "I get it, but you're not helping her like this. Come take a walk with me."

Rage, and strength, seemed to seep out of Sloan. He paled as he glanced toward the room where two more officers and a statuesque black woman in a crisp skirt suit were standing. The woman said something to the officers and started over.

"I didn't... She fell." Sloan pressed his eyes shut, leaning against the wall when Dominik released him. "I need to be with her."

Dominik squeezed Sloan's arm, watching the woman as she spoke to the officer. And got him to back off with a few sharp words. The man didn't look happy, but he didn't argue with her.

She came over, a professional smile on her lips, but a fair amount of compassion in her eyes. "Mr. Callahan, my name is Tina Dejesus. I am with the Department of Justice, Victim Services." She held out her hand and appeared to relax a bit more when Sloan straightened and shook it respectfully. "I am an investigative social worker, and we have received a referral on your family. I need to interview you all separately to address the allegation."

"The allegation." Sloan stared off at nothing, almost as though he were in shock. "They think I hurt her."

"The doctor was required to file a report due to the nature of some of the injuries, but I'll be speaking to Oriana shortly. Maybe you can take a walk with your friend and meet me in the family room down the hall in about fifteen minutes?" She smiled when Sloan nodded absently. "I understand that this situation must be very stressful, but it will go smoothly if you're willing to cooperate. Oriana is receiving the best care. I'm sure you'll be able to see her soon."

Silence for a few, long minutes, then Sloan took a deep breath and inclined his head. "Yeah. I don't want her upset. Just...please tell her I'm not far. If she asks for me—"

"Someone will let you know." The social worker met Dominik's eyes, as though assessing whether or not he'd make things better or worse. At his level look, she grinned. "Your players are clearly devoted to you, Mr. Callahan. You must be a very good coach."

Sloan let out a lifeless laugh. "Dominik was in love with Oriana. He probably still is. If I don't come back, send your officers to the parking lot to find my body."

Nice. Dominik ground his teeth, refusing to react to the social worker's questioning look. As Sloan made his way toward the elevator, Dominik remained at his side, wondering why he'd even bothered. Yes, the team needed their assistant coach, but the head coach could manage without Sloan.

A few days behind bars would be good for the man. He might not deserve it for the edgeplay that had likely freaked out the doctor, but from what Max had told Dominik, Oriana had been left alone after the scene, which is how she'd cracked her skull on the bathtub. To make things worse, Sloan had lost his cool when he'd been asked to leave the hospital room. He was an idiot and he was lucky anyone cared enough to keep him out of jail.

They were outside before Sloan decided he wanted to talk. He actually stopped by the smokers and bummed a cigarette, his hand shaking as he lit it. "Thank you for coming. I don't know why you did, except you want to tell me how badly I fucked up. Have at it."

"You don't smoke, Sloan. What the fuck are you doing?" Not exactly what he'd planned to say, but it made him sick to see Sloan with a cigarette between his lips. The man was smarter than this. "You want a fucking drink while you're at it? We have a game tomorrow."

Sloan choked out a laugh, walking out into the parking lot and leaving Dominik half running to keep up. "This gets out and I won't be there. The league takes domestic abuse pretty seriously."

"True. But you aren't abusive. Oriana consented; this won't go further than a few questions about what happened."

"You sure about that? The doctor called the cops because of 'violent injuries.' The nurse who put Oriana in the hospital gown told me and Max to leave, then the doctor joined her. And the cops showed up." Sloan pressed the heels of his palms to his eyes. "Max was able to get back in, but I haven't seen her since."

Dominik wasn't sure he would have been reasonable in the same scenario, but he was here to make sure Sloan didn't aggravate things. So he faced Sloan, arms folded over his chest, waiting for the man to look at him. When he didn't, Dominik cleared his throat.

Looking worn out, Sloan lifted his head.

"This whole thing is a mess, but you can't lose control. Oriana needs to see her Doms are there for her. That everything is going to be okay. Do you think she'll believe that if she finds out you were about to be arrested?"

"The cop kept calling me a sick freak. Said I would pay for what I did to her." Sloan rubbed his lips with his fist. "I ignored him at first, but then the doctor wouldn't let me in the room. I heard her crying. She didn't know what was happening. Max told the doctor he was her husband and they couldn't keep him out. But...I don't have the right to be with her. That never occurred to me before."

Damn it, Dominik didn't want to feel for Sloan, but he did. Regardless of their past, Dominik knew he'd never really fit in the relationship. But Sloan did. He was as important to Oriana as Max was, but the law would never acknowledge his place in her life.

From day to day, the three of them could live as though none of that mattered, but in times like this, the world they lived in would always push Sloan aside. A fact he'd never had to face before now.

Moving on had been hard. Dominik still wondered what he could have done differently so he could still be one of the men in Oriana's life. But for the most part, he'd accepted that it wasn't meant to be. What they'd had wasn't solid enough to fight for.

What Sloan had with her was worth every barrier they'd have to cross, but at the moment, there was a wall standing between him and the woman he loved that couldn't be moved. All Sloan could do was wait there until she could meet him on the other side.

This had nothing to do with Dominik, but he couldn't help wanting to stand by Sloan and make sure the man knew he wasn't alone. Dominik had no doubt that Sloan would be there for him if someone had made the call and said he was the only one who could get past the haze of anger and pain. He hadn't hesitated when Max had asked it of him. There was nothing he wouldn't do for friends and family. And like it or not, he considered Sloan a little of both.

He let out a heavy sigh and took the cigarette from Sloan, dropping it to crush it into the dirt. "Enough of the fucking bullshit. You're a good Dom. I didn't train you to fall apart when things get tough. Pull your shit together and figure out what you're going to do next. The woman you love is in the hospital. Everything you do from this point on will be about her. About making sure she has everything she needs."

"What can I do for her here, Dominik? They're going to try to keep me away from her—who knows for how long? She'll be in the hospital for days for the head wound."

"And if they do, you're going to make sure this isn't harder on her. You talk to her on the phone, you send her flowers, and you don't give her any reason to worry about anything besides getting better."

Raking his fingers through his hair, Sloan let out a quiet groan and shook his head. "I can't fucking believe this shit. We've got to talk to a social worker."

"That's what you get for being a kinky fucker." Dominik grinned when Sloan laughed. Some might figure it was too soon to joke about things, but he could tell Sloan had calmed down enough to deal with the drama like an adult. This wasn't the first time the police had to get involved in something like this. Hell, he'd heard of cases where rough sex led to an investigation. Shit happened.

They spoke for a bit longer, walking around the perimeter of the hospital grounds. When they went inside, the cops watched Sloan as he headed for the family room, while the social worker motioned Dominik over.

"Mr. Perron asked if you could sit with Oriana while I speak to him. At this point, I don't see any reason to keep Mr. Callahan away from his partner, but unfortunately, hospital security is insisting he leave after I've questioned him."

"They won't even let him say goodnight to her?" Losing his own temper wouldn't help anyone, but it was starting to seem like Sloan and Oriana would continue to pay for the doctor's overreaction. "They're taking this a bit far, don't you think?"

"It may seem like that, but your friend wasn't exactly reasonable when this all began." She pulled a file folder out of the huge purse slung over her arm and headed back toward Oriana's room. "If all goes well, I'll see if I can get him a few minutes with her."

"Thank you."

She smiled, holding the door open as Max came out. "I should thank you. This could have turned out a lot worse."

Max held out his hand, then pulled Dominik in for a rough hug as they shook. His throat worked as he swallowed and looked back into the room, and Dominik tightened his grip on the other man just long enough for Max to school his features. Then he let Max go with the social worker and stepped into the room.

Golden-mahogany hair spilled across the pale blue pillow case, eyes closed and normally light olive skin deathly white, Oriana was still one of the most beautiful women he'd ever known. He moved silently, hoping not to wake her. The lights were low, but he could still see the harsh bruises on the side of her head, with half a dozen stitches holding the torn flesh together.

He inhaled slowly, imagining how fucking scary it must have been for Max and Sloan to find her—probably unconscious and bleeding out on the floor. Max's voice had broken when he'd mentioned that she hit her head on the side of the bathtub. And how he'd left the floor soaking wet.

Finding out what happened had brought back all kinds of messed-up emotions for Dominik. Mostly anger, but he couldn't really blame anyone for the accident. And seeing Oriana, he couldn't even be irritated at Sloan's reaction.

If she were still mine, no one could have forced me out of this room.

Which, considering how pissed off Sloan must have been, it was surprising that only three cops were here. Sloan must be going soft.

Lips slanted in a wry smile, Dominik settled into the armchair by the bed. It creaked as he shifted and Oriana's eyes shot open.

"I didn't mean to wake you, sweetheart." He leaned forward, catching himself before he could reach out and touch her. Her men would be back before long, and he needed to be here as a friend. One who didn't touch her cheek and hold her as though he had every right to. Because he didn't. Not anymore.

Which didn't hurt as much as it once had. He wanted her happy and healthy. He still cared about her. But the loss was more of a distant ache than a fresh wound.

Oriana tried to lift her head and groaned. Then pressed her eyes shut and sighed. "I'm surprised that you're here. Did Max call you?"

"Yes."

"He shouldn't have. I'm sorry, it's not fair of him to drag you into this." She winced as she adjusted her head on the pillow. "Not that I don't like seeing you, but you have your own life and—"

"He called because of Sloan." Not that she'd be happy about that, but he didn't want her feeling guilty about him being pulled away from living his own life. Dominik and Oriana had finally gotten to a good place. And they were damn well going to stay there. "I'm not sure how much you know about what happened. The social worker questioned you?"

She frowned, nodding slowly. "Yes. She asked if things were okay at home. If I was ever afraid and if there were a lot of arguments. I got dizzy and sick and she told me we could take as long as I needed, but I didn't want to talk to her at all. She seemed satisfied when I told her neither Sloan nor Max have ever done anything to me that we hadn't discussed first."

"You do understand why they had to ask, though? There are women who..." His words trailed off as he remembered some of the bruises he'd seen on Sahara when she'd first joined the Cobras' Ice Girls. Those hadn't been marks made during consensual edgeplay.

Fuck, the look on her face when she'd asked if Sloan had hurt Oriana... He'd been too distracted to do more than tell her it wasn't like that. And then they'd fought and he'd left her with the cab.

He had to call her. Apologize and somehow make things right.

She might not give him a chance, but he couldn't blame her. She'd been through too much to deal with a man treating her as badly as he had.

You're an idiot, Mason.

Oriana reached out and touched the back of his hand. "What is it?"

Well, they were friends, right? No reason not to tell her. He'd earned a few people telling him he'd fucked up. "I was on a date. The way I left—"

"With who? And before you beat yourself up, you said you came for Sloan. He's the assistant coach and it's the playoffs." Her passion for the game came through nice and clear, no matter how much pain she was in. He couldn't help but grin at the irritation on her face. "If this chick doesn't understand that the game comes first, she's not the right girl for you."

"Easy, tiger." Dominik laughed, turning his hand in hers to stroke her knuckles with his thumb. "She respects the game; I just wasn't clear with her. She thinks I came for you."

Biting her bottom lip, Oriana met his eyes. "But you didn't."

"No." His brow furrowed and he cleared his throat, feeling strangely uncomfortable. "But I'm glad I came."

She didn't say anything. Her eyes were on something—someone behind him.

Sloan stepped up to his side and put a hand on his shoulder. "So am I."

Chapter Five

Sahara was so relieved when she got home, she walked straight in and got to the kitchen before she realized something was off. Her door hadn't been locked. And there was someone in her house.

The urge to scream lodged in her throat, and she froze when she saw Grant sitting at her kitchen table. When he stood, she knew she had to run. But her body ignored the command her mind was screaming. He came toward her, and she winced as he put his hand on her arm.

"I didn't mean to scare you. I swear, the door was unlocked when I got here." His grip tightened when she finally calmed enough to try to pull away. "You have to listen to me. Sit down. We'll figure out who did this."

He pointed at the far wall. The window seat Scott had made her was in pieces, the wood chopped up like someone had taken an ax to it. But she didn't see an ax. Or any weapons. Not that he needed them to hurt her, or worse. Grant didn't want to kill her, did he?

This wouldn't be the first time she had wondered that, but she wasn't the scared girl who'd once stayed with him because she was too afraid to get away. Or because she let him convince her he was going to change.

"My friends are waiting for me. I have to go." She twisted free and put some distance between them. She knew the exact amount of space she needed to avoid the swing of his fist. It was easier when he was drunk. Unfortunately, he seemed perfectly sober. She'd have to pick her words carefully. "I'll file a report with the police. Thank you for watching the place for me."

His eyes narrowed. He stepped forward, his jaw hardening when she skidded back. "You don't believe me. You still think I'll hurt you."

"No, it's not that, Grant. If I keep my friends waiting, they'll come looking. And they won't buy your story about—"

"My story? Are you fucking kidding me?" He brought his hand up and she cringed, but he simply raked his fingers through his hair. "I know you were out with Dominik Mason. And that you two argued. There are pictures online, and I'm not surprised that it didn't work out. He's not right for you. I came here to prove that you could count on me to be your friend. Like we talked about."

Okay, she wasn't sure he was listening to himself. Even if there were pictures of her and Dominik, how would he have seen them unless he was checking up on her? A phone call would have been reasonable. Showing up at her home…?

But pointing that out would piss him off. So she forced a smile and nodded. "That was thoughtful of you. I appreciate it. Maybe we can talk tomorrow?"

"Because your 'friends' are waiting? Don't lie to me. I saw you pull up in a cab. And get out alone." He reached for her again, then slammed his fist into his thigh when she shifted again. "Stop being such a fucking drama queen. Did you mean a word you said about us being friends?"

"Yes." She bit into her inner cheek, fighting not to tremble. The terror that tightened her throat made it hard to breathe. She had meant it. She'd been that fucking stupid. The rage in his eyes proved he hadn't changed at all. "Please, Grant. You have to understand how this looks. I'm a little freaked out. I'll stay at a friend's house and—"

"Whose house? Not Dominik's, he ditched you. Did he see how nuts you can be?" Grant smirked when she bit her bottom lip. "That's it, isn't it? You went nuts on him and he lost interest. Smart man." He shook his head. "I don't want to fight with you. Just sit down. Tell me how many guys you've pissed off and maybe we'll get a better idea of who could have done this."

She'd never reach the door with him standing, but maybe if she got him to relax a little, she could make a run for it. She nodded, moving toward the table. He pulled out a chair. Sat down.

Spinning on her heels, she bolted to the front door. She heard him behind her and knew she hadn't been fast enough. His hand flattened on the door before she could open it. His other hand latched on to her jaw, fingers digging in until she cried out.

"Why do you do this? I'm fucking trying, Sahara!"

Reacting without thinking, she drove her knee up into his groin. He let out a shout and stumbled back. She opened the door and took the stairs two at a time, losing both her shoes before she reached the parking lot. In her car, she fumbled with her keys. Got it started.

Grant stepped in front of the car. Hit the hood and shouted at her, but she couldn't hear what he was saying. Panic had her blood pulsing in her ears. She leaned on the horn and hit the gas.

He jumped out of the way just in time to avoid getting hit.

Tears blinded her as she drove, but she was afraid to stop. She hooked up her phone to her Bluetooth and tried calling Jami. No answer.

She couldn't call Akira. Cort would find Grant and kill him. Right now, she wasn't sure she cared if Grant wasn't around, but…damn it, no. She didn't want him dead. And she really didn't want Cort back in jail.

Red and blue lights flashed in the rearview mirror. She pulled over and quickly dried her tears. Damn it, could tonight go any worse? She rolled down her window and thunked her head back against the seat when she saw the woman in uniform, whose dark brown hair was pulled back in a tight bun, was none other than Officer Laura Tallent, who was in a relationship with *two* of the Cobras. Sahara didn't think Laura was much of a gossip, but she told her Domme—the fourth in their interesting quad—everything.

And her Domme, Chicklet, was best friends with the Cobras' assistant coach. So one way or another, everyone would find out about her getting pulled over and why if she didn't come up with a good excuse for driving erratically. Or fast. Or whatever she'd done.

They'll find out anyway if you report this. Which you should.

"Fuck my life." Sahara pulled out her license and registration, holding them out before Laura could even ask. "I'm sorry, Officer Tallent. I didn't realize I was speeding."

"You weren't. You drove through three stop signs."

Of all the... Sahara pressed her eyes shut. Running stop signs wasn't much better than speeding. She'd been so distracted, she could have driven straight into another car. Or a person. Her whole body started to shake and bile rose in her throat. Her eyes teared as she struggled to keep from throwing up or passing out.

"Sahara, are you okay?" Laura's professional demeanor softened as her deep blue eyes widened with concern. She leaned closer to the window. "I can't see you being this upset about a ticket. What's going on?"

There was no easy way to explain, and Sahara felt too damn raw to hold anything back. "Someone broke in to my house. He was still there when I walked in and I was scared, so I took off. I should have called the cops, but I just needed to get out of there. I can't believe I was so fucking stupid. He won't change—I really wanted to believe he'd change. My life is so much better now and I could have forgiven him."

"Whoa, wait a second. Did you know the person who broke in to your house?"

Sahara nodded and met Laura's eyes. "Yes. It was my ex-boyfriend, Grant Higgins."

"Shit. All right, are you willing to file a report? If you're too shaken to drive, you can call someone to pick up your car and I'll bring you to the station." Laura straightened when Sahara nodded again, looking relieved to have a purpose beyond discussing something so personal. She was a great cop and a good woman, but Sahara had never seen her hanging out with the other Cobra ladies.

She had her job and she had Chicklet. Sahara wasn't sure how her two men fit into the relationship; the few times she'd seen them at the club, the balance seemed a little uncertain. Not that Sahara could ever hope to make sense of it, she couldn't imagine managing more than one other person in her life like that.

Not like any of that mattered. Laura would take care of whatever needed to be handled. Privacy meant a lot less than safety right now, and Sahara just wanted to get as far as possible out of Grant's reach.

Who could she ask to get her car though? They'd have to come pick her up after; she couldn't expect Laura to babysit her all night.

If she managed to convince Laura and Chicklet not to tell anyone—she needed someone who wasn't in a relationship. Someone who wasn't into gossip.

There was always Pischlar. She trusted him enough to scene with at the club. He had a weird relationship with his best friend, Ian White, but they'd been spending less time together recently. And even if White was with him, he never did seem to pay much attention to what was going on around him.

The man wasn't stupid, despite what many seemed to think. He just looked at the world in such a straightforward way that subtle bullshit went right over his head. Almost as though he felt, if people really wanted him to know what was going on, they'd tell him directly. If not, it wasn't his business and he didn't need to worry about it.

"Can you call Shawn Pischlar?" Sahara climbed out of the car as Laura opened the door. Then leaned against the hood while Laura pulled out her cell phone, one brow lifted in question. "I'm afraid if I talk to him now, he'll assume the worst."

Laura grinned, her eyes sparkling with wry amusement. "I'm sure him getting a call on your behalf from the police won't give him the impression that this is good news."

Damn it, she's right. Sahara combed her fingers into her hair, dropping her head back and groaning.

One hand up, Laura shook her head. "Don't worry, I'll make sure he knows you're all right. If he sees my number and assumes there's a problem, he'll think it's about White or Vanek."

Not much better. Maybe this was a bad idea.

But it was too late. Laura apparently had Pischlar on speed dial. Which, considering Pischlar was one of the few who could handle White, wasn't all that surprising.

"Hey, Shawn. No, White's not in trouble. Excuse me? No, Raif doesn't want another..." Laura's cheeks reddened. "I really wouldn't know, *Sir*. You'll have to ask her."

Oh boy. Yep, very *big mistake.*

"In case you didn't notice, I am calling from my work phone—yes, I'm absolutely positive it's not White. Sahara's dealt with an emotional trauma and she's not fit to drive. I'm bringing her to the station to file a report. She wanted to know if you could pick up her car."

After a brief pause, Laura smiled and nodded. Sahara felt some of the tension ease from her chest.

"Yes. I radioed in for a unit to meet me here. They'll have her keys. I'll give them your name." Laura's brow furrowed slightly. "I'm not sure how long this will take. She might not want you to... Fine, I'll tell her."

After hanging up, Laura met Sahara's eyes. "He'll meet you at the station in about twenty minutes. He said not to speak to anyone without a lawyer. I do think the poor boy's spent too much time with the trouble triplets."

The slight Southern drawl in Laura's tone made Sahara smile. She could almost forget why she was going to the police station as she sat in the back of Laura's car, staring into the darkness. Could almost forget why she couldn't go home.

But just almost. The one good thing was this wasn't like the last time she'd had to escape Grant. Back then, she'd pushed away so many friends for daring to show concern that she'd had no one left to turn to. If she hadn't gotten the opportunity to come to Dartmouth and perform with the Cobras' Ice Girls...?

She had no idea where she'd be now. Maybe just miserable and depressed like she'd been for far too long while stuck in that relationship. More than likely, Grant would have killed her. She'd gone back and forth between believing he'd eventually have beaten her to death and convincing herself there was no way it would have gone that far. He'd gotten progressively more violent near the end, but...

Damn it, after tonight, it made even less sense than ever that she'd defend him. She'd lost her home, possibly twice now. She'd alienated family and friends. Why couldn't she just see him for what he was?

Because they don't know him. And I do. I've seen him kind and gentle and sweet.

She'd also seen him cold and cruel and vicious.

Reporting him won't change anything. His lawyers will be calling you in the morning.

Let them. She refused to cower again. At least no one else had gotten hurt because she'd tried to leave it all behind her and not look back. She couldn't even quite explain why she felt so fucking confused and guilty, but taking part of the blame was almost easier than believing the man she'd loved was that heartless. That he could tell her how much she meant to him one minute, then beat her down the next.

They pulled up in front of the station. Laura came around the car to meet Sahara on the sidewalk. A weariness had stolen into Laura's eyes, and she sounded worn out as she rested her hip against the side of her car, making no move to go into the station.

"You seem uncertain, Sahara. I can't force you to come in and file a report. I'm sure you know that if he can hurt you, he'll do the same to any woman he's with. Besides that, you're not safe. If he's gotten to the point that he's breaking in to your apartment, there's no telling what he will do next." She took a deep breath. "If you file a report, and follow through with pressing charges, we can bring him to court. Maybe get him out of here for good."

If the charges stuck. And if Grant's lawyers didn't find a way to make her look like a liar or a slut or whatever else they could manage to discredit her testimony.

Jaw clenched, she met Laura's steady gaze. The woman was probably used to victims being unable to follow through. And seeing the terrible consequences. Sahara wouldn't be yet another one of them.

"I'm doing this. I won't lie, I'm scared to death. But I refuse to give him that kind of power again. This is my home and I'm not running or hiding. I'm ready to do whatever I have to." Sahara's heart raced, almost as though saying the words out loud meant she was ready to climb into the pit and face whatever came at her. And she wasn't ready.

But there was no going back now.

Laura's smile was brilliant as she pushed away from the car. "You have no idea how happy I am to hear that. Come on, sweetie. I'll take you to the victims' advocate. He's a great guy."

Great or not, by the time Sahara was done filling out the report, answering all the questions, and having pictures taken of the bruises on her face, she wasn't sure she could keep from bursting into tears any longer. To file a restraining order, she had to bring up parts of the past she'd tried to bury deep. Reliving it all had her feeling like she'd gotten another beating. Like every officer in the station could see each and every bruise Grant had ever left on her body.

But when she came out of the back office, she spotted Pischlar, who was getting suspicious looks from the cops around him even though his black jean jacket covered most of his tattoos. He did look a bit like he could have been brought in wearing cuffs with his semi-mohawk and plug earrings, but all she saw was the understanding in his green eyes. He strode right up to her and took her in his arms, making it easy to toss aside her shield and take the strength he offered. His solid chest, the steel of the muscles in the arms he wrapped around her, the fact that he hadn't said a single word, but somehow knew exactly what she needed, all made him exactly *who* she needed at that moment.

Her nose and her eyes were leaking though, and she was suddenly worried about getting his shirt wet. She sniffed and peered up at him. "Get me out of here, Pisch?"

"Not a problem, pretty girl." He put his arm around her shoulders, nodded to Laura, and then guided Sahara out to the street. After opening the passenger's side door of her car, he waited for her to get settled, then crouched down and rubbed her thigh. "Where to? Do you want to go home?"

"No!" She covered her mouth with her hand, trying to gulp back the panic that had burst out with her reply. The very idea of going home made her skin crawl. Grant would come back. He wouldn't care about the restraining order. "Bring me to a hotel or…or something. I don't want to wake up Jami or Akira." Her throat tightened. "I did it again. She was right. Cort was right too, but I was horrible to him and—"

"Enough of that now, *Liebling*. They'll both understand." His lips pursed slightly and his brow creased in thought. "I don't like the idea of bringing you to a hotel. Are you comfortable coming back to my place? If not, I'll see if Chicklet—"

"I'm fine with you. I love Chicklet, but she's just as likely to hunt down Grant as Cort is."

"But you don't think I am?"

"Are you?"

The edges of his lips quirked and he shook his head. "No. I'm seeing to you. Higgins will get what's coming to him." Pisch reached up and gently touched her chin, running his fingers along her jaw. "This his handiwork?"

"It's nothing." She brushed his hand away gently. She hadn't seen the marks, but after the looks she'd gotten, it was probably ugly. A constant reminder of yet another mistake. One she didn't need. "Can we go somewhere? I don't care where at this point. I just don't want to be here anymore."

He nodded quickly and stood. "Consider us gone. And I won't mention what happened again, but I'm here if you need to talk."

"I appreciate this so much, Pisch." She hugged herself as he shot her a small smile before closing the door and moving around the car.

True to his word, Pischlar didn't bring up anything during the drive. He turned the radio on, cranking the volume when he noticed her singing under her breath. When they got to his apartment, he led the way, opening the door and letting her in without comment.

His apartment was cleaner than that of any guy she'd ever known, but not so polished that she was afraid to touch anything. Pulling off the disposable blue booties she'd gotten at the police station to cover her bare feet, she ducked into the bathroom to toss them in the trash, then went to the living room.

While she perched on the sofa, Pischlar disappeared into the kitchen. She heard the sound of running water.

"Feel like a tea? I have soda too. Or beer?" His tone was relaxed, like she was just here to hang out.

Which made him even more awesome. She smiled and stood, walking over to the doorway of the kitchen. "A tea would be nice."

"Regular or herbal?"

"Do you have chamomile? I need to get my sleep for the show tomorrow." Her smile faded as she realized, unless some kind of miracle happened, she'd be at the Forum while Grant was there. And he would find her.

Pischlar put down the kettle and closed the distance between them, cupping her cheeks in his hands. "Listen to me. Even *if*, by some fuckup in the legal system, Grant is at the game, you have nothing to worry about. He's not getting anywhere near you. I'm not big on violence, but I'll make an exception if I need to. And you know very well that goes for the rest of the team."

"People are going to find out, aren't they?" She didn't want anyone to know. She was ashamed, and she knew she had no reason to be. Well, except for the fact that she'd kept it a secret and given Grant the chance to come at her again. Or worse, victimize someone else.

Since they'd broken up, Grant had only been seen with high-profile models, but that didn't mean he hadn't hurt any of them. She could hope he hadn't. He was charming at first. The perfect gentleman.

If he'd gotten violent with one of them, word would have spread, right? They wouldn't put up with him treating them badly.

You did.

Yes, but she wasn't anyone special.

What the fuck is that supposed to mean?

Okay, she knew she wasn't making any sense. She was tired of being in her own head. Maybe she'd feel better in the morning. Maybe things would be clear.

"Sahara, look at me." Pischlar smoothed her hair away from her face. "You're not alone anymore. You've done nothing wrong. Actually, I'm damn proud of you for taking the steps you needed to, but I get why you didn't before. You are a strong, beautiful person. You've been through hell. And I can't promise it's over, but you are going to let us help now. You're never going to have to face him again without either one of the guys or a fucking cop by your side.

Think about that, rather than whatever else is going on in that pretty little head."

"Oh, Pisch." She gave him a playful shove and laughed. "You were doing so good until you pulled the 'pretty little head' thing."

He put his hands up in surrender. "My bad. I blame the language barrier. It's a compliment in German."

She wrinkled her nose at him. "Bullshit."

"True." He winked and headed back to the kettle. "But you smiled and laughed, so my job here is done. I take blow jobs as tips."

Her eyes went wide as she stared at his back. "You did *not* just say that."

"Okay."

The man was impossible. But he was right. She was smiling and the stress had been shelved for the moment. She also knew he was joking. If Pischlar wanted a blow job during a scene, he'd never been shy about putting her on her knees.

Her cheeks heated as she considered the times he'd done just that. They'd only scened a handful of times, but often enough to move past the "getting to know you" stage. She'd kissed him. Had her hands and her mouth on his dick. Had his fingers inside her and his lips and his tongue…

Not the time to be thinking about that, girl. He's a friend.

A very hot friend.

Stop it!

Pischlar patted her arm. "Here's your tea. And get that look off your face or I'm gonna put this on the counter and get you up on that table."

She ducked her head and pulled out a seat. He chuckled and set the mug down in front of her.

The front door swung open and slammed into the wall, shattering the lighthearted, flirty mood.

"Damn it, White! I have neighbors!" Pischlar rolled his eyes and patted her shoulder before heading into the hall. "Are you drunk?"

"I took a cab. Don't nag, man." White stumbled into the living room and collapsed on the sofa, his white shirt and tie both undone and wrinkled, but of a quality that told her he'd probably started the night dressed nicely. He raked his overgrown brown hair away from his face and dropped his head back on a cushion. "Can I ask you something?"

Coming up behind Pischlar, Sahara sipped her tea, feeling horrible for being yet another who'd apparently decided Pischlar needed to take care of them tonight.

At least she was sober.

Pischlar crossed the room and took something out of White's hand. A flask. Lovely.

He glanced back at her and mouthed, "I'm sorry."

"Hi, Sahara!" White sprawled back on the sofa. "Maybe I should ask you too. I want to ask Tim. But Tim's gone. Fuck, I miss him."

Oh boy. Sahara inhaled slowly. The mention of Tim brought a stab of pain to her chest. Apparently, White was a sad drunk. And he hadn't dealt with Tim's death very well, so every time he drank, he probably relived all the emotions he hadn't faced.

She wasn't much better though, so she wouldn't judge. There was a reason she rarely picked up so much as a beer anymore.

"What happened, White?" The stance and tone was very different than the open sympathy Pischlar had shown her. Almost defensive, like he knew whatever White would say would hurt. "You asked me to help you dress appropriately for your first date with the new girl. Unless you acted like a caveman, she should have been—"

"Do I look gay?" White sat up and looked down at the creases in his dark gray dress pants. "I brought her somewhere nice. I was on my best behavior. I remembered the fork and everything."

"Yep, that definitely makes you gay." Pischlar sighed. "Don't keep me guessing. Other than letting another man suck your dick, nothing you've ever done makes you gay. Unless you opened the conversation with how bad Richards is at giving blow jobs."

Sahara bit the inside of her cheek to keep her jaw from hitting the floor. *White and Richards?*

White scowled at Pischlar. "Why the hell would I do that? That would be stupid."

"So what *did* you do?"

"Nothing! Well, okay, this guy was hitting on me. And I was trying to be nice, but then he slipped his number under my glass and the chick saw him. She acted all weird after, so I had to show her I wasn't into him, but..." White frowned. "Well, maybe I didn't have to. She was kinda stuck-up. But when he grabbed my ass, I was pissed. So I slew-footed him. He went down. People freaked. And she took off and told me not to call her. She said she *knew* I was one of *those*."

"That's it?" Pischlar shrugged. "Caveman then. I warned you about that. Not many chicks get off on the guy they're with throwing his weight around."

"Uh-huh. But she'd asked me about *you*. And when I said you were cool and we were friends...well, she asked how *good* of friends. Like, huh? Not sure what she meant. She asked for details. I told her we watched *Avengers* last week. She looked bored." White rubbed his temples. "The first time the guy came on to me, she looked all happy. Then she was all mad when I tripped him and said I don't like dudes touching me."

"Ah. Okay, I get it." Pischlar shook his head and turned back to the kitchen. "You need water. And better taste in women. I'm happy you took a cab. When did you start drinking?"

"After she left. People were staring at me and I hate that shit. You know how much I hate it." White accepted the bottle Pischlar brought him, tipping it to his lips to drain half. "I left and found a bar. Another guy came on to me and I almost punched him. But it was Ford's bar, so he stopped me. And he didn't charge me for anything. I talked to him. He's awesome. I love Ford."

"I bet. Did he hit on you too?" Pischlar had White's flask in his hand. He glared at it, then set it aside. "I'm sure he gets where you're coming from."

"He does. But then Cort came in and he got all weird. They talked. No touching, but I kinda wondered...maybe they want to be gay? Can someone want that? Like...why would you? I'm confused." White groaned and plunked down on the sofa. "I bought a bottle. And drank most of it. Cort told me I needed to go home. But I wanted to come here." His brow furrowed. "You mad at me?"

"Why would I be?" Pischlar grabbed a blanket off the back of the sofa and laid it over Sahara's knees as she settled into the armchair a few feet away. "I'm an awesome friend. Feel free to tell me all about your fucked-up night. I clearly have nothing else going on."

White cocked his head and glanced over at Sahara. "But she's here."

"Yes, she is."

"Did I interrupt?" White chewed on his bottom lip, and Pischlar made a strained sound as he spent more time than necessary fixing Sahara's blanket. "I shouldn't have come. I'm sorry."

"Don't be." Pischlar sighed. "I'm being an asshole. *I'm* sorry. I just don't get why you let your agent set you up with chicks. They're either shallow or stupid. Or, like this one, want things you can't give them."

"What did she want? I figured she was just mad because of what I did. That was stupid. I just don't like random people touching me. And he thought I was gay. And I'm not."

"Right."

"You don't believe me."

"Does it matter?" Pischlar disappeared into the hall, returning with another blanket for White. "We have a game tomorrow. Drink your water. I'll get you more. And you're gonna forget that girl."

"Okay." White flung an arm over his face. "I need better girls. I'm no good at this. It was more fun when you came out with me. They're nice with you."

"They expect nothing."

"Which is cool. I'm tired, Shawn. Can I crash here?"

Pischlar went still and stared at White as he closed his eyes. He spread the blanket over the other man, looking like he'd been punched in the gut. "Stay. But don't call me that. I'm Pisch. Or Easy. Always 'Easy.'"

Damn it, Sahara couldn't ignore what she'd seen. Or the pain in Pischlar's eyes. White wasn't perceptive sober. Drunk, he'd flung out his issues carelessly and Pischlar had taken a few hits. She rose from the chair and wrapped her arms around him from behind.

"I'm sorry I was part of all the drama you had to deal with tonight. Let me make it better?"

Arching a brow, Pischlar looked over his shoulder at her. "How?"

"I need to be held tonight. And so do you. The rest can wait for the morning." She pressed a soft kiss on his cheek. "Please?"

"Yes." He drew her before him and wrapped his arms around her waist, breathing into her hair. "That sounds like the perfect fucking plan."

Chapter Six

"I own a hotel."

Dominik blinked and looked over at Hunt, who was sitting on the bench a few feet away from him with the bottom half of his equipment on, staring at his phone as though he'd been struck dumb. Dominik shook his head, sure he'd heard wrong. "What?"

Hunt plunked his phone onto his sports bag and raked his fingers through his close-shaven hair. The poor boy looked just as confused as Dominik was. "Not sure how that happened. I have to talk to my dad. He has power of attorney because I don't want to deal with all the money shit. He pays my personal trainer and my manager and... I guess he thought it was a good investment?"

What the hell? Dominik's jaw hardened. He'd heard about this happening to other players. Not just the young ones either. It wasn't any of his business, but why the fuck was Hunt finding out about this right before their first game in the goddamn playoffs?

Other players were filling the room, and Dominik was sure Hunt didn't want everyone to know, so he shifted over and kept his tone low. "He *thought* it was a good investment? I'm guessing it's not?"

"No. Fuck, I shouldn't worry about this now. I got some bills in the mail, and I was like 'Huh?'" Hunt rubbed the bridge of his nose and took a deep breath, picking up his phone again when it *dinged*. "I couldn't get ahold of my dad, so I sent everything to my accountant. He just emailed me. There's all kinds of repairs I need to pay for.

And late payments and interest... I'm kinda fucking broke. I don't get it."

Damn it. If this got out, Hunt would be dealing with more than money problems. The press loved stories like this. Dominik wasn't an expert on investments, but he knew a few of the players were. If nothing else, he could help make sure this didn't get the young goalie off his game.

He put his hand on Hunt's shoulder. "Listen to me, kid. There's nothing we can do now, but tomorrow we'll talk to a few of the guys. They'll have some great ideas for you and know all the right people. Keep it quiet until then, all right?"

"Yeah. I can do that." Hunt paled, still staring at his phone. "My credit cards are frozen. My accountant said he's talking to the bank in the morning, but I'm in deep."

"If you don't have good people to help you manage your affairs, Hunt, we'll find some. This is some nasty business, but you've got us. Give me the fucking phone." Dominik held out his hand, breathing a little easier when Hunt handed it over without question. "Get this out of your head. The game is *all* that matters. I've got you. 'Kay?"

"'Kay." Hunt rubbed his thighs irritably. "But me being fucked doesn't matter since I'm just the backup. And Bower's on fire!"

Dominik smiled at that, glancing over at the starting goalie who was bouncing his daughter on his knee. Under normal circumstances, wives and children weren't allowed in the locker room before games. But nothing lit Bower up more than those few precious moments with his baby girl. And his fiancée, Silver, and their man—Dean Richter, the team's general manager—didn't need anyone's permission to be here. Media wasn't allowed in before playoff games, and everyone was cool with whatever worked for their star goalie.

"He is, but you're a big part of the team, and you damn well know that. I expect you to be on the bench, ready to step into the line of fire if you're needed. Understood?" Dominik gave Hunt a hard look, and Hunt ducked his head and grinned.

"I'm on it!" He pushed to his feet and strode over to Richards, the team's youngest player, and hooked an arm around his neck. "Those strippers fucking loved you! Tell me that didn't get you off!"

And this is why I'm fine with getting old. Dominik rolled his eyes, chuckling as Richards did the same. A few of the players were bisexual, but they kept to themselves and the media didn't have the opportunity to make a story out of most of the relationships. The trashier reporters had tried, which was Hunt's reasoning for trying to make things "easier" for Richards. And even though Richards was only attracted to men, he was young enough to go along with all his friend's crazy plans.

If it kept up, Dominik would tell Hunt to back off. But so far, it had been pretty harmless. Hunt looked out for the rookie and was supportive. He didn't want anyone messing with the kid, which was fine, but his attempts to throw women at the rookie were questionable.

When Richards was ready, he'd likely tell Hunt to back off himself. But Dominik had a feeling he enjoyed spending time with Hunt and understood that the other young man had been raised with an old-school mentality that needed to be gently shifted to reality. And the reality was, Hunt's outlook was changing more than Richards's ever would.

Relaxing back against the edge of his stall, Dominik observed the rest of the team like he did before every game. The trouble triplets—Vanek, Demyan, and Carter—were kneeling around Demyan's adopted daughter, Casey. Looking at pictures she'd probably drawn at school. Scott Demyan was becoming downright respectable as a father and staying out of trouble so he might lose his spot with the trio at some point, but that wasn't a bad thing. The other two? Dominik reserved judgment.

Over on the other side of the room, Shawn Pischlar and Ian White had their heads bowed as they spoke quietly. Pischlar looked up and a brilliant smile spread across his lips.

Dominik's lips thinned as Sahara hurried across the room and wrapped her arms around Pischlar's neck. She patted White's cheek and let out a soft laugh.

Whatever was going on with them was new. Yes, she'd played with Pischlar at the club, but it was never serious. Pischlar didn't do relationships, and Sahara hadn't wanted one at the time.

He'd hoped that had changed, but maybe he'd read her all wrong.

Or maybe you fucked that up when you ditched her during your date.

Possible, but he didn't regret being there for Sloan. Or Oriana and Max. He couldn't imagine Sahara doing differently if Jami or Akira had called her. He wished he'd had a chance to talk to her, to iron things out, but after being at the hospital most of the night, he'd gone home and crashed. Then went back with Sloan to get an update on Oriana's condition.

She was stable, but there were complications and she needed more tests. Sloan still wasn't allowed in the hospital, but when Dominik had come back and given him an update, he seemed more relaxed than he had just hearing it on the phone from the nurse.

Speaking of Sloan, he walked in with Max, looking tired, but determined. They parted near the coach's office and Max went to his stall to change, glancing over to give Dominik a nod, mouthing, "Thank you."

Inclining his head, Dominik smiled. Despite the mess of his first real date in far too long, he was happy with the progress that had been made. Both Max and Sloan seemed focused. The tension between all of three of them was gone. He couldn't ask for more.

But he had a hard time keeping his eyes off Sahara as she hugged White and kissed Pischlar's cheek. He was on his feet before he had a chance to think of what he'd say to her. Or worry if she wanted to see him.

He caught up with her in the players' lounge and spoke softly. "Sahara?"

She jumped and spun around, almost falling over on her cute little bright pink heels. Which almost matched her cheeks. He grabbed her wrist as she flailed and pulled her close to steady her on her feet.

"Dominik." She wet her lips and turned her head, but he'd already seen the bruises. She'd tried to cover them with makeup, but the discoloration was still obvious.

And as he put his hand under her chin to make her face him, he could tell by the placement that they had been made by a big hand. Not quite as big as his, but with strength that hadn't been held back.

She had seen Grant Higgins yesterday—she'd told him as much. But these marks hadn't been there when she'd been with Dominik.

"What happened?" He managed to keep his tone calm. As angry as he was, he needed her to know he was in control. That she didn't have to worry about his reaction. "Was it Higgins?"

Her eyes teared as she nodded. "Yes, but he won't come near me again. I'm surprised you hadn't heard. I have to go see Mr. Keane—he wants to hear what happened from me before this goes public. I'm honestly shocked it hasn't already."

"Higgins showed up at your house last night?" Damn it, he should have seen her home himself rather than put her in a cab. The phone call from Max had him thinking of nothing but keeping Sloan out of jail. And making sure Oriana was okay.

Sahara shrugged and dropped her gaze. "He broke in to my house. He was there when I walked in, and I had to kick him in the balls to get out of there."

Dominik swallowed, torn between pride and a deep, acidic rage. The encounter could have ended so much worse. "That's my girl. I'm... Damn it, Sahara. I'm sorry. I should have stayed with you."

Hiking up her chin, Sahara met his eyes. "It is what it is. Pischlar picked me up at the station. I'm staying with him for a bit. I'm not sure when—"

"Sahara! Damn it, sweetie, are you okay?" Silver burst into the lounge, holding up her cell. "I can't believe I had to find out about this on Facebook! Your ex was just charged with breaking and entering. The Islanders said that he won't be playing tonight, but other than that, they're not saying much. His fans are trying to start shit. Idiots!" Silver pulled Sahara into her arms. "I've got you—I hope you know that? The press is swarming the halls, but Keane has security clearing them out."

"Oh." Sahara pulled away from Silver, all the color gone from her cheeks. "I knew it would get out, but not this fast…"

"Honey, it's the playoffs. All the guys are being watched. But your followers are defending you and you know the team will. Keane asked Becky to meet with him for a press release. We have less than an hour before the game. Becky will probably want to talk to you." Silver shook her head and carefully brushed her fingers across Sahara's jaw. "I could kill that man. You!" She pointed at Dominik. He narrowed his eyes in warning, but she didn't seem to notice. "Talk to the guys and make sure none of them does anything stupid out there. He's not playing. This isn't to affect the game."

"Sweetheart, I'm pretty sure neither Richter nor Bower tolerate you speaking to them that way. And I sure as hell won't." Dominik tried to keep the anger out of his tone, but he needed to be alone with Sahara. To make sure she was all right before she was dragged in front of the cameras and reporters. "*You* need to back off."

Silver's cheeks reddened. She stomped her foot, her heel clicking sharply on the tile. "This isn't about you being a Master at the club."

"No, it's about respect. I don't work for you, princess."

"You work for my family. Dean will—"

"Then he can speak to me himself." Dominik shook his head, not too impressed with Silver going back to her spoiled rich girl attitude. She may think she was being professional, but she was crossing the line into diva territory. And the focus should be on what was best for Sahara. He turned to her. "You don't have to speak to anyone if you're not ready. I can take you home."

"I can't go home, I don't feel..." Her lips parted as though what he'd said had just registered. "Dominik, you have to play. The team needs you."

"Do you need me, Sahara?" Fuck, he never missed games for personal reasons. He'd even played once with a fractured ankle. But he couldn't see past those bruises.

Dropping her gaze, Sahara hugged herself. "I appreciate the offer, but I don't know. I can't think about... Please don't be upset, but staying with Pischlar is the best thing for me right now. And I want to perform. And forget about...everything."

He inclined his head, schooling his features to show nothing but acceptance. She wasn't rejecting him for another man. Not yet anyway.

There was no place for bitterness. If he was going to support her, he had to do so completely. Pischlar would keep her safe. Comfort her.

Do all the things Dominik had lost the chance to do.

"Talk to Becky. I'm sure she'll field any questions if you're not ready to answer them." He cupped her cheek in his hand, loving the way it felt to touch her and have her lean toward him as though she wanted to be near him. He tucked a strand of hair behind her ear. "I'm not upset. Say the word and I'll be there."

"Thank you." She put her hand on the back of his and inhaled slowly. "I did enjoy our date. Maybe we can do it again sometime? And leave our phones at home?"

"Definitely." He smiled, dropping his hand when she slipped away to follow Silver out.

He stood there for a few long moments, groaning as he realized, despite her questionable delivery, Silver was right. If Higgins's arrest had gone public, the guys needed to be told what happened. The last thing they needed was to see it on Twitter or Facebook or whatever their social addiction happened to be.

Or worse, on the ice.

Stepping into the locker room, he looked around, catching Sloan's eye as the other man glanced up from where he was having a heated discussion with Max. Lips drawn in a hard, thin line, Sloan nodded.

"All right, men. Listen up." Dominik folded his arms over his chest, waiting until conversation died before he continued. "This is gonna piss some of you off, but don't you fucking forget why you're here. And the people out there in the stands, the fans *and* our family, need us to prove they've put their faith in the right team."

"Fuck that." Demyan rose from where he'd been sitting with Zach. Casey was nowhere to be seen. Becky had probably taken her out at the first sign of trouble, along with Bower's baby. Which meant Demyan didn't have any reason to hold back his rage. "I just heard. And the game don't fucking matter."

"That's not how she feels. She's getting ready to go out there." Dominik felt a strange calm come over him as he considered his own words. And then his doubt was gone. "Can you do any less?"

* * * *

Both Chicklet and Laura were in Keane's office when Sahara walked in with Silver. She'd expected Becky, but she was nowhere to be seen. She frowned and glanced over at Silver.

"She texted me to say she was bringing the kids to the wives' lounge. I'm heading there now so she can come up." She rubbed

Sahara's arm, then gave Keane a hard look. "She's been through a lot. Be nice."

Keane sat forward, smiling pleasantly. "Miss Delgado, I've heard some concern about your unique manner of speaking to the players and the staff. Is this something we should address with the board in the near future?"

Silver blinked at him. "What? No, of course not. Anyone who's complaining is one, a wimp, and two, friends, family, or people I go to the club with."

Chuckling, Keane stood, something about his bearing making Sahara want to back right out of the room. She'd pretty much gotten over her crush on him. Kinda sorta. But that didn't change the effect he had when he got that dominant air about him.

"My dear, I do think you'd regret making this a club issue. With the number of Doms you've irritated, you may end up regretting your transgressions for a very long time." His steps were slow and steady as he approached Silver, but she, like Sahara, seemed frozen to the spot. "I will speak to your Master. If it's attention you require, I'm certain he can see that you get it. However—" he spoke close to Silver's ear "—if it's discipline, I am more than willing to do my part."

The color left Silver's cheeks. She almost tripped on her way to the door. "I'll talk to him, Sir. And I'm sorry. I just want to make sure Sahara will be okay."

"She will be." With that, Keane turned away from the closing door and stood in front of Sahara, making her feel like a little bunny that had hopped right up to a lion roused from a long, refreshing nap.

How the hell had she ever thought she could interest a man like him? Admiring him should be done like one would admire a force of nature.

From afar.

Keane grinned and suddenly he was the kind gentleman she hadn't been too intimidated to share the same air with. The one she dreamed would take her on limo rides and bring her flowers and maybe fly her around in his helicopter...

Chicklet, who Sahara had forgotten was even in the room, nudged her and spoke in a mock whisper. "You're staring, pet."

Someone, please shoot me.

Over by the window, Laura shot her a sympathetic look.

Taking her hand, Keane led Sahara deeper into the office, pulling out a chair in front of his desk. "You are too easy to read, Sahara. Please, have a seat. This won't be long."

"Okay." Sahara sat, chewing on her lip as Laura came over and took the chair beside her and Chicklet stepped out into the hall. Frowning, Sahara glanced toward the door. "Why did she leave?"

"She's here to make sure you get home safely. If that's what you choose to do. If not, she will accompany you to the Ice Girls' locker room. We're taking your security very seriously." Keane's tone was soft, but completely professional now, making it impossible to see him as the Dom who wore leather and wielded a whip at the club. He was too proper. The dark blue suit, his dark hair with its gray streaks combed into a perfectly neat hairstyle, all made him nothing more than her boss.

Which was exactly what he was.

"Now, Officer Tallent has given me the official statement about the incident, but I'm hoping you can give me a little more. Only what you're comfortable with, of course, but considering that this will be a high-profile case, I want to be sure the team is in the position to fully support you." His brow furrowed and he leaned forward. "Which we will do, regardless. But there has been mention of your having invited Mr. Higgins into your home. That you had rekindled the relationship."

"That's a lie!" Sahara's breath caught as she shot out of her chair. Her stomach twisted and she wasn't sure if she was going to pass out or puke. Neither made any sense. She'd known there'd be rumors. Grant had a lot of fans, and they weren't going to be nice about her getting him arrested. "He came over yesterday morning and I told him we could go out for coffee. I didn't even let him in my house then. I may be stupid, but I'm not *that* stupid. He was telling me about losing his mother and I felt bad and…"

Laura reached out and took her hand, giving it a squeeze. "None of us will doubt anything you say, Sahara. We went over this last night. But when my brother brought him in, he got in touch with his lawyers. They encouraged him not to contact you, but he didn't waste any time calling a friend who was more than happy to spread 'his side' of the story."

Sahara slumped back into her seat. She'd expected the gossip to spread like wildfire. Even expected Grant to call her a liar. But to pretend they were together? That she'd accuse him of breaking in for...for what exactly? Why would anyone even believe his story? It was crazy!

Then again, why wouldn't they? Better to think she was some crazy, scorned girlfriend than see a handsome sports hero as an abuser.

She put her hands on her knees so Keane wouldn't see how badly she was shaking. And she took a slow breath so she could speak very clearly. "I should have charged him with domestic abuse when I first came here. You encouraged me to, but I was so happy, I figured I could just move on. That's not an option anymore. He won't stop unless he's forced to. I'm afraid to be in my own home, and I refuse to live like that anymore. I'm staying with a friend, and I will go to court and do whatever the law needs me to do to keep him from doing this again. To me or anyone else."

"I'm very happy to hear that. And I believe you will be happy to hear, since charges have been laid against Higgins, the league has suspended him indefinitely. They are likely releasing a statement as we speak." Keane leaned back in his chair. "We are in a unique position because you are one of our own. I doubt Higgins's team will make any big announcements other than supporting the league's decision, but we will most certainly make one in regards to you. The question is, what are you comfortable with?"

Fiddling with the hem of her skirt, Sahara considered the question carefully. Like it or not, people would be paying close attention to how the league handled the situation.

"The situation." Yeah, she liked thinking of it like that. Distancing herself. Imagining it was happening to someone else. A friend whom she could hug and say, "You can do this."

Before she could answer, Becky burst into the room, sounding breathless. She came up behind Sahara and wrapped her arms around her shoulders before kissing her cheek.

"I'm sorry it took so long. Casey saw something on one of her favorite sports blogs and I had to assure her you were okay. The blog was on your side, but they were telling everyone you'd been choked and were still in the hospital." Becky touched her cheek. "Oh, honey. Why didn't you call me? Or Scott? He's so angry I think Sloan might bench him. He told me to ask you to stay with us. When Pischlar said you were going home with him..." Becky held up a hand as Sahara's lips parted. "Don't even worry about it. Zach will deal with Scott. And White was actually quite helpful. He may not be the sharpest tool in the box, but he knows his boy."

"White isn't stupid." Of all the things Becky had said, one would figure the last thing Sahara would focus on would be the slight against White's intelligence. But she just couldn't absorb the rest. And White, like Pischlar, had kept her sane this morning while she'd been waiting for the phone calls from Grant's lawyers. Calls that never came. "He swore he wouldn't get in a fight with Grant even if he was allowed to play. And he'd do his best to make sure no one else did either."

Becky gave a quick nod. "That's good, but thankfully, we don't have to worry about him. We will do a quick press release. It's up to you whether or not you'd like to be there. Or if you'd like to wait to talk to the district attorney before you say anything publicly."

"I want to wait. Talking to the cops was bad enough." Sahara winced and looked over at Laura. "No offense—it would have been ten times worse if you hadn't been there."

"None taken, honey," Laura said with a small smile. "I think you're handling this very well, and we're all proud of you. The DA is a great guy and he's dealt with high-profile cases before." She handed Sahara a card. "Call him if you have any questions. I have to get back to work, but Chicklet will be with you all night. Not that we expect Grant to show up, but we're not taking any chances. He's got some rabid fans that came to see him, and we don't want them coming after you."

Sahara rubbed her arms to stave of the sudden chill, realizing that those fans would be a bigger threat than Grant for the next few weeks. He couldn't find her at Pischlar's, but the fans would be at this game, and possibly the next one. She'd have to stick to the restricted areas of the Forum. Stick by Chicklet in the parking lot. And pray that they would leave when the Islanders did and never come back.

"I'll stick with Chicklet—until I'm with Pisch anyway. I feel safe with him and White."

"That's good..." Laura glanced over at Keane, who was dealing with paperwork and giving them some semblance of privacy. "Umm...Pisch is a great guy, and I'm happy you're comfortable with him. We were afraid you'd be avoiding men for a while. The thing is, he's..." Her brow creased as though she was struggling to find the right words. "He's not the relationship type. You know what Scott's reputation was? Well, Pisch's isn't much better. He has some kind of standard, but I'm afraid, if you get too attached, he'll make his usual graceful exit from your life."

Nothing Sahara didn't already know, so she let out a light laugh. "He gave me the speech the first time we scened at the club. Don't forget, I played with Ford too. And we're still friends." She shrugged, something hurting deep in her chest as she accepted the reality of her future. One she'd hoped to change only last night. "I'm not ready for a relationship. It's better if I'm with someone who doesn't want more."

"Hon, you don't know that."

With the way that she'd reacted toward Dominik? Yes, she knew she was still too much of a mess to consider a life with anyone. The fact that she'd gone from not dating to considering something long-term was proof of how seriously *not* ready she was. She'd have to learn to stand on her own before she headed down that particular road.

"I do. But it's fine." She pushed out of the chair and met Keane's eyes as he lifted his gaze. Strange, but besides her reaction to his heady dominance, she hadn't felt the pull from him that she'd experienced every single time she'd been in his presence. She had his full attention, but she wasn't looking for some kind of signal that he might be interested. Which made it easier to smile back at him without the slightest bit of shyness. "Thank you, Sir. For everything."

He studied her face for a moment. Then stood. "No need to thank me, Sahara." He came over and gave her a hug that was almost paternal. Which made her past crush even more awkward. "If there's any way I can help you, please let me know."

"Yes, Sir."

"And as for being ready, there's no rush. You're still very young." He patted her arm gently. "I do hope to see you at the club again soon. During times like these, our close community can give you the escape you need. You could use some time out of your busy head, sweetheart."

A suggestion, not an offer. But that was fine. Pischlar would have no problem playing with her. He was safe. She wouldn't lose her heart to him.

But as she said goodbye and walked with Chicklet to the Ice Girls' changing room, she couldn't help thinking back on those golden eyes and that warm smile. One that didn't make her feel just safe.

Dominik had made her feel alive.

Chapter Seven

The team was starting to head out to the ice, but Max stayed put when he saw the number flashing on his phone. Private number, so it could be the hospital. And he could only think of two reasons Oriana would call right before a game.

Either there was really bad, or really good, news. If it was bad, he didn't expect to hear Oriana's voice at all. Jami had gone to keep her company while he and Sloan were here, and the girl wouldn't hesitate to let him know if something went wrong. She didn't hate the game anymore, but the girl had her priorities straight.

As much as he loved her, he had to admit Oriana's obsession with the game went beyond most of the players'. Which is why he'd insisted she have company.

"I wasn't going to call, but I figured good news would keep your focus where it belongs." Oriana sounded tired, but upbeat. A positive sign. "The latest blood test looks good. I'll be here another day or so just to be safe, but my doctor said the platelets in my blood are at a better level, and as long as I continue to respond well to the medication, I shouldn't need surgery."

"They were considering surgery?" He'd known that she'd had to go through more tests, but surgery hadn't been mentioned, even after the troubling results.

Oriana sighed. "Worst-case scenario. But if the next scan shows improvement, I can go home. They couldn't fit me in until tomorrow, so I won't know more until then."

He nodded, leaning against the wall by his stall and combing his fingers through his hair. "I'll be there right after the game. But I'm glad you called me. Looks like they've got everything under control."

"They do. But you don't sound relieved."

"I am; I just hate that you're stuck in the hospital. I know how much you were looking forward to this game, sugar."

"Jami's got it up on the TV. I see the other guys warming up, so get out there!" She let out a sharp breath, as though raising her voice had hurt. "I'm going to let you go. Give Sloan a hug and a kiss for me."

He snorted. "In front of the guys? I'm sure he'd love that."

"Blame me." Her tone was soft and slightly playful. Which was more reassuring than anything she'd said. "Just make sure he's not blaming himself. And win this one for me."

"I'm on it, love." They exchanged goodbyes and he hung up, tossing his phone on top of a hoodie in his stall. He ambled toward the entrance to the rink, almost knocking Vanek over in his rush. He grabbed the younger man by the shoulder. "You good?"

Vanek frowned at him. "Why didn't no one say Oriana was hurt? First Sahara, now Oriana? What the fuck happened last night?"

Jerking his chin to the hall, Max continued forward. "Completely unrelated. Oriana hit her head on the bathtub."

"Because of a scene?"

"Because I'm an idiot and I left the floor all fucking wet." Another jab of guilt slammed into his chest, but he did his best to hide it from Vanek. The kid was one of their best players. He needed his head in the game. "She's doing better. Called me to make sure I didn't worry, so don't you start." He gave Vanek a hard pat on the back. "And you heard what Mason said about Sahara. She's tough and she didn't let that son of a bitch stop her from performing tonight. So you're gonna follow her lead."

"Yeah, well, it's a good thing he ain't here. He'd be leaving on a stretcher." Vanek gave a feral smile, then jammed his mouthguard in his mouth before stepping onto the ice.

So much for getting the kid's head in the game. He caught Zovko's gaze and Zovko inclined his head in response. The man would keep an eye on his sub. And Max would too. Was the best they could do.

Sidling behind the bench, Max gestured Sloan over. Speaking low, he told him everything Oriana had said. Sloan's throat worked hard and he hunched his shoulders.

Well, hell. Max rolled his eyes and decided to follow his sweet wife's instructions. He looped an arm around Sloan's neck and gave him a big, loud smooch on the cheek.

Growling, Sloan shoved him away. "What the fuck, Max?"

Max grinned, seeing the flashes from cameras all around. "Sorry, Coach. Lady's orders."

"Fuck me." Sloan's cheeks reddened as Shero chuckled behind him.

That's been established as a no. Max considered saying it out loud, but he wasn't a sadist. Or a masochist. Pushing Sloan any further wouldn't be very smart.

Besides, Oriana needed to see him out there, ready to play the game.

Puck drop and he skidded back to block a shot, passing across the ice tape to tape with Demyan. Play moved out of the Cobras' zone and he raced to hold his position as the forwards set up. Vanek and Pischlar snapped the puck back and forth between them as Demyan took point. Kral, the defenseman paired with Max, held the line.

Demyan took a high stick from the Islanders' defense as he fought to screen the goalie. Blood trickled down his lip. He licked it away after shooting the ref a dirty look. The Islanders' defense clipped the puck toward Max.

He couldn't look away from the blood. There wasn't much, but all he saw was Oriana on the bathroom floor. A puddle of red spreading on the tiles.

Forcing himself back to the present, he put his stick down to block a pass. Too late. He scrambled after it as the Islanders went on a breakaway. Dove just short of the shot on net.

Bower's glove went up.

The goal light flashed.

Fuck. Max slammed his stick into the ice on his way to the bench. *What the hell was that?*

"You all right?" Sloan asked, his hands on Max's shoulders as he sat. "That was damn sloppy."

No kidding. Max glanced over at Demyan, who was getting his lip taped by one of the trainers. Another trainer offered Max a bottle of Gatorade. He took it, murmuring thanks. "Just saw shit that caught me off guard. I'm over it."

"Like fuck you are." Sloan shoved away from him and went across the bench to talk to Shero. Shero nodded at whatever he was saying.

And Max was held off his next two shifts.

By the time he was waved onto the ice, he'd managed the tunnel vision the guys needed him to have. One of the Islanders took a puck to the face as the Cobras went on the attack, and he barely blinked. The mess was cleaned up, and Zovko took the face-off and tucked the puck back to Max.

Straight saucer pass to White. Vanek crowded the net, jumping out of the way for a clear shot.

Goal! Now that's how it's done!

Center ice. Zovko was thrown out of the face-off and Vanek took his place. Words were exchanged. The puck hit the ice.

Vanek's gloves followed. His tone was shaky as he circled the Islanders' forward, Peters. "You don't get to talk about her like that. You wanna go?"

Peters snorted. "Not happening, little boy. You got a crush on her?" He stuck close to Vanek, who'd scooped up his gloves as play resumed. "Consider yourself lucky. She'd ruin your career, just like she's trying to do to Higgins."

"You don't wanna fight, why don't you fuck off?" Vanek charged to the corner to dig out the puck. Then he started chirping. "You married, meathead? Punch your wife with those big hands?" He freed the puck with his skate and kicked it to Zovko. "You find her sexier all bruised and bloody? You look like the type."

Damn it, Vanek. Shut up!

An Islanders defenseman pinched in on the left, retrieving the stray puck and firing at the net. Bower made the save, but the rebound landed right between Peters's feet.

Thankfully, he was paying more attention to Vanek than to the game. Kral got the puck to Max. He skipped it to Carter.

And all hell broke loose. Peters grabbed Vanek by the back of his jersey. Zovko hauled Peters around and tossed his gloves.

With a feral smile, Peters did the same. "Defending your boyfriend, man?"

"Yes." Zovko cracked Peters in the jaw. Nice hit, and he held his own as Peters nailed him with several rapid punches.

Even fight, so Max wasn't worried. He kept out of the way, with an eye on Vanek, who was being held back by one of the Islanders. The guy was talking calmly and didn't resist when Carter came to pull Vanek away.

Not everyone on the team was an asshole. The few that were just gave the rest a bad name.

The refs let the two men go at it. The crowd cheered every time Zovko got a good hit in. But it had been a long shift and both guys were getting tired.

Max waited for the refs to separate them. He saw Zovko's helmet fly with a brutal punch.

And everything seemed to slow as Zovko went down. He was out before he hit the ice, so he didn't brace for impact. Or protect his head.

Blood pooled over the ice. Max didn't move as the trainers skidded up to Zovko's still form. Barely acknowledged Vanek's shout of fear.

"Come on, big guy." Bower hooked a hand to Max's elbow and slid him over to the bench. He glanced back. "Carter, get our boy out of the way!"

Seconds later, Vanek was pinned between Carter and Demyan. A stretcher was brought out. The fans stood and clapped as the players helped carry Zovko off the ice.

"Shit." Sloan approached, his skin gray and his eyes wide. Of everyone's reactions, Sloan's hit Max the hardest. The man had no issues with blood. Or hadn't. Players had been hurt before, and Sloan was the one who got the team back out there with assurances that their teammate was in good hands.

But he wouldn't be that man tonight. Not after what had happened to Oriana.

The ice was cleaned yet again, and the ref spoke to both coaches—the Islanders' and Coach Shero—and Carter was pulled in to serve Zovko's penalty. Vanek was benched, pale and lifeless and completely unresponsive with a trainer sticking close to him, speaking low.

"Perron!" Shero came over and gave Max a firm shake. "You've seen worse. I know you're going through a personal issue—no, don't look at me like that. I adore Oriana, but she would be the first to remind you that this is the playoffs. The men are shaken. They will follow your lead." He squeezed Max's shoulder. "Can I count on you?"

Can he? Max wasn't sure he could promise anything. He'd already fucked up once because he'd had trouble not seeing Oriana whenever blood spilled. And when he'd finally managed...

But Shero was right. Oriana was watching. She'd be worried about Zovko. About the whole team. She didn't need to see him fall apart when they were counting on him to step up.

"I got this, Coach. You worry about him." Max looked at Vanek, wishing the trainers would get him off the bench. Between Vanek's own injury, learning about Oriana's, and seeing Zovko go down, the kid couldn't be expected to continue playing like everything was fine.

Shero nodded and went to the trainer. Together they led Vanek off the bench.

The game continued, but no matter how hard Max tried, he could tell the guys were distracted. His attempts to score resulted in multiple pucks ringing off the post. Carter ended up back in the box twice for stupid penalties. Then Demyan did the same.

When Richards was called on a questionable interference penalty, then thrown out for mouthing at the ref with just three minutes left in the game, Max resolved to accept this defeat. They were down 6-1.

He still played his hardest, still shouted encouragement to the men who didn't look like zombies out there.

But he was fucking grateful that the press wouldn't be allowed in the locker room after the game. The team needed some space to get their heads on straight.

Which seemed unlikely at this point.

The team that left the ice after the loss wasn't the one that had made it to the playoffs. And if something wasn't done, they wouldn't have a chance at making it past the first round.

* * * *

Nasty damn loss, but Dominik had no regrets. He'd put his all into the game. His team was a mess, but he had a few ideas of how to deal with that. First thing would be getting an update on Zovko's condition. And since Vanek would no doubt be by his side until someone forced him to leave, he'd bring the kid to see Oriana as well.

And Sahara.

Knowing the young man's history, growing up seeing his mother mistreated by several different men, Dominik wasn't all that surprised that he'd shut down completely. But the team needed him. After quickly dressing in the locker room, Dominik went on the hunt for Vanek, wondering if he'd left still in his equipment. His stuff had been bundled haphazardly into his stall, so there was no telling if he'd even gotten changed.

"Mason!" Max raced down the hall after him, taking a few gulps from the open bottle of water in his hand, then swiping the spill from his lips. "You looking for Vanek or Sahara? They're both in the parking garage with Chicklet."

Dominik inclined his head. "Got it." He strode toward the parking exit, glancing over at Max, who kept pace with him. "What makes you think I'd be looking for Sahara?"

Max snorted. "I tend to be quite observant."

Dominik rolled his eyes. *Damn voyeurs.*

"I also noticed she's been spending a lot of time with Pischlar and White." Max gave him a sideways look. "You're not into sharing, so—"

"Leave it alone, Max." Dominik knew his tone told Max he'd hit a nerve.

He also knew Max assumed their friendship gave him leave to keep pressing if he thought there was a good reason. So, naturally, the man continued as though Dominik hadn't interrupted. "You haven't played at the club for a while. You're not training anyone. You and Sahara have great chemistry."

Apparently they *were* having this conversation. Dominik sighed and resolved to get it over with quickly. "Sahara isn't ready for a relationship. I could have overlooked the fact that she's not a sub, since I have no interest in the lifestyle any longer, but I'm too old for casual flings."

"Ah, I see. And I reckon all this was discussed on your first date?"

"What does it matter? We went on a date to see if we're compatible. We are not." The situation had been far from ideal, but when did life ever lay out the perfect circumstances? It was best that they'd both gotten out before either of them could get hurt.

Letting out a low whistle, Max put his hand on Dominik's arm before he could go any farther into the parking garage. "I might be way off base, but I think the whole date thing was a mistake."

Hoping Max had a point, and wouldn't waste time getting to it, Dominik waited as patiently as possible.

The insufferable man grinned. "I can just see it. You trying to be all 'I'm not a Dom' and her being all newbie submissive. Waiting for that presence that gets her all hot. That must have been one hell of a date."

Clenching his jaw, Dominik waited a few beats before speaking so he wouldn't let his irritation show. "It wasn't a horrible date. I enjoy being around Sahara. She's sweet and easy to talk to and I'm comfortable with her. She's brave, trying to move on with her life after what that bastard did to her. Even trying to forgive him."

"Which will make her an awesome friend."

"I don't want..." Damn the man. Dominik groaned and rubbed the back of his neck. "Friendship is not all I want from her."

Folding his arms over his big chest, Max nodded slowly. "Clearly. But she's starting off from an insecure place, and you're giving her a man she doesn't know. A man *I* don't want to fucking know. Being a Dom wasn't a hobby for you and it isn't why things didn't..."

And this was where Max would stop pushing. Which was understandable. Their friendship had survived, but he likely felt some responsibility for how things had turned out between Dominik and Oriana.

It was long past time to lay that to rest. "Oriana loves you. You give her what she needs. I don't resent you for that." He rolled his shoulders. "We weren't right for one another. I love her, I always will, but I want her happy. She needed me to let her go."

Max's lips twitched up in a wry smile. "If you have a bird and you let it go…"

"Exactly."

"But what about Sahara? You let her go. Does she know she can come back?"

No, I pretty much told her not to. Dominik grimaced and lifted his head to see Pischlar and White walk past, likely going to wherever Sahara was waiting. He'd pushed her into Pischlar's arms without even meaning to. And accepted that she had made her choice.

Only, was it a choice? After dealing with Grant, she'd probably gone to the only safe haven available. He couldn't blame her for turning to the one who'd be there for her, no strings attached. She was still young enough that her experience was limited to boys. And men like Grant.

The idea of her being with Pischlar, with any man, for any length of time didn't sit well with him. But they hadn't reached the point of any kind of commitment.

He wasn't in any hurry to get there. If there was anything between them, it would develop in its own time. With her seeing that he wasn't waiting around, but he'd never be too far.

Like it or not, offering his friendship might be the best thing. For now.

At least Pischlar won't be possessive. I don't have to worry about stealing another man's woman. He observed Sahara with the other two men. Her quick smile at a joke Pischlar made, before she looked over as though to make sure Chicklet hadn't gone far. The quiet parking garage seemed to make her nervous.

I would have her out of here already. Home with me. Safe.

She'd be safe enough with Pischlar and White.

Shallow reassurance, but it would have to do.

He made sure his strides were clear as he got closer and smiled as her eyes met his. The warmth in her returning smile made him wish he didn't have to wait for her to find her way back to him.

But it will be worth it.

Chapter Eight

Sahara had to tear her eyes away from Dominik to pay attention to the conversation going on around her. The last she'd caught was that Chicklet was taking off, understanding, but a little irritated, that Vanek had taken a cab to the hospital rather than wait for her.

Before Pischlar and White showed up, Sahara had been grateful for Chicklet's company. But now she just wanted to get out of here. And Chicklet didn't seem to want her to leave with them.

"You can't be serious, Chicklet." Pischlar sighed, not looking overly upset, but maybe a little tired. "You trust me with your sub, but not with Sahara?"

White snorted. "She trusted you to fuck her sub. And Zovko was right th—"

Chicklet's fist caught White right in the eye. White stumbled back against Pischlar's car, making no effort to even protect himself when Chicklet fisted her hand in the collar of his shirt.

Her eyes were as deadly as a snake's, her tone not much better. "I'm getting real tired of your mouth, boy. Does privacy mean anything to you?"

"Easy there, Chicklet." Dominik gently pulled Chicklet away from White. "We need the big brute in one piece. And your men need you. Go on, I've got this."

Nodding jerkily, Chicklet straightened the sleeves of her leather jacket. "Fine, but you best make sure she don't get hurt. And I'm talking about more than her asshole ex."

Inclining his head, Dominik watched Chicklet head for her Jeep. While Sahara found herself watching him. He was...very calm.

That's a good thing. Right?

He arched a brow as he glanced over at White. "Do you have a death wish, Bruiser?"

"No! What the fuck did I do?" White frowned, turning to Sahara. "You didn't know about Pisch and Vanek? I figured you girls talked about everything."

Sahara's cheeks heated. She hadn't been privy to that information. Staying that way would have been fine with her. "Umm...no. But it's okay. I won't say anything."

Pischlar stretched his arms behind his neck, cracking his knuckles. "Awesome. I suppose I'll have to wait a bit before asking her for a copy of the video though. So you owe me, White."

White blinked at him. Then his eyes went wide. "There's a video? Damn, you're..."

"Easy?" Pischlar looked quite pleased with himself. "Yes. I'm also exhausted. If not for you busting in, Sahara and I would have had a quiet night."

That got White apologizing, but Sahara didn't pay much attention to him. For some reason, she was desperate to see Dominik's reaction. He'd seemed all right with her staying with Pischlar, but did he think they were involved?

"So much on your mind. Pischlar can help you with that." Dominik chuckled when she stared at him.

Pischlar cut White off, his eyes going a little wide. "Is that an order or an offer, Mason?"

"Neither are mine to give. I appreciate you being there for Sahara. She's special to all of us." Dominik brushed his fingers down her cheek, then took a step back, his eyes on her. "You know what you need right now, sunshine. Take it. No regrets."

Her chest felt tighter, even as some of the weight on her lifted. Whether or not he'd worded it that way, Dominik was giving her permission to do whatever she wanted with Pisch. She wasn't sure what she'd expected, but not this.

"Dominik..." She closed the distance between them and put her hand on his arm before he could walk away. "I don't understand."

He kissed her forehead. "I think there's a few things we both need to work out. I'd rather do that before we try to start something, only to say goodbye later."

"Can I still call you?"

"Whenever you want."

"Can we hang out? Maybe go back to the theater?" She probably sounded pathetic, but this confused her more than when he'd put her in the cab to go see Oriana.

He nodded, a warm smile on his lips. "I'd like that. And I take back what I said about the club. You're more than welcome there."

She swallowed hard and nodded. Her heart was racing, so fast she was light-headed. Maybe he'd decided he'd be willing to train her if she wanted, but that was it.

Well, he might have decided not to go beyond training, but she... Okay, she hadn't really considered very much in the last twenty-four hours. She'd been afraid and clung to the one person she was sure of. And she wasn't ready to let go.

Even though she knew nothing would come of being with Pischlar.

She took a deep breath and let her hand fall. "We almost had something. I don't want you to think you're losing me, like you lost—"

He put a finger over her lips. "Hush. I don't think that."

"Why?"

"Because you're not her."

* * * *

Over an hour later, back at Pischlar's house, Dominik's words still haunted Sahara. Her biggest fear had been not measuring up to Oriana. When she went to the club, she always looked to the more experienced subs for how to act. Following Silver's lead never got her very far. What Bower and Richter put up with wasn't the norm.

Subs like Oriana were clearly preferred, but showing the kind of graceful submission she did was hard. Sahara had tried, but there was a limit to the number of Doms willing to play with a newbie. Pischlar's interest in her had been nice after weeks of going to the club and not finding anyone willing to give her a shot.

When Sahara played with Pischlar—and once with Pischlar *and* Ford—it had been fun. She'd been able to relax and go along with whatever they wanted to do. But she craved something more. Mr. Keane's complete control over the subs he scened with was everything she thought a BDSM relationship should be like. For the longest time, she'd gone to the club hoping one day he'd look at her and show the same interest he did in them, but he only scened with women close to his own age. And despite her embarrassing effort to look more mature, he'd rarely spared her more than a fond glance.

She'd moved on, but her needs hadn't really changed. Mr. Keane had been her ideal Dom for a reason. She just couldn't put her finger on why exactly.

Dominik was different. She'd only ever seen him with Akira, training her with no intention of keeping her. At one point, Sahara had considered asking him for the same, but she was too close to him already to delve into something temporary. If she let him in, she'd want to give him everything.

She already wanted to.

I'm not ready.

If only she weren't such a mess. Maybe then she could be the right woman for him.

What's it gonna be? More therapy? A complete personality transplant?

Tension gathered at the base of her skull as she rejected the idea. She didn't need to become someone else. He'd either like her for who she was, or he wasn't worth her time.

He does. And he is.

Her groan drew a soft laugh from Pischlar, who was cooking up some grilled cheese sandwiches in the kitchen. He came out with a tray full of sandwiches, plates and cutlery, and tomato soup divided into three bowls. After setting the tray on the coffee table, he placed a plate in front of her and grinned.

"Help yourself. Do you want a soda? Or some tea?"

"A tea would be nice." Sahara took one of the sandwiches off the stack and put it on her plate. Damn, that smelled good. Nicely browned with cheese oozing out from the sides. The soup wasn't from a can either. She inhaled the sweet aroma, her mouth watering.

"Thank you so much, Pisch. I have to warn you though, treating a woman like this will make her want to keep you!"

Pischlar's eyes widened in mock horror as he reached for the plate. "That's a scary thought. Maybe I should toss this and—"

Sahara batted his hand away, laughing. "Don't even think about it! And you don't have to worry about me. I'm good just playing with you."

He gave her a crooked grin, then plopped down on the armchair, glancing back over his shoulder. "You done yet, Bruiser? Food's ready!"

The creak of a door and then White came down the hall, still wet from his shower.

And wearing nothing but a towel. He combed his fingers through his damp hair and headed for the empty space on the sofa beside Sahara. Her cheeks heated as he bent down to grab a grilled cheese sandwich. His towel wouldn't hold for long.

With all those muscles so close to her, she couldn't help wishing it would fall so she could ogle the rest of him.

The way Pischlar licked his lips, he was having those very same thoughts. But he tore his gaze away and cleared his throat. "The lady and I would like some tea. She's a guest. You're not. You've gotta earn your food."

Biting the sandwich in half, White chewed quickly, then dropped the other half on the third plate. "Your food's worth more than me just making tea. Want anything else, man?"

Shaking his head, Pischlar waited for White to disappear into the kitchen before mumbling, "Nothing you're willing to give."

Poor Pisch. Sahara wanted to hug him, but before she could express any kind of pity, he was smiling again.

He brought his spoon to his lips, one brow arched. "Might wanna eat before that gets cold."

Right. Eat. No thinking about him not being with the man he was so clearly in love with. Or her inability to love anyone. She dipped her spoon into the soup.

The first bite had her forgetting about thinking too much about anything. Creamy yumminess, sinfully good. She let out a soft sound of appreciation and polished it off, using pieces of her sandwich to clean the last, delectable drops.

They were both finished before White came with the tea. He didn't seem to mind though. He simply set the mugs in front of them and dug into his food.

"While we're on the subject of you being a 'guest,' Sahara," Pischlar said, as though the conversation hadn't even paused after his instructions to White, "I have an idea."

"Oh?" Sahara sipped her tea, keeping her eyes on Pischlar. She didn't think he'd want her to pay to stay here, but she would if he asked.

He was a Dom, so maybe he'd want her to do chores?

"Yes. I need to know your limits first."

She almost choked on her tea. The casual atmosphere had cleared all thoughts of any kind of scene from her head. Which shouldn't have surprised her. Pischlar had a way of keeping her slightly off-balance no matter how often they played together. Even saying she was willing was no guarantee it would happen, tonight or any other time.

He'd seen her limit list at the club, so his asking now likely meant he had something different in mind.

"Umm...well, they haven't really changed." She set down her mug so she wouldn't spill if he caught her off guard again. "I'm not big on pain, but I don't mind a little. I don't like being called names. No slapping in the face..."

Inclining his head, Pischlar leaned back in his chair, completely at ease. His eyes were attentive though, in the way some Doms had that made you feel like they would catch any errant thought. He eyed her hands fiddling with the hem of her skirt.

She folded her hands on her lap.

"You'd indicated an interest in exploring more sexual contact in your recent scenes. Originally, you didn't want penetration."

"Jesus, Easy!" White glanced at her, leaning forward a bit like he wanted to protect her. "What kind of fucking conversation is this? She's not some chick you can just..."

Pischlar gave White a tight smile. "I can just what? We're negotiating. You've been at the club often enough to know how this works."

"I don't play."

"But you observe. Maybe you should stick to that." This was the first time Sahara had ever heard Pischlar being short with his best friend. Or with anyone really. His posture hadn't changed, but she wasn't sure what to make of his tone.

White's jaw hardened. He moved to stand. "You want me to go, I'll—"

"Sit." Pischlar smiled when White immediately dropped back down. "Good. Now, I have no problem with you being here, but if Sahara does, you can crash in the guest room." He turned his focus back to her. "But first, how much are you comfortable with, sweetheart? I think Mason was right. You could use a release. What it consists of is up to you."

Her heart raced as she stared at him, half wishing they didn't have to talk at all. It had been a long time since she'd felt the calm of giving up control. No matter how confused she was about life in general, she couldn't deny how much she craved the simple peace of a scene with a Dom she could trust.

Dominik had told her to go for it, so she didn't have to worry that playing with Pischlar would change anything between them, right? Would he be pleased that she'd taken his advice? That she'd gone after exactly what she needed?

Part of what she loved about submitting was not having to make any decisions. The ability to just let go, to worry about nothing but the pleasure of her Dom of the moment, was incomparable. But now she had a nagging little voice in her head that wanted Dominik's approval.

Which he gave.

But what had he meant, exactly? He wasn't here to tell her how far she should go. While he might have wanted her to find some release, he wasn't nearby, offering his warm smile of approval. Or his dark frown when she pushed the boundaries for a reaction.

"Tell me what you're thinking, Sahara." Pischlar had shifted over to sit on the table in front of her, and she hadn't even noticed. But his hands wrapping around hers steadied her. "Do you still trust me?"

"Yes." She didn't even have to consider her answer. This man was her friend. Playful or not, he'd been her only Dom for over a year. The only one who'd taken the chance on introducing her to a lifestyle she was clueless about. Sure, it had been BDSM-lite, but it had been enough to leave her wanting more. "I guess...I just wonder if it's always going to be like this. Just playing for a little bit, then nothing for weeks. I guess I want it to be real."

Lips twitching at the edges, Pischlar nodded. "I think you'll find that soon enough. But you know it's more than I can give you."

"I know."

"Do you think tonight will tide you over for a little bit? We have a couple of days after the next game before we head to New York. I can bring you to the club in a week or so for a more intense scene if that's what you're looking for."

"I'd like that." She let herself fall into his seize-the-moment mentality. And glanced over at White, who looked like he thought he shouldn't be here. Maybe she could accomplish a little more than subspace during the scene. "White, you should stay. But the rules for you won't be the same as the ones for Pischlar."

White's throat worked as he swallowed. "What do you mean?"

Even Pischlar had cocked his head, looking curious to know what she was up to.

She batted her eyelashes sweetly at White. "We've never done anything together. I'd feel much more comfortable if we shared some limits."

"That sounds fair." White's brow furrowed. "What limits?"

Smiling, Sahara pointed to the center of her chest. "Anything you do to me, you should be able to do to him, or let him do to you. Naturally, I'll let the two of you decide which."

Letting out a rough laugh, Pischlar stood and pulled her to her feet. "You're topping from the bottom, pet."

"Not at all, Sir. I'm not submitting to White."

"Or to me, by the sounds of it." Pischlar slid his hand into her hair, tugging to tip her head back. "The only thing you get to decide is whether or not I can fuck you tonight. If White wants to play, he and I will discuss his limits."

White rose to stand beside Pischlar. "I'll do it."

Perfectly still, Pischlar released his hold on her hair and stared at White. His eyes were guarded, but there was a hunger within them that told Sahara she'd been right to manipulate the scene in his favor, even if it wasn't very good submissive behavior.

"You wanna repeat that? You are aware of what she's asking?"

Folding his arms over his chest, White scowled at Pischlar. "I heard her. And I'm not stupid."

"I never said you were."

"No, but you and everyone else treat me like I am. You pointed out that I should know more about the lifestyle." White took a deep breath. "I don't know as much as I should, but I know a lot of Doms train with other Doms. So train me."

With a shake of his head, Pischlar moved away from her. He walked over to the window, gazing out to the street, lost in his own thoughts.

Sahara bit her lip. All right, maybe this *hadn't* been such a good idea after all.

The silence stretched out. White made an aggravated sound and took a few steps toward Pischlar. "If you don't want me—"

"Clear off the table, White." Pischlar's tone had changed. It had an edge of command to it—the solid, unwavering one that made goose bumps rise all over Sahara's flesh. He didn't turn around until White began to clear the table. "No sex tonight. And that only includes actual penetration." His gaze leveled with hers, cool and calculating. "I will touch you and taste you, Sahara. White may as well, if he's game for what that entails."

His words reached White, who promptly walked into the doorframe and let out a shocked grunt.

Pischlar's lips slid into an evil smile. "She's tempting, isn't she, Bruiser?"

Wetting his lips with his tongue, White didn't move a muscle. Or speak. He didn't seem sure of the appropriate response.

A throaty chuckle and Pischlar slipped to her side. Circled her, brushing her hair over one shoulder. Kissing her throat. "Don't be shy, Ian. She's not." He undid the first few buttons of her blouse. "Come here."

Shivering, not because of the cold, but because the adrenaline was giving her a heady rush, Sahara watched White close the distance between them. He kept his hands fisted by his sides, like he was afraid he couldn't resist touching her if he relaxed even a little. His eyes were hooded with lust, and he inhaled roughly as though he'd forgotten to breathe.

Such a big man, so strong, but while she felt the slight pull of attraction to him, nothing compared to the commanding presence of Pischlar. He wasn't the type of Dom most women thought of when exploring BDSM, but from her experiences at the club, she knew he was one of the most respected in their community. His easygoing nature was a sheer veil, concealing a man who exuded control as effortlessly as he glided on blades across the ice.

He brought his hand up to the back of White's neck. "The pretty skirt and blouse don't hide much, but they're in our way. Take them from her."

Leaning toward her, White brushed his cheek against hers, his fingers on the buttons of her blouse as he whispered, "Are you okay with this?"

With the scene? Yes. But she hated being asked once the negotiations had been done. She couldn't be too irritated with White though. Not with Pischlar's lips twitching slightly like he'd heard and was waiting for her to rethink the situation she'd put herself in.

"I'm fine, White. I promise, I'll safeword if I need to." She nibbled on her bottom lip, considering. "Will you kiss me?"

White froze with her buttons half undone. He shifted so his lips were close to hers. And shook his head. "No. I'm sorry, but that's kinda personal and this is a one-time thing, right? Friends fooling around?"

Pischlar didn't give her a chance to answer. He let out a laugh that was so cool it made her shiver. "That's right, White. Nothing serious. I've never found kissing alone to be an issue, but we can follow the *Pretty Woman* regimen if you'd like."

"Don't be an asshole, Easy." White traced the tips of his fingers over the exposed flesh of her ribs, as though trying to soothe her. Or himself. "You've got your 'Don't try to keep me' lecture. She has limits. This is my thing."

"Fair enough." Pischlar stroked the side of White's neck with his thumb, his tone softening as White's eyes drifted shut with a quiet sound of pleasure. "I apologize."

"No need. Just keep doing that." White finished with the buttons without opening his eyes. "Fuck, a bit more pressure and I'll do anything. I should have added a massage to my demands."

Pischlar chuckled as he worked the muscles of White's neck with his hand. "What demands?"

Eyes open now, White grinned at Sahara, then slid her shirt off her shoulders. He bent a little to reach the zipper at the back of her skirt. "Guess I really didn't need to make any, did I?"

Heat spread over Sahara's cheeks, and she couldn't help combing her fingers through the soft, messy brown hair that almost reached White's shoulders. These two men might not be the forever kind, but they made her feel beautiful and desirable. Special and cared for.

"You're gonna be a handful, Bruiser. If it takes you this long to get her undressed, the poor girl is going to get bored." Pischlar circled them, coming up behind Sahara and deftly unfastening her bra strap while White peeled down her skirt and helped her step out of it. "I've seen you get a girl out of her clothes much faster."

Once he'd straightened, White cupped Sahara's cheeks in his hands and caressed her bottom lip with his thumb. "They didn't mean nothin'."

Hand up, Pischlar made a dismissive gesture. "Enough with the sappiness. Damn, no wonder you're single." Pischlar removed Sahara's bra, tossed it aside, and then swooped her up into his arms. "Save the sweet talk for the ladies you're taking out to dinner. This one's on loan." As he lowered her to the table, he gave her a playful wink. "I've actually read some fun books about Doms lending their subs to others. My favorite involved a cage, but with such short notice—"

Sahara rolled her eyes and giggled. "I'm not on loan."

By her side, White released a low growl. "You're not putting her in a fucking cage."

That made Sahara laugh. And Pischlar was soon chuckling and trying to calm the protective male. He also seemed to be using every possible opportunity to touch White, and so far, White didn't appear to mind.

Progress! Her inner cheerleader did a little dance.

Laid out on the table, she settled in for a playful scene, maybe a bit like the one she'd done with Pischlar and Ford. She'd never given Akira any details because it was hard to even meet Ford's eyes without remembering everything he'd done with his hands and mouth and tongue. He was pretty intense, but she hadn't felt a strong connection with him. And she'd always known Pischlar was in charge.

And yet, she'd never had trouble interacting with Pischlar in public. He was the type of man who could see you at your worst, drunk out of your mind, or embarrassing yourself on a Murphy's Law kinda day, and he'd treat you no differently once you'd pulled yourself together. Almost like it had never happened.

Which was probably why it was so easy for her, and several of his teammates, to fool around with him. The next day, nothing changed. There was no jealousy—none that she'd ever seen anyway. He gave nothing his lovers could hang on to besides the memories.

"Are you with us, Sahara?" Pischlar tipped her chin up with a finger, smiling down at her when she nodded. "Good girl. Now give White your wrists. He will hold you while I toy with you. Are you still good with the club safeword?"

"Yes, but I doubt I'll need it." She lifted her wrists over her head, bending her knees slightly, relieved that she'd been left with her panties. For the moment anyway. Being topless was all right, but she needed to get used to White's presence before she was completely exposed.

As White clamped his big hands around her wrists, Pischlar strolled out of the room like he'd forgotten about both of them. Sahara wasn't worried; she trusted White and she wasn't in the headspace where she'd need the presence of the Dom she'd submitted to. That probably wouldn't happen at all tonight.

However, White looked irritated. He knelt at the end of the table. "What the fuck is he doing?"

Sahara shrugged. "I don't know, but you sure do swear a lot."

He cringed and muttered an apology.

"No big deal. Just try to relax and enjoy the scene." She licked her lips, then widened her eyes in mock fear. "Unless he's getting his really nasty toys. Floggers and butt plugs and canes—"

A creak of the floorboards was the only thing that warned them of Pischlar's presence. He dropped his toy bag on the floor with a loud thump and smirked. "Oh my."

Jaw clenched, White moved to stand. He practically snarled when Pischlar put a hand on his shoulder to still him. "Listen, pal. I'm not watching while you hurt her. She said she don't like pain."

Pischlar's brow twitched up. "Do you?"

"Huh?"

"Do you enjoy pain, Ian? It's a very simple question—one I suggest you consider before you continue speaking. You asked me to train you, which means you will be as respectfully submissive as our lovely Sahara." His gaze drifted over to her. "Who will not tease those who are unaware that she's joking."

Uh-oh. Sahara pressed her lips together, wondering if she could warn White not to push without getting herself in more trouble.

White released her wrists and stood. "This isn't her fault. You're gonna fucking tell us what you're planning to do. And who the fuck likes pain?"

"Would you like a list?"

"You're being an asshole again."

"Am I?" Pischlar's head tilted to one side. "How serious are you about training with me, Ian?"

Blinking and taking a step back as though his brain had just caught up, White hooked his thumbs to the top of the towel still wrapped around his waist. "I'm serious. I've just never... This whole scenario is kinda freaking me out."

"Play doesn't bother you at the club." Pischlar's tone was gentler, as though he had been prepared for the reaction, but was waiting for White to face it himself.

"I'm not part of the scenes. It's none of my business, and they're all together, you know? She's not mine. Or yours. And cages and whips and... that's too much."

"Very well, but from this point on, you'll find a better way to voice your objections. I don't appreciate being sworn at during a scene. Or given orders by my trainee." Pischlar folded his arms over his chest, no less intimidating in his faded jeans and white muscle shirt than any Dom in black leather. "If you understand and take your punishment, we can continue."

Sahara bit her lip hard, waiting as White stared at his feet. Not that she was an expert or anything, but he didn't seem submissive enough to accept a punishment. His pride might push him to hang in a bit longer. Pischlar wouldn't accept a half-assed attempt though.

White was full of surprises though. He lifted his head to meet Pischlar's eyes, his stance relaxed. Which probably had a lot to do with trust. The man wasn't his best friend for nothing.

"I'll take it. And I'll stop fu—messing this up." He gave Sahara an apologetic look. "I'm like a bear in a tea shop. I hope I didn't get you in trouble."

Damn, he's adorable. She was used to bigger men being rough and gruff and mean. Well, the ones she'd known through...

Nope, no thinking of him!

Anyway, White was different. Kinda fitting that he'd screwed up the old saying "bull in a china shop". He was more a bear than a bull. A big teddy bear she just wanted to cuddle up with.

If the teddy bear was really, really hot.

Pischlar laughed. "White, take off the towel and get back in position before she decides to pet you rather than screw around with you. She's got that tender look on her face that she gets when she's playing with Luke's puppy."

Sahara ducked her head when White's cheeks reddened. Damn Pischlar for reading her so well.

"You sure know how to make a man feel good, Pisch." White dropped the towel, then thunked down on his knees before Sahara even got a chance to catch a glimpse of the whole package.

Darn it.

Before White could shackle her wrists in his hands again, Pischlar grabbed a fistful of his hair and tugged his head back. He spoke with his lips close to White's. "I can make a man feel very good. And I will. And you're going to regret every single second of it. Because while we're going to make Sahara come so hard and so often she won't be able to stand, you won't be getting off, no matter how much you beg."

"Why the fuck not?" White tried to pull free, but Pischlar's muscles tensed as he tightened his hold.

"Punishments are rarely fun. Still want to play?"

"With how determined you seem to be to get me to back down? You're damn right, I'm still playing."

Wrists held, eyes closed, Sahara tried to brace herself for Pischlar's full attention falling on her. She heard gloves snap and swallowed hard.

"Keep your eyes closed, *Schatz*." He trailed a finger over her belly, a small, slightly cool and moist line.

Which grew colder, then heated. And continued heating. She squirmed as the heat spread.

"How does that feel? And White, don't you dare let her go."

Sahara inhaled, putting the sensation in perspective so she could give an honest answer. "It almost burns, but it's not horrible."

A soft laugh and Pischlar ran his hands up over her ribs. "Good girl. How about this?"

His hands were covered with the stuff. She gasped as the cooling turned hotter and hotter. His hands circled her breasts and she whimpered. He wouldn't...?

He did. Her back bowed as he rubbed the gel-like substance over her nipples. They hardened and the sharp, tingling feeling expanded, making her pant as she fought for some relief from the lick of flames that tormented her.

"Oh fuck!" She tugged at her wrists and White's grip tightened. So much for him not being all that submissive. He was following orders perfectly. "Pischlar, please!"

"Please what, pet?" He blew on her nipples, and she almost shot off the table. "Does that help?"

Evil man! Sahara groaned as the air cooled, then heated her flesh all over again. She didn't realize Pischlar had stopped until she felt cold metal against her hip. *Snip*. Then again on the other side. *Snip*.

Her panties were pulled away.

"They were so pretty too. I promise, I'll replace them." Pischlar's tone was full of laughter. He was having way too much fun torturing her, but she hesitated to call him a sadist.

This wasn't pain. Exactly.

Close enough though.

"Keep your hands where they are, Sahara. White, can you let her go for a sec and open this for me?"

The low whistle White let out didn't mean anything good. "Are you for real?"

"Yes. But you're going to have to wait your turn. I can tell you're curious."

"Maybe..." White cursed softly, then returned to restrain her. "Brace yourself, baby."

Her thighs were spread far enough to accommodate Pischlar's shoulders. She heard a crunching, which seemed out of place.

White cursed again.

Pischlar's mouth closed over her clit.

At first, all she felt was the erotic teasing of his tongue. A sigh of pleasure escaped her. Her clit throbbed and sparks of heat raced up her nerves. It felt so good, she forgot about the burning sensation still covering her breasts.

Until the fire spread to her clit, much more intense than the flames hovering over the rest of her. Her lips parted and her hips bucked. Her core clenched as everything came together, overwhelming her resistance, leaving her with no choice but to experience everything at once, to be aware of every inch of her skin. All alive and sensitive and sparking with pleasure on the edge of agony.

Echoing *snaps*. The gloves. Pischlar's bare hand touched her thigh. Comforting her.

"Where are we, *Schatz*?"

Where? Sahara frowned, then realized what Pischlar was asking. "Green, Sir."

"Very good. You may come when you please this first time." He kissed her thigh, then pushed something hard deep into her pussy. A long, slick dildo. Before she could adjust, he had the vibrations going. He licked her clit, pumping the solid rod in hard and fast.

She couldn't hold anything back. She tossed her head, screaming as the heat, the rough, fucking motion, and the manipulations of his tongue brought her to a fierce climax that held her in the throes of pleasure for so long she wasn't sure it would ever end.

But it did, fading slowly, leaving her twitching every time Pischlar shifted the dildo. When he withdrew it, she gasped through her parted lips, jumping when he ran two fingers over her pussy, wetting his fingers with her juices.

"You may open your eyes now, Sahara." He smiled at her when she opened her eyes. Then he turned to White. "Let her go. And open your mouth."

The second White let her go, Sahara sat up. She was still tender, but her curiosity overrode the lingering pleasure. Pischlar was so tempting, offering up his fingers like a special treat. He was handling White like a puppet on a string, but Sahara didn't see it as a bad thing. White wouldn't be going along with the game if he weren't interested.

He just needed a few hard shoves in the right direction.

Knowing this, she wasn't all that surprised when he looked at her while he sucked on Pischlar's fingers. She leaned forward, licking her lips just as he was. She could sense Pischlar was trying to carefully draw White deeper into the scene. Her need to please him had her wishing she could help.

"Stand up, *bärchen*." Pischlar stepped back to give White some space. Then he motioned to her. "Let's see if you do as well holding him as he did for you, Sahara."

There was no hesitation in White's movements, but plenty in his eyes. Sahara had no clue how she'd hold him if he didn't want to keep still. She wrapped her hands around his wrists and her fingers didn't touch. Her grip was weak.

Restraint was symbolic though. White was being given a chance to prove he could submit. She'd never understood why a Dom would want to train by first being a submissive, but there were probably reasons behind it. Reasons that made her uncomfortable, because she didn't want to imagine any of those she'd happily kneel to kneeling to anyone else.

But seeing White struggling to give up control didn't bother her.

Weird.

Donning fresh gloves, Pischlar picked up a container of balm from where he'd left it on the sofa. He approached White as he dipped his finger in. "Don't move."

And White didn't budge, but he inhaled sharply as Pischlar drew a line of the icy-hot balm across his pelvis. He groaned as Pischlar covered his chest with it, jerking at the attention Pischlar paid to his nipples.

"Fuck that burns," White muttered, his fists clenching below where Sahara held his wrists. "Other than torturing me, what do you get out of this, Easy?"

Pischlar moved in closer to whisper in White's ear. "You're taking it because I've asked it of you. I control everything you feel. Discomfort and pleasure and pain. It gives me a fucking high to know I can give you everything, or nothing."

Whatever Pischlar did next had White dropping his head back and groaning. Sahara tried to get a better look, clenching her thighs at the wave of lust that ran over her when she saw Pischlar's hand between White's thighs.

She'd seen submissive men before, but few were as big and tough as White. She could picture him with a whip in his hands. Toying with a bound sub, his powerful body working as he fucked her.

But under Pischlar's command, he was like a tame wolf. One you expected to snarl rather than come to heel. Rather than making White seem tame, the whole scene proved that Pischlar was fucking good at what he did.

She wasn't sure whether she should be scared for, or jealous of, the person he someday decided to claim.

The way White fought to hold still, Sahara could tell he was getting close to climax. She kissed the back of his shoulder, quietly hoping Pischlar would stop teasing, forget the punishment, and give the man his release.

A hard pounding at the door ruined any chance of that. White eased out of her grip and headed for the bathroom—likely to grab his clothes. Pischlar reached down and tossed Sahara her shirt, bra, and skirt.

Her panties were done for, but she got everything else on in record time as Pischlar went to see who had come by for a visit in the middle of the night.

"Where is she?" Ford's voice came from the hall, nice and calm.

He must be alone. If Akira or Cort had come with him, they'd be pushing into the house and making a damn scene.

"Won't you come in, Ford?" Pischlar sounded like he got visits around two a.m. every night. And didn't mind at all. "I'm assuming you won't be allowed to sleep until you make sure Sahara's in one piece?"

Ford grunted, stepping in with his hands stuffed in his pockets and his shoulders hunched. "Something like that."

Sahara folded her arms over her chest and glared at him. "If you knew where I was, you knew I was safe. This is ridiculous."

With narrowed eyes, Ford looked from her to the toy bag on the floor. He ran his tongue over his teeth. "You were assaulted two nights ago and neither of your closest friends have heard from you. Akira has been on the phone all night with Jami and Silver. She needs to see for herself that you're really all right. For all she knew, you had gotten drunk and were letting whoever was nice take advantage of you."

"I haven't gotten drunk in months!" Sahara's face heated as rage simmered in her veins. She wasn't sure exactly why she was so mad. She loved that her friends cared, but she was an adult. She could take care of herself!

Clearly. A snarky voice in the back of her head found her funny.

She ignored it. "I appreciate the concern, but as you can see, I'm fine. Please tell Akira I'll call her in the morning."

"She's still up. How about you call her now?" Ford pulled out a cigarette, put it between his lips, but didn't light it. Hopefully that meant he would be leaving soon. "Maybe you think it's unreasonable, but with what Akira went through herself, she's imagining the worst. Please tell me you get that?"

Fuck. Sahara swallowed hard and nodded, going to her purse to get her phone. Akira had been raped when she was a teenager. She was in such a good place now that it was easy to forget how far she'd come. They had done self-defense courses together and exchanged horror stories. There was nothing they didn't talk about.

But the second Sahara had issues with Grant, she'd gotten back into the same old habits. She'd pushed away the people closest to her.

Only, this time, she'd known she was doing it.

The first ring hadn't even finished before Akira picked up. She spoke so softly, Sahara could hardly hear her. "Sahara? I didn't tell him to go, I swear."

Turning away from the men, Sahara pressed her fingers to her lips. "Even if you had, I...damn it, I really screwed up. I didn't want to tell you what happened because of Cort's reaction when he saw me with Grant. I was afraid he'd kill him."

"He wouldn't get a chance. If I ever get my hands on that man, I'll—"

"You're going to stay away from him. I'm pressing charges. I don't want any of my friends paying for my stupidity."

Releasing a soft sigh, Akira hesitated, then cleared her throat. "Why Pischlar? He's a nice guy, but he's temporary. You need a future, babe."

"I'm not ready for a future. I need right now." Sahara wasn't sure how much she should share, but she'd held back enough. So she just told Akira everything. "I talked to Dominik and he was cool with me coming here. He told me to 'take what I need.'"

Akira groaned. "Damn Doms. All right, fine. Have fun. But you can't keep putting your life on hold. One of these days, you'll have to start living it."

"I will. Consider this my last act of complete abandon. And...well, it's not just for me. Having me play along..." She lowered her voice in case the guys were listening, though they seemed to be ignoring her. "White was more comfortable with Pisch than ever. You know Pisch is in love with him, right?"

"Yes, but White's an idiot."

"He is not."

"About Pisch, he is. But enough of them. I reserve the right to raunchy details, but can I give you some advice?" Akira sounded unsure, like their relationship wasn't what it had been. But she continued before Sahara could tell her nothing had changed. "Don't let this stop you from wanting more. You're ready; you just haven't accepted it yet. And Grant scared you into hiding again."

"I'm not hiding." Well, technically she was, but that wasn't what Akira meant. "You didn't see how I reacted when Dominik got a call from Max and had to leave. I was all jealous and insecure, and I don't like myself when I'm like that. I need to work on me before there can be an 'us.'"

She could picture Akira nodding. Hear the understanding in her tone. "I get that. But promise me one thing?"

Considering how rarely Akira asked for anything, Sahara agreed without a second thought. "Sure."

"You may have screwed up, but everyone does. Pressing charges was a big step—one you were too afraid to take before. Unless you're still holding out for Keane—"

"I'm not."

"Good to hear. Just don't ignore opportunities because you're afraid to take them. I don't know if Dominik is the one for you, but I've never seen you open up to another man the way you do with him. Pischlar is safe because he asks for nothing. There's no risk." Akira paused. "You'd be taking a chance with Dominik."

"I know." Sahara glanced back toward the men. White had joined them, fully dressed, and nothing in his expression betraying the scene Ford had interrupted. "And he's not going to wait around forever."

They finished up the conversation and Akira asked to speak to Ford. Whatever she said seemed to satisfy him, because he left shortly after.

Which was when things got awkward. Sahara waited for Pischlar to say something, but he simply picked up his toy bag and went to his room to stash it. White went to the kitchen to do the dishes. So she started tidying up the living room.

A few minutes later, Pischlar returned, glanced from her to White, and burst out laughing. "You're both *incredible*. Why can't you understand life is so much simpler when you learn to roll with the punches?"

White dried his hands on a dishrag and leaned against the fridge. "Easy for you to say, Easy. Nothing fucking bothers you."

"Yes, but I'm not sure what's bothering you." Pischlar looked White over. "I promise, nowhere on you does it say 'My best friend was jerking me off.' You're not even hard anymore."

Sahara stared at the back of Pischlar's head. Damn, he certainly wasn't going to make White more comfortable being all blunt. She couldn't blame White for not being in the mood—she was pretty out of it herself.

"I don't get you. What we did wasn't—*isn't* my thing. You know that. Why don't you just drop it?" White tossed the dishrag over the side of the sink. "Pretend it never happened."

Nodding slowly, Pischlar moved to White's side. "That is one option. The other is we forget the rest of the world and finish what we started. I bind Sahara to my headboard so you can taste her delicious pussy while I suck your dick until you come. Entirely up to you."

And with that, Pischlar strolled back down the hall and disappeared into his bedroom.

Rubbing his hands over his face, White groaned. He muttered something she couldn't hear, then lifted his head to meet her eyes.

She couldn't help but smile at him. A glance at the front of his black jogging pants proved he was more than interested in Pischlar's offer. But he wouldn't budge unless she was willing to join them. Like the kissing, it was his way of holding on to his ideas of what he should want.

Helping him with his illusions really wasn't any hardship.

"Come on." She held out her hand, her smile widening when he took it. "You want this as much as I do."

He pulled her against him, bending down to gently kiss her throat. "I want you."

No point in arguing with him, so she tugged his hand and led him to the bedroom. He could deal with reality tomorrow.

And so would she.

Chapter Nine

The morning of the Cobras' second playoff game and Oriana was finally clear to be released from the hospital. A day later than planned, but her scans had been pushed back because there was only one MRI scanner and an emergency had taken priority. Regardless, the medication was working, and other than advising Oriana to watch for specific symptoms, the doctor seemed optimistic for a full recovery.

She'd hated being in the hospital, and leaving had seemed like the only thing she could look forward to, but that morning, Max had come in early to wait for her release papers with her. And Sloan had come in not long after. She wasn't sure what strings had been pulled, but she'd seen him out in the hall with a man in a suit, whom she'd overheard apologizing for any "unpleasantness" Sloan had experienced. The team provided a lot of money for research and equipment in the hospital, but she wasn't sure how she felt about threats being used to give her and her men special treatment.

One of her siblings was behind this, she was sure of it. But she'd wait until she was done soaking in Sloan's presence before she gave them hell. She'd missed him. She hated seeing the circles under his eyes and knowing he probably hadn't slept well while she'd been here.

I'll tell them no more power plays and give the hospital a big donation.

She didn't feel too guilty. None of the maneuvering would have been necessary if they hadn't assumed the worst. Hitting her head and being stuck in the hospital was nothing compared to being forced away from one of her men. She felt like she'd been punished for being hurt.

Curled up in a chair on Sloan's lap made the last few days irrelevant. She was going home. The rest could be forgotten.

Silver and Ford showed up to see her out, Silver bearing an expensive Tiffany vase—which had Sloan making a face out of her sister's view when he saw it—full of yellow tulips. Ford had gone a little more traditional with a Squishable panda plush and a single white rose.

A short time later, everything signed and her gratitude expressed to her nurses, Oriana sat in a wheelchair as Max rolled her down the hall. Hugging the panda, she grinned up at Ford when he squeezed her hand.

His expression was the protective look of concern that had been planted there every time he'd come. He jerked his chin toward someone approaching.

Their father. With his wife Anne and several men she didn't recognize.

Her throat closed up. Max locked the wheelchair and stepped up beside Ford.

Sloan, smart man that he was, put his hand on Silver's arm, preventing her from lurching forward and likely saying all the words she'd held in for too long. Her father had shown little interest in any of them, unless "acting" fatherly could work in his favor. Oriana had spent more time than any of them trying to earn his love. But she'd finally accepted the fact there was no love in him to be given.

Standing a few feet in front of all of them, their father folded both hands over his cane. He was wearing a dark navy blue suit, but that did nothing to hide the dangerous man he could be when provoked.

"Mr. Delgado." Sloan sounded calm. A very good sign. "We weren't expecting to see you."

Leaning heavily on his cane—he'd been in a wheelchair the last time Oriana saw him, his health must have improved—Anthony Delgado glared at Sloan. "I don't know why not. She is my daughter. Now get out of my way, you monster. I heard what you did to her."

Your daughter? Oriana had to fight to hold back the tears. Even after a DNA test, her father had insisted she wasn't his. He'd readily claimed Ford, but wanted nothing to do with her.

Why now? She couldn't believe he'd suddenly had a change of heart.

Max shifted to stand closer to Sloan. "I'm not sure what you heard, sir, but any concerns have been laid to rest."

"Bullshit. The social workers spoke to her and she was too afraid to tell them the truth. Either that or…" Anthony let out a heavy sigh. "My own health prevented me from looking after my children as I should have, but Oriana's never been all there. My lawyers are looking into it. She really shouldn't be allowed to make decisions like this, and once a judge sees how incompetent she is, he will agree that she should be with her family."

I am with my family. Oriana had needed space from her father to build her own life. To find her own strength and believe she was worthy of love and respect. There were times she missed him, but seeing him now made her wonder if she wasn't just missing the idea of a parent who loved her unconditionally.

He would never be that man.

Without Sloan to hold her back any longer, Silver behaved in her typical, rash way. She strode forward and jabbed her finger right in the center of their father's chest. "You're insane if you think we'll let you get away with this. What do you want? Money?" She poked him again. "I'll give you whatever you want if you'll stay the fuck out of our lives."

"Silver." Ford wrapped an arm around Silver's waist and hauled her back. "You're not helping anything. Calm down."

Anthony laughed. "No, let her go, Ford. She's proving why she's unfit to care for her mentally unstable sister."

Oriana put her hand over her mouth. She was going to be sick. She needed to get out of there. She wanted to go home and pretend none of this was happening. She spotted a familiar woman a few steps back from her father and his lawyers. She couldn't remember the woman's name, but she was a reporter Silver'd had issues with in the past.

They needed to get Silver out of here. Oriana needed to get out of here. She wouldn't help her father air the dysfunctional Delgado relationship to the press.

"Sloan, bring Oriana home." Max put his hand on Sloan's arm. "Please."

With a sharp nod, Sloan turned his back on her father and came to her, bending down to cup her cheek. "Listen to me. Silver's probably right. He wants control over you because he thinks he'll get his hands on your money. Max and Ford will take care of this. I'll try to get Silver to leave with us."

Her head throbbed when she inclined it to show she agreed. The tightness in her chest made it hard to get a word out. "Doesn't he know I don't have any money?"

"You're married to Max. He's pretty well-off."

"And you."

"Not officially, but yes, my money is yours."

"That's not the point. It's not really *mine*. He can't very well go into your accounts—" Or could he? If he proved she was unable to care for herself, and somehow took her away from Max and Sloan, maybe he could have access to funds as a caregiver.

"Enough, pet. You won't be found incompetent." He kissed her softly, rising to take control of the wheelchair. "Silver, there's another set of elevators at the end of the wing. Come with us, I'll need you to sit with Oriana while I drive."

As their brother and Max argued with their father and his lawyers—who had finally joined the conversation—Silver seemed far more interested in being heard than going anywhere. She hissed something at Ford when he tried to propel her away with a firm grip on her shoulders.

Max made the decision very easy for her. "Could you call Asher, sugar? I'm sure he'll get this straightened out right quick."

"Consider it done." Silver tugged the jacket of her pale pink skirt suit straight and glared at their father. "Have fun wasting the little money you have left on lawyer's fees, old man."

When Silver spun on her heel and headed for Oriana, their father called out. "You might not believe me, Silver, but I'm trying to do what's best for my children. Maybe you wouldn't have had so much trouble after your child's birth if you'd been with real family."

Eyes wide, Silver never slowed her stride. She kept pace with Sloan as he rolled Oriana down the hall. Didn't say a word.

But Oriana's heart broke for her when she saw the tears spilling down her sister's cheeks. What her father had tried to pull hurt, but not nearly as much as what he'd already done. Silver had broken free from him a long time ago, but Oriana suspected she'd always hoped to have her daddy one day. He'd had her fooled when he'd given her the team, but he'd hoped to manipulate her.

This was a fresh wound for both of them. One that would be ripped open again and again until they finally got Anthony Delgado out of their lives for good.

Oriana reached out and laced her fingers with Silver's. The trembling smile her little sister gave her made it a little easier to breathe.

They had each other. And their men. The team was their extended family.

Everything else they would get through. Together.

* * * *

Having Sloan and Oriana out of hearing was comforting, but Max hated that he had to stay here, listening to the crazy old man rather than give his wife the homecoming he'd planned. Maybe it was excessive, but he and Sloan had put together a little party.

Nothing huge, Oriana needed to rest, but she would be happy to see their close friends and family. And maybe that was exactly the distraction she needed after all this.

Unfortunately, he was still supplying roadblock services for her heartless father.

"You are her husband. How could you let the man who abused her leave with her?" Anthony's lips twisted in disgust. "I had hoped she'd made a decent choice with you, but clearly I was wrong."

The man wasn't pulling any punches. At least Oriana didn't have to hear any more of his nonsense.

Better Delgado aim his venom at Max than his children.

"You have my number, Anthony." Once, Max would have called the man Mr. Delgado. But he wouldn't give him that respect. He'd called him "sir" out of habit. Not because he meant it. "Please have your lawyers call me. Oriana needs time to recover."

Anthony bared his perfect, fake teeth in a sneer. "She will recover in my home where she belongs. I won't have my daughter manipulated any longer."

This time, Ford didn't wait for Max to take the lead. He let out a gruff sound. "Your daughter? When did you decide she was your daughter again? This whole performance shows how little you care for her! Do you think she needs this kind of stress?"

Moving closer and reaching out as though to touch his son's arm, Anthony sighed when Ford jerked away. "I am so happy that you've become close to your sisters, son. But you're clearly just as misguided as they are. Hopefully, in time, you will see that I'm doing what's best for you all."

Ford retreated a step and shook his head. "I became your son when it was convenient for you and the man who raised me. As far as I'm concerned, I have no father."

"You're young. You'll change your mind." Anthony smiled. "The last name you claimed says it all." Sympathy filled his eyes. "I was sorry to hear about your old man. He was once a dear friend."

"Why am I not surprised?" Ford snorted. "You've done enough damage for one day. I'm going to see how my sister is doing. Her and Silver are the only good that came out of you being my mom's sperm donor."

Ford was done. He strode away in the same direction his sisters and Sloan had gone. Max moved to follow, but one of the lawyers cleared his throat and approached him.

"This is all very unfortunate, but we will, of course, insist on a new caseworker to assess the situation. The evidence against Mr. Callahan is damning, and you would do well to not make yourself an accomplice." He handed Max a card. "If you decide to do what's right and testify against him, please call me. We will make sure Oriana gets the best care."

Max crumpled the card in his fist. "I will make sure she's taken care of. And strong enough to deal with whatever you throw at her."

The man shrugged and returned to Anthony. Max didn't waste any more time on them. He hurried to catch up to Ford.

He found the young man outside, trying to light a cigarette, his hands shaking. After the third try, he snarled and punched the cement wall. Blood ran down his fist and the cigarette hit the dirt. He didn't react to the pain.

Simply pulled out another smoke.

"You're a mess. Come on, Ford, I've got a kit in my car." He made sure Ford would follow, then headed to his SUV to grab the first aid kit from his trunk. With Sloan's temper, he made sure to keep it well stocked. He pulled out a bottle of sterile saline water. "Let me see."

Holding out his hand, Ford didn't say a word as Max cleaned, then covered his busted knuckles with practiced ease. Once the adrenaline passed, Ford would be in pain, but nothing appeared to be broken.

At least they were at the perfect place if he'd done more damage.

Ford tried to light his cigarette again and seemed to get more agitated with each failed attempt. Max didn't approve of him smoking, but this wasn't the time for a lecture. So he took the lighter and held the flame until the cherry glowed.

"Thanks." Ford leaned back against the SUV and sighed. "What a fucking mess. Do you think Oriana's okay? And Silver... Fuck, how could he bring up her kid? I might have had a twisted childhood, but at least I didn't grow up with him."

Max wasn't sure how to reply to that. Ford's father had died in prison less than a year ago. After having run the Kingsley empire for decades. When Max had first met Ford, he'd thought he was a rich boy playing at being a thug. But he was a product of his upbringing. The Kingsleys were ruthless and Ford had tried to fit in.

It said something about his character that he'd finally broken free and become a good man who loved his sisters. And their little niece.

"That bastard doesn't get to take any more of our time than he already has. The doctor approved a small gathering for Oriana, but no longer than a couple of hours." Max playfully shoved Ford toward the passenger side of the SUV. "Get in. Bower is bringing Amia and Casey. Nothing cheers Oriana up as much as seeing the Cobra brats."

Ford snorted as he snapped his seat belt. "Yeah, I'm sure she loves you calling them that."

"Chicklet started it. So, naturally, no one objects." Max grinned. "Wouldn't mind a few more added to the brood though. You and Akira—"

Eyes glazed in the distracted look of a man in love, Ford ducked his head and smiled. "Me and Cort are ready, but Akira has plans. She wants her figure skating school set up first so our kid can get the best training as soon as he or she can stand in skates. I hope the kid ain't into hockey, because Akira has their whole career set out for them."

"Ah." Max wasn't sure what to say. The likelihood of Oriana carrying a child wasn't good, but he couldn't imagine trying to plan his son's or daughter's life like that.

"Okay, it sounds nuts, but it's not really that bad. She's fine with whatever our children want to do, but the minute one is into figure skating? Well, they'll have the best of everything. Not much different than Cort building a bike from scratch for our son to ride when he's old enough."

True. Max glanced over at a red light. "Or your daughter?"

"*Hell* no. Cort doesn't want our daughters around bikers." Ford chuckled. "We've had some interesting conversations."

"And your input?"

Ford's brow furrowed. He shook his head. "I just want to be a better father than either of mine. If I manage that, I'm good."

Fair enough. One thing Max was grateful for was that if they ever managed to bring a child into their home, the kid would have his father. And Sloan's and all kinds of extended family. They would never want for love.

"How goes the adoption?" Ford stared forward, making it clear he'd heard something. "I know you've gone to a few agencies, but…"

Yeah. But. "We've been turned down several times."

"You make good money. You have a stable family." Ford frowned. "What's the problem?"

"Two gay men can have trouble adopting. Do you think they consider a poly family stable?" Max thought over some of the conversations they'd had with adoption agencies. They'd even been told to lie on the applications. Alone, he and Oriana would have little trouble adopting. But Sloan wouldn't legally be the father.

Sloan had insisted the legalities were irrelevant since they hadn't mattered when they'd said their vows. Why now?

Max had resisted the idea, but Oriana went along with what her most alpha Dom wanted. Sloan hadn't cared who fathered her child, but he wanted to be fully involved. And he might have been able to adopt a child that wasn't his if Max was the father. Or Max could have been the one signing the papers.

But either one of them having no rights?

The experience in the hospital had been enough to prove Sloan's point. What if they had a child and one of them couldn't make important decisions? Which one of them would have to wait until the "right" person was contacted?

Maybe a private adoption would work. They were still looking into their options. Which would be put on hold until Oriana was healthy again.

When they parked in front of the house, he took note of all the familiar cars and smiled. The only people truly important to Oriana who were missing were himself and Ford. Nothing her father had done could ruin all that those who cared for her could give.

He spotted Dominik's truck and slowed his pace. Max had brought Dominik back in, maybe not all the way, but enough to open doors that had been firmly shut. With Oriana in such a vulnerable state, would it be more difficult for her to remember why it hadn't worked out between them? Max would accept whatever she wanted, but what about Sloan?

Won't be an issue. Dominik's moved on.

Had he? Really?

To be honest, Max wasn't sure. In a perfect world, friendship would be enough. But if today proved anything, it was how imperfect the world really was.

Chapter Ten

Dominik hadn't planned to intrude on Oriana's homecoming, but a text from Sloan had him ditching his plans for the day and swinging by a local bakery for her favorite treats. He'd gotten here about half an hour ago, ready to herd the team out, concerned that a crowd might overwhelm her, but people were calm and Oriana was soaking in recaps of the game from the players.

Becky had stopped by for a short time with Bower and Dean and the little ones, staying just long enough for Oriana to cuddle the little girls. The players stuck around longer because Oriana was asking so many questions, yet they filed out as soon as she started looking tired. She had food enough for a week or so with all the casseroles the players' wives brought. Everyone wanted to show their appreciation and support.

And he wasn't surprised.

Tim had been the heart of the team, but Oriana was a big part of the reason they still had a team at all. It was no secret how much she and her siblings had done to keep the Cobras' franchise alive.

He chatted a bit with everyone, then prepared to make his exit, giving Oriana one last hug and a kiss on the forehead as Max and Ford joined them. Dominik's leaving would prompt most of the stragglers to take his lead.

But before he could say anything, Oriana put her hand on his arm. "Could you do me a favor?"

Anything. The word came to his mind, but it didn't leave his lips. He meant it, and yet, not the same way he once had. So he simply nodded.

"I haven't heard from Tyler or Chicklet and the guys are saying Zovko is hurt badly. Could you check on him and give Tyler my love?" She bit her lip and shook her head, wincing as though the motion hurt her. "I don't mean it like—"

"I know what you mean." Dominik squeezed her hand and stepped back. "I'd planned to stop by at some point today, so it's not a problem. Just get some rest and get better so you can come watch us play. You won't be in any condition to deal with the insanity at the Forum until at least the third round. So we have our work cut out for us."

She smiled. "Yes, you do. And...thank you for being here. For being such an amazing friend."

Once, the distinction might have hurt. He still expected it to a bit, but they'd reached the point where it felt right. "I always will be, sweetheart."

On his way out, both Max and Coach Shero caught up with him. The coach gestured that they'd talk outside and slipped out the open door. Max pulled Dominik in for a rough hug.

His tone was low as he spoke. "We good? Fuck, I know this can't be easy. I keep expecting you to tell me and Sloan to get lost. We have no right to—"

Dominik snorted and put his hand on Max's shoulder. "I should take offense to you questioning my friendship." That word was becoming his new mantra. "You're my teammate and like a brother to me. Everything else is in the past. All I ask is you stop bringing it up."

"Done." Max breathed a sigh of relief. "See you in a few hours, man. And thank you for coming."

Nodding, Dominik said goodbye and made his way out. He was getting uncomfortable with the constant gratitude. Hopefully, this would be the last of it.

Coach Shero was waiting by his truck. "Dominik, I hate to dump this on you at the last minute, but I could use your help. I'll follow you to the hospital—I apologize, I couldn't help overhear that you were going, and I need to check on Vanek and Zovko myself. The boy's listed as a game-time decision."

"Reasonable, but I don't see what that has to do with me." Dominik hoped he sounded more direct than blunt. He needed a nap if he was going to be fresh on the ice. "Do you need me to speak to the men?"

"No, actually, I'm going to need you to host one for a time if you're willing." Shero rubbed his hand over his lips, his eyes showing how exhausted he was. Finding a replacement for Zovko couldn't have been easy. "There's a young man we'd planned to bring up next season. We've been discussing an entry-level contract with his agent for some time. He's damn good and he could be a game changer."

There were at least five men on the farm team Shero could be talking about, so Dominik just nodded for him to go on.

"The thing is, he's got responsibilities that need to be taken care of. They could distract him if not handled carefully. I spent all day yesterday and this morning convincing his agent and his coach we could manage anything he requires. I would have approached Callahan, but clearly, that's not an option." Shero looked uncomfortable. "You have a stable home and you've roomed with rookies before."

Ah...is that all? Dominik shrugged. "I have plenty of space. He can stay with me."

"You may want all the details before you commit."

"If he's good enough for you to go to all this trouble, I don't care about the details. Let's go see Zovko and Vanek. You can tell me more on the way to the room." Dominik smiled to soften his words, but he was just eager to get the insanity of the day over with so he could focus on the game. He envied the players with wives whose sole focus during the playoffs was to make sure their men had no distractions. Several of them even sent children to relatives and spent all their time watching what their husbands ate. How much they slept.

All right, he didn't need anything that extreme, but it would be nice to share some of the burden. To go home to someone who'd listen and then tell him nothing mattered but what he did on the ice.

He pulled onto the street, picturing Sahara doing exactly that. She came from a long line of hockey players. She would understand...

Damn it, he had to stop picturing her in unrealistic roles. He'd done well giving her time and space to get where she needed to be before even considering a relationship. He refused to put any pressure on her. Or himself.

But he had to admit, over the months that they'd gotten closer, he'd considered how easily she'd fit into his life. Even when he'd struggled with the idea that Oriana was no longer part of his future, the idea that Sahara might be kept slipping in.

The next step was up to her. Which was hard to swallow. He could only stand back and hope the carefree life Pischlar offered wasn't all she wanted. Anyone could ignore their own needs. And she had more reason than many to prefer things uncomplicated.

He had to stop seeing her with his collar when he still hadn't decided if she craved the weight of it around her neck. He had only just accepted that he wouldn't turn his back on the lifestyle; he'd simply stop training subs he couldn't keep.

Thankfully, he pulled into the hospital parking lot before his mind could delve any deeper into things he had no control over. He joined Shero halfway across the lot and let the man distract him with the rookie he'd be inviting into his home.

"He should be arriving in about an hour. I hate to rush you, but I need to give the driver picking him up your address. If you're sure—"

"I'm sure. But tell me more about the kid. Does he need a babysitter or just a place to stay?" Dominik followed Shero down the hall, figuring he knew where Zovko's room was. "You said he had responsibilities? Will I need to make any big changes right away or do I still have time for a nap before the game?"

"I don't see that being an issue. He'll need to rest as well." Shero shook his head as they took the elevator up to the sixth floor. "The information I have is limited, but I know he has family in Ontario. You may have more than one person invading your home."

"You haven't even given me his name yet." Dominik grinned at Shero's flustered look. "Give the driver my address. I'm assuming the whole entourage won't be there today?"

"No, of course not. There hasn't been much time..." Shero said. "His name is Heath Ladd."

The name was familiar. "I'm sure I've seen his stats. A smart choice. And no drama that I know of."

"He's a good kid. His coaches think he'll fit in without making waves."

"Perfect."

"Are you sure you don't want me to find out specifics? We're asking a lot of you."

"He needs a bed to sleep in. Some guidance. If he has a mother or a sister that needs to stay with him while he settles, I'm fine with that. I have a few spare bedrooms." Dominik tried to think of anything else that could make things difficult. "I can drive him where he needs to go if he doesn't have his own car. I can keep him away from the press. He's eighteen, right?"

"Yes."

"Not a drinker? Is he prone to being late or slacking off?"

"No." Shero seemed much more comfortable discussing the young man's habits than he had been making the request. "He's always the last to leave the ice. His coach did mention he's not very talkative, but he takes instruction well. He had a trainer he was close to in London, but I have several in mind to work with him. He's dedicated. A sniper. I'll put him on the third line to start off, but I see him making it to the second or first easily."

"Which is exactly what we need." The idea that Zovko wouldn't be playing with them indefinitely was hard to swallow, but that was the reality of their sport. And the reason management kept their options open. He reached for the door. "Are they expecting us?"

Shero nodded. "They knew I'd be stopping by today. Even I wouldn't drop in unexpected with Chicklet standing guard over him. But I don't see them having an issue with you being here as well."

Inclining his head, Dominik rapped his knuckles softly on the door. Chicklet opened it seconds later. She met his eyes, trying to put on a brave face.

He was having none of that. "Come here."

Her strong body leaned into his as he wrapped his arms around her. She was a tall woman, all wiry muscle and badass attitude, but she loved unconditionally and had claimed Raif Zovko as one of her own. That he was a Dom as well didn't matter. She'd be hovering over him, all her protective instincts on high alert until he was strong enough to tell her it was unnecessary.

Which, hopefully, wouldn't take long.

"How is he?" Dominik asked when she pulled away, letting her wipe her tears before joining her in the private room.

She went to Zovko's bedside, putting her hand on Tyler's shoulder. The young man was half-asleep in a chair he'd dragged right next to the bed. He barely lifted his head to greet Dominik, struggling to keep his eyes open as he put his hand over Chicklet's.

"Surgery went well. They put a metal plate in because parts of his skull caved in. He's sleeping a lot." Chicklet shook her head, looking helpless and frustrated. "I wish I could tell you more, but it's day to day. He needed a blood transfusion yesterday. Thankfully, we're the same blood type."

"I can donate to anyone. I could have done it." Tyler dropped his hand to his lap. "Still don't get why you didn't let me."

"Because you're getting back on the ice as soon as Coach here thinks you're ready." Chicklet turned to Shero. "He hasn't slept in two days, so I don't know if..."

Shero shook his head. "We'll manage without him for another game." He focused on Tyler. "If you can't come to New York, the team will understand. But we could use you out there."

Tyler nodded, but he didn't comment. The game clearly wasn't a priority.

Not that Dominik could blame him.

Looking at Zovko, Dominik had a hard time seeing the same strong, vibrant man he'd come to know over the past few months in the pale, lifeless form on the bed. Zovko's usually perfectly styled, chin length hair was limp. Dark shadows surrounded his closed lids. The heart monitor showed his pulse was strong, but he looked vulnerable and drained.

Maybe it would be different if he woke and showed the indomitable spirit they all knew him for, but he needed to rest and heal. And his loved ones could do nothing but wait and hope for the best.

Damn it, Dominik wished he had more to offer than the same platitudes they'd likely heard from everyone. At least with Oriana, he'd been able to calm Sloan down. Talk to Max. And her. The accident had been frightening for them all, but compared to what Zovko was going through, Oriana had been lucky.

Approaching Tyler, Dominik crouched down to meet the younger man's eyes. "Don't worry about the game. If you need anything, you give me a call. All right?"

Eyes tearing, Tyler nodded quickly. He grabbed Dominik's wrist before he could stand. "Thank you."

The gratitude made it hard to leave, but apparently Dominik had something to offer after all. With everyone reminding Tyler it was the playoffs, the team needed him, Zovko would want him with his team…all the kid wanted to hear was that he was exactly where he needed to be.

But, while this was where *Tyler* needed to be, Dominik had to get home. Welcome the new rookie. And pray he could manage a power nap before he hit the ice.

He got to his truck and sat there for a while, craving a few moments of silence to get his shit together. The past couple days had been so hectic focusing on the game himself was going to be a challenge.

Taking out his phone, he flipped it idly in his hand. Then he went through his callers and pressed Sahara's number.

"Hello?" She sounded happy to hear from him, but uncertain, as though worried something was wrong.

The smile on his face lightened his tone. "Hello, sunshine. I hope I'm not calling at a bad time."

"Not at all. I'm just relaxing a bit before the game." She paused. "Don't you guys take naps? Like toddlers?"

He couldn't hold back his laugh. Yes, calling her had been a very good idea. "Something like that. I had to come see Zovko first."

"How is he?"

"Stable. Which is the best that can be expected right now."

"I guess, but that was scary. And poor Tyler…this is too much like his own injury. He's not playing tonight, is he? I know you guys are supposed to tough it out, but he loves that man."

My feelings exactly. Not a conversation he could have with most of those on the team, but Sahara wasn't in the game mentality. And neither was he, obviously. "I made sure he knew he can take the time he needs. Zovko will probably insist that he play, but maybe, once he's able to do so himself, Tyler will be ready."

"I'd imagine so." Sahara's voice relaxed, as though she'd settled into a comfortable chair. "So aside from that, how are you? I heard Oriana went home today... You don't mind me mentioning her, do you?"

"Not at all. She's a friend. I saw her, spoke to Max, and I think they're going to be fine. How are your boys?"

"Pischlar and White? Good, I think. Being here is...uncomplicated."

"Good." He wasn't feeling the word, but he was happy for her. She needed uncomplicated after what she'd gone through. "Are you ready for tonight?"

"Yes, but you guys better win!" She giggled. "Don't want to put too much pressure on you, but the last game *sucked*."

"I agree."

"Can you score one for me tonight? I've always wanted someone to do that."

He opened his mouth, tempted to tell her to ask Pischlar or White, but that would be petty. He'd told her he was fine with her doing whatever worked for her right now. And he was.

But her asking him something like that caught him off guard. He needed a few minutes to come up with a logical reply.

Any reply.

Any time now.

"Dominik?"

"Yes." He cleared his throat. "I'll score one for you."

"That means something, doesn't it?"

He steadied his breaths, leveling his tone. "No more than you want it to, sunshine."

She hesitated. Then exhaled loudly. "I kinda want it to. Is that weird? I'm a head case, right? Don't worry, you can be honest."

"I always will be, Sahara. And no, you're not a head case." He rested against the headrest. "I'll be in New York for a few days, but when I come back, I want to see you."

"Won't I see you tonight?"

There was something in her voice, a quiet longing. Which shouldn't be there if Pischlar had succeeded in distracting her. If they were both her Doms, Dominik would give the man a call and see what more could be done.

But this wasn't a partnership and Pischlar was no more than a casual, temporary lover. *Very* temporary if Sahara decided she needed more.

He grinned and shrugged. "I don't see why not. I'll introduce you to my new roommate."

"Uh…I didn't know you were looking for one." She released a small, irritated sound. "Is she nice?"

Her jealousy was something they'd have to work on. He could point out that she was hardly in a position to judge who he lived with while she was staying with two other men, but he'd rather build up her confidence than press her insecurities.

So he clarified. "*He*. And I don't know, I haven't met him yet."

She laughed with obvious relief. "So stupid…I'm sorry. I guess he's a rookie you're looking out for? I should let you go so you can focus on him."

"Yes, I'm about to join him at my place. But do me a favor, pet."

A soft, rapid intake of breath, so close to the phone she must have it pressed right against her face. "Yes, Sir?"

"Don't call yourself stupid. I don't like it."

Nothing. Then she laughed nervously. "Sorry. I nodded, but you can't see me. I won't anymore."

"Good girl." He shook his head at himself, both loving and hating how natural the dynamic between them felt. Loving it because he didn't doubt they could have a good, strong relationship. Hating it because they weren't there yet. "I have to go now, sunshine. Watch for that goal."

After he hung up, he drove home, feeling fully at ease for the first time in a while. Things may be complicated with Sahara on the whole, but tonight, they'd be very simple.

Light the lamp. Make her smile.

And win the game.

* * * *

Sahara bit back a grin as she stood with Akira in the bedroom Jami shared with Sebastian and Luke. Holding up one of each of their home jerseys, Jami dropped back on the bed and groaned. She had a tough decision to make.

And both Sahara and Akira were trying very, very hard to be sympathetic.

In nothing but jeans and a bra, Jami lay on the bed, the jerseys on either side of her, her hands over her face. "This sucks! Why isn't it this hard during the regular season?"

"Because they take turns?" Sahara bit her lip. Exchanged a look with Akira.

They burst out laughing.

"You're both horrible bitches and I hate you." Jami sat up and smirked. "Besides, they don't always take turns. Sometimes—"

"TMI!" Sahara slapped her hands over her ears and hummed loudly.

Akira was just about on the floor, hardly breathing through her laughter.

Sticking out her tongue, Jami returned her attention to the jerseys, petting the numbers with a fond expression on her face. "They both know I love them. They lost while I was wearing Luke's jersey, so… But I don't want him to think I blame him—"

The sharp snick of boot heels came from the hall as Chicklet strode into the room, right up to the bed, and picked up the jersey with "Ramos" and "11" on the back. She held it out to Jami. "Get dressed. You will not be late on my watch, and you're being ridiculous."

Jami wrinkled her nose the second Chicklet turned to leave the room again, but she quickly donned the jersey. And kept her voice to a whisper when she spoke. "How much longer are you going to need your own security detail, Sahara? Not that I don't love Chicklet, but…*damn*. She's miserable. And before you remind me, I know how scared she is for Raif, but why isn't she with him? Can't Cort or Cam trail you?"

That would probably be easier on everyone, but the conversation before Chicklet had come to pick her up hadn't gone well. Sahara's attempt to release Chicklet from her team-appointed job as bodyguard had been taken as an insult.

"I promised to tell you when I was leaving Pischlar's place, but you don't need to come. He'll drop me off at Jami's. Tyler and Raif need you more than I do."

"They need me sitting in the damn hospital, completely useless, more than you need me watching your back?"

Sahara winced, wishing she'd worded that better. *"No! I mean, I'll be fine and you should—"*

"I'll be there in ten minutes. Be ready."

Chicklet had been hired because Mr. Keane thought Sahara would be more comfortable with a woman, but she'd be fine with Dominik's brother. Having Cort watch her would be awkward after what she'd said to him, but she'd rather swallow her pride than keep Chicklet away from her men when they needed her.

"I tried to suggest she stay at the hospital, but she gets all the details of the case from Laura, so... Well, she's not convinced that I'm safe out on my own." She hugged herself, grateful for the long, black wool jacket that covered her uniform. She was suddenly very cold. "Grant's out on bail, but I haven't heard anything from him. The crazy calls I've been getting are from his fans. As well as the Facebook messages—"

"Death threats." Akira corrected with the same irritation she showed anytime Sahara tried to downplay the situation. She folded her arms over her chest. "And one of the crazy bitches found your apartment." Her lips thinned when Jami's eyes went wide. "I'm not surprised you didn't know. Sahara doesn't want us to worry. Because that's the priority."

"Damn it, Sahara." Jami drew her knees to her chest and wrapped her arms around them. "What happened?"

Sahara dropped her gaze to the floor. "My landlord said someone spray-painted 'Lair' all over my door."

Akira's brow shot up. "You mean 'liar'?"

"I think whoever wrote it *meant* liar." Sahara rubbed her arms. Laura had tried to joke about it when Sahara had called her, but finding any humor in it was difficult when both the team and the police were taking the threats seriously enough to have her constantly watched. Despite Chicklet's presence, there was a unit parked outside

Jami's house. The last straw had been the message posted on Sahara's Facebook wall, detailing an orgy of violence that took a truly twisted mind to think up.

At least the woman who'd left that hadn't been difficult to track down. The arrest had brought even more attention to the case.

Sahara had changed her phone number and texted the new one to all her close contacts. Stopped going online at all. Didn't spend much time outside. Or anywhere public.

If she hadn't had Jami and Akira, she would have felt very alone. Fooling around with Pischlar and White had been fun the first night, but after that, simply…shallow. Not that they weren't sweet to her. Tender and attentive, always making sure she enjoyed herself.

"Uh-oh. She's all lost in thought again." Jami nudged Sahara into the hall, hooking her arm on one side while Akira took the other, making the hallway very crowded. "What's wrong, babe? You know you're safe, right? Whether it's Chicklet or—"

"*Or?*" Chicklet slapped a magazine on the coffee table as they stepped into the living room. "Why would there be an 'or'?"

Damn it, Jami's getting as bad as Luke and Tyler at keeping her mouth shut. Sahara worked her arms free and held up her hands. "No reason, I was just saying I felt bad keeping you away from Raif. And that maybe we could get Cam to take over."

Chicklet grunted and grabbed her leather jacket. "I'll talk to Mr. Keane. He's the one who hired me, and the team needs Cam on the road. Cort would be a better option. He's got a hearing soon."

She didn't sound mad. Or insulted.

Sahara nodded quickly. "Sure. I'd be fine with Cort. Or whoever—"

"Not whoever, little girl. I would like to be with my man more, but I won't leave you with someone I don't think can watch you as well as I can." Chicklet opened the door and led the way out, surveying the street before heading over to the black SUV the team had loaned her. She gestured for Sahara to get in the backseat with Jami. "You've made your point. It will be considered."

Another nod and Sahara sank back in her seat, silent for the ride to the Delgado Forum. Jami and Akira seemed lost in their own thoughts, which was good. There wasn't much to say.

Once they were inside the restricted area of the Forum, Chicklet left them to go talk to Mr. Keane. There was enough security around that Sahara didn't need a constant shadow. They were early, and she and Akira were already dressed, so there wasn't anything to do besides hang around.

She turned toward the Ice Girls' locker room. Akira and Jami started in the other direction.

"Hey, where are you going?" Akira crossed the short distance and grabbed Sahara's hand. "The wives' room is ten times nicer than our locker room. Have you been there yet?"

Umm, no. Sahara laughed and dug her heels into the carpeted floor. "Why would I go there? I'm not married to a player. And Jami's the only one engaged to…two."

Jami let out a happy sigh and admired her engagement ring. "I'm one lucky bitch, eh?"

"Yes, but that still doesn't explain why *I* have any business in there." Sahara had met some of the players' wives in New York. Longtime girlfriends were sometimes accepted into their ranks, but it was a dubious honor. They could be damn catty, and Sahara wasn't in the mood to deal with cliquish behavior.

Akira rolled her eyes. "Oriana is usually Queen Bee in there. And when she's not running the show, Silver is. She's probably there with Becky and the babies right now. You'll see, it's great."

Babies. Yep, Akira knew just how to convince her. Sahara giggled as Akira pulled her, half running, to a room all the way down the hall from the locker rooms. She pushed the large wooden double doors, slipping in as quietly as she could, feeling like a kid late for class when the women inside looked over at her curiously.

The room was a bit bigger than the locker rooms, and much more stylish than the players' lounge. All the décor was still in the team's black and gold, but there were glass and mirror accents, as well as softer golden shades to lighten up the room. With leather sofas on one side, and several tables on the other, the set up was perfect for the players' families to relax in before the game started and between periods.

Silver wasn't here, but Becky was. In a crisp, tan skirt suit with a white shirt and snazzy nude heels Sahara was so going to beg to borrow, she was perched on a black leather armchair, bouncing Amia on her knee and watching Casey color a huge poster on the floor with several of the other Cobra kids.

A smile lit Becky's face when she spotted Sahara and she stood, lifting Amia to her hip and crossing the room to give Sahara a hug. "Hey, sweetie. How are you?" She eyed Sahara's chin, likely checking out the fading bruises. "You look better."

"I'm feeling it. Everyone's been amazing, and I've had tons of support from the team. Thank you." She didn't really want to talk about her situation though, so she turned to Amia and gave the little cutie a kiss on the cheek. She had such soft, light brown curls, darker than they'd been only a few months back. "She's starting to look more like Casey. They could almost be sisters."

Becky nodded, laughing as Amia made a grab for the tiny unicorn pendant that Sahara wore on a delicate gold chain. "Yes, but she's got a bit of all her parents. I swear, the looks she gives me!" Becky gently pulled Amia's hand back and the baby proved her point by staring at her with annoyance. "Tell me that's not Dean right there!"

It really was, which was interesting since he wasn't her biological father. But he was her daddy in every way that counted and she mirrored him in many ways.

Another grab and this time, a pointed "No," from Becky got Amia's lip sticking out in a pout.

"And that's so Silver." Becky winked.

Coming closer, Akira giggled, offering the baby her thicker bracelet to play with. "I was going to say that looked just like Ford when he's not happy. Maybe we should call it the Delgado pout!"

The women around who were pretending not to listen joined in on the laughter. Several came forward to introduce themselves. Not surprisingly, most seemed to have popped right out of the magazines strewn on the table near the kitchenette. At least one of them was on two of the covers.

Sahara braced herself when the woman, who was a few years younger than her, came over and thrust out her hand. "Jackie Littlefield. The guy who has a full beard all season, Peter Kral, is mine. I just recently put a ring on it."

An inch taller than Sahara, with long, slick black hair and startling, pale gray eyes, Jackie exuded so much warmth and confidence all at once, Sahara wasn't sure how to react. Or what to say. She didn't want to make an ass of herself.

She glanced at the woman's left hand, ready to gush over a huge diamond. But the ring wasn't gaudy at all and very pretty. "Congratulations. Can I see?"

Jackie beamed and held up her hand. "It's a Disney engagement ring. I fell in love with them and couldn't choose. I'd considered the Mermaid one, but he got me Aurora and said it suited me better." She bit her lip as she gazed down at the pink sapphire, which had small hearts formed with diamonds on either side. "His ring is bigger. I was afraid I'd embarrassed him, getting down on one knee in front of his whole team—"

Jeanette, the wife of Beau Mischlue, came up behind Jackie and gave her a hug from behind. "It was the sweetest thing I've ever seen." Her French accent made her voice soft, but she spoke English much better than her husband. "Beau teased me after, asking why I hadn't thought of that when I bugged him for so long about getting married. The men were all jealous."

"Maybe, but I don't want him thinking the ring is to make a statement."

"Why not? Besides, the bigger the ring, the more challenged the bunnies are." Jeanette flicked her wavy brown ponytail over one shoulder. "You trust him?"

"Of course! I wouldn't marry him if I didn't."

"Good. Then no worries. The ring is perfect for his big hands." Jeanette glanced over at Sahara, then at Jami and Akira. "Jami, have you set a date? We should have a big party to celebrate. If your father doesn't like it, he won't be invited."

"Jeanette!" Cecilia Brends, the tiniest of the women, even though she was the mother of four kids, put her hand over her lips and shook her head. "You can't say things like that! You'll get your husband traded."

"*Eh?* We go to Montreal. I will miss you, but we can visit." Jeanette winked at Jami to show she was joking. "You're a big girl now. I remember you as a little bundle of trouble. Looking at you makes me feel old."

"I don't feel old. I would give up my Gucci purse to know what it's like to be with *two* of our guys." Cecilia let out a dramatic sigh. "Two like Mirek and I'd probably have eight kids. And I'd need to be committed."

"Looking at Ramos and Carter, I think Jami might be able to give the team the whole next generation. Enjoy that tiny body now, honey."

"Jeanette!"

Jami's cheeks were red. Akira was doing a horrible job of not laughing at their dear friend. Someone needed to change the topic before Jami regretted coming in here.

Not that Sahara much wanted the attention on herself. Maybe they could talk about hockey?

She cleared her throat. "So...do you watch all the games here? You've got a nice view of the ice. And what do you think of our chances for the post-season?"

Beside her, Jami gave her a grateful look and squeezed her hand. Jeanette latched on to the subject, proving to be very knowledgeable about hockey. She threw out a few questions and comments that Sahara couldn't help but respond to.

Tests. Not catty exactly, but close. Sahara braced for her to move in for the kill.

Jeanette cocked her head, studying Sahara with curiosity. "Most of the Ice Girls know about the game. A bit. But you grew up with it, didn't you?"

Name-dropping would sound like bragging, so Sahara just nodded. "Yes. And I played until I was in my late teens. I wanted to be the next Manon Rhéaume, but I wasn't good enough. And my grandfather always said he doubted a woman could play anything but goalie with the men."

"He's been right so far. But the women's teams are amazing to watch. It would be good to see them draw more viewers." Jeanette visibly relaxed, as though she'd decided she didn't need to keep interrogating Sahara. That didn't mean she accepted her, but she didn't see her as a threat. "You've told us little about yourself. Are you dating one of the men? Or several? We've decided we really don't care either way, but we don't let just anyone in here. Akira gets a pass because Cort looks out for our men. And Ford is a darling."

Ford? Sahara blinked at Akira, who smirked, then shrugged.

"I'm...staying with Pischlar?" Sahara winced as the words came out of her mouth. Pischlar was pretty easygoing about life in general, and there wasn't much she could do that would piss him off. Implying they were together might be an issue for him. "White's there a lot too. I mean, it's not anything. I'm not dating either of them, we just... I needed..."

Fuck, that was stupid.

Pischlar might laugh about her awkwardly blurting out private details, but White certainly wouldn't find it funny.

And she now had the full attention of every woman in the room. Jami let out a soft groan behind her. Akira scowled and shook her head.

Jackie let out a piercing whistle that made everyone jump. "Just about warm-up time! Who's going to the box with me? I'm not missing that look Peter gives me before the game starts while you bitches gossip."

"We have to get ready for our routine, but as soon as we're done, we'll join you." Akira grabbed Sahara's arm and Jami's hand. "Jami, you should check on Sam. Make sure she's doing okay. She hardly looks like she's pregnant, eh?"

They got out of the room just as conversation turned to who *did* look pregnant. And then half ran down the hall before stopping to stare at one another. And start laughing like crazy women.

"So much for trying to show you how great it is in there. They're really nice though, Sahara. You'll love them once you get to know them." Jami tugged her bottom lip between her teeth, pressing her hand to one blazing red cheek. "Hanging out with guys so much makes me forget how much more...open women can be."

"Oh, it was fine. I've dealt with a lot worse. The Ice Girls..." Sahara hesitated, not sure she wanted to say too much about them. Jami worked at the Forum, like Sam, but she'd been promoted to an usher. She was technically part of the Ice Girls, but only as a backup if one of the others got hurt. So she wouldn't be performing tonight.

And hadn't all season.

Jami rolled her eyes and made a dismissive gesture with her hand. "You know I'm not as into performing as you two. Don't hold back on my account." She hooked her arm with Sahara. "Tell me Justina's learned to stick up for herself?"

Sahara shook her head. Justina was one of the youngest of the Ice Girls. An amazing performer, but she was shy and insecure and had a weight issue—not a real one, she was as fit as any of the girls. But she was a medium to their extra small.

The Ice Girls' old coach had made it more of an issue and gotten herself fired. After Silver ripped her a new one. The Ice Girls knew better than to openly bully Justina, but Sahara was sure the girl still overheard the odd nasty comment. She was always quiet in the locker room. Stuck close to Akira and Sahara.

"I think she'd quit if she didn't love the team and being out there so much. We're supposed to be doing a big photo shoot this summer. She's already trying to get out of it. But she's only talking to me and Sahara." Akira frowned. "Silver might be able to help, but I hate bugging her. She's so busy with work and the baby. And now with Oriana being hurt...?"

"We need to take Justina out and work on her confidence." Jami tapped her bottom lip with her forefinger as they continued to the Ice Girls' locker room. "Maybe bring her to the club?"

Sahara went still with her hand halfway to the door. "Are you serious? She might be submissive, but what goes on there would scare the hell out of her."

"Not with us holding her hand."

"BDSM isn't the solution to everything, Jami."

Jami rolled her eyes. "Yes, I'm aware. But some of the players who go there are just a *little* kinky. And there's always Pisch. He'd be great for her, and you're not keeping him."

True. But if Sahara was starting to feel uncomfortable with the lack of substance in the relationship, Justina would be a wreck after the first time she let Pischlar close. She doubted he'd go near Justina; she just wasn't his kind of girl. She needed at least the hope of more from the start.

What does that say about you?

Nothing. Sahara wouldn't start tearing herself down about what she should have done. She didn't judge Pischlar for his carefree attitude. She wouldn't start doing it to herself. This wasn't the fucking 1800s. So long as she was a single woman, she could do whatever she wanted.

But that lifestyle didn't appeal to her anymore. Which was also fine.

Except, they weren't talking about her. So she focused on the reasons why Jami shouldn't be giving Justina a nudge in Pischlar's direction. "The girl hasn't dated anyone since I've known her. Pischlar would show her a good time. Then he'd break her heart. If he didn't crush her in the first five minutes with his "You can't keep me speech." I heard it and I was all right. She wouldn't be."

"It's not really a speech, he…" Jami ducked her head when Akira gaped at her. "So not getting into details, Sebastian made it clear to Luke and me that if he wanted our sex life out in the open, he'd play at the club. He doesn't bring us there very often anymore. He likes his privacy."

Well, that was new. What had changed?

Not that she could ask, since Jami had brought up privacy, but would Sahara sharing her experiences be weird now?

Akira apparently didn't share Sahara's reservations. She turned away from the locker room and folded her arms over her chest. "Did something happen? Is you and Luke being engaged a problem?"

"No, of course not. Sebastian just…he's not interested in sharing anymore. He did when he thought I needed it, but we've renegotiated. I think all the talk about Pisch playing with Tyler got to him." She shrugged. "Luke's uncomfortable with rumors, and Sebastian is trying to protect him. Not that I think you'd say anything, but when my Master gives me an order…" She smiled, her eyes dreamy. "Things are perfect. I don't know how else to explain, but I hope you understand."

"We do." Sahara had no doubt Akira felt the same. "No more sex talk."

Jami shook her head. "That's not what I mean. Just…certain things I can't tell you. I am more than willing to listen to any dirty details you want to give me!"

Sahara smirked. "Well then, there's probably a few interesting things about White you'd want to know. The things that man can do with his tongue..."

She cut herself off and opened the door to the locker room.

"Hey!" Jami called as Sahara ducked inside. "You can't stop now!"

"We're gonna be late. Love you!" Sahara blew Jami a kiss and hurried to her locker, grinning as Jami stuck out her tongue before slipping out of sight.

Just a little bit of time with her friends had Sahara feeling a million times better. She laced up her skates, waited while Akira gave the group their routine pep talk, and then followed the group out to the ice. Above, on a platform, a few of their girls danced with pom-poms like regular cheerleaders. The routine on the ice would be quick—just enough to rev up the crowd and keep them entertained before the elaborate light and music show came on to introduce the players.

Almost half of the seats were still empty, but they had a nice-sized audience. Sahara glided out around one half of the rink, three girls a few paces behind her, while Akira circled the other side. The lights dimmed and the spotlights followed them. The song "Dangerous" by David Guetta came on.

Speeding up, Sahara pushed into a leap, spinning before landing across from Akira, who mirrored her as she began to dance. Gold and red lights flashed, pulsing in a way that distorted their movements. The cold didn't touch her as she moved to the beat, every choreographed motion perfectly natural after weeks of practice, her muscles burning as she twisted and grinded down, fast, then slow and precise.

The Jumbotron screen showed them, then the dancers on the platform who kept with their rhythm, every step a reflection, so much passion in every gesture the crowd couldn't help but be sucked in to the excitement.

All the screaming, the cheers, hell, even the catcalls made Sahara's heart beat a little faster as she smiled and rushed away from the rest of the group to do another leap, landing only to spin in place until the world became a blur. She had given up her dreams of playing hockey so long ago, but she'd still found a way to be part of the sport she'd been born to love. Some of her best memories were from sitting out there in the stands, high above the ice but feeling every check into the boards, every fight, every goal, and every win as though she were right there with the players.

Maybe the Ice Girls weren't all that important, but they were a link between the fans and the team. Their dancing and their cheering expressed so much of what the crowd experienced. The opinions of the critics were irrelevant. Once they were done, all that mattered was they were all screaming for the same result.

A home ice win for the team that represented them all.

When they finished, they quickly cleared the ice and raced back to the locker room. Sahara changed into her sneakers and ran with Akira up to the wives' box to see the puck drop.

By the time they got there, the anthems had both been sung. The puck hit the ice and the crowd roared as Dominik took possession. He jetted between the Islander forwards, evaded their defense, and snapped the puck at the goal.

The lamp lit up and the cheers were deafening. Sahara jumped, clapping and screaming until her throat was sore. There was nothing like a goal within the first second of a game to set the pace.

"Sahara!" Akira grabbed her arm, bouncing as she pointed down at the ice. Then at the huge Jumbotron screen.

Huddled among his men, Dominik grinned, accepting their praise, but he was looking up, as though searching for someone. Ramos moved closer, saying something to him before pointing up to the wives' box.

There was no way he could see her, but Sahara could feel his eyes on her as he clearly mouthed the words "For you." Then winked.

Her heart forgot how to beat properly. She pressed her fingers to her lips, skittering out of view of the camera when she saw her own shocked expression on the screen. Around her, all the wives and girlfriends were giggling. Whispering excitedly.

But she hardly noticed them. She had a hard time staying put. She wanted to go down there and hug Dominik and thank him.

There were no words for how that gesture made her feel. Yes, she'd asked him to score a goal for her, but there'd been no guarantee. But he'd done it. He'd actually done it.

Screw diamonds and flowers and sweet words. That 1-0 on the scoreboard meant more than any gift her man could give her.

He's not your man.

Not yet. But he would be.

You're not ready.

She told herself to shut up and laughed, drawing a few curious glances. Maybe she'd needed some time to figure out what was going on in her own head, but all her doubts were gone. Not only because of the goal. The goal had just pushed her to accept all she could have if she let herself believe she deserved to be happy.

And she was happy. She couldn't remember the last time she'd been this happy.

The only problem was, she'd put up her own roadblocks. Yeah, she and Dominik had talked, but he would need more than an "I'm ready" to show him she'd done a complete 180 and wanted to give them a real shot.

She wished she could tell him this instant, but he didn't exactly have an office job where she could just call him up. Or text him.

He might notice one of those great big signs…

Okay, she had to pull herself together. He'd made an awesome gesture without going over the top. There was no mistaking where he stood.

All she had to do was find a subtle—and *rational*—way to do the same.

Chapter Eleven

Dominik's goal ended up being the only one, though the rookie, Heath Ladd, came close more than a few times. While the other players had trouble breaking out of the neutral zone, Ladd cut into the opposition like a hot blade through butter. The kid was fast, so he seemed to be on a different pace than everyone else on both teams.

But his efforts only resulted in repeated rings off the post.

The crowd groaned. The team gave Ladd quiet words of encouragement.

The boy reacted to neither. He was calm to the extreme. Composed.

He did, however, let himself smile a little when the Cobras won. Dominik kept an eye on him, hoping to get a clue about how to deal with the boy by how he interacted with the team. So far, he was polite and practically mute. He grinned at Bower when the game ended, waiting near the boards for the rest of the guys to finish congratulating the goalie.

Holding back, Dominik watched Ladd approach Bower.

"Great game, mate." Ladd rubbed his glove across his lips. "Been wantin' to see ya play."

Bower straightened to his full height, a big grin spreading across his lips. "Yeah? Well, thanks, kid. You were pretty good yourself. I think you'll get your first goal in New York for sure."

Ladd shrugged. He'd apparently said all he was going to say, but it was better than the one word replies everyone else—including

Dominik—got from the boy. Maybe he could use Bower's help to get the boy settled. The younger players had tried welcoming the rookie, but he'd nodded and grunted a lot to all their questions.

Carter, who was usually friendly with everyone, had muttered at one point, "The new guy's stuck-up."

Easy to assume, but Dominik had a feeling Ladd was observing them all, trying to figure out where he fit in.

Which, in the playoffs, would have to happen quickly.

Back in the locker room, Dominik changed into jeans and a hoodie, grabbing his jacket before joining Ladd at his stall. The younger man had a long-sleeved shirt, but he hadn't brought along anything warmer. He'd come straight from London with a small suitcase and his hockey equipment. The weather down here was unseasonably warm, but this close to the ocean, nights still hovered close to freezing.

Poor kid was going to have a hard time getting used to the weather. Hopefully, the rest of his things would be shipped over soon. He had a one-way contract, so he didn't have to worry about being sent back down. He'd been in Ontario for almost a year, but after looking Ladd up online, Dominik had found out that he'd had been in Russia as a junior. So the cold wasn't a new thing, but he hadn't been prepared for spring in Nova Scotia.

At least Dominik was parked inside. So tonight wouldn't be too bad, but if Ladd's stuff didn't get here before they flew to New York tomorrow, he'd need to pick up a few things. Dominik would lend him something if he needed it—the kid would drown in most of his stuff though. He was tall, but wiry.

"Ready to go, Ladd?" Dominik called out. He had to fight not to laugh when he caught Ladd staring at Bower. Tyler and Richards had been like that with Zovko when he'd joined the team. Sometimes younger players got a case of hero worship. Bower had had an amazing season, so it wasn't surprising that a boy who'd fought the odds and become one of the first—if not *the* first—Australian-born player to sign in the league would look up to him.

So long as it was just admiration, there'd be no issue. If it was more, he'd have to talk to the kid. Lusting after a guy involved with the man who handled your contract wasn't a good way to start a stable career.

Ladd tore his gaze away from Bower and nodded at Dominik as he hefted up his sports bag. "Yeah, mate."

That was it. Dominik sighed, not even sure why it irritated him that he couldn't get more words out of the kid. Taking a nap hadn't been difficult after he'd shown Ladd around his house. The boy disappeared into his new room and didn't make a sound until Dominik told him it was time to get ready to go. He'd told Ladd to help himself to food, a shower, whatever he needed.

A few "Thanks." A "Nope" when he asked if the kid needed anything else. A shrug when he dug a little deeper, wanting to know if the rookie had any questions.

Maybe Ladd was shy. He'd get over it. So long as he was an asset on the ice, his social skills were irrelevant.

Leading the way down the hall, Dominik pulled his phone out of his pocket to text Sahara. He'd wanted to see her before going home, but she was likely hanging out with her friends. Introducing her to Ladd didn't seem like such a great idea anymore. The boy was so closed off, had met so many people tonight, any more would be awkward.

He could always drop Ladd off if she did want to spend time with him though.

Dominik: Hey, sunshine. What are your plans for the night?

Sahara: Looking for you. I went down to the locker room as quick as I could, but you're not here!

Chuckling, he stopped by the door to the parking lot and held up his hand for Ladd to wait.

Dominik: I apologize. I needed to get Ladd out of the locker room. He hasn't made the best first impression.

Sahara: Ladd? And where are you? You said I could see you tonight.

Dominik: I did, didn't I? He's the rookie rooming with me.

Sahara: Oh…I guess you have to take care of him then. I don't want to bother you…

Silly girl. He was well aware of her insecurities though, so he wouldn't tease her. He was pleased that she still wanted to see him.

Actually, he had an idea. An insane one, but it was about time he made a move to see where they were at.

Dominik: Step out of the locker room and you'll see me.

Suddenly, she was there. Her cheeks were flushed, as though she'd rushed straight from the Ice Girls' locker room to meet him, which was probably why she hadn't seen him. She ducked her head as she quickly crossed the distance between them. The pleats of her tiny black skirt bounced off her thighs beneath her snug, black leather jacket. Her hair was in a high ponytail, swinging over her shoulders.

She came up to him, looking like she wanted to throw herself into his arms, but had changed her mind at the last second. Tonguing her bottom lip, she glanced over at Ladd, who was still standing somewhere behind him, completely silent.

"Hey." She stuck out her hand. "I'm Sahara."

Ladd moved up to Dominik's side and gave her hand a gentle shake. "Heath Ladd."

"Nice to meet you. And I'm sorry for stealing Dominik from you, but…well, I'm going to." Her cheeks grew even redder as she met Dominik's eyes. "I want this. I want everything. I don't know exactly what that means, and I know my timing is terrible, but I couldn't let you leave and not tell you." She inhaled roughly. Glancing at Ladd again, she visibly relaxed when she saw he'd taken out his phone and looked comfortably distracted. Her focus returned to Dominik. "If you need proof that I'm ready, just tell me what to do. This is new and scary, but it's everything I want. You…you're more than I deserve, but—"

He lifted his hand to press a finger to her lips. She was adorable, trying to offer herself to him, all while bracing for rejection. There had been no way for him to get them to this point until she opened that particular door, but now that she had, he was more than willing to take over.

"Enough." He ran his finger over her lips, then cupped her chin. The bruises were faint, but still a constant reminder of why he hadn't pressed his claim before. "Are you sure? You were very clear about needing something casual. And I don't blame you."

"And I appreciate you giving me space. But I don't need it anymore." She peered up into his eyes, leaving no doubt as to what she needed now. "Have you decided you're still a Dom?"

"Yes." The admission was both liberating and terrifying. He couldn't give a woman a simple relationship. He would always be all or nothing.

She nodded. "Then be mine."

He smiled and reached out for her, wrapping one arm around her waist even as he tipped her chin up. It was time to lay all his cards on the table and see if she would take the bet...or fold. "Come with me."

Her brow furrowed. "Where?"

"To New York. We've wasted enough time. You need a break from the hell you've been through." He leaned close to her, brushing his lips over hers, tasting the sweetness of them with a flick of his tongue. "And I need you. I need to have you close so I don't worry. So I can work my magic and convince you that you deserve everything I have to offer."

She went perfectly still, her lips parted and her eyes closed. For a split second, he worried that he'd put too much pressure on her. She'd been through a lot and this was a big step. Even if she wanted to come, her mind would probably set up all kinds of obstacles. Her team might need her for practice. It was too last minute. She was the offspring of legendary players; she wouldn't want to distract him from the game.

He had a counter to any objection she might come up with, but he didn't want to be selfish. She had a life that he didn't want to stomp all over. Plans that he wasn't part of. He was willing to wait if that's what it took to be part of her future. The opportunity had been there before, but he hadn't taken it. He'd been concerned about how vulnerable she'd been after Tim and Madeline's death. He'd given her time and space. Both of which she might still need.

"Yes." She met his gaze, no doubt or hesitation in her eyes. "Let's do this."

She didn't move. Held her breath as she lowered her gaze in the perfect act of submission. His pulse raced as he claimed her lips, lifting her to press her against the wall so she was completely helpless in his arms. She gasped as he deepened the kiss, exploring her mouth in a way he'd avoided before. He'd denied himself, and her, the depth of his passion because he couldn't put himself out there again only to see a woman he cared for in the arms of another man.

Training was one thing. He'd enjoyed it with Akira. But he couldn't do it again. His life had been on hold for long enough. He needed to take that next step. To find someone he could call his own.

That Sahara had played with Pischlar didn't bother him. The man wasn't interested in claiming anyone. Or...well, any woman anyway. He'd likely claim White if given the chance.

Which might end up being the only real obstacle. Because Sahara had played with White as well. What if she had feelings for him? White wasn't as easy to read.

"I know Pischlar likely gave you his speech, but what about White?" Dominik didn't want to hurt the guy. As much as he wanted Sahara, he had to be practical. If there was something between her and White, it would have to be handled carefully. "I don't want to put pressure on you, but I don't share well."

"I..." Sahara glanced over at Ladd—Dominik had completely forgotten the rookie was there. "It's not an issue. We played, but it was mostly because I see how Pisch feels about him. I made it okay, but the rest is between them. I'm kinda hoping it will work out, but I can't keep up the games. I opened the door. But now I...want something that's mine."

"Do you think I will be yours, pet?"

"I hope so." She rose up on her tiptoes to kiss him. "I'm going to go home, get some sleep, then pack. Call me when you get a chance and tell me what time the team's heading to New York. I'll grab a flight and meet you there." She squeezed his hand, practically bouncing in place. Then she turned her attention to Ladd. "It was great to meet you. I hope you weren't planning to share a room with Dominik? I should have asked, but he offered and—"

Pulling her in to claim her lips and quiet her, Dominik chuckled. Her excitement was contagious, but Ladd had heard more than enough. "He'll be fine. I'll get you all the details in the morning."

"Okay." She took a deep breath and laughed. "This is insane, but it feels right."

It did, but Dominik wouldn't let himself get carried away. Having her with him on the trip was a step in the right direction, but who knew where things would go from here? At least she had family out there if things didn't work out.

Either way, there was no reason to ruin the anticipation for her. He gave her a hooded look and wrapped her ponytail around his hand, whispering against her lips. "Pack light, pet. I tend to fully enjoy what you've given me to play with when I'm not on the ice."

She shivered, the flush in her cheeks returning as her eyes widened. "I will. But maybe something pretty in case we go out to dinner or—"

"No need, I'm not bringing you to show you off, Sahara." He brushed his lips over hers one last time before letting her go. "Sleep well."

* * * *

Sahara was too excited to sleep much that night. She ended up going to Jami's house and trying to be very, very quiet as she paced around the guest room. Exhaustion finally took over, and she crashed for a few hours. But she woke bright and early, dressing in the jogging pants and Cobra T-shirt Jami loaned her before heading to the kitchen.

At the stove, making scrambled eggs and breakfast sausages, Sebastian glanced over at her, amusement lighting in his dark brown eyes. "Are you hungry?"

"Not really, but I should probably eat."

"*Sí, pequeño*. But help yourself to coffee first. It is fortunate that you will sleep on the flight." He pushed the eggs around the frying pan with a spatula, then transferred them to a plate. "You were restless last night, yes?"

Damn it, she'd kept him up. She frowned as she went to grab a mug and fill it with coffee. "I'm sorry, I didn't mean to bother you."

"No bother at all. I had much on my mind as well and spent hours in my library, reading." He filled another plate with sausages and brought them to the round table in the small, brightly lit breakfast nook. He returned to the kitchen to grab the toast when it popped. "My loves weren't disturbed, and Luke's sister could sleep through the world splitting in two. I did wonder what was troubling you, but there's no need to tell me more than you are comfortable with."

There were some of the Cobras she considered friends who she could share just about anything with. Except the subject of Grant. Scott had even gotten some awkward details about her period once when he'd demanded to know why she was moody. Pischlar knew her entire sexual history.

She had a comfortable relationship with Sebastian, but she'd never really confided in him. He and Luke were kinda like friends because of all the time she spent with Jami. Not people she'd go to with her problems... She didn't want him worrying either, though.

"Actually, for once it's something good that kept me up. You know I'm heading to New York today?" She took a sip of her coffee, wrinkling her nose at the bitter taste. She'd been too distracted to even think of adding sugar or cream.

Chuckling, Sebastian came over and passed her the sugar dish. He opened the fridge and pulled out the cream. "Yes, you and Jami discussed your trip extensively last evening. She wishes she could come as well."

"Why doesn't she?"

"She won't leave Samantha. And Luke would not do well with his sister underfoot during such an important game." Sebastian made a dismissive gesture. "Not something I care to discuss further. You were explaining why the trip to New York is a good thing?"

She nodded as she fixed her coffee so it was actually drinkable. "Dominik wants me there. I want to spend time with him. I was kinda worried I'd be a distraction too, but he's been doing this long enough to know what he can handle. And he can handle me just fine." She choked on her coffee, realizing she'd just blurted out *way* too much. "I mean—"

"I know what you mean. And you're right, Mason will have no issue doing whatever is necessary. With you and on the ice." A movement near the table had his eyes narrowing. He snapped his fingers and let out a sharp "No."

Luke's puppy, Bear, dropped his paws back to the floor and slunk up to Sebastian with a hesitant wag of his tail.

He patted the dog's head and continued. "I'm surprised it took you both so long to realize how well you're suited. Perhaps I shouldn't be. You share the same aversion to considering your own best interest."

Sahara blinked, joining him at the table and picking up one of the empty plates to serve herself at his pointed look. "We do?"

"Yes. Mason was comfortable training subs for a time. Too comfortable. I was not surprised to hear he rushed to the hospital when Oriana was hurt. I expect it had more to do with either Perron or Callahan, but I may be mistaken. The point is, he keeps all those he cares for. Has a need to watch out for them." Sebastian lifted his mug to his lips, studying her face as though gauging her reaction. "You found shelter with one who does the opposite. Pischlar cares for many, but he holds them at arm's length. He can't hurt you and you can't hurt him. I believe that's very important to you."

"It used to be." She put her mug down beside her untouched plate full of food. "I'm a wreck. I don't know what's going to happen with Grant and the trial. I don't know if I can do a real relationship. But...I want to try."

He inclined his head. "This is good. Because I believe Mason reached the same decision. I would warn you to guard your heart if I believed Oriana still owned most of his, but she doesn't. He is not a man to play games. He enjoyed training because he could invest himself fully in his students. He is a man who does nothing halfway."

"So you approve?" She wasn't sure why Sebastian's approval mattered, but it did. Her friends were biased. He wasn't. So maybe a different perspective was exactly what she needed. "He's the captain of your team. He needs stability, and I'm not sure I can give him that."

"He knows what he needs. He's no different than you in his hopes for the future. None of us are, really." Sebastian cut a piece of sausage with his fork. Snapped his fingers and smiled when Bear came to sit beside him. When the puppy held still for a full minute, he tossed her the piece of meat, which she caught in midair. "Happiness doesn't always come when we're in the right place in our lives. All we can do is latch on to what we're offered and not waste a single moment. Know that, whether things are hectic or calm, those who truly love you will be there in the end."

Sahara took a bite of toast, nodding as she thought over his words. "You're not just talking about Dominik. I pushed Jami and Akira away for a bit. That was a mistake."

"It's good that you're aware of this. I try not to meddle, but I don't take kindly to those who make my girl sad." His tone sharpened, just a little. "Don't do it again."

She bit her lip, not sure if he was mad at her for upsetting Jami or if his warning was just that. Sebastian had always been pretty easygoing, but if it had been him in the parking lot instead of Cort that day when Grant showed up? She wouldn't have been able to get rid of him so easily.

And if she'd treated him like she had Cort, they wouldn't be having a pleasant conversation right now. He gave respect where it was earned.

She was just happy she hadn't done anything to lose his.

"I won't." She took a few more bites and cleared her throat. "So, you guys played better yesterday. What are you expecting in New York?"

Before Sebastian could answer, Jami shuffled into the dining room with Luke a step behind her. They both slumped into their chairs.

Sahara took the opportunity to go grab them some coffee.

"It's too early for all the serious talk. You're both nuts." Jami mumbled thanks when Sahara handed her a mug. "The team has to win the next two games. Take the series back home and end it. Anything other than that will piss me off."

Luke snickered, inclining his head when Sahara gave him his coffee. "No pressure, right? Just for that, boo, we're gonna bring both games to overtime."

Jami groaned. "You are a pain in my ass!"

"Not lately. You're always 'too tired.'"

"I have a *real* job."

That escalated quickly. Sahara stared into her coffee, wishing she had a newspaper to hide behind. Or her phone. Maybe this was karma for what she and Dominik had pulled in front of Ladd.

The smile disappeared from Luke's lips. "Seriously, Jami? You want to talk about this right before we leave?"

"*You* brought it up. She should go back to school so she can get a 'real job.'"

"*She*". They were discussing Samantha. Nothing seemed to get Jami and Luke butting heads more than anything involving his pregnant sister. Sahara refused to take sides. Jami thought Luke should forgive his sister for stealing from his mother—*and* Jami—because she was family.

But family often left wounds that took the longest to heal.

"She got fired again! She got caught stealing from one of her coworkers!"

"She has issues!"

"Clearly!"

"Enough!" Sebastian smacked his hands on the table as he stood. "Why am I only hearing of this now?"

"Because Jami texted me last night. I saw the text this morning and she said not to be mad. So I was trying not to be." Luke gulped down his coffee. Rubbed his lips with the back of his fist. "I mentioned Sam going back to school, and now Jami's throwing it in my face. Because I'm an unreasonable asshole when it comes to my sister. Well, we know whose side Jami's on." He pushed away from the table. "I'm going to the gym for a bit."

Sahara shrank into her chair as Sebastian reached out and grabbed Luke's arm. She shouldn't be here. They had too much going on to deal with yet another person in their home. She should have considered that before accepting Jami's invitation to spend the night.

"This will be resolved before you leave, *niño*." Sebastian gave Sahara an apologetic look. "You must catch your plane soon. I will drive you. Chicklet informed me earlier that Cort has been assigned to watch over you, so we will be picking him up and he will be on your flight."

Oh fuck. Sahara had planned to talk to Cort, but…not yet. In the near future. Next week if absolutely necessary?

But Sebastian was pissed and she wouldn't aggravate him more. So she simply nodded and watched him drag Luke, with Jami following, to their bedroom.

Her phone buzzed. She pulled it out of the pocket of her borrowed sweatpants and grinned.

Dominik: When is your flight leaving?

She checked her watch.

Sahara: Three hours. I'll have to chill in New York for a bit before you get there.

Dominik: Not alone?

Sahara: No. Seb just said Cort's coming with me.

Dominik: Good.

Sahara: Yeah, not so much. I was horrible to him. We haven't talked since. It's gonna be...weird.

Nothing for what seemed like a long time. Then she saw that he was typing.

Dominik: Cort's a good guy. But if he gives you a hard time, let me know.

Sahara: Why? This is my mess.

Dominik: Call me. I'm tired of typing. And I need to hear you're all right.

She took a deep breath, then clicked his number on speed dial. For some weird reason, just hearing "Hello" from him put her at ease.

"Hey. I'm sorry if you're worried. I'm really fine."

He snorted. "A 'fine' from you could mean many things. You're finally letting me in, pet. I don't take that lightly."

"What does that even mean? I'm going to spend time with you, but you're not taking on the drama that follows me everywhere." She sighed. "I've decided not to pack it. I'm not checking a big bag. You said to pack light."

"I did. But I want you, Sahara. All of you." He spoke softly, choosing his words carefully. "The team is less worried about Higgins at the moment than they are of his fans. I'm grateful that Cort can keep you safe. He will understand why you pushed him away. You pushed everyone away. You will resolve the situation. My only concern is you make the trip in one piece."

"You get that you're worried about puck bunnies, right? *He* hasn't come near me. His lawyers are doing a good job keeping him away."

"But you *will* accept the protection offered."

"Yes. I'm not stupid. One of those fans spray-painted my door. And the threats online..." Goose bumps rose on her arms and she rubbed them to warm herself. "I won't take chances, but I won't give them any more power than they've already taken."

"I'm not asking you to. But let us help, Sahara. Whether it's Akira, Jami, their men...or me." Dominik sighed. "Indulge us. We couldn't stop Grant from hurting you. But we want to believe we can prevent him from doing it again."

This isn't your problem. I chose him. I let him back in! Her eyes teared as she considered how willing she had been, all of a week ago, to believe Grant was a new man. She thought of his mother. Such a sweet woman. There had been times she'd talked to her about things she wasn't willing to go to her own mother with. Sahara had a normal relationship with her parents. Regular calls. Visits at holidays that could be trying, but still nice.

Her mother wasn't one Sahara could discuss anything unpleasant with. She was fragile. Always had been. Her father was proud of Sahara's every accomplishment. A little more focused on her brother who was sixteen and in the minors, but they had a legacy to carry on.

None of this was what Dominik wanted to hear. He was worried about *her*. And she'd given him plenty of reason to be.

That had to stop if they were going to have anything worth holding on to.

"I've already promised not to drop the charges. Whatever security the team decides I need, I'll accept." She sighed. "But I miss things being simple. The worst outcome being whatever people said about pictures of us together online."

He let out a rough laugh. "You haven't seen the comments, have you? Wait...don't you dare look for them. But I want you to promise me one thing."

"I can do that. Depending on what you want, Sir."

"You're incorrigible. All I ask is you come to me if anyone brings up anything that you think will be a problem. We are doing this together." His tone was strained. "People can be cruel. But you're not alone."

She dropped onto the sofa in Jami's living room and pulled her knees to her chest. If Dominik was willing to deal with all the craziness she was bringing into the relationship, she could handle whatever *his* fans had to say about her. She'd grown up hearing crude remarks at school about her grandfather, her uncles, and her father. Her mother had never "lowered" herself to acknowledging any of the fan mail or the way girls threw themselves at Dad, but Sahara had to deal with her own friends acting like idiots. She was prepared for just about anything.

"I know that. But I can't wait until I'm actually with you. Maybe then all the press and the mess I've gotten myself into won't seem all that important." She was going to sound like a selfish bitch, but she needed to make one request before she let him go. "Just promise, when we're together, you'll let me be useful? I don't care if it's washing your feet or ironing your clothes, I really, really, don't want to be a burden."

"That has to be the simplest thing you've asked of me so far." There was a smile in his tone, one that warmed her almost as much as his arms did when he held her. "You'll be in New York a few hours before me, but I've put your name on my room so you can check in if you'd like."

"I'd say they won't let me check in that early, but you guys probably have the whole floor." She'd never gone on road trips with Grant, so she wasn't sure what to expect, but she'd been around the hockey lifestyle enough to know about the special privileges given to the team. As a child, she'd experienced some of them. The league had changed though. So she'd just have to wing it. "And I guess the pictures will help."

"Don't forget your promise, Sahara."

"What promise?"

"The comments. No reading them. I won't have anonymous assholes upsetting you." His voice was soft, but firm. "And one more thing."

He wasn't holding back with the orders. And she loved it. She twirled her hair around her finger and grinned. "Are you gonna tell me not to pack any panties?"

A sharp laugh, then he groaned. "Brat. No, I'd like you to pack everything you normally would. With one addition." He paused. "Bring the red dress."

Less than an hour later, in her apartment with both Sebastian and Cort standing guard, the red dress was the first thing that went into her suitcase. She packed in record time, sure her cheeks must be beet red from her thoughts of Dominik's reaction to the silk nightgowns she'd chosen. She had a feeling her suitcase would be lighter on the way home if even half of her fantasies played out. The delicate straps wouldn't survive her lust, never mind his.

At the airport, after going through security and finding her gate with Cort, she settled in to wait for the flight to board. Her mind wandered to how things would be now that she and Dominik were taking the next step. Maybe she was thinking about it too much. He'd been tender with her, but even before their first date he'd warned her that she wouldn't get more than a kiss. What if the same restrictions applied? He'd mentioned wanting to spend time with her. And he wanted her to bring panties.

"Stop that." Cort leaned back in his seat, rubbing one hand over his shaved head. He scowled when the man beside him cringed. Then sighed when Sahara blinked at him. "Sorry, you tapping your foot like that is driving me insane."

She hadn't even realized she was doing it. She crossed her legs and smoothed her flowy, white and blue knee-length skirt. They hadn't exchanged more than the barest pleasantries. She didn't want to annoy him. Especially when she still hadn't figured out how to apologize.

"I'm sorry." She brought her fingers to her mouth absently but caught herself before she started chewing her nails. She hadn't done that since she was a teen. Not a habit she wanted to start over.

There were about ten minutes left before they boarded and were stuck in separate seats. Cort wasn't a big talker. She might as well get the apology out there so their time together wouldn't be awkward.

"I should have told you before, but I really *am* sorry. I shouldn't have been such a bitch to you." She stared down at her hands on her knees. "You're a better friend than I deserve."

He gave her a sideways look. "You consider me a friend?"

"Yes. I know part of what you did was because Akira was worried, but you risked going back to jail because you were worried about me." Talking to him was getting easier. The weight of guilt lifted a little from her chest. "And, now that I think about it, you scaring him off was probably the best thing that could have happened. Who knows how much worse things would have been if..." Her throat tightened. It wasn't hard to imagine how bad. If Grant hadn't lost his temper so quickly, if he hadn't broken in to her apartment, she'd still be convinced he'd changed.

"Hey, shit happens. I ain't even mad." Cort took her hand and gave it a little squeeze. "I've seen situations like this end badly. I'm just happy you're all right."

All that worry for nothing. She should have known Cort wouldn't hold a grudge.

But it seemed almost too easy. Like she should have to earn his forgiveness. Or at least explain herself a bit more. She took a deep breath.

He held up a hand and shook his head. "Don't. You've been through enough. Akira is over it. I'm over it."

"But—"

"But you can't forgive yourself. Not sure how to help you with that, sweetheart." His lips quirked up to one side. "How about you buy me a beer when I get my ankle monitor off? You can be part of celebrating my freedom."

She smiled at him, loving the idea. "Deal. It shouldn't be much longer, right?"

"Next week I go before the judge and either get pardoned or go to jail." He didn't seem upset by the prospect, so he probably expected the judgment to go in his favor. His grin widened as though he'd seen her thoughts playing out on her face. "They let me travel with the team now. So long as I don't fuck up, all that's left is the paperwork."

So long as he doesn't... She bit her bottom lip hard. If Grant had pressed charges, the outcome might have been very different. She would have been responsible for Cort losing his freedom.

"You're doing it again. Stop." He stood and slung his black rucksack over his shoulder. "Don't dwell on what might have happened. It didn't. Let's just get on this plane and see where things go from here."

"To New York." She joined him in line, rolling her small suitcase behind her. "Other than that, I have no clue."

He chuckled, putting his arm around her and giving her a quick hug. "Ever think there's nothing wrong with that? Change don't happen when you're doing the same old shit."

"Very true." She gave him a little nudge with her elbow. "Anyone ever tell you you're pretty smart for a thug?"

With a loud snort that got a few startled looks, Cort shook his head. "Not lately. But thank you."

"My pleasure." She giggled when he rolled his eyes at her, then held out her ticket and passport to get scanned before heading down the jet bridge to board the plane. She was happy and relaxed, more than she'd been in a while. The people who mattered to her hadn't abandoned her, no matter how many reasons she'd given them to. She was out of Grant's reach. For good this time.

Most importantly, she wasn't running from a chance at love anymore. She was, quite literally, flying toward it, full speed. And the future was looking pretty damn awesome.

Chapter Twelve

The future was going to have some unexpected roadblocks. Sahara stared at her phone when she got off the plane. Her mother had texted her, all excited about her visit.

And apparently she had read the comments Sahara was forbidden to read. Along with some new ones.

Mom: Honey, we need to talk. He looks like a very nice young man, but you must see how difficult things will be for you both? I wasn't going to bring this up at all, but… Well, I think we need to talk about this. You've made poor choices in the past.

Poor choices? Her mother didn't know all the details about what Grant had done to her. How bad things had been. Mom had mentioned once that she didn't like how angry Grant sounded sometimes, but that wasn't that surprising. All the men in her mother's life treated her like she was made of delicate crystal.

Did she think Dominik was a violent man?

Sahara didn't want her mother getting all stressed and calling everyone they knew to discuss her concerns. She had a bad habit of airing family drama. And there was no way Sahara was going to become her new headliner.

She thanked Cort for putting her suitcase in the trunk of the cab and climbed into the backseat as she called her mother.

"Hello, my darling. I hope you had a pleasant flight?" Her mother sounded perfectly relaxed. Which probably meant she was sitting with a bunch of her friends and putting on what she called her "brave front."

This conversation should probably wait until they were alone. Sahara chewed on her thumbnail as Cort climbed into the backseat, giving the cabbie directions to the hotel. "Yes, it was fine. I just wanted to let you know I was here. I'm heading to the hotel, but we can have dinner later tonight if you want?"

"I'm with my girlfriends for bingo, honey. But why aren't you staying with us? There are rumors, but…well, I'd assumed you were just coming to support the team. You got my text, didn't you?" Her mother let out a heavy sigh. "I hope I didn't upset you, but with all the talk of Grant being arrested and you seeing so many different men…"

"I was staying with a friend, Mom. I'm only seeing one man, but it's very new. *Too* new for me to be bringing him to meet you and Dad." The very idea of bringing Dominik to meet her parents scared the hell out of her. Her father would be all moody and her mother would gush and start talking about weddings. Sahara was "at that age," after all.

As much as she loved her family, she didn't miss their attempts to rival their favorite Broadway plays in entertainment value.

"Well, I'm happy to hear there's only one man. Please tell me it's not the one with all the tattoos?" Her mother clucked her tongue. "You're too old to be going through a reckless phase."

At Cort's amused sideways glance, Sahara realized her mother was speaking loud enough for him *and* the cabbie to hear both sides of the conversation. Time to end it.

"No, I'm not dating Pischlar. He's just a friend." Her mother didn't need details of a past friends-with-benefits relationship. They weren't that close. "I'm seeing Dominik. The captain of the team. I'll tell you all about him later, but right now I'm with a friend and being very rude."

"But you said it was a new thing. Maybe you'll meet someone suitable now that you're home—did you hear that Roger is dating again? It's about time; his wife died two years ago."

Sahara shook her head and laughed. "Sometimes I wonder if you actually hear yourself, Mother. Please don't try to set me up with any of your friends' sons while I'm here. I have to go, but I'll call you later."

The fact that her mother let her end the call was a miracle. Stuffing her phone in her purse, she turned to apologize to Cort. Which she seemed to be doing a lot lately.

He waved it off, chuckling. "Don't even worry about it. Just tell me I ain't gonna have to go with you to meet the parentals and it's all good."

"I wouldn't do that to you."

"Good. Because if she has a problem with Pisch, I don't want to know what she'd think of me."

They made their way into the hotel, checked in, and parted ways at the door to Dominik's room. Cort had been given a room on the same floor as the rest of the team, but it was at the other end of the hall. He made her promise to text him if she planned to go anywhere, pulling out his phone before she even closed the door.

She smiled as she heard his voice go all tender. "Hey, man, how you doing? Did you go see your sister?"

The room was bigger than she'd expected—more of a junior suite actually. There was a sitting room with a small blue loveseat and two armchairs, set around a simple black coffee table, and a flat screen TV up on the opposite wall. The bedroom had a king-size bed covered with a white duvet and a neatly folded golden throw.

Her stomach got weird and fluttery as she stared at the bed. She would be sleeping here for the next four nights. In Dominik's arms.

You won't be sleeping the whole time.

Heat spread across her cheeks, trailing over her breasts and down between her thighs. She closed her eyes and pictured Dominik here, his eyes on her as she stripped for him. Or maybe he'd take her clothes off in a rush. She still couldn't get the idea of him ripping a few out of her mind. For some reason, the image made her all hot and needy.

But you can't expect him to spend all his time getting you off.

Maybe not, but she was an independent woman with no issues taking care of herself. With some time to kill, she filled the Jacuzzi tub to take a nice long and *very* satisfying bath. Then she showered and donned a short-sleeve, white blouse with a simple, black skirt, and a pair of strappy, black sandals. Her phone buzzed with a text from Dominik saying the team was almost at the hotel, so she quickly did her makeup and threw her hair into a stylishly messy bun. Double-checking for her room key, she messaged Cort that she was headed down to the lobby and hurried out to the elevator.

He met her before the elevator reached their floor. "Excited?"

Ducking her head, she let out a soft laugh. "Is it that obvious?"

"You're practically glowing, sweetie. Do I need to have a chat with Mason about treating you right?" Cort had that protective look in his eyes, and she had a feeling Akira had said something. Considering Akira's past involvement with Dominik, she didn't see it being anything bad.

She studied Cort's face, curious. "You know Dominik. Do you think I have anything to worry about?"

"No. But the talk never hurts." He shrugged like it was no big deal. "I could leave it to your dad. Just didn't want to piss you off if you want me to mind my own damn business."

"Did you have 'the talk' with Jami's men?"

He grinned. "Seb had it with *me*. And Ford. Not long after Jami warned us not to hurt Akira or she'd feed our balls to Luke's dog."

"Fair enough." Sahara wondered how Dominik would react to all the warnings. She wouldn't encourage Cort to threaten him, but maybe it would be good for the men to have a conversation. And make up for her being a bitch when Cort had been justifiably worried about Grant. "Say what you need to. Just remember that he's your friend. And I'm a grown woman."

The wicked smile on Cort's lips didn't bode well for how his talk with Dominik would go. Then again, Dominik would likely take it in stride. Be amused at best, or mildly annoyed at worst. If she talked to him first, he'd understand why she hadn't stopped Cort from saying anything.

But when they met up with the guys in the lobby, she abandoned the idea of any kind of playful chat.

Most of the team was distracting the media while a tight-knit group moved quickly in her direction. Pischlar gave her a grim look while Dominik stepped up to her side and looped an arm around her shoulders.

He didn't even give her a chance to ask what was wrong. "Don't panic, it's nothing huge. There was bad turbulence on the flight and some of the guys are shaken. Coach wants them away from the media, so the ones who made it through fine are taking all the interviews."

Sahara nodded, glancing back at the men who were being interrogated by the press. She was pleased to see Tyler, since that meant Raif was probably doing better and had told him to come. Both Tyler and Luke were making big hand gestures—it looked like they were doing charades and the answer was "plane crash." Scott was a few steps behind them, smirking and adding to the story in a way that had several of the reporters abandoning Sloan and Max's calm retelling for the more elaborate story.

Zach gave Scott a sharp elbow in the side and took over. The reporters began to lose interest as he laid out the bare, undramatized facts.

"Do you need me to go back to the room and wait?" It made sense for Dominik to be here if the media was questioning players about the flight. He was the captain after all. "I don't mind—"

"Actually, I was wondering if you could check on White. Pisch and Richards are with him, but he might be more comfortable talking to you." Dominik made a face, his focus on Heath Ladd, who seemed to have drawn a crowd despite his aversion to conversation. "I'd have Ladd room with Pearce if I thought the man could teach him how to handle the media with short answers, but Demyan needs his man to keep him on the right track. Right now, the reporters seem to think the rookie is shy. If they keep pushing, he might end up giving the media a sound bite they'll have a field day with. I need to keep an eye on him."

Oh…so this isn't just about the interviews? She tried not to let the heart-wrenching disappointment she felt show. "Do you need me to get my stuff out of the room then? I can probably crash with Cort. I mean, he's guarding me anyway and Akira trusts me, so it wouldn't be weird."

Cort cleared his throat behind her. "It would be a little weird."

She frowned at him. "You're not helping."

He shrugged. "How about you stay where you belong and the kid rooms with me? Problem solved."

Dominik stroked the base of her neck with his thumb and grinned at Cort. "I appreciate the offer, and I may consider it, but not because I needed to find a good place for him. I'd already planned to put him in with Mirek Brends. Unfortunately, Sahara tends to assume the worst."

"I didn't—" *Yes, you did.* "I just—" Ugh, she was going to smack Dominik if he didn't stop looking at her like she was the cutest little thing. "It's not funny. I'm trying to be helpful."

"Thank you, pet. But I need you to stop assuming I'll set you aside. For any reason. I let you believe that once because I had something come up. I won't do it again." He bent down and pressed a light kiss on her lips, which made her feel a bit less like hitting him. "I want to keep an eye on Ladd while he deals with the media, then get him settled. I need you with White. I shouldn't be long."

He gave her a long look, as though to make sure she understood he wasn't abandoning her, then squared his shoulders and made his way through the throng of reporters and hotel staff surrounding three-quarters of the team. She watched him for a minute, then forced herself to walk back to the elevators.

This was good. He was trusting her to take care of one of his players. One who she'd fooled around with, but that didn't matter. What bothered her wasn't that he was asking her to help him out, she wanted to be there for him.

It just seemed like, no matter what they did, something—or someone—was always keeping them apart.

* * * *

"You are aware that shrugging when you're asked if you thought you were going to die is not an appropriate response, right?" Dominik was tempted to shake Ladd when the boy's shoulders lifted. The quiet had seemed like a good thing at first, but after two days of one-sided conversations, he had half a mind to hand the rookie over to Chicklet for her special brand of conditioning. "I thought your coach said you were easy to deal with."

Now *that* got a reaction. Ladd's face lost all color. He stopped right in the middle of the hall, shaking his head. "I'm trying to be easy, mate."

"Dealing with a mute, who isn't actually a mute, isn't easy. It's frustrating as hell." Dominik scratched his scruffy jaw. His playoff beard was still pretty short since they were only a week in, but he was so accustomed to keeping all but above his lip and his chin cleanly shaven that the stubble was uncomfortable. And, naturally, since he was already annoyed, everything was irritating him at once

He studied Ladd's closed-off expression, wondering what it would take to get through to him.

"I thought Brends would be a good choice—his English isn't great and he's trying to work on it—but I don't think you'll be very helpful. So there are two options. You can stay with one of the teams security guys, who may throw you if you annoy him, or our backup goalie, Dave Hunt." Who also might throw Ladd, but who was more likely to ignore him. "Take your pick."

Ladd looked like he was going to shrug again.

Dominik's lips thinned. "Do that again, and you'll sleep in the goddamn hall."

"The goalie's fine."

"Good. I'll let him know." This should be interesting. Dominik texted Shero to get Hunt's room number, then motioned for Ladd to follow him. He continued eyeing the rookie, not sure if he was more frustrated because of the kid's silence or because it had just been a long fucking day. The turbulence hadn't bothered him too much, though he'd admit it had been unsettling being jolted around for half an hour. Their flight had taken longer than expected, so they hadn't been cleared to land for what seemed like forever.

He was hungry and tired and needed a damn shower. He wanted to go back to his room, hold Sahara in his arms, and stay with her until he had to get back on the ice for morning practice. He didn't mind the responsibilities of being the team captain, but people were asking more and more of him and the return was nothing but sleepless nights and no time for himself.

Which wasn't Ladd's fault. The kid was just the final straw.

Once they reached the door to Hunt's room, Dominik lifted his fist to knock, eager to finally have a few minutes to spend with Sahara before the next obstacle came up.

Ladd cleared his throat. "The reporters were bloody morons, so I ignored them."

Damn it. Dominik chuckled, unable to deny the satisfaction of having actually gained some ground with the kid. A few more minutes wouldn't hurt. "Yeah, well, you know the scripted answers you always hear us giving?"

The rookie nodded.

"Much more effective in getting them to leave you alone. Nodding, shrugging, and shaking your head just make them want to keep digging. Give them a whole lot of nothing and it will be painless."

Another nod. And a smile. "Right, mate. I'll try that."

The boy was learning to use his words. Not a huge improvement yet, but Dominik didn't feel like he'd wasted his time.

He and Sahara had more than earned a few uninterrupted hours.

And they would have them, even if he had to steal her away to claim them.

Chapter Thirteen

What the fuck... Shawn Pischlar stared at White's muscular back, which was all stiff and tense, not sure how to even finish the thought. There were a few options that could work.

Like what the fuck had he been thinking? What the fuck was he gonna do now? What the fuck was going to happen to the friendship he'd done his damn best not to ruin?

Until the goddamn flight.

Coach always made sure Shawn sat with White, even when things had been tense between them. Yeah, it had hurt to find out White had fooled around with Richards after all the "I'm straight" talk, but Shawn knew how his best friend's brain worked. Richards was safe because the kid didn't ask for much. He'd probably invited White to come hang out in his room to watch a movie and gone along with whatever drunken suggestions White made.

And I wasn't really jealous that night. More like... Hell, he couldn't finish that thought either. Anything to do with White messed with his head. People might assume Bruiser wasn't all that bright, but Shawn was the stupid one of the two of them. He felt sorry for Richards—the kid didn't need a confused straight dude messing with him.

Shawn shouldn't have messed with *White*, but this past week they'd gone further than he'd ever expected. He wouldn't fool himself into believing that he would have gotten his hands on White without Sahara's help, but they were all having fun, so no harm, right?

If he'd left it at jerking White off and sucking his dick once in a while, maybe they could have continued just fucking enjoying each other.

He just never fucking learned.

The flight to New York was short, but they'd been sitting on the plane, waiting for clearance to take off, for what seemed like forever. Shawn slid the window cover up to look out at the runway, counting the planes ahead of them and trying to guess how much time they had left. The pilot had announced a twenty-minute delay.

Twice.

The engine growled and the plane shifted forward. White grabbed Shawn's knee. "Please close the window, man."

Not even bothering to ask why, Shawn slid the cover down. White always hated flying, but some flights were worse than others. And the bruising grip on Shawn's knee made it clear that this would be a bad one. He had a few tricks to distract White—on a trip to LA, he'd actually read to the man until he passed out and slept the whole way. But that was before Tim's death. After, the focus had changed to keeping White awake. Bruiser had nasty fucking nightmares about being crushed in a car, or a mine, or sometimes both.

Heights had always been an issue, but flying seemed to combine all his fears into a debilitating terror that had several team therapists struggling to find the right kind of therapy to get White past it. So far, they'd made little progress.

White was doing his yoga breathing thing though, so he wasn't at panicking point yet.

They hit the runway. The plane sped up.

The grip on Shawn's knee tightened even more.

"If I'm gonna be out with a lower-body injury, mind squeezing a bit higher, pal?" *Shawn laughed, hoping White would see the humor and relax a little.*

Instead, he dropped his head back and groaned. "Don't fucking tempt me."

"Wouldn't dream of it. But I'll tell you this. You're gonna fuck me before you die." *If he let himself consider that statement, he'd get damn depressed. But it made a good joke.* "Obviously, that means you'll live a very, very long time."

The slight slant of White's lips was close to a smile, so Shawn sat back until they'd reached the altitude where he could put a movie on his iPod. He'd ordered the new Avengers one special because he knew White hadn't seen it yet.

"You'd seriously let me do that?"

Movie all ready to go, Shawn sat back, arching a brow as he tried to figure out what the fuck White was talking about. "Let you do what?"

"Fuck you."

All right, did we both die? *Shawn rubbed a hand over his eyes and groaned.* "Don't say shit like that to me, Bruiser. People who aren't fucking don't need to have conversations about it."

White nodded slowly. He pressed the call button for the flight attendant, then ordered two whiskeys on ice. Apparently he needed both to continue the chat he wouldn't let go.

He cleared his throat when they were alone again. "But...you've sucked my dick, man. And other stuff. So it's not like we're just two people—besides, only Sahara's ever gotten you off."

Fuck me. *Shawn didn't usually worry too much about being overheard, but Sahara had already flown to New York. To meet up with Mason. Shawn and she had talked, and he and Mason were cool, but the man didn't need fucking details from White.*

Thankfully, Mason was sitting at the other end of the plane with the new kid.

"I don't really give a shit who gets me off." *Shawn let out a strained laugh that White didn't catch.* "You want to fuck me, then it's pretty simple. Unbuckle your seat belt and go wait for me in the bathroom."

What should have shut him up about fucking made White's face go red. He sat there for a bit, staring at his hand, which was still on Shawn's knee.

Then he got up and walked down the aisle between the seats, disappearing into the bathroom.

In the hotel room, Pischlar watched White, standing a few feet away, staring out the window. Sahara and Richards were both in the room, looking uncomfortable. Sahara's eyes were on White, and she was chewing on her bottom lip in that way she did when she was thinking hard. She better not blame herself for how weird things were between him and White.

Neither of them had been thinking of her on that plane.

Strangely enough, White's fear of flying made it so no one even blinked when Pischlar followed him to the bathroom, then went in and locked the door. He'd done it before when White had gotten sick. Hell, so had a couple of the other guys.

The second he was clear of the door—barely, because the bathroom was just a bit bigger on their charter flight than one on a regular plane—White pulled him close, tugging at his shirt and kissing his throat. Shawn bit the inside of his cheek to keep from moaning and undid White's jeans. He freed White's dick, stroking the already rock-hard length.

There wasn't much time. Someone would eventually come knocking at the door to see if Shawn needed help. Which, depending on who it was, might have once gotten a yes.

If this weren't White in his hands, with his lips on Shawn's throat, moving against him like he'd gone wild with lust. Shawn didn't expect this to last. Didn't expect another chance.

He pulled a condom and a small pack of lube from his wallet.

"You sure, man?" White panted, speaking in a whisper. "This is fucking crazy, but I can't stop thinking about you."

Don't fucking go there, Bruiser. *Shawn swallowed hard and laughed softly. "I'm sure. You wanna buy me dinner first?"*

"Why you gotta be like that?"

"Fuck me, White. Before you change your mind."

Hands braced on the sink, Shawn almost came the second he felt the head of White's dick pressing into him. So fucking slow, so gentle, it was obvious White had only ever done this with girls. He kept his hands on Shawn's hips, easing in with gradual thrusts until his pelvis was flush against Shawn's ass.

"Fuck, Shawn." White bit the side of Shawn's neck, thrusting in a little harder. "Am I hurting you?"

"Don't call me Shawn." He felt White stiffen as he tensed and forced himself to relax. "I'm not fragile. You're more likely to break me if you don't start moving."

White's breath came out in a laugh, close to his ear. "But we've got to be quiet."

"Yeah." Shawn's grip tightened on the edge of the sink as White pulled out, then thrust in hard. "Fuck yeah."

The man might be straight, but White wasn't a selfish lover. He figured out all the right places to hit and kept aiming for them. He rode Shawn hard, reaching around as he neared his own climax to wrap his hand around Shawn's dick. He stroked in time with his thrusts, then brought his free hand up to cover Shawn's mouth when he came.

And fuck, Shawn was pretty sure he'd never come that hard. If White's hand hadn't been there, he would have shouted loud enough to get the captain of the damn plane back here. So much blood had pumped through his cock that he was pretty sure his brain was fucking done for. He used the last of his strength to pull his pants up after White pulled out.

Which probably explained what had come out of his fool mouth.

If they were alone, Shawn might try to talk to White. Take back what he'd said. But he had a feeling the only reason White wasn't telling him to get lost was because Sahara and Richards were here.

And Richards was only here because he fucking sucked with the press. The rookie tended to blurt out whatever came to his mind. Not in the blunt way some of the other players did either. More like he was being given a test and didn't want to fail.

Hell, just last week, Rebecca Bower, who ran public relations, had bitched to Coach Shero about Richards's latest mess that she had to clean up. He'd been asked what he'd thought about the ref who'd given him three penalties during the last game of the series. And he'd answered with brutal honesty.

The answer got him a fine from the league and a talking-to from just about everyone.

Which was nothing compared to him spilling how they watched the Islanders' goalie and knew he was weak high stick side. Wouldn't you know it, the goalie had miraculously learned to close up that particular hole.

Coach Shero had agreed to keep Richards away from the press until they could teach the kid to go with the damn script.

And Sahara? Well, she was probably here to make sure they all behaved themselves. Richards lived with Coach Shero because the man seemed to think White would corrupt him.

Maybe Shawn should leave the coach a memo, letting him know he had nothing to worry about anymore.

The quiet was getting awkward. Shawn decided to fix that the only way he knew how. "You guys wanna fuck?"

Richards's jaw practically hit the floor. Sahara put her hand over her mouth, then glanced over at White.

Shawn ignored them. He was fucking tired of tiptoeing around everything. If this kept up, he'd be just as sad and boring as the rest of them. He relaxed back on the bed on his elbows. "Come on, kid. White says you're lousy in the sack, but I think he lies."

Slamming his fist into the window frame, White let out a growl. "Why do you always fucking do that?"

"Do what?"

"You know what."

Actually, Shawn had no fucking clue. Did White have an issue with Shawn being an easy fuck? Hadn't seemed that way on the plane.

He ground his teeth as he remembered when he'd slipped from his status quo in the cramped bathroom.

"You okay?" White ran the cold water, washing his hands then wetting his face. "I, uh...fuck. We shouldn't have done this here."

"Not sure it matters where we did it. Are you cool?"

"Yeah." White ran his fingers through his hair. "Hey, is this going to change anything with us? I mean, Sahara's gonna be with Dominik. If she wasn't, then maybe..."

"Because you're straight. And having pussy in the bed keeps you that way, right?"

White drew in a sharp breath. "Why you gotta put it that way? We're having fun. I thought you only flipped out when people expected more from you. I don't."

"Fucking good thing. Don't fall in love with me or anything, Bruiser. I'll break your heart." Shawn was doing his best to steel his own before it bled out in his chest. He'd known White was only experimenting with him because Sahara had offered herself as a consolation prize.

"Don't worry, I won't."

The plane shook and the seat belt light came on. White's face lost all color as he reached for the door. Shawn grabbed White's arm to steady him.

White jerked away.

A brisk knock sounded on the door. Sahara bolted from her chair and ran to the door, probably hoping to see Dominik.

Dean Richter, the team's general manager, stepped into the room. "Sahara, you're looking well."

"Thank you, Sir." Sahara moved to let him in. "Is everything all right?"

"Everything's fine. I wanted to discuss something with Pischlar. If you don't mind—"

Shawn stood and strolled up behind Sahara, slouching against the wall as he inclined his head at Richter. "I've got nothing to hide. What's up, Mr. Richter?"

Richter's lips thinned. "Very well. I appreciate you wanting to defend your teammates, but social media isn't the place to do it. We're in the playoffs, and you're not a young man without experience dealing with this kind of thing."

Fucking PR, always checking our posts. On the bus, heading to the hotel from the airport, Shawn had checked out Facebook so he wouldn't worry about the fact that White was ignoring him.

There was a new picture of Richards up. The kid had done a magazine shoot and he looked fucking hot. It was a badly kept secret that the rookie hung out in random gay bars, and he had quite the following. A few twinks had left admiring comments.

Some random asshole had started calling them, and Richards, nasty fucking names. Richards shared the photo and called the guy out. The guy told Richards he'd pound his ass.

The idiot probably hadn't considered how fucking sexually his words could be interpreted. So Shawn had commented to clarify:

If you're threatening the kid, you're gonna have to go through me and the entire team, asshole. If you're hitting on him? Get in line. If you're really horny, and half as hot as your picture—wait, no way you're fucking Jon Snow???

Anyway, PM me and we can hook up. I'll give you a pounding you'll never forget.

Shawn's fans loved the comment. So did Richards's. It had over 300 likes.

But Shawn had been waiting for someone from management to come give him shit. "I'll get Richards to delete the post. One sec." He called over his shoulder. "Richards, delete that post! I got us in trouble!"

"Richards is in here? With you?"

Well, I'm fucking flattered. Shawn smirked. "Yep, he was sent in here so we could babysit. Wasn't he taken away so we wouldn't corrupt him? It might be a good idea to decide what your priorities are."

The veins in the GM's temple looked about ready to burst. "My priorities are simple. You can't be advertising your sexual activities on your public profile. Or his. I expect you to be a professional."

"On the ice and in the locker room? Absolutely. But I won't have the team dictating my personal life." Shawn straightened. "If I decide I want to fuck Richards, or White, or anyone else, it's not a goddamn PR issue."

Dean's brow furrowed. He shot Sahara an apologetic look, but he didn't back down. "That may be true, but you're going too far, Shawn."

"Are we friends now, Dean?" Shawn gritted his teeth. "I don't recall anything in my contract limiting my sexual activities."

"Perhaps not, but the contract does dictate your conduct in public. If you have an issue with that, we will set up a meeting with your agent to discuss it further."

"Fine." Shawn was done with this conversation. And with this whole fucked-up day. "Is that all?"

Movement at his side, with a far too familiar scent, had him bracing himself for whatever White was about to say. Should be interesting. "Fuck, Pisch, what are you doing? Your contract is up this year. Do you want to be traded?" He put his hand on Pischlar's shoulder. "It's simple. You can't fuck the whole team."

Really? Shawn laughed. He hadn't even considered his contract. Maybe a trade would be a good thing. "You don't get to make that decision." Shawn shoved White's hand off his shoulder. "Besides, Silver almost pulled it off, so it can be done."

* * * *

Shit! Sahara sidled into the hall, trying to get out of the way and slamming into Dominik just as Dean rammed his hand into the center of Pischlar's chest. Pischlar's back hit the wall and Sahara winced.

"Should we get Landon?" Sahara whispered as Dean said something to Pischlar only he could hear. She'd never seen Dean lose his cool, and Landon was probably the only one who wouldn't risk his career getting in his face.

Dominik shook his head and gently pulled her aside. "Not unless you want Landon to kill Pisch. You don't need to see this. Go back to my room."

Dismissed. Again. She backed up as the raised voices inside the room echoed into the hall even after the door slammed shut. It opened again and White stormed off toward the elevators, not even sparing her a glance. Richards came out seconds later, closing the door softly.

Leaving Pischlar with Dean. And Dominik, who could only do so much to keep his boss from beating the crap out of a player who'd clearly lost his sense of self-preservation. Maybe bringing Landon into the chaos *was* a bad idea, but there had to be someone who could take control of the situation. She paced a little farther down the hall, then back, her phone in her hand as she considered her options.

She could do exactly what Dominik had suggested, but she hated feeling useless. Pischlar was her friend and he was hurting and this was probably her fault. She'd tried to help him get closer to White, but clearly something had happened to ruin whatever progress he'd made. The way he was acting, she had a feeling he *wanted* Dean to trade him.

Which Dean would realize when he calmed down. Granted, he'd still be furious, but he wouldn't let Pischlar use him as a way to sabotage his own career.

There was only one person she could think of who would get through to Dean. And the timing was horrible, but when was the timing ever good for all hell to break loose? This *was* the playoffs. The most important thing was the team remaining a team.

"Sahara? Is everything okay?" Silver asked the second she answered the call.

Sahara chose her words carefully. "No one is hurt. Well, besides Pischlar. And I think I'm partially to blame."

She gave Silver the abbreviated version of the situation. Smiled at Silver's calm request. Then went back to Pischlar's room and rapped on the door hard enough to be heard over the shouting.

Dominik opened the door and frowned at her.

"Please excuse me, Sir." She slipped by him and held her phone out to Dean, who had taken his suit jacket off and looked ready to beat the shit out of Pischlar. Or continue doing so, if the blood on Pischlar's mouth was anything to go by.

Dean straightened. "Not now, Sahara."

"Will you get on the fucking phone, Dean!" Silver's voice could be heard, loud and clear. "If you don't talk to me, Sahara *is* getting Landon. And if you risk our starting goalie for your macho—"

Dean took the phone and moved to the hall, calming visibly.

That felt damn good. But Sahara wasn't done. She walked over to Pischlar, facing him as he dropped into the chair she'd abandoned earlier. Crouching in front of him, she met his eyes. "Please don't do this. I'm not sure what happened, but the team needs you."

Pischlar groaned and nodded, rubbing his hands over his face. "Damn it, I really fucked up. I'm easy. I'm not supposed to care about anything."

"That's not true and you know it." She gave his forearm a little shove so he'd look at her again. "You love him. Is it Richards? Did him being here get to you?"

"Naw. The kid's all right. And he's going through his own shit." Pischlar swiped the blood off his lips with his thumb then scrubbed it on his pants. "White wasn't in his seat when the plane started jerking around. Neither was I."

"So he got scared. That's okay. He'll get over it."

"Oh, he's over it. He made that perfectly fucking clear." Pischlar shrugged. "I should have let it go a long time ago. Just glad the games are over. Trying to figure out what the fuck he wanted was exhausting. Now I know."

"I don't think you do. Whatever happened might seem like it ruined what you guys had, but that doesn't mean—"

"He fucked me. He's a pretty good lay. But most definitely straight." Pischlar smirked, looking a bit more like himself. Confident and completely carefree. Which wasn't as reassuring as it should be. "We might have fucked a few more times if you were still with us, but I'm happy that you've finally got someone worth your time."

Her throat tightened as she finally absorbed the entirety of her role in destroying Pischlar and White's friendship. Having a woman involved had made fooling around acceptable in White's head. He really had no idea how Pischlar felt about him. He probably wouldn't connect Pischlar blowing up at Dean to his rejection. He'd probably be confused by how things would change.

But they would. Because, as "easy" as Pischlar was, he had a big heart that he usually protected with a bomb shelter's worth of walls. He'd opened the heavy steel door for White. And been blown to pieces.

She couldn't fix this. But she still needed to do *something*. She took his hand in both of hers. "Do me one last favor. I know I have no right to ask you for anything, but it's important."

Pischlar's brow furrowed. He nodded.

"Apologize to Dean and don't screw up your standing with the team. You belong here."

He pulled his hand free and patted her cheek. "How about you let me clean up my own mess? If you were my sub, we'd have a chat about your meddling."

"Funny, I was just thinking the same thing." Dominik's shadow fell over her, a canyon depth to his voice and a sharpness to his eyes that made her feel like a little mouse trembling as a hawk spiraled above. "The GM needs to speak to our friend, pet. And you and I will have that chat."

She stood, ready to tell him off for being so high-handed when she was only—

"Oomph! Hey!" The room tilted as he swooped her up and slung her over his shoulder. "Dominik! You can't—"

"You've been around the lifestyle long enough to know what asking me to be your Dom meant. To put it simply, I can." He gave her ass a hard smack, tightening his grip on her waist as she squealed and tried to wiggle free. "And I will."

The first smack hadn't hurt much, but the second stung enough to steal her breath. She stopped fighting as the burn spread and her thighs clenched. She was embarrassed, especially when she caught both Pischlar and Dean watching her with mirrored expressions of amusement, but she enjoyed Dominik taking charge.

Part of her whined that she shouldn't let him get away with this. That she was an independent woman and he was acting like a caveman.

A more honest part of her mind admitted she didn't mind it in the least.

Chapter Fourteen

The struggling had been kind of cute, but Dominik was pleased when Sahara went still even as her heart pounded against his shoulder. He left the room, trusting that Dean and Pischlar were both mature enough to hash out their issues without any more bloodshed, and headed to his own room at the other end of the hall.

Life had thrown so many roadblocks in front of him and Sahara it would be easy to come to the conclusion that fate just didn't want them together. Strangely enough, it was Pischlar's comment, "If you were my sub…" that had pushed Dominik to stop trying to dodge the roadblocks and simply set a new course.

Sahara shared his need to care for others. Not a flaw in itself, only, as he observed her putting her own needs aside to help her friends again and again, he couldn't help but wonder if half the roadblocks weren't put there by her. And him.

Not intentionally, of course. But they hadn't made their budding relationship a priority. Life wasn't easy, and sometimes happiness was hard earned. A good Dom puts his sub's well-being above everything else.

He needed to put Sahara first if she was going to be his. And it was about time that he claimed her.

"I hope you don't have plans for the night. I have no intention of letting you leave this room." He gently lowered her to her feet so he could take out his key card. "We likely have a few things to discuss, but unless the limits you had at the club have changed, I don't see the need for much conversation."

As he opened the door, she stood by his side, looking up at him as though she'd lost the ability to speak.

"Perhaps I should clarify. We will not discuss Pisch and White. Our exes are not relevant tonight—unless I hit a trigger with you, in which case, it may be unavoidable." He ran his thumb down her cheek when she dropped her gaze. "Let me take care of you, Sahara. There's nothing more important to me right now."

Her throat worked as she swallowed. She looked up at him, so vulnerable he wished he could just hold her close and erase everything that had ever hurt her. "The...chat? Are you going to punish me?"

"Do you need to be punished?" If they had been together longer, he wouldn't hesitate. But they were still getting to know one another in many ways. A punishment might do more harm than good at this point.

She wrinkled her nose and took a step into the room, sliding over so he could close the door. "I don't know. You told me to come here, but I called Silver. It was the right thing to do, but I completely ignored your request."

"If you considered it a request, you were free to do whatever you thought necessary."

"True."

"But it wasn't." He gave her an understanding smile when she bit her lip. Most of her submissive experience came from Pischlar, who, while a good Dom, didn't have many rules for his subs to follow. She had a natural aversion to disappointing those she respected, which would be useful.

They were starting on a good foundation of mutual respect and affection. The chemistry was there, even though they'd both ignored it so often it was a tiny spark in the kindling, which could either flare into a full blaze or die.

Stroking the flame while he brought them to the next level would be quite satisfying. Sahara was a passionate woman. And he'd denied himself a taste of her for long enough.

"Strip and wait for me by the bed. I haven't gotten a chance to shower since the flight and I need it." He didn't wait to see if she'd follow his orders before pulling off his shirt and heading to his luggage for a change of clothes. He refused to lay a finger on her until he was clean, but more importantly, he was interested to see *how* she'd respond to his vague instructions. A sub's interpretation of her Master's instructions disclosed much about her needs. And he had yet to learn all of Sahara's.

He followed her movements from the corner of his eye, noting that she went to stand by the bed before she began to work on the buttons of her white blouse. The way her brows drew together told him she was thinking very hard about something.

There was no way he'd miss seeing her body fully exposed before he left the room, but he had to find out where her head was at.

"Stop." He strode up to her and tipped her chin up with a finger. "What was that thought?"

She blinked as though she'd forgotten he was still there. Then she licked her bottom lip, bringing his attention to the lush, glistening swell. "I was trying to decide if I should kneel. I don't want to assume anything. I need to do this right."

Good girl. He wouldn't voice his approval yet, but her honesty was refreshing. And her choice of words made things very clear. She needed directions that left no room for failure.

"Don't kneel just yet, pet. Stand at the end of the bed, hands clasped behind your back. When I return, I want nothing obstructing this beautiful body that now belongs solely to me." He loved the shade of pink high on her cheeks, showing just a bit of shyness. "Keep going, Sahara."

She took a deep, bracing inhale and removed her shirt. The skirt went next. Both were left on the floor. He preferred his subs to take care of their things, but he wouldn't interrupt the reveal for a lecture.

She held his gaze as she reached back to undo her bra. For a dancer, her movements were stiff. She was feeling exposed and likely a little off-balance. He didn't need a performance though. Having her strip like this was meant to remove more than the material that concealed her from him. She would be naked in every way possible.

He watched her carefully to make sure he wasn't pushing her too far, too fast, but the stubborn set to her jaw pleased him.

He smiled when she bent down to peel off her panties before straightening and squaring her shoulders. He circled her, stopping behind her to observe the way she entwined her fingers at the small of her back. Despite her spine and shoulders being held stiffly, her hands were relaxed.

"Very pretty. Are you cold, pet?" He ran his hands down her arms, feeling the goose bumps that had risen all over her flesh. Her tiny pink nipples were hard and she was trembling. He wouldn't leave her for even the brief time it would take him to shower if she were truly uncomfortable.

She shook her head. "Can I be honest, Sir?"

"Always."

"I'm nervous. I want to make sure I do everything right because, the way you look at me, it's like you believe I can. Like I'm perfect." She lowered her arms to her sides, opening her hands in a beautifully subconscious show of submission. "I'm not, but I'll try my best."

Pressing his lips to her shoulder, he wrapped his arms around her, holding her in a strong embrace as he whispered in her ear, "It will be easier if you don't try. I'm not asking you to guess, sunshine. When you submit to me, all I need is for you to let me take control. So long as you're with me, so long as you hold nothing back, you're doing it right."

Her eyes filled with warmth as she gazed at him over her shoulder. He couldn't resist stealing one last kiss before he released her. It was times like this that made him wonder why he had waited so long to claim her as his own.

But, more importantly, made him grateful that he finally had.

* * * *

The sound of the shower cutting off pulled Sahara from her daydreaming and she nibbled on her bottom lip in anticipation, watching the bathroom door. When Dominik had first left her here, she'd wondered if she'd go nuts waiting and fail to follow his simple orders. She had really, really wanted to join him in the shower. Lose herself in his kiss and soak in every drop of pleasure he could give her.

Just imagining how amazing being with him would be had made the time pass so quickly, she'd succeeded in doing what he'd asked of her without any effort at all. The challenge would be staying put when he came through that door. She was so aroused she might just jump him.

Very bad submissive behavior. There will be no jumping of the Dom. A giggle escaped her as she pictured the look on his face if she actually threw herself at him. He'd probably be amused at first, but then he'd punish her. Which might be hot too, but she'd earned enough punishments for one day.

She'd pleased him simply standing here, ready to surrender control. His approval meant more than the brief satisfaction she'd get out of touching him as quickly as she wanted to.

The door opened, and one look at him tested her resolve to remain where he'd left her. He'd brought clothes into the bathroom, but he must have changed his mind about getting fully dressed because he was wearing nothing but a pair of black Calvin Klein boxer briefs. Droplets of water still glistened on his skin, trailing down the smooth brown flesh over bulging muscles that swelled as he stood just a few feet away from her.

His eyes burned with hunger, and her breath caught as he closed the distance between them. He lifted her in his arms, his mouth slanting over hers as he brought her to the bed. He lowered her, never breaking the kiss, his hands in her hair as he held her still so he could explore her mouth with torturously slow dips of his tongue.

Heart slamming into the cage of her ribs, Sahara clung to his broad shoulders, moaning as he tugged at her bottom lip with his teeth. He gentled his kiss, looking into her eyes in a way that made her heart skip a few beats. In that moment, she had no doubt that he'd chosen her and had no regrets. Despite how often they'd pushed away from one another, the pull between them had always drawn them back. Now that they'd stopped resisting, it was like the connection had snapped into place.

She wasn't sure why, but the pool of overwhelming lust and happiness gathering within made her dizzy and brought tears to her eyes. She pressed her eyes shut tight, digging her fingers into the muscles of his arms, struggling for composure. If she didn't regain control, she'd say something stupid. Something that, no matter how amazing being with him felt, was too soon to say.

"Sahara, look at me." His hand curved under her jaw. When she looked at him, she saw concern in his eyes. "Don't consider your words. Tell me exactly what's on your mind."

The tears spilled and she tried to turn away to hide them, but he wouldn't let her. So she gasped in enough air to speak. "Can I have this? I want it so bad. I need for it to be real, but life can be so horrible and I'm afraid if I let my guard down, everything good will be taken away."

He dipped down to kiss her tenderly, in a way that made her feel precious and cared for. "I can only promise to do everything in my power to keep you safe. Nothing is more important to me than giving you a reason to smile. A reason to hope the good things can last."

More tears, but she wasn't ashamed of them anymore. If anyone could understand them, it would be Dominik. "You're that reason already. Is that weird?"

"No. It means I'm off to a better start than I was on our date." He grinned when she rolled her eyes, then latched on to her wrists, pulling them off his shoulders and drawing them up to the bottom of the headboard. "My first mistake was refusing to give you more than a kiss, even if you begged. I won't deny myself any longer."

"Do I still need to beg?" She would. Actually, it was starting to seem like a very good idea.

He shook his head. "All you need to do is tell me if you have any hard limits. And take whatever I choose to give you."

Hard limits? She wasn't sure her brain was working well enough to think of a single one. But she knew Dominik too well to give him that answer. They'd slowed the rush of lust enough for some negotiation. And she wouldn't put the same restrictions on him that she'd put on Doms at the club.

"Pain scares me; I'm never sure if it will trigger..." Her words locked in her throat and she tipped her head back, trying to push away the flash of memories trying to play out in her mind. Screaming.

Fists. The throbbing agony in her face when she was stupid enough to piss off Grant. "Fuck, I'm sorry. I—"

"Shh, it's all right, sunny girl. Keep your eyes open. Stay with me." He stroked her cheek with his thumb. "I don't enjoy much pain play. But when I smacked your ass, did it bother you?"

She frowned, thinking back on exactly how she'd felt in that moment. "I was embarrassed, but that was because Pischlar and Dean were watching."

"Very good. So we will keep punishments mild, and you will tell me if you have flashbacks or the slightest twinge of fear." He smiled in a way that gave her all the warmth of his approval. "And bondage?"

"I like bondage." Her cheeks heated. She hadn't even hesitated.

He chuckled. "Noted. Stay put, I have just the thing for you."

She hadn't let go of the headboard, but she lifted her head just enough to watch him go to his sports bag. Her brow furrowed—he didn't keep his toys in there, did he? Not that she'd complain, but she knew, probably better than most, how nasty hockey players' sports bags could smell. She'd once told her mother, "I love the way daddy smells when he comes home from a game." Her mother had laughed, taken out her father's sports bag, and handed her a pair of his gloves.

Yeah, nothing compared to the stink. That was exactly why players got so riled up being face washed on the ice. There was nothing quite so rancid, no matter how clean the guy was.

When Dominik returned with a roll of hockey tape, she let out a sigh of relief. He arched a brow at her and she grinned.

"I was a little nervous about what you kept in there."

He snorted as he pulled out a length of tape and tore it with his teeth. "Would you have used your safeword if it was a big rubber cock?"

Ewww! She nodded, wrinkling her nose and pressing her thighs together. "'Red,' 'hell no,' and maybe 'Are you nuts, Sir?'"

"Respectfully, of course."

"Of course. One must show the proper regard to mentally unstable Masters."

His laughter and all the joking might have seemed odd, considering how ready they'd been to pounce on one another, but she loved how relaxed they were with one another. She'd never really laughed with Grant. Maybe when he tickled her, but she'd always hated that. And if she'd acted like this before sex? He would have lost it.

A tug at her hand and Dominik taped one wrist to the headboard. "Stay with me, pet. I see the shadows in your eyes, telling me he's here with us. You need to tell him to fuck off."

Her eyes went wide. Then she giggled. "I don't see how that would be helpful, since he's not *actually* here."

"He's in your head. He doesn't need to hear the words, but you need to say them." He taped her other wrist, then came to sit at her side, sliding one big, warm hand over her belly to rest on her hip. The contrast of his dark skin against her pale flesh, his gentle caress, had her focusing on his touch rather than the horror that tried to worm its way into her thoughts. "Maybe add a mental knee to the balls. I can't tell you enough how impressed I was that you fought him off."

She inhaled deeply, his pride in her like a gasp of fresh air and light after being trapped in muggy darkness. "I'm not that weak little girl anymore."

"You were never weak. He's a monster." Dominik's lips quirked. "Now, fuck off, Grant."

At first, she wondered if he was reminding her of the words she had to say, but then she realized he needed to speak them himself. If they let him, Grant could easily linger in the depths of their consciousness. But Dominik was making sure he was tossed out with the trash. Where he belonged.

"Fuck off, Grant!" Sahara jerked her knee up, feeling a little silly and laughing at herself. But somehow, sharing this with Dominik stole the power Grant still had over her in a way that hadn't seemed real with all the therapy. She'd taken steps to get out of his reach, but he'd always been with her.

No more. With Dominik by her side, the only power she'd hand over would be done willingly.

"Better?" Dominik leaned over her, stroking her side, his eyes telling her he sensed she was in the right place for them to move forward. He smiled when she nodded. "Good. Now, the tape will give you the illusion of restraint, but if you really need to be free, all you have to do is pull hard."

She bit her lip, wondering why he'd wanted to make it so easy. She'd had real restraints at the club. "I won't."

"We've never played before, Sahara. Don't take it as a bad thing." He tucked her hair behind her ears. "Until I can be sure of all your triggers, I'd prefer an easy release. We'll get you some wrist cuffs for next time. I gave away all the reusable toys and restraints I had when I decided I no longer wanted to be a Dom."

"I'm glad you changed your mind."

"You changed it for me. Pushy little sub." He cupped her cheek with one hand, claiming her lips in a deep, passionate kiss. "I think we've done all the talking necessary for the moment. Let me see what I have to play with."

He moved down, brushing his lips along the length of her throat, pausing when she moaned in pleasure at a sweet, tingling sensation. Her neck had always been sensitive, but few men gave the area much attention. Dominik however, lingered, using his teeth on the same spot. Sucking lightly, he turned the sweetness into spine-bowing pleasure. She whimpered, grinding her heels into the sheets as her core clenched in need.

His lips slid lower, along her collarbone, between her breasts, where the rough texture of his playoff beard teased the swell. He rubbed his cheek over one breast, and her nipple tightened at the sharp spark in her nerves. He turned his head to take the hard little nub between his lips, pulling until she writhed beneath him.

She had to fight not to tug at her wrists. She wanted to guide him to her other breast to ease the ache of desire, but he was already there, rolling his tongue around her nipple, lifting both her breasts so he could give each the attention of his mouth.

A little farther down and he gently bit the skin of her belly in a way that was almost ticklish. She jumped and he pinned her hips, holding her still so he could move on to the dip of her pelvis.

Her lips parted as his tongue traced down to the edge of her mound. "Please…"

He bit the inside of her thigh. "Not a sound, my girl. Hold it in until you can't help but cry out. Then I want to hear it all."

She gasped between her parted lips as he spread her thighs. Being quiet while he had his mouth on her seemed impossible, but she wanted to please him. His fingers opened her and the tip of his tongue slid between her folds. His teeth closed around her clit and tugged.

The pleasure cut through her, razor-fine along her nerves, bringing her to the point where she needed to be closer to him, all while wanting to twist away to escape the intensity of the sensation. He laved over her clit with his tongue, dampening the edge, then pressed down, drawing a lazy circle over the hyperstimulated nub. He pressed her thighs farther apart and slicked a finger between her folds.

Not a sound escaped her, but she had to choke back a "Yes!" when his finger penetrated and her core clenched around him. A slight bend of his finger and all her restraint escaped her. She arched, crying out as her climax took her up and up and rocked her body like a small earthquake.

Another finger filled her, drawing out the pleasure until she sank into the mattress, completely drained. She'd gotten so used to toys and different stimulants to get her off that she hadn't expected Dominik to bring her release with only his fingers and his mouth.

Maybe she should have held back longer. She tightened around his fingers, feeling self-conscious. He wanted a sub who would give him control, but she hadn't waited for his permission. She hadn't even thought to try.

He withdrew his fingers, slipping off the bed to grab something out of his suitcase. Not looking at her, he exhaled slowly. "I'm not sure what to make of that expression, Sahara. Talk to me."

She pressed her eyes shut. Then remembered his telling her he wanted her to look at him. When she opened them again, he was standing by the bed, studying her face.

"A good sub waits for permission to come." She chewed on her bottom lip, still a little swollen from his kisses. "Oriana would have—"

"Clearly not for the same reasons, but Oriana has no more place in here with us than your ex does. Do not compare yourself to her again." He didn't sound angry, but his gaze was hard as he held hers.

"You were told to be silent until you couldn't any longer. That was permission."

"But I—"

"You are still new enough to try to assume to know what I want. What you will work on is not attempting to guess what I want from you. I will be very clear." His tone softened. "You are my sub. You will learn to please me, and I appreciate that it's important to you. But your pleasure is mine to give or deny. Denying you would be pointless if you don't know what you're missing. We're not there yet."

"I'm sorry." Damn it, she'd messed up again. Why couldn't she just get this right? "I won't do it again."

"You may, but that's not a bad thing. Stop thinking you should know everything." He brought something to his mouth. A condom package that he tore open with his teeth. "Should we stop to discuss what you didn't do wrong, or shall we continue?"

All she could do was nod, but it satisfied him. He covered his length, then returned to the bed to kneel between her thighs. He ran his hands up and down her calves, bending down to press a light kiss above her knee.

Her whole body hummed in anticipation of his taking her, and heat pooled deep in her belly. She prepared for him to hold back, to tease her until she couldn't resist begging for him. Instead, he lifted her knees over his muscular arms, holding her with one hand while he used the other to guide his thick length into her.

Deep, long thrusts brought him deeper and deeper, the way he glided almost all the way in, then drew out until only the broad head of him remained, stimulating her in a way no man had before. He held her legs and hips off the mattress so she could do nothing but take whatever he gave. Which was everything.

His gaze on her face, reading every reaction, moved her beyond absorbing the sensations. She'd let men fuck her before and had managed to shield her heart, knowing it had no place when they were just getting off. With "the ex" she'd been more involved, but too often the focus had been on making him happy.

With Dominik, she hadn't even had a chance to put up her defenses. And she didn't want to try.

"I love the way you look at me, pet." Dominik helped her wrap her legs around his waist and braced one hand by her head, changing the angle of his thrust, his rhythm harder and faster. Sweat beaded at his temples and on his chest, causing his skin to glisten like dark amber in the glow of the lamplight. "So much trust. With your body and your heart."

"I couldn't give one without the other." She moaned as he hit a spot deep inside that sent a spike of pleasure sizzling along her nerves. Her thighs clenched against his hips. "Not to you."

He slid one arm under the small of her back, lifting her to him while hitting that same spot over and over, driving her up to the heights of ecstasy, his pelvis grinding against her clit until she hit the peak. The orgasm burst within like a morning glory sparkler, blazing bright white in the center and shooting out tiny flashing stars.

Her vision blurred and her back arched. She pressed her face into the curve of Dominik's neck as he gathered her close with one last powerful thrust.

Tugging the tape from the headboard, Dominik held her against his chest as he rolled to his back without pulling out of her. His dick had softened, but there was an intimacy to simply lying there with him inside her, her whole body wrapped around him.

After her pulse finally slowed and her head cleared, she realized she was just as sweaty as he was. The cooling moisture felt kinda gross. She'd never laid around this long after sex, and there was something nagging at the back of her mind that she'd forgotten. Something important.

"I should go take a shower. I'm icky." She rose up, combing her fingers through her hair, which was sticking to her face. From the corner of her eye, she noticed the time. It was almost three a.m. And he had a game tomorrow. "Shoot, you need to get some sleep. If you play badly because of me, I'll never forgive myself! Why didn't you tell me?"

He chuckled, picking her up as he sat, easing out of her and placing her on the bed beside him. "Next time, we're doing a scene that's intense enough to keep you from worrying so much after. We have a two-hour practice around noon. I'll be fine." He kissed her forehead, drawing her to her feet as he stood. "Let's take a shower, then I will be a good Dom and get some sleep."

Okay, he's smiling, so he can't be too upset, right? She hadn't even considered for a second that lecturing her Dom might not be smart. She ducked her head and gave him her sweetest smile. "I'm sorry, I wasn't trying to tell you what to do."

"Don't be. You will learn." He gave her ass a little swat as she headed for the bathroom. "I still owe you a punishment, and I've found spankings in the shower to be quite effective."

Lips parted, Sahara spun around to walk backward. "You wouldn't!"

He smirked and arched a brow.

Oh yeah. He so would.

Bianca Sommerland

Chapter Fifteen

An irritating buzzing and the sun glaring through curtains, that should have been closed, rudely jerked Dominik from sleep. He flopped his arm over his eyes and groaned, deciding he would take a couple more minutes. Blindly reaching out, he found the source of the noise and managed to hit the snooze on his phone.

Blessed silence.

He frowned when he listened closer. It was way too quiet. He sat up, found the other side of the bed empty, and lunged off the bed, grabbing his jeans as he called out, "Sahara?"

Nothing.

Damn it, had she woken up and regretted what they'd done? The night had gone well. Granted, he'd definitely need a nap before the game, but they'd made love several times and her "punishment" had been more for his amusement than anything else. He wouldn't push for discipline so soon.

But maybe she hadn't seen it that way? She'd been practically glowing with happiness all night, but he could have missed something.

Regardless, she shouldn't be alone. If she was upset, she might not have thought to call Cort to go with her. There was a good chance Grant had been released if they didn't have enough evidence to charge him. And his crazy fans were dangerous. Anything could have happened to Sahara while he'd been dead to the world.

The lock clicked on the door to the room. It opened, revealing Sahara with a tray of coffee and a paper bag in her hands. Cort held the door for her, flashed Dominik a knowing look, and then disappeared into the hall.

"Good morning!" Sahara came over to the bed, putting the coffee and whatever was in the bag on the nightstand. Her smile faded as she met his gaze. "Please tell me you're not angry. I wanted to surprise you with breakfast and..." Her wide eyes teared. "I did it again. I keep fucking up. Please don't be mad."

Fuck. Good going, Mason. He shook his head, pulling her into his arms and making a soft, shushing sound. He had been worried, but he should've given her more credit. He wasn't even sure she knew her need not to "keep fucking up" was likely a defense mechanism. Having a man angry with her had resulted in painful consequences in the past.

Spankings might not be a trigger, but he'd have to be careful how he expressed his displeasure. He kissed her hair and tipped her chin up with a finger. Her damp cheeks and the fear in her eyes broke his heart.

"Sahara, I was worried. I'm not thrilled that you didn't tell me you were going out, but you brought Cort. That's what he's here for." Dominik wished *he* could be the one protecting her, but he had too many responsibilities toward the team and he didn't want her to feel trapped by his side. "Can we start over?"

"It's my fault. I didn't think and—"

"You were doing something sweet. I take it that's a no to starting over?" He inhaled slowly, trying to think of a way to pull her out of the sandpit of guilt he'd inadvertently knocked her into. Considering the source of her reaction, he recalled what had worked last night. "Fuck off, Grant."

Her brow furrowed, but then she let out a shaky giggle. "Yes. Damn it, I'm a mess. You're not him, and I know that. I'm sorry."

"Please stop apologizing. Your past isn't going to disappear just because we're together now. But you're not dealing with it alone anymore. Part of any relationship is complete honesty. I'm afraid of not being able to keep you safe. That doesn't give me the right to demand you not leave my sight." If they were in a 24/7 style

Master/slave relationship, he could, but he doubted that would be a good fit for either of them. And short of putting her in a bubble, he'd have to accept there were limits to his ability to protect her. "You were trained to walk on eggshells around that asshole. I won't have you doing it with me, so please tell me when I frighten you. Even if it's just with a look or my tone of voice."

She nodded, biting her lip when he reached over to grab a napkin off the tray for her to blow her nose. After she'd composed herself, she slid over to sit on the bed beside him. "You didn't frighten me really. I guess part of me is still stuck on what I did wrong in my last relationship. I don't want to ruin what you and I have."

"You won't. Besides, you're feeding me. My mother taught me to be very, very nice to the person who is bringing me food." She giggled again and the tension eased from where it had gathered between his eyes while trying to get her in a better frame of mind. He ran his hand over her hair. "I owe you a treat. Would you object to a foot rub after breakfast?"

She picked up the paper bag, shaking her head as she pulled out a huge breakfast sandwich with eggs and bacon and cheese on a fat croissant. His mouth watered even as she mumbled something.

He took the sandwich, but he waited to take a bite. "What did you say?"

Her lips thinned. "Doms don't give foot massages."

"And subs typically don't tell their Doms what they can do." He bit into the sandwich and made a throaty sound of pleasure, wanting her focused on how much he appreciated what she'd done, rather than on her slip of protocol. They'd work on that. Later. "This is amazing. Did you get yourself something?"

"Yes, they had my favorite kind of muffins." She dipped her hand into the bag. Licked her lips as she held up a chocolate muffin. "Triple chocolate with white chocolate chunks. There's a bakery right down the street that I always went to when I lived here. They actually sent me a box of them when I moved and told me to visit. They were so happy to see me; they've known me since I was a kid."

Dominik watched the memories play over her face, giving her blue eyes a far-off look and bringing a smile to her lips. All the sadness and fear had been erased from her features. He loved seeing her like this.

"I'd love to check out the bakery if we have a chance while we're here. I've never had chocolate for breakfast, but I'd be willing to try if it's as good as you say." Watching her savor the muffin, pinching pieces off and slipping them between her lips before licking her fingers clean gave him a craving for something besides food for breakfast. His dick hardened, completely on board.

He glanced at the clock on the nightstand. Unfortunately, he didn't have time to indulge before practice. *After, however...*

Sahara watched him with an impish grin on her lips. She broke off a big piece of muffin. "I usually don't share, but for you, I'll make an exception." She fed him the piece and leaned close, her lips brushing his ear. "Are subs allowed to threaten their Doms? Because if you keep looking at me like that, the Cobras are going to lose their captain for the rest of the day."

Catching her wrist, he sucked two of her fingers into his mouth.

She inhaled sharply and pressed her eyes shut. "Ugh, it's too bad I love hockey, or I'd seriously try to make you stay."

"You can come watch us practice. You'll have to hurry though if you want to do your hair and makeup and whatever it is you do to get ready." Dominik made quick work of finishing his sandwich. Only then did he notice Sahara standing in front of him, arms crossed over her chest, a petulant scowl on her lips.

He cocked his head.

She let out an irritated huff, motioning down at her snug gray Batman T-shirt and blue jeans. "You told me to pack light. Now you want me to fuss over my makeup and hair? What's wrong with how I look?"

Well now, this was certainly no way for a sub to behave. He was half tempted to spank her. Or laugh because she was adorable when she got all riled up. He didn't want her to lose this beautiful confidence, so a gentle rebuke would be enough.

"There's nothing wrong with how you look. Those painted-on jeans are fucking hot, and I do believe I have a new fondness for 'the Batman.'" He rose to stand over her, giving her a little taste of intimidation while watching her carefully to make sure she wasn't truly afraid. "There's a habit I have of being considerate to those I care for. I didn't want to assume you'd be comfortable dressed like that all day. I think you're perfect as you are."

"Oh." She looked appropriately contrite. "I'd be in trouble if you weren't in a forgiving mood, wouldn't I?"

He inclined his head. Hell, he was going to have trouble keeping a straight face around this woman. She was practically bouncing on her heels and her lips were quivering as though she was fighting back a laugh.

"I won't say I'm sorry, because that seems to annoy you. But I'll try not to forget you think I'm hot." She hopped up on her tiptoes and kissed his cheek. "We better go. If you're late, your coach won't be so nice. And I won't be allowed to come to games with you anymore." She pulled out her phone. "I better text Cort and tell him I'm heading to the arena with you. He can go with your brother."

With that, she headed straight out the door. He followed, shaking his head, more than a little relieved to see she'd returned to her sassy, outgoing self. The insecurities remained beneath the shimmering surface, but he had a feeling they would dissolve over time.

Time was rarely generous though. As soon as he stepped out of his room, he saw her on her phone, a strained expression on her face. He closed the door, keeping pace with her as she began to walk toward the elevator. He couldn't imagine Cort giving her a hard time, but either way, he had to let her handle this unless she let him know she needed his help.

Before long, it became clear that the caller wasn't Cort.

"Mother, please don't try to make me feel bad. This is crazy!" She groaned and rubbed two fingers between her eyes. "We *just* started dating. We'll come back to New York eventually. He has practice and—no, you can't talk to him!"

Dominik pressed the button to call the elevator. He studied her face, curious to know if there was more behind her shaky confidence besides an abusive ex.

"He'll tell you exactly what I just did. Ask Dad. It's the playoffs and there's no time for—" Her throat worked as she swallowed. She didn't speak until they were past the hotel lobby. "Hi, Daddy. Yes, he's right here." Sahara held out the phone, mouthing, "I'm sorry."

Dominik gave her a mock warning look as he brought the phone to his ear. "Hello?"

"Mr. Mason, I was speaking to my wife this morning, and she mentioned that you're dating my daughter. Her mother and I are both understandably concerned." Mr. Dionne continued before Dominik had a chance to agree. "Her mother asked if we could all meet for coffee. Sahara seems anxious that it will conflict with your schedule, but I'm sure you could spare half an hour?"

Not really a request, but Dominik didn't blame her father for being protective of his daughter. And meeting her parents to ease their fears was more than reasonable.

But Sahara isn't comfortable with it. This isn't a decision I'll make without her. He cleared his throat as they stepped out onto the sidewalk. "I will see what I can do, sir. Can Sahara call you back once I clear things with my coach?"

"Please do." The call ended.

He handed Sahara her phone. "Is there a reason you don't want me to meet your parents?"

Her cheeks reddened. "No! It's...well, don't you think it's weird? I mean, meeting the parents happens after you've been dating at least a few weeks. Besides, you don't know my mother. She'll interrogate you, and you'll be so fed up when it's over that you'll never speak to me again."

Sliding his hand beneath her ponytail to take a light hold on the back of her neck, he brought her to a stop to face him. "There is absolutely nothing either of your parents can do that will make me leave you."

"But they—"

"Nothing." He stroked the side of her neck to soothe her. "I won't tolerate cheating or lying. Both are things you can control. Nothing else will come between us. Do you understand?"

"Yes." She closed her eyes, leaning into his touch. "Why do you have to be so wonderful? I keep waiting for the alarm to go off and wake me up."

He grinned, pulling her close because that deserved a kiss. She was pretty damn wonderful herself.

"Dominik!" A shout from behind, coming from his brother Cameron stopped him with his lips a breath away from Sahara's.

Rolling his eyes, he put his arm over her shoulder and turned to greet his younger brother. "Your timing is excellent, as usual."

Baring his teeth in a remorseless smile that proved he'd interrupted to be a jerk, Cam shrugged. "Sorry, Mom just called. She's meeting you after practice and she wanted me to find you. She got tickets to the game too."

All right, this is freakin' hilarious. Dominik burst out laughing, and both Cam and Sahara stared at him like he'd gone nuts. He motioned for Cam to walk with them, since the arena was only five blocks or so from the hotel.

"This isn't funny, Dominik. You were right, I should have gotten changed." Sahara gazed back at the hotel longingly. Her foot missed the curb, and Dominik latched on to her waist to keep her from face-planting. Unfortunately, her knee made contact. With a puddle. "Oh my God! I have to go change now! I can't meet your mother like this!"

She tried to slip out of his grasp. He tightened his grip. "Oh no, you don't. You come with me. Cam can fetch you a change of clothes."

Cam sputtered. "I can?"

Dominik smirked and pulled out his key card. "A nice dress maybe? What would you be comfortable in, Sahara?"

Sahara shot him a grateful look. Then gave his brother a sweet smile that melted the big, tattooed man on the spot. "There's a nice white one with purple flowers. And my white heels and…umm, I can't wear this bra." She blushed. "There's only one other one in my suitcase. Are you sure you don't—"

"Naw, it's fine." Cam gave Dominik a sideways glare, but he was all charm with Sahara. "Not like I haven't handled bras before. I'm kinda impressed that my brother doesn't mind me handling yours though." He winked at Sahara, then took off. "See you in a bit!"

If Dominik didn't love the cocky bastard, he'd probably strangle him. He sighed and draped his arm back over Sahara's shoulder. Dealing with his brother was worth seeing her relax a little about the introductions. They would get through the awkward ritual of parental introductions and carry on with their lives.

How bad could it really be?

With a rough inhale, he pulled Sahara a little closer.

You just had to ask that, didn't you?

* * * *

"You must be Sahara." A tall black woman with kind, golden brown eyes behind wire-frame glasses approached Sahara in the stands by the rink, a broad smile on her lips. Her pale gray pantsuit looked custom-fitted to show off her curves while giving her a professional appearance.

Sahara nodded and stood, not sure whether or not to hold out her hand to shake the woman's—this was clearly Dominik's mother, first impressions were important. Before she had a chance to decide, Mrs. Olivia Mason drew her in for a firm hug.

"No need to look so frightened. You should see some of the girls Cameron brings home. The boy has absolutely no taste." Olivia held Sahara at arm's length, still smiling. "I've seen your shows on the ice. You're a talented young lady."

"Thank you, ma'am." Sahara smiled back, relieved that so far the woman didn't seem to hate her. "Your sons speak of you often. I know Dominik is thrilled that you were able to come."

"Ha! No need to humor me, young lady. I heard that your parents insisted on meeting him. My presence is only adding to the pressure on you both, and for that, I apologize." Olivia lowered into one of the seats and patted the one beside her. She continued when Sahara sat. "Tell me, will your father be hard on my son or will he give him a chance to prove himself?"

Good question. Sahara considered her answer carefully. "Honestly, I don't know. When I was a teenager, my dad used to invite half his team to hang out at our house before I went on dates." She shook her head and laughed. At sixteen, she'd been embarrassed by the veiled threats the players aimed at any boy who'd dared to ask her out. She wasn't a little girl anymore, and she doubted Dominik would be intimidated by the veterans. "I'm a little more worried about my mother completely humiliating me. Or making Dominik uncomfortable. She has…strange ideas about things."

Olivia nodded slowly. "Perhaps, but she probably just wants to assure herself that you're in a better place. Mothers don't always know how to voice their concern without being overbearing. I've had mine. Meeting my children's significant others didn't always alleviate them, but one hopes simply showing interest will give our babies somewhere to turn when life gets tough."

"You're right. And I should be grateful my parents care so much." It was hard to convince herself her mother really did. Most of the time, unless she could brag about Sahara's accomplishments, it seemed like she was just dealing with an inconvenience.

Dominik's mother patted the back of her hand. "Be grateful, but don't forget that you're living your own life. Parents don't always have to approve. And if they disapprove of my son? Well, I fully support you respectfully telling them where to shove it."

Covering her mouth to smother a giggle, Sahara turned back to the ice to watch Dominik. Practice was almost over, but he was still going hard, working with the trainers on shots and speaking to Sloan during the final stretch led by the rookie, Heath Ladd.

When the men were dismissed, he lingered on the ice, exchanging a few words with different players. But his focus seemed to be on Heath.

The rookie was going around the ice, shoveling pucks toward the net. Which was nice of him, it left less work for the trainers when they went around to pack everything up.

Unfortunately, the backup goalie, Dave Hunt, didn't see it that way. He snarled something when a stray puck hit his skate, then slammed his shoulder into Heath's.

Heath opened his mouth, shut it, and turned away. When Hunt grabbed his arm, he tried to twist free.

Dominik skated up to separate the pair. He grabbed Hunt by the front of his shirt, then shoved him toward the bench exit. For a few long moments, he watched Heath continue to clean up the scattered pucks. Shaking his head, he headed off the ice.

"Prepare yourself, my dear. The children have put our boy in a foul mood." Olivia snickered as she stood. Once they reached the end of the seats, she hooked her arm to Sahara's. "I think he gets it from Joshua, honestly. That boy... I'm not surprised he's leading soldiers now. He used to try to quiet down Cam and my girls when they were rowdy. Dominik was the only one who really listened to him. Bless them, I remember coming home after work and seeing them both trying to clean up the mess the others had made."

Sahara tried to picture Dominik as a little boy. It wasn't hard to imagine him being serious and responsible. Looking up to his older brother and trying to take care of his mother. "You seem like you're a very close family."

"We certainly are." Olivia put her hand on Sahara's forearm. "You'll love Joshua. He's the perfect gentleman. And smart. He could have done anything he wanted to with his life, but he chose to serve our country. Dominik wanted to as well, but Joshua insisted he play. The military would have been good for Cameron, but I guess it wasn't meant to be."

Nodding, Sahara listened to Olivia brag about her children, her daughters, one who'd had beautiful babies and took care of her, the other who was still in law school. She sounded so proud of them all. Which must be amazing. She couldn't help but wish her mother was a little more like Olivia.

They met Dominik outside the locker room. He had showered and dressed in black slacks and a white shirt. She was glad Cam had brought her a change of clothes, or she would have felt underdressed next to him.

But when his eyes met hers, what she was wearing didn't seem to matter. He seemed to see more of her. Deep inside, where she was the same girl who wore jeans and scuffed her knees and cried for the stupidest reasons. He saw everything and still smiled and reached out to take her in his arms.

He pressed a kiss on her forehead, then pulled his mother in close on his other side. "I see my two favorite girls have met. And are getting along. That's good."

"She's a sweet little thing. I think I'll be warning you along with her father to be good to her." Olivia winked at Sahara, the mischief in her grin making it obvious where Cam got it from. "Where are we joining them?"

Not at a café. Sahara glanced at her phone, wanting to die on the spot as she whispered the answer.

Olivia's eyes went wide. "That's one of the most expensive restaurants in New York! How did they even get a reservation?"

"Well, my mother likely name-dropped. My father isn't a huge name, but my grandfather was. She might have brought up Dominik as well." Which shouldn't have come as a shock. Her mother did whatever worked to get what she wanted. "I'm sor—"

"That word, Sahara," Dominik warned in a slight growl. He grinned at his mother when she frowned at him. "My girl would apologize for a rainy day if I let her. She's working on it."

"Good." Olivia took Sahara's other arm as Dominik took her hand. "Never you mind, sweetie. I've heard the food is delicious, and our boy must be fed before the big game."

Sahara felt a little better, but that only lasted until they pulled up in front of the restaurant in a cab and opened the door to hear a woman's shrill voice berating a busboy.

Speaking of first impressions...

"Mom!" Sahara hurried to her mother's side, drawing her attention from the poor young man who was red-faced and holding up his hands to defend himself. "I'm begging you. Stop."

"I opened my own door! Do you know how humiliating that is?" Her mother huffed, looking over at the limo idling on the curb. "And your father is no help. *He* said he'd rather have a smoked meat sandwich! After all the trouble I went to reserving us a table."

Sahara blinked at the limo. "Is Daddy still in there?"

"Yes! Can you talk to him? I won't have him spoiling our dinner. Your new man should know who your family is. Have you told him about your grandfather?" She eyed Dominik, who was standing back with his own mother, talking out of the side of his mouth. "He dressed very casually. And so did you. What were you thinking?"

Can I disappear? Is that an option? Sahara hadn't expected this to be fun, but so far, a nightmare was putting it lightly. "I'll talk to Daddy. Why don't you go make sure they have our table ready? They might have forgotten."

The expression of horror on her mother's face over the very idea of the table not being ready might be laughable, but it got her rushing inside. Away from Dominik and Olivia. So they wouldn't have to deal with her alone.

Opening the door to the limo, Sahara slid inside and fell into her father's arms. "Can we grab Dominik and his mom and just drive away?"

Her father laughed. "I wish. No, cookie, we have to keep her happy. But I have something to tell you which may explain why she's acting a little crazier than usual."

A little? Sahara had never seen her mother scream at anyone like she'd been screaming at the busboy. She usually showed her disapproval with sharp little barbs of cruel comments. She'd looked downright unstable out there.

Was her mother sick? Sahara pulled away from her father and hugged herself. If her mother wasn't doing well, then Sahara was a horrible daughter for even being annoyed at her. But why had he waited to tell her?

"You're doing that thing you do. I blame your mother for that. It's not the end of the world." He sighed. "We're getting a divorce."

Her mouth went dry. This was better than her mother having a terminal illness, but...she couldn't picture her parents apart. Even when her mother nagged and complained and demanded the world, her father took it in stride. He had for as long as Sahara could remember.

"Cookie, we stopped living together when your brother went to play for the juniors. I've met someone and...I think she can make me happy. I know I make her happy, and I didn't realize how much I needed that." He took her hand and gave it a little squeeze. "I think I was always waiting for you and your brother to grow up and set out on your own. Please don't hate me."

"I don't, but...why come with her today? If you'd asked to meet Dominik on your own, I would have said yes."

"I know you would have, but your mother and I have an agreement. We keep up pretenses until the divorce is finalized. Since I admitted to infidelity, she gets a bigger share of our assets. She'll be able to continue the lifestyle she knows." He took a deep breath. "And I'll be free."

Staring down at her hands, Sahara struggled to find the right way to ask the one thing she really needed to know. "Did you cheat on her?"

"No. We were legally separated for two years before I met Debbie—yes, maybe I should have told you, but you were going through so much, and it took every ounce of restraint I have not to hunt down the asshole who hurt you and kill him." He rubbed a hand over his face. "The only reason I didn't is because your brother needs me. He's fired three of his last managers. He's a bit more like your mother than I want to admit, but he's young enough to change."

Fredrick, her brother, was talented, but she couldn't deny that he had the entitled attitude their mother had taught him. Since he was ten years younger than her, they hadn't really grown up together. Either she'd been figure skating or playing hockey. Or he'd been out there trying to be the next Dionne in the league.

She wasn't sure how she felt about her parents' divorce, but she had to admit, it would be the best thing for her brother. Her mother would stick with her friends, and her father would have a chance to give his son a new outlook on life.

"I'm not mad and I don't hate you. But do me a favor?" She smiled when he nodded. "Be nice to Dominik. He's…everything I ever needed. He's an amazing man, and he really cares about me."

"Agreed, but if he ever lays a hand on you…" Her father cupped her cheek. "I'm sorry I couldn't protect you."

She tugged at her bottom lip with her teeth. "I get why Dominik hates me using that word. Don't be sorry. I made my own mistakes and I'm stronger now. Of all the things I've done in my life, I'm prouder of the day I walked out that door than anything else."

They left the car and went inside when they saw both Dominik and his mother already had. The hostess led them to their table. Which was surprisingly quiet.

Olivia gave Sahara a sympathetic smile as Dominik pulled out her chair.

Sahara sat, smoothing her hands over her skirt.

Her mother being quiet was a good sign. Maybe the worst had passed.

* * * *

Gulping back her third glass of wine since she'd sat down, Sahara's mother leaned forward and giggled. Dominik hated that Sahara had to see the woman like this, but there wasn't much he could do except be a sounding board for all her frustrations when this was over. Even if it meant he'd have to ease out each and every word of how hurt and embarrassed and ashamed she'd been.

"Grant Higgins thought he was such an amazing man, but after four years with my daughter, he never managed to knock her up? He clearly didn't want to marry her, but a baby would have been nice. She'd be set." Sahara's mother reached for another glass of wine. Her husband pulled it out of reach. She grabbed Sahara's glass of water and gulped it down. "Those people commenting on your pictures are right though. Have you ever considered what you'll be putting your children through? The world can be cruel to the mixed. Even the bible says 'let the Jews stay with the Jews and the Gentiles stay with the Gentiles.'"

Between Sahara's shocked expression and the way her father went perfectly still and stared at his wife like he'd never seen her before, the blatant ignorance the woman was spouting was something new. Many of her words were exactly what had been written in the comments he'd asked Sahara not to read.

"You don't actually believe that, Mother." Sahara pressed her fist against her lip as though she physically needed to hold in her words. When she lowered her fist to the table, it was clear she'd decided to speak her mind. "Daddy just told me about the divorce. You're unhappy, and I'm sorry that you're suffering. But the things you're saying are disgusting."

"Disgusting? My dear, you don't seem to understand the world. Either you're hiding bruises or choosing a man who will condemn your children to a hard life."

"If you keep this up, you'll have nothing to do with my children if I ever decide to have them! Half of the reason I hid the bruises was because I knew how ashamed you'd be if I didn't!" Sahara slammed her hand down on the table. "Grant *beat* me. I'd rather he'd have killed me than have given him a child to hurt as well."

Dominik pushed away from the table, feeling sick to his stomach at the cool way the woman was regarding her daughter. He held his hand out to Sahara. "Let's go."

Sahara took his hand, then turned to his mother. "I'm so sorry. I was afraid this might be awkward, but…I wasn't expecting this."

His mother shook her head, already moving to Sahara's other side without even acknowledging Sahara's mother, who was hissing something to her father. The man had his head in his hands and seemed to have mentally and emotionally retreated from the entire situation.

"Remember what I told you, Sahara." His mother hooked her arm to Sahara's. "You told her where to shove it. Well done. Now let's go find my boy something to eat."

They made it to the door before Sahara's father caught up with them. Sahara was holding back tears and shaking. The man should have gone to his daughter first. But he put his hand on Dominik's arm.

"That wasn't fair to either of you. My wife considers news spreading of Sahara being beaten by her ex an embarrassment. I consider it a failure. I wasn't there for her, so there was no reason for her to come to me. I spent her childhood either playing the game or wishing I still could." His eyes narrowed as he met Dominik's. "If that's all you can give her, let her go. She's been through enough." He shook his head. "If not…well, you may not have been 'dating' long, but there's been speculation about you and my daughter for quite some time. Her mother may be obsessing over future grandchildren. All I care about is that you not play games with my little girl."

Dominik gave the man a stiff smile. "She's not a little girl anymore, Mr. Dionne. And thankfully, she no longer needs you to protect her. I owe you nothing, but I assure you, I'm not playing games."

"Then what are your intentions? Will you marry her?"

So far, the discussions had gone to kids and marriage. Neither had Dominik panicking, but he wanted to keep the pressure off Sahara. She needed to know what a normal relationship—with a bit more negotiating—looked like before they approached either subject.

His mother adored her after only a couple of hours. So he could leave them together while he settled this clusterfuck.

"If we reach that point, I will be sure to let you know. Now, I have to go prepare for the game tonight. Please make sure your wife doesn't show up at the arena. With how much she had to drink, I doubt security will let her through the door." He'd damn well make sure they didn't if he had to. Maybe he should clear this with Sahara, but she needed someone who had her best interests at heart. And that would always be him, no matter who else should be first in line. "I'll leave you to say goodbye to your daughter."

"Of course." Sahara's father hunched his shoulders and crossed the distance between him and his daughter. He hugged her, but he didn't say much. The man seemed completely lost.

But Sahara squeezed him tightly. Assured him everything was fine.

She told Dominik's mother the same after they dropped her off at her hotel. Since Dominik was with Sahara, Cort wasn't busy. And he'd been perfectly comfortable making sure Dominik's mother got to the arena for the game.

Dominik grabbed one of the team's rentals and drove Sahara around the city for a while, giving her the time she needed to say what was on her mind.

"My mother texted me." She laughed, but it was one of the saddest sounds he'd ever heard. Choked and strained. As though she was making it just for him. "If we get married, she'll pay half. And she saw the perfect wedding dress."

There were so many things he could say. He could assure her that it would be a long time before they had to worry about her mother's involvement in their nonexistent wedding. He could tell her she'd look beautiful in any dress. He could change the subject.

But he expected her to be honest. So he said the first thing that came to his mind. "If we ever get married, we're eloping to Vegas. Jami and Akira can come with their men. But that's it."

Sahara let out a bubbly laugh and rested her head on his shoulder as he drove aimlessly, his only destination somewhere that he could return from in time to hit the ice.

"If you ever propose, tell me that again." She exhaled slowly, brokenly, making him want to hold her and tell the rest of the world to fuck off. "And I'll say yes."

He reached for her hand and held it tightly. It was way too soon, but her words made the idea of asking one day that much more real.

Chapter Sixteen

Center ice in the Barclays Center arena, Dominik stood with the starting line as the Canadian anthem was sung. Over to his left, he could hear Carter belting out the words at the top of his lungs. He'd adopted the ritual after researching the percentage of games they won when he sang compared to the ones they lost when he didn't.

Other players had their own rituals. Demyan had clearly taken the fifteen minutes he'd gone missing from the locker room with Pearce to carry out his own. He had teeth marks on his throat and his dirty blond hair was a mess. Dominik chuckled as he caught Demyan glancing back at the bench with a lazy smile of satisfaction.

The strangest superstition had to be Bower's. The goalie had once asked the trainer to retape his stick during the anthem because he hadn't noticed it had gotten messed up during practice until the last minute. They'd gone on a five-game winning streak after, so naturally Bower now couldn't play with the same tape he used during practice.

At the moment, one of the younger trainers was standing with Bower's stick in his hand, waiting for the slight pause between the anthems to finish with the taping. A few feet behind him stood Cam and their mother.

Dominik frowned, confused. Since when were family allowed down by the benches before the game? Cam usually watched from the press box, and his mother had a ticket right behind the penalty box.

Neither looked upset, so they weren't waiting to give him bad news. That made it a little easier to breathe, because his mind couldn't help but go over worst-case scenarios. One of his nieces or nephews getting really sick or hurt. Either of his sisters having called because they needed their mother home for some kind of tragedy.

He refused to consider Joshua. He missed his brother, but he'd drive himself insane considering all that could go wrong.

The announcer, who was actually the chief executive officer and owner of the Islanders, stepped onto the red carpet that had been rolled out for the anthem singers. His bald head glistened under the spotlights as he spoke into the mic, a broad smile on his ruddy face.

"In honor of the men and women at home and overseas who serve to protect our great country, the Islanders would like to welcome the West Point Military Academy marching band. We would also like to present a special guest who came a very long way to watch his brother play professionally for the very first time. This player is a veteran of the league, but his brother's service prevented him from attending any games."

Dominik held his breath. Blinked and shook his head, sure he was seeing things as a man followed the marching band onto the red carpet.

"Please give a warm round of applause for Staff Sergeant Joshua Mason."

The rink rushed by as Dominik abandoned his spot with his team. He slammed into his brother, swallowing back a sob as Joshua's arms wrapped around him. He pulled away for an instant to make sure there was no sign of pain on his brother's face. His last letter had said nothing about coming home. His letters never revealed much. Not where he was. Where he was going. He tended to focus on questions about how Dominik was doing. The team. Their mother and siblings.

Joshua looked fine. Healthy and whole, if a bit tired. He nodded to Dominik as though to assure him that all was well. Then he pulled him back in for another hug.

"How?" Dominik shook his head, laughing as he quickly dried his eyes with the sleeve of his jersey. "Can you stay? You're gonna watch the whole game? Maybe hang out after?"

Grinning, Joshua turned as their mother and Cam joined them. He held them all, kissing Mom's cheeks before he gave his reply. "I'll be here for the whole game. And you can thank Mom and Cam for setting this up. Cam talked to both teams and they were all for it. But we're on a time limit. Go win this fucking game and—"

"Joshua! Language!" Their mother looked around as though worried the cameras might pick up her son swearing and judge her.

Inclining his head, Joshua kissed her forehead, then motioned for Cam to take her arm and help her off the ice. The carpet helped, but a wrong step could still put someone on their ass. "I'm sorry, Mom. Let me sing the anthem and I'll come sit with you. Dominik, I'll see you after the game."

Dominik watched Cam and their mother walk away. Then he grabbed Josh's hand and drew him close. "This was incredible. Thank you."

"My pleasure. Just don't make me regret it, little brother." Joshua gave him a light shove and Dominik took the hint.

He got back on the blue line with his team, accepting every big stupid grin from his guys with a nod. The band began to play. His brother's deep voice joined them.

This time, Carter wasn't the only one singing. Dominik let his voice join the tens of thousands in the stands. His whole body trembled with excitement as he absorbed the enormity of the chance he'd been given.

Today, it was his turn to make his brother proud.

* * * *

Sahara stood in the press box with Cort by her side, not even trying to hold back her tears. But out of the many she'd cried over the years, they weren't tears of pain or despair. She wasn't sure she'd ever been happier for anyone in her life.

The cameras had only caught Dominik's expression for a split second before he'd moved too fast for them to follow, but the shock and joy had been amazing to witness. He loved his brother so much, but he didn't often let his fear for him show. He'd been strong for his family. For her.

He deserved this moment, and she loved his family for giving it to him. Cort had let her in on the surprise when she'd first come up and she'd been holding her breath, watching Dominik the whole time even though she couldn't make out his face so far away.

"People are gonna talk, you know." One of the player's wives, whom she hadn't met and seemed too aloof to introduce herself to, sniffed as Sahara dabbed at her eyes with a tissue. "They'll say the Islanders wanted our captain distracted so they'd have the advantage."

Sahara frowned at the woman. "This is Dominik Mason. He's the captain for a reason. He's excited to have his brother back, but his head will be in the game."

The woman shrugged and focused on the play on the ice. Sahara bit her lip when she saw Dominik miss an easy pass. He recovered quickly, but his wild shot ended up on an Islander stick. He raced to block a pass, dropping hard to cover the goal. The Islander forward changed direction and snapped a pass to another, who sent the puck flying in a blur toward the net.

Carter put himself in the line of fire. The puck struck his skate.

He went down.

The ref froze the play when the Cobras regained possession. The trainers came out, standing back when Carter waved them off. He rose on his blades. Then dropped back to his knees.

"Shit." Sahara watched the trainer help Carter up. He was maneuvered off the ice with only one skate down. "If his foot is broken—"

"He'll still play." Cort grinned when she glanced over at him. "I know the game. Wanna bet he'll be gone for five minutes, then be right back out there?"

She shook her head, knowing full well Cort was right. Her father had played with broken bones in his foot. He'd come home some days, his foot so swollen she wasn't sure how he'd get his skate back on. The team doctors had their ways though, and with the stick of a needle and some ice, most would play if they could stand.

By the end of the first period, Carter was back, looking perfectly fine. He wasn't favoring one side, so maybe it was just a bruise. Or a fracture that would turn into a full break after a few more games.

Hockey players were crazy.

The score was still 0-0. Sahara spent the beginning of the break chatting with Cort and Dean, until Dominik's mother and brothers were invited up for some refreshments. Sahara sat beside Olivia, sipping the wine a few of the wives had suggested she'd need to keep herself sane for the next two periods. Drinking in front of Olivia had been uncomfortable at first, considering how her own mother had behaved, but Olivia was as good as her son at reading Sahara.

"Enjoy. I'm having some too so we can toast our quick exit from the nuthouse." Olivia rubbed Sahara's shoulder, then took a sip of the wine the attendant had brought them. "Mr. Richter, I should thank you for how well you've been treating my boys. Honestly, I thought you would spend five minutes with my youngest and then shove him on the next plane back to Chicago."

Dean looked over at Cam and shook his head. "He's been on his best behavior, Mrs. Mason." His lips quirked up to one side. "But if he ever gets out of line, I promise, you'll be the first one I call."

"Hey! What about Dommy? Did anyone tell you about the fight he got in with the assistant coach? Over some chick?" Cam was grinning the entire time he ratted out his brother, but then Joshua cuffed him upside the back of the head. And all eyes turned to Sahara.

She remembered the fight all too well. And didn't even want to think about it. She trusted Dominik. He said things with Oriana were in the past, and she wouldn't question him because his brother had a big, stupid mouth.

Insulting Cam in front of his mother wouldn't keep Sahara in her good graces though, so she simply shrugged. "He gets in fights so often on the ice I hardly noticed."

"Not as often as he used to. Which is good." Dean sipped his coffee. "The league is changing, and fighting isn't as accepted as it used to be. A lot of players who were primarily fighters are finding themselves without contracts. Thankfully, that wasn't the case with Dominik. He's exactly the leader the team needs and one of our best defensemen."

Dean's praise had Sahara's chest swelling with pride. She exchanged a glance with Olivia, who had a huge smile, as though Dean had just presented her a gold medal.

"I did an excellent job with all my brood. However, I have to admit, when he was little and I had to get him up at five a.m. to hit the rink at six, there were times I hoped he'd find a new hobby. Like playing the saxophone or juggling." Olivia snickered when her sons gave her horrified looks. "You're both to blame. You always wanted to come, but you'd whine the whole way. His coaches were saints for putting up with the lot of you. Joshua grew up fast, but for the longest time, Cam would cling to my leg and hide from everyone. It was interesting, to say the least."

The conversation about the men as children seemed to fascinate Dean, but he tilted his head to one side as though something had occurred to him. "What about your daughters? Did they enjoy going to the rink?"

"When they were very small, yes. But after they hit about five or six, they lost interest in sports." Olivia gave him a nod of understanding. "Your little one may be very different, what with all her parents so involved in the game. I was happy when my daughters wanted to do girly things, so I encouraged it. Raising three boys without a man around was difficult, but I managed a good balance on my own I think. The girls were in their teens before I really saw the effect of not having a father. Amia is blessed to have two."

Sahara finished her wine, not sure she had anything to add to a conversation about kids. Or if she even wanted to take part after her mother's crude comments about not having had them with Grant. She loved Amia and spent a lot of time with Scott's daughter, Casey, but the idea of having children of her own one day...

Well, it wasn't as frightening as it had once been. She still made sure *never* to forget her birth control pills though. When she'd been with Grant, the idea of getting pregnant used to make her physically ill. He'd brought it up a few times, but she'd always used the excuse of her career to get him off the subject. The truth was, even though she hadn't been able to convince herself to leave him for the longest time, there'd been no way she'd give him a child to take out his anger on.

One of the girls at the self-defense classes she'd taken with Jami and Akira had told them about how her boyfriend had pierced holes in condoms to get her pregnant. He'd thought having a baby would make it harder for her to leave him.

Which might have been true if he hadn't beaten her to the point that she'd miscarried.

Only on the worst days had Sahara ever considered that her fear of him meant she should get away from him. And fast. But all the nightmares of having children with him, all the fear, the skills she'd gained over time with different shades of makeup for all the stages of healing bruises, had been easy to forget on the good days.

"Sahara, are you all right?" Olivia took her hand, something in her eyes saying she already knew the answer.

Sahara laughed and put down her second glass of wine. "Yes, but I need to stop drinking. I'm getting all maudlin."

"Understandable after what you went through today." Olivia stood and held out her hand. "Come, I want to see what kind of goodies they have on that table. They certainly spoil the men who run the show, don't they?" Leading Sahara to the tables set up along the length of the wall, Olivia took two plates from the stack and handed one to Sahara. "I expect you didn't eat much today with all the excitement. Oh! Deviled eggs! I love these. Do you?"

Not sure she even wanted to think about food, never mind eat, Sahara nodded absently. She trailed after Olivia, letting Dominik's mother fill her plate while she commented on the appetizers and pastries laid out.

They brought their plates to the high tables in the corner and sat on the stools. Cort came over a few seconds later, joining them with nothing on his plate but a chocolate muffin. He switched their plates without saying a thing and drew Olivia into a conversation about Joshua's military service.

"Umm...excuse me?" Sahara pointed at Cort's plate, then the one he'd stolen from her. "What are you doing?"

He popped one of the deviled eggs in his mouth and chewed slowly, his lips curving upward as he swallowed. "I just got off the phone with Akira. She said you hate any kind of boiled egg, and if you looked sad, I should find you chocolate." He wiped his mouth with a napkin from the dispenser on the center of the table. "You're welcome."

Olivia snickered and continued with her favorite subject.

And Sahara ate her muffin. Which, strangely made her feel much better after she'd devoured half of it. Polishing off the rest, she eyed the table. She was actually pretty hungry. Excusing herself, she went back to the table to get in line behind the wives and management who'd gathered.

Her spine stiffened as she caught what the woman, who'd earlier mentioned Dominik being distracted, was saying. "I'm not saying they're right, but it's interesting that very few people had a problem when Oriana Delgado was with him. Oriana's exotic though. I'm not sure where Silver came from. Those skinny little blondes seem to be everywhere."

"I'm sure most of them bleach their hair," another woman remarked with a sniff. "What's sad is they're not dating different races out of love. It's a new fad."

"Some fad!" the first woman sneered. She glanced over, spotted Sahara, and then lowered her voice a little. But not enough that Sahara couldn't hear every word. "I honestly think this one enjoys the drama. No one pays much attention to those sluts parading around the ice, but she's constantly in the media for something."

Appetite lost, Sahara went back to the table. Both Olivia and Cort were watching her with concern, but she shook her head. "I don't want to talk about it."

The women were cruel, ignorant bitches. She could have spoken up, but she wasn't going to give them the satisfaction of upsetting her. If she ignored them, they'd eventually go away. Or get bored.

People who set out to hurt others usually stopped striking out when they didn't get the reaction they wanted. The lesson hadn't been an easy one to learn. Once, she'd been the type of person to fight back.

But sometimes you just had to be still and quiet. Wait for it to be over. Then find somewhere to lick your wounds. Alone.

Only, she wasn't given the chance.

Slipping out of the press box, she'd planned to head to the bathroom for a few minutes, but she ended up almost walking into a man she was pretty sure she'd seen around the Delgado Forum. A girl in her early teens with bright pink hair stood beside him, holding a fussy toddler. The little boy hiccupped, his face red, as though he'd been crying.

"Excuse me, ma'am, but I was told Mr. Richter would be here." The balding man looked frazzled. "My name is Dale Pritt and I represent Peter Kral and Heath Ladd. I was to bring Heath's brother and sister to wait for him."

Brother and sister? Sahara nodded and opened the door, leading the trio into the room she'd just left. "He's right in here." The poor kids were dragging their feet, utterly exhausted. She smiled at the girl. "My name's Sahara. Your brother is my boyfriend's roommate. It's a pleasure to meet you."

The girl scowled. "I bloody well doubt it. We weren't even supposed to be here." Her scowl faded and a gleam of satisfaction shone in her eyes. "But I called his manager every hour for two days and he finally said he'd bring us."

"Well, the flight must have been exhausting." And Heath's manager deserved a raise. He had taken off to talk to Dean, so Sahara led the kids to the refreshment table. The boy hadn't spoken yet, so she crouched down, holding a plastic cup. "Do you want something to drink? Maybe a snack?" She glanced up at the girl to include her in the offer. "I can find you somewhere comfortable to watch your brother play."

"Bran don't talk much. He likes apple juice though." The girl folded her arms over her chest, eyeing the table. "I like Mountain Dew."

After pouring both drinks, Sahara led the kids to the table where Olivia was still sitting with her sons. Olivia and the guys were completely into the game, and Sahara wanted to see how the team was doing. But first, she had to make sure the kids were comfortable.

The girl hopped up on a stool and mumbled thanks when Sahara handed her the cup of Mountain Dew. Bran blew his overgrown, curly blond hair that made him look just like Heath, away from his eyes and held his arms up to Sahara. She lifted him up against her hip, and he took his apple juice.

Watching them, the girl finally cracked a smile. "He likes you. You look a bit like our mom did when she was younger. He's only seen pictures though." She bit her lip and stared at her soda. "My name's Kimber. Like the gun."

"That's a cool name."

"Thanks." Kimber gazed down at the ice. "Can I tell you something?"

"Sure."

"I don't know anything about hockey. Heath told me he would teach me, but he's always busy. I want to be at as many of his games as I can." She squinted up at the Jumbotron. "Like, are both teams losing?"

"Nope, they're tied. And if this keeps up, they'll go to sudden death." Both kids stared at her, wide-eyed. She grinned. "One thing I know is hockey. I'll teach you all about it."

A few minutes later, Dean came over and suggested Sahara bring the kids to the cushioned seats on the small balcony in front of the press box. He'd gotten someone to find blankets for them, so they were all cuddled up as they watched the game.

By the end of the third, Kimber had a pretty good grasp of the game. By the beginning of the first overtime, both kids were asleep.

Sahara managed to stay awake long enough to watch her man score the winning goal. In the third overtime.

Those men... She yawned as she closed her eyes, just for a minute. *Are freakin' machines.*

Chapter Seventeen

The game was won in triple overtime. The team kept their celebration short on the ice out of respect for the fans, but when they got to the locker room, the excitement was deafening. Dominik slapped a few of the guys on the back as he made his way to his stall. His body was slick with sweat and he was eager to get under the cool spray of the shower.

First things first though. He gestured for Ladd to come talk to him, needing to see where the boy's head was at before the reporters were allowed in. Coach Shero and Sloan had kept media exposure to a minimum during the home games, but Rebecca Bower had argued that the fans needed as much access to the team as possible while they were on the road.

Which probably explained why the PR lady was having what looked like a very serious conversation with Richards. He'd get another chance to give scripted answers. If he failed, he could end up back in the minors. He was a promising young player, but he'd proven to be a liability and might need another year or so to mature.

Ladd would come under the same scrutiny. Mason planned to give him a brief prep, which hopefully wouldn't come off as another lecture.

The boy took a seat, tucking his shoulder length hair, slightly curly with the dampness of sweat, behind his ears. He stiffened when Hunt strode by. Fisted his hands on his knees.

Dominik frowned. "You never did tell me what the issue between you two is. Are you still sharing a room?"

Nodding, Ladd hunched his shoulders and stared down at the floor. "He was fighting with his dad on the phone. Asked me what I thought about the hotel deal."

Finally. Progress. Ladd talking in full sentences was nothing short of a miracle.

Except, Dominik doubted him shrugging at Hunt had caused the rift. And Ladd wasn't elaborating.

Time for a little nudge. "What did you say?"

"He's too old to need his daddy."

"Just like that?" Of course like that. Dominik groaned. "You must have had friends on your team in Russia? Were you this blunt with them?"

The shrug came so automatically, Dominik doubted Ladd realized he'd come to rely on it as a form of noncommittal communication. But then his lip quirked as though he'd remembered something. "Didn't mean to do that. Ah…took me a while to learn Russian."

"A lot of Russian players speak English."

"Yeah, but they didn't talk much."

All right, this was going to be a bit more difficult than Dominik had expected. Ladd had been pretty young when he'd played in Russia. Without parents around, and with his naturally intense focus, even a coach might have missed how little the boy was developing socially. Dominik could work on that with him, but Hunt probably wasn't the best guy to stick him with to fix this issue.

Unfortunately, putting Ladd in another room at this point might be difficult. And the two rookies really should work out their differences.

"I get that you grew up without your parents, but you had your sister. You care what she thinks, don't you?" He studied Ladd's face as he cocked his head, thinking it over, then nodded. "All right, well, Hunt is grateful for how his father dedicated himself to pushing him to the top. Right or wrong, this is his situation. A little compassion would go a long way."

The ruckus coming in as the door to the locker room opened told Dominik he'd run out of time. He sighed and put his hand on Ladd's shoulder.

"The reporters will want to talk to you. You've seen interviews with other players in the league? The same old answers they all say?"

"Yeah, mate. But what's the point?"

"The point is your new fans get to see your pretty face and hear you talk." Dominik chuckled when Ladd made a face. "This isn't the minors anymore, kid. Get used to it."

The flood of cameras and mics kept Ladd close to Dominik's side as the questions began. Dominik didn't have to keep his full attention on the reporters surrounding him; they rarely came up with anything new. One mentioned his love life and he laughed it off with a "No comment."

He heard every one of Ladd's answers, and his smile grew wider as he heard "Give 100%" no less than three times.

Good boy.

A New York reporter spoke over the others. "You were notably silent during the last interview. During this one, your answers don't even make sense." He glanced at his notepad. "'Are any players hiding injuries?' got 'We're all giving 100%.' You gave the same answer when asked about gay players in the locker room. Is there a reason behind you avoiding questions because, to many, it comes off as arrogance not befitting a young player?"

"Last interview was about the flight." Ladd blinked at the man. "I'm not afraid of flying. No point in acting as though I am."

"Then give us something worth sharing."

"Like?"

The reporter was getting frustrated. "Again with the evasions. Can't you answer one damn question?"

"Yes. Do your research, find something to ask me, and I will."

Oh fuck. Dominik shook his head. Ladd didn't notice.

The reporter frowned. "Excuse me?"

"Questions. Do you blokes have any? No?" Ladd finally caught Dominik making a cutting motion and flashed a smile. "Then no comment."

The locker room cleared out. The men were oddly quiet as they showered and changed, considering they'd just won a game. But Ladd's interview would be all anyone would talk about for days.

Dominik waited until the locker room was completely empty to let the boy have it.

"Where, in any interview, have you ever heard a player tell reporters to do research?" Dominik didn't wait for an answer. The kid could bring up the Leafs, but fuck that. "You sounded like an arrogant asshole. 'Find something to ask me'? What the hell was that?"

"They already think I'm arrogant. The last interview, they wanted to know which players might play badly because of the flight. How would I know that?"

"You're not expected to. Deflect!"

"I said 'No comment.'"

"Way too fucking late and you know it. You gave the media so much to play with." He sat back in his stall, not sure if he really wanted to deal with the kid anymore. For now, Dominik needed to get to his hotel room, hold Sahara, and forget this whole fucked-up day.

His phone rang and he checked the number. It was Cort.

"Hey. How's Sahara?"

"Sleeping. She's got two little kids with her—did you know your rookie has a little brother and sister?"

"No. He failed to mention them." Dominik glared at Ladd and the boy paled.

Cort paused. "I was gonna bring them down, but security's got barriers up at the players' exit because there's a crowd waiting for you all to come out. Be safer to bring her with the little ones out a side exit. Is it cool if we meet you at the hotel?"

"That's fine. Thanks, Cort." Dominik pressed end and stuffed his phone in his bag. He straightened and laced his fingers behind his neck, shaking his head. "Let me guess. You thought you'd impress me so much with you performance and behavior that I wouldn't even notice the kids? You let me assume you had an older sister staying with you."

Ladd hunched his shoulders. "I wasn't sure when they'd be able to join me. Mr. Pritt was working out the details."

"Which you were going to share with me when exactly?"

"When I decided if *I* wanted to stay with you. This all happened real fast. I just got custody when I proved I had a stable place in Ontario." Ladd braced his hands on his knees and stared at the floor. "Kimber and Bran were in foster care for two years. Bran almost got adopted. I didn't want to risk losing them again."

Well, fuck. The kid was in way over his head. There was no way Dominik would abandon him now. "Did they have a nanny in London? Is she coming too?"

Ladd shook his head. "She didn't want to move. She was watching them until I was settled, but Mr. Pritt had my permission to bring them down when I was settled. Not sure why they're here."

Dale Pritt was a damn good manager, well-known in the league, but he wasn't a family man. He'd likely pulled as many strings as possible to bring Ladd to Dartmouth. Relocating his siblings was likely part of his contract.

A huge responsibility. One Dominik hadn't really considered for himself, but regardless, he'd help Ladd in any way he could. He patted the rookie's shoulder. "Come on, sport. We'll manage. But you've got to promise me one thing."

"Anything." Ladd looked up at him, his eyes filling with hope. The kid had probably braced himself for the worst.

Not surprising, really. From the little Dominik knew, the young man hadn't had it easy. Felt pretty awesome to be in a position to change that for him. "We're in this together, so no more surprises."

"Yes, sir."

"Don't call me sir."

"Sorry." Ladd slung his sports bag over his shoulder and followed Dominik out to the parking garage. He hesitated in front of the SUV. Glanced over at Dominik. "Hey, Mason?"

"Yeah?"

"Thanks, man."

Dominik inclined his head, then climbed into the driver's seat of his rental. He waited for Ladd to get in the passenger side and rolled out, slowing when he spotted a few dozen fans, several in Cobra jerseys, waiting at either side of the barriers security had set up. He wasn't sure letting Ladd around the fans was a good idea considering his mess with the press, but he didn't have the heart to just keep driving when they'd been out here waiting so long.

Tapping the steering wheel, Dominik slowed to a stop and spoke very slowly and clearly so the kid wouldn't misunderstand a damn word. "You smile, say thank you and you're welcome when appropriate. You got it?"

Ladd nodded, inhaling roughly. He rolled down his window and his whole demeanor changed as he reached out to take the hat of a little boy whose father lifted him up to reach over the barrier. "Hey, buddy! Did you enjoy the game?"

Dominik signed a few hockey cards, nodding and smiling while keeping half his focus on the rookie. A few people had their phones out. Social media getting an unedited glimpse of Ladd might make or break him.

"It was *awesome*! I wasn't sure Mom would let us stay, but Dad called her and she said it's the playoffs," the boy said excitedly. "We flew all the way and I was hoping I'd get to meet you. Is it true you're from Australia? Did you ever see a wild kangaroo?"

"Only when I was about your age." Ladd signed the hat with the boy's Sharpie. "I spent a lot of time in Russia, but before that I lived on a farm near Sydney. Seen a lot more wallabies. And possum."

"That's so cool! What about killer crocodiles?"

"Never met one of those. Be pretty neat though." Ladd plunked the hat on the boy's head. "Probably safer watching them on TV."

The boy laughed, the father thanked Ladd, and the small crowd dispersed, smiling and laughing with the joy of the win. Dominik pulled onto the street, driving the few short blocks to the hotel, going over what he should say to the rookie.

His interactions with the press still needed work, but the fans were going to love him. If he could share some of the warmth he'd shown the little boy to their teammates, he'd be in a much better place.

Ladd didn't seem to mind the silence as they made their way from the parking below the hotel up to the team's floor. After they got off the elevator, Ladd checked the text his manager had sent him with the room number where his brother and sister were staying. Sahara was still with them, so Dominik followed Ladd, who opened the door soundlessly.

Shutting the door quietly behind him, Dominik stepped softly to avoid waking Sahara or the children. The manager rose from a chair in the corner, whispered goodnight, and slipped out.

The bathroom light was still on, but the rest of the room was dark. The room had two double beds, one with a blanket completely covering a tiny form. In the other, Sahara was curled up next to a little boy who was hugging her arm and sucking his thumb.

She looked so sweet, Dominik hated to disturb her, but Ladd would want to sleep with his baby brother. He motioned for Ladd to gently move his brother's arm. The toddler instantly latched on to Ladd's hand, grumbling a little and sucking harder on his thumb.

But he didn't wake up. And neither did Sahara, even when Dominik lifted her up in his arms and cradled her against his chest. He smiled at Ladd when the rookie eased onto the bed, fully dressed, with his brother still clinging to him.

Ladd smiled back sleepily. "G'night, mate."

"Goodnight, sport."

A few minutes later, in his own room, Dominik lowered Sahara onto the bed and covered her with the duvet. Even in sleep, he could see some of the strain of the day casting shadows beneath her eyes. She curled into a tight ball on her side, her golden hair draped across the white sheet, looking so vulnerable he didn't feel quite right stripping all his clothes off to lie next to her.

He took off everything but his boxers and climbed into the bed, still careful not to disturb her. But despite his best efforts, she let out a soft groan and rolled toward him.

Without opening her eyes, so she was probably still half asleep.

"Today was bad." She snuggled up against his side, relaxing when he eased her head onto his shoulder. "I'm so happy you don't hate me."

Why would I ever hate you? His jaw tightened as he considered what she might have done that she'd feel guilty about. Maybe she was still interested in Pischlar? That would be hard to swallow, but it wouldn't make Dominik hate her.

I won't share.

Running his hand absently over her hair, he pushed the baseless fears aside. Nothing she'd said or done lately gave any indication that she wanted anything other than a monogamous relationship with him. Her time with Pischlar and White had been mostly to bring the two men closer.

If he really considered how her day had gone, she was probably reacting to how someone who should love her unconditionally had treated her. Maybe she believed her mother hated her.

More likely, her mother simply believed she was looking out for her daughter. In a way that did more harm than good.

In the end, Dominik couldn't worry about Pischlar. He couldn't erase the hurtful things her mother had said or done.

But he could make sure she never doubted his place in her life. So he pressed his lips to her hair. "I couldn't hate you, my sunshine." He breathed in the sweetness of her, fresh like a sun-kissed meadow at dawn. Then he whispered, "But I'm most definitely falling for you."

Chapter Eighteen

Sahara was never sure what woke her so early in the morning. The only time she'd ever really slept in was when she used to let go and drink too much just to numb the pain. Strangely enough, that had happened more often once she'd been free of Grant than when she was still with him.

Or maybe it wasn't so strange. While she'd been with him, she'd been in a constant state of anxiety. She woke each day and prepared herself to speak carefully, to smile prettily, and to avoid doing anything that might upset him.

People talked about abuse, and it was so easy to sympathize while not being part of the frightening scenario. Even when she was. Of all the things she remembered of their relationship, the first time he'd hit her stuck out the most.

She'd just walked in the door after visiting her parents. A guy she'd had a crush on when she was very young had complimented her dress. Her father had playfully threatened his teammate and nothing had come of it. They all knew she was with Grant.

When Grant asked her how her day was after practice, she'd laughed and told him the story.

His eyes narrowed. "Were you trying to get his attention? Your dad is a good man, but I'm surprised he didn't say anything about what you're wearing."

She looked down at the yellow sundress Grant had always loved. "I was looking forward to seeing you tonight. I wore your favorite dress."

"For another man."

Laughing, she shook her head. "No, I'm so over him. He's just a few years younger than my dad. I just didn't feel like getting changed."

"Why? Aren't I worth the effort?" He came closer, staring at her, a strange look in his eyes. "You're with me. Why would you go anywhere without me looking like that?"

She rolled her eyes and shrugged. "Damn, I didn't know it was a big deal. Relax."

"Relax?" The back of his hand hit her cheek. Her shock kept her silent, even as she stared at him. "You know I love you! Why are you playing games! Fuck!" He backed away from her, showing more pain than she felt, even as her cheek throbbed. "I love you so much. Stay away from me. I can't believe I just did that."

Covering her cheek with her hand, she walked away from him. Locking herself in the bathroom, she leaned against the door and tried her best to figure out what had just happened.

Then she heard the broken sound of Grant's sobs. He never cried, and hearing him falling apart broke through the anger and bruised pride in her that wouldn't tolerate what he'd done. He hadn't hit her that hard. He regretted lashing out; he'd even told her to leave.

But she loved him, so she'd stay and they'd work through this. He'd made a mistake.

And so had she.

The sex had been great that night. He'd been so attentive and she'd truly believed he'd never hurt her again. Only, he never did change. She'd only gotten better at making excuses for him. For so long that it had become normal.

She shivered and went over to the window to close it, but the slight breeze was unseasonably warm. The chill was from her memories, and this morning they seemed more determined than ever to drag her into the past.

Her therapist had often reminded her to focus on her breathing when this happened. She'd recommended yoga, but she fully approved of the self-defense courses. Anything that made Sahara feel in control. That reminded her she wasn't stuck in that horrible cycle of abuse anymore.

The control thing might be difficult, considering how much Sahara needed Dominik to take charge, but she wasn't waking him up because she was dealing with her damn issues. Not that he'd mind if she did, but no matter how often he assured her he accepted her, flaws and all, she couldn't just accept herself this way. She wanted to be stronger. To feel like she was actually making progress.

Flashbacks could ruin a whole day, but she refused to let herself sink into the same old hopeless pit. She changed into a pair of gray jogging pants and a white tank top and did some stretches in the sitting room, sensing some of the shadows within retreat with each satisfying tug in her muscles. About fifty jumping jacks got her blood pumping, and she moved smoothly into the routine one of her trainers had taught her. A mix of self-defense and jujitsu, which she'd planned to take regularly but had to put off until the hockey season was over. The idea of being able to take down an armed opponent appealed to her.

Not so much because she thought she could beat someone holding a gun to her head, but if you could block a knife, blocking a fist didn't seem so hard. Strength and size weren't the deciding factors.

One precise movement after another, Sahara let the focus on her body smother the unease in her mind. The routine was almost like a choreographed dance, only she could see every attack and counterattack. She moved faster, letting out a rough sound with each kick and punch. Sweat beaded at her temples and ran between her breasts, and she smiled as she saw the faceless assailant in her head go down for good.

There wasn't so much as a breath of warning or a scuff on the carpet, but Sahara sensed Dominik watching her. Her cheeks heated as she glanced over at him. "Ah…I hope I didn't wake you up? I was trying to be quiet."

His lips curved into a soft smile as he approached. "You were, but I've gotten spoiled by having you sleep beside me. I thought you might have gone to get breakfast again—"

"I could if you're hungry. I was thinking of bringing you to the bakery if you've got time."

"I'd love to, but—"

"It's not far. And they have more than chocolate." She used the front of her shirt to dry some of the sweat from her face, hating that he was seeing her all gross after watching her kick some imaginary ass. "Do you mind if I get changed first?"

He shook his head and folded his arms over his chest. "Stop interrupting me. I was going to ask about the workout. Is that the self-defense you were learning with Scott and the girls?"

"Some of it."

"Are you self-conscious that I saw you?"

She wrinkled her nose. Then nodded. "I haven't done the routine in a while, but it relaxes me. I should have waited until I got home."

Dominik arched a brow at her. "Why?"

"Why?" She blinked, not sure what he was asking. Why did it relax her, or why wait until she got home? Nibbling on the side of her lip, she shrugged. "To avoid embarrassment?"

Letting out a light laugh, Dominik took her by the wrist and pulled her against him, his kiss like a sweet reward for her honesty. "We'll have to work on that. If it relaxes you, maybe you should do it more often. You still take courses regularly, yes?"

"Semiregularly?" She tried to remember the last time she'd actually gone to the community center where Scott volunteered once a week. Scott had called her last month to ask her why she hadn't been around. And she hadn't been back since.

Her only excuse was the Ice Girls had been working hard on the pregame shows, but Scott was in the starting lineup on a team in the playoffs and she couldn't remember him ever missing a class.

Nodding, Dominik tipped her chin up with a finger. "Consider this my first nonsexual command as your Master. You will continue the classes. If they aren't challenging enough, choose another form of self-defense to expand on."

Or what? A petulant little voice in her head asked. She couldn't completely ignore the side of her that demanded independence, but the stronger part of her, the side that craved his control, prevailed.

She inhaled slowly, sweet anticipation sizzling in her veins. "So my submission will go beyond the bedroom?"

"Yes, unless you object?" Dominik smiled when she shook her head. "Good. Now try some of those moves on me. They're more than punches and kicks. That spin and elbow to the floor was interesting."

Her very favorite move, one she still couldn't believe actually worked. Nothing compared to the elation she'd experienced when she'd executed it successfully for the first time. Her instructor had even put her in front of the class a few times to demonstrate.

Why the hell did I stop going?

She grinned at Dominik. "It's a takedown, but I've only ever done it on a mat. I wouldn't want to hurt you."

His brows shot up. "Hurt me? Sunshine, I'm sure you're very good, but look at me."

"I am. Learning self-defense against small, weak men would have been pointless, don't you think?"

"True, but I'm not concerned that you'll hurt me." The edge of his lip twitched into a challenging smirk. "Show me what you've got."

She squared her shoulders, not sure if he was teasing her or pushing her to prove herself. Either way, he was about to get exactly what he'd asked for. "Fine, but don't say I didn't warn you."

He bared his teeth in a broad smile, turning to pick up the coffee table and move it to the other side of the room. Returning, he took an attack pose, knees bent slightly, hands up as though prepared to block a punch.

Naked except for his boxers, Dominik's majestic form was bared before her in a way that was both alluring and intimidating. All those bulging muscles, the smooth brown flesh of his wide chest and thick legs, he was a powerful man who could—and had—simply throw her over his shoulder and have his way with her. Which wasn't a problem.

But the reason she felt so comfortable with him was because she knew that strength would never be used against her. If she actually had to use her moves to fight him off, one of them would end up in serious pain.

Probably her, but she wouldn't go down easy. If he underestimated her, she'd have a fighting chance.

This wasn't about being able to fight him though. She was confident in her ability to defend herself. She needed him to be as well.

"I'm not attacking you, you're attacking me." Not bothering to take a stance, she motioned him forward. "Don't give me a warning.

Come at me like you imagine someone who wanted to grab me would."

Dominik's smile faded. His jaw ticked, but he gave her a firm nod. Then he lunged, reaching for her.

She latched on to his wrist, turned into him, and used his own momentum to flip him over her hip. His back hit the ground and he let out a grunt. She drove her elbow down, letting out a shout of triumph.

But the satisfaction vanished when Dominik jerked away with a wince. Her elbow had connected with his mouth. And his bottom lip was bleeding.

"Oh my God, I'm so sorry! One sec, I'll get something." She jumped to her feet, ran to the bathroom, and grabbed the box of Kleenex. She ripped out a handful as she rushed back.

Sitting up, Dominik gave her a crooked grin as she knelt beside him and gently pressed the tissue to the small split. "It's not that bad. But I stand corrected. My girl is damn tough."

"I didn't mean to actually hit you." She'd *never* hit anyone this hard during her courses. Yes, she'd warned him that he could get hurt, but she'd been concerned about him falling hard on the thin carpet. She chewed her bottom lip, moving the tissue a little, relieved to see at least the bleeding had stopped.

"Sahara, I'm impressed. And, more importantly, you weren't trapped in fear or sadness or letting anything hold you down. You're strong, and this is one of the first times I haven't seen you doubt that." He took her hand, prying open her fingers to take the red spotted tissue. "I'm willing to spill a bit of blood if it means you'll see the woman I do every single day."

Fuck, I love this man. Sahara leaned closer to him, staring into his eyes as she pressed her hand to his cheek. She wasn't ready to tell him yet, but the emotion spread like a straight shot of strong spirits once the burn passed and all that remained was the warmth circulating through her veins. Her skin felt like it was glowing and she needed to touch him. To kiss him. To let her body tell him what words couldn't even express.

He wrapped his arms around her, pulling her up to straddle his thighs. "You won, fair and square. Name your prize."

She didn't even have to think about what she wanted. But how to tell him? Would he understand that it was the only prize she would ever need?

"Let me surrender to you, Dominik. Like I'm not fragile and full of triggers. I need to be your submissive in every way possible. Even if only for today, I need to feel what it's like to completely give up control."

His fingers slid into her hair and he tugged slightly until she met his eyes. His expression was impossible to read, but she had a feeling he was trying to gauge the reasons behind her request. She knew he'd say no if she were asking so she could prove she was as good as Oriana or any of his other past submissives. But she wasn't sure if he'd say yes even if he saw how desperately she needed to fully offer herself to him.

A sub might kneel for a Dom, but if he didn't want her at his feet, the act meant nothing.

He inhaled slowly. "You're not asking to play. You're asking for something real."

"Yes."

He inclined his head. "Then that is exactly what I will give you."

Bubbly excitement burst in her chest and she pressed her eyes shut, biting her tongue to keep from saying something stupid. The proper reply would be "Thank you, Sir."

Not difficult, just say it!

"When do we start?" No, that was all wrong! She giggled when he gave her a level look. "Sorry. I mean, thank you. Thank you so much, Sir. I swear you won't regret this."

Chuckling, he lifted her off his lap, rising smoothly above her and holding out his hand. She offered her hand, but he took hold of her wrist instead. Drawing her to her feet, he swiftly spun her around, pinning her against him with her back to his chest.

His breath caressed the flesh of her neck as he brushed his lips along her throat. Then he whispered in her ear, "I'll regret nothing, Sahara. But you might."

She shook her head, absolutely positive anything he did to her would be perfect.

"We shall see." He released her and stepped back, leaving her to steady herself as he strode toward the bedroom.

Her brow furrowed, she followed him. Wasn't he going to give her an order? Restrain her, maybe spank her? Something?

Standing in the doorway, she stared at him as he swiftly dressed in a pair of black jeans and a black T-shirt. "Sir?"

"This room will be tidy when I return. And you will be wearing the red dress, waiting for me." He glanced around the room, shaking his head. "You will learn to take better care of your things."

"Okay…" She wrinkled her nose. They were starting her submission with chores? And he was leaving. "When will you be back?"

"Shortly." He stepped up to her, tapping her under the chin when she scowled at her feet. "Have you forgotten what you asked for already, pet?"

"I can't submit to you if you're not here."

His lips twitched with amusement. "You can, and you will. That will be your first lesson."

"What's the second one?"

He kissed her forehead, then headed toward the door, not answering until he was halfway out.

"Patience."

Chapter Nineteen

A little more than an hour passed before Dominik was on his way back to the hotel, carrying a bag full of fruit and a black paper bag with black ribbon handles. His strides were long and he'd worked up a bit of a sweat in the trek to the fruit stand, the kink shop, and back. In New York, with a quick Google search, finding the stores that suited his needs hadn't been difficult. Resisting the urge to take a cab and cut the travel time in half had been the real challenge.

The lesson of patience wouldn't be taught if he rushed though. They'd reached another level, and his heart swelled as he envisioned the beauty in Sahara's triumph, the moment when she owned her strength without a slip of doubt. Neither her mother nor Grant could take that strength from her if she continued to nurture it. And he would help her in every way he knew how.

That she'd slacked on her self-defense training, despite how much it empowered her, concerned him. Was she trying to please her mother by not being too tough? After meeting the woman, it wasn't a stretch to believe Sahara had very skewed ideas of how a "lady" should behave. Her upbringing could have a lot to do with how long she'd tolerated Grant's abuse. Grant was the kind of man her mother would approve of. The right earning bracket. The right family.

The right color.

Her mother's ignorance had stung, but he wouldn't allow the woman to take up space in his mind. Whether or not Sahara chose to train simply for an outlet, or because she was damn good at it and wanted to explore competing or eventually training others, he would make her see the benefits. Dealing with the memories of her abuse was much like dealing with the death of a loved one. In a way, the young, innocent woman she'd once been had died during her suffering. And time didn't erase what she'd lost.

But time would teach her how to keep living. To close that chapter in her life and learn how to manage when her book fell open on those dark pages. If sparring with him, or with those she trained with, gave her a sense of peace, then they had the master key to all the doors she needed to open to move on.

And it was having that key within reach that had him willing to accept her complete submission.

He was eager to explore Sahara's needs and discover how well they aligned with his own, but she needed some space from him to fully absorb what it was she'd offered. Her comment about not being able to submit if he wasn't there made it very clear that she expected him to take her submission from her.

He would, but only once she was able to hand it to him, fully committed to everything the gift entailed. She had been spoiled with Pischlar, receiving instant gratification for the barest act of surrender. There had been no true power exchange between them, and yet that was what she asked of—and what she *needed* from—Dominik.

To reach that point, they would need to go back to the basics. Negotiations had been done, trust was established, but neither of them really knew how deep her submissive nature ran.

After today, they'd have a much better idea.

In the hall on the way to the hotel room, he spotted an elderly cleaning lady with pure white hair in a bun under a hairnet, slight in her pristine uniform, but something in the way she moved and the bright sparkle in her brown eyes showed energy that belied her age. She stopped pushing the card and smiled at him.

"Good morning, sir."

He glanced at her name tag. "Good morning, Ethel."

Her gaze followed him as he stepped up to his door, pulling out his key card. "Very sweet girl you have, sir. Not at all like the others."

"Others?" Dominik frowned, wondering if some of the guys had picked up chicks and left them in the rooms for housekeeping to deal with. He didn't see any of the rookies pulling that kind of crap, but he wouldn't tolerate any of his men making the hotel staff's job more difficult.

"Oh, don't you worry yourself, young man. I raised twelve children, I can handle a few rowdy boys and their women. But she was so polite and tipped me just for letting her have a few things to clean with." The skin around her eyes and lips crinkled as she laughed. "I've never heard someone apologize so much for not letting me do my job, but it seemed so important to her, I didn't have the heart to insist. Please let me know if either of you needs anything else."

Dominik grinned, even more eager to see how Sahara was doing. He inclined his head. "I will. Thank you."

He opened the door to the hotel room quietly and stepped inside. The fresh scent of lemon cleaner filled the room. The carpet looked like it had been vacuumed and everything in the sitting room shone.

After pulling the door shut, he moved into the bedroom. The bed was made and the suitcases were nowhere to be seen. Leaving the bags on the bed, he continued to the bathroom and met Sahara's eyes in the mirror as she ran a soft bristle brush through her silky, golden blond hair.

She gave a little start and spun around to face him. "I was almost ready for you, Sir. I was going to kneel by the bed and wait and—"

"And you did everything I asked of you." He folded his arms over his chest and leaned against the doorframe, taking a moment to admire the way the red dress caressed her sweet curves. Her heels made her legs look incredibly long. The dip of her neckline showed a tantalizing amount of cleavage but left plenty to the imagination. She was so well put together it was hard to believe she'd spent most of the last hour cleaning, but she was so desperate to please him she'd probably scurried around from the second he stepped out, needing to follow his orders as perfectly as humanly possible.

"You did very well. I believe you've earned your reward." He backed into the bedroom with a crook of his finger for her to join him. Then he pointed to the floor by his side. "Now you may kneel."

She knelt gracefully, looking relieved. He had a feeling she considered kneeling a true act of submission and had been waiting for the chance to do it for him. A plus, considering he planned to have her in this position a lot today.

"Close your eyes. I will give you your first gift." He waited until she pressed her eyes shut, then reached into the black bag for the thick, red velvet blindfold he'd bought for her. He stood, moving behind her to pull it over her face and tie the red ribbons over her hair. "I will take everything from you before the day is done, Sahara. Your sight, your ability to speak, then lastly, what you will be able to hear. I will control all you feel, what you taste, and every movement you make."

Drawing in a sharp breath, she nodded.

"You will always have the ability to express your limits. I will respect them, but I will constantly be easing you toward them until I have a better understanding of each and every one. You will be observing high protocol until I release you from it. Do you understand?"

A tiny tremor shook her, but she gave another nod. "Yes, Sir."

"Good girl. Now, I have one last question." He paused, the edge of his lip twitching when her brow furrowed. She was probably thinking very hard about what else he might expect from her. No need to keep her guessing. "Do you object to having another Dom involved in our scenes?"

He didn't share, but he did have plans that would involve the assistance of another Master. Not something she'd expect from him, which meant she would be kept slightly off-balance.

Exactly where he wanted her.

* * * *

What's the right answer? Sahara tried to shake off the light-headedness that had come over her from the moment Dominik had left. She'd quickly ditched her irritation over having to clean and focused on how pleased he would be when he saw the room. Asking housekeeping for rags and spray cleaner and the vacuum had been a little embarrassing, but Ethel had been so nice about it Sahara had actually felt pretty damn good knowing she'd taken some of the burden off the old woman's shoulders. Yes, cleaning the rooms was

Ethel's job. The rest of the players had given her plenty to do though, and she'd already looked worn out.

Sahara had also been rather proud of how well she'd done. She kept her own apartment pretty clean, but only by her own standards. Ten minutes rushing around, and she never had to be embarrassed having guests over.

Cleaning to impress Dominik meant so much more. She'd thought back on how well he cared for his things and knew Olivia had probably kept a very tidy house. He'd be uncomfortable in a messy room and Sahara wanted to show him she could easily meet his standards. Every surface she polished, every bit of clutter she straightened up, was a small gesture of her willingness to serve him.

And, strangely enough, she found she didn't want him to thank her or act like she'd done anything special. He'd been right when he'd said he didn't have to be there for her to submit to him. Simply knowing he'd be pleased was all she'd needed.

His question still hung between them, though. Was this a test? Did he need some assurance that she didn't need another man in their relationship to be happy?

No. This was Dominik. He wouldn't suggest another Dom being involved just to make sure she'd say no. She didn't understand his motivations, but only one answer felt right.

"I won't object to anything you choose to do to me, Sir." She wet her bottom lip with her tongue, knowing she'd just left the door wide open for so many scenarios she wasn't sure she was ready for. But she trusted him completely, so there was no need to deny him anything. "While you were gone, I realized how fulfilling everything I do for you can be. I need to continue with you close. I'm not sure if that makes sense."

"It does. You're embracing your submission beautifully, and I'm happy to be the focus of what you need to give. The housekeeper actually spoke to me, and I was very proud of you." His voice sounded more resonant now that she was shrouded in darkness, almost like he was all around her, his deep tone sinking straight into her like tremors vibrating from the floor beneath her knees. His words settled over her, a blanket of soft, warm approval that she could curl up in like a contented little kitten.

He chuckled and touched her cheek. "I love that little smile. Your need to please goes beyond submission. It's too soon to say if we can delve into a 24/7 lifestyle, but I think something close to that would suit you."

Yes, please! When she'd first gotten interested in BDSM, her only interest had been spicing up things in the bedroom. With Dominik, she couldn't see those limits applying. She would still give her all to being an Ice Girl. To being a much better friend than she'd been in the past, but she needed him to be part of every aspect of her life. To sense him with her even when he wasn't. Or couldn't be.

Like he'd been this morning.

"Open your mouth, pet. You'll need your strength." He touched her bottom lip with his thumb, then pressed something cold into her mouth.

She bit down and the sour sweetness of the orange slice burst on her tongue. She chewed, swallowed, and then parted her lips for another. Once she'd finished the orange, he fed her some strawberries. Raspberries. And a kiwi.

Once she was done, he made her drink from a bottle of water. He used his thumb to dry her lips, then bent down to kiss her. "I enjoy having you eat from my hand. Unless we are in public, or have company, this is how you will eat from now on."

Intense, but she loved the idea. They weren't playing with the concept of a power exchange anymore. Instead of wading in the shallow end, he'd swum in deep with her hand in his, guiding her beyond the rough current until they were floating in the gentle waves together. She didn't need to feel the earth beneath her feet to hold steady. All she needed was to know he'd never be too far to keep her from being pulled under.

There was silence for what seemed like a long time. She relaxed back on her heels, for once not feeling the least bit impatient. She'd never felt so content. So at peace.

"Give me your wrists. I'd like to see how these look with the dress." Dominik wrapped a soft cuff around one of her wrists, then the other. He didn't clip them together, but he moved them around her wrists gently as though testing the fit. "A deep red in tooled leather. They suit you."

"Thank you, Sir." She wanted to touch them, but how still was she supposed to be?

Dominik touched her cheek, letting out a soft laugh. "You're overthinking again, pet. If it makes you feel better, ask for permission to move or speak, but remember what I told you about guessing."

"Well, I'm guessing you wouldn't take off the blindfold to let me see the cuffs."

"That's a good guess."

"But may I touch them? And am I allowed to touch you?" She wasn't sure their scenes today would be much fun if she wasn't allowed to reach out to him. If she couldn't see him, then she needed some other way to know if he smiled or frowned. Which seemed very important right now.

Latching on to her wrists, Dominik brought her hand up to his face and kissed her fingertips. "Unless you're bound, or I've asked you to hold a position, you're always allowed to touch me."

He released her wrist and stayed close to her. She hesitated for a few seconds, then traced her fingers over his lips. She could picture his broad smile so clearly it was as though the blindfold had been ripped away. Without her vision though, his skin seemed smoother, hotter. His beard was prickly against her fingertips at first, but the thickness along his jaw was soft.

She expected him to stop her any time now and continue with the scene, so she slid her hand to the back of his head, leaning up for a kiss. She gently nipped his bottom lip, parting her lips when his hands delved into her hair and his tongue met hers, first teasing a little, then moving in a sensual way that made her moan with desire.

This kiss seemed to last a long time, but at the same time, was over too soon. She gasped when he drew away from her and only his hand on her shoulder kept her from tipping forward.

"Do you still want to feel the cuffs, Sahara?" Dominik's thumb ran up and down the side of her throat. "If so, do it quickly. I have plans for this beautiful mouth."

"I'm sure I'll have plenty of chances to check them out." Sahara grinned, then licked her lips. "But I'll wait on whatever plans you have as long as you please, Sir."

"Cheeky little sub." He tugged her hair but didn't sound too upset. "Hands by your sides and open that pretty mouth."

Lips parted, she held still as she heard him unzip his jeans. The head of his cock, hot and smooth, brushed over her bottom lip. Eased into her mouth slowly. She flicked her tongue over the slit at the tip, tasting the slick saltiness of precum. He moved deeper and she wrapped her lips around him, letting the wetness on the skin of his dick moisten her lips as he drew out.

As he pressed in and pulled out repeatedly, she held him loosely, feeling he wasn't in a rush to get off. She'd seen other subs please their Masters like this, but she'd never gotten the point. Blow jobs were usually to get a guy off quick or foreplay. This seemed like neither.

She wasn't sure what the motivation for those men and women was, but for herself, the act was intimate. Simply giving pleasure, while asking for nothing in return. He could fuck her mouth hard and fast and she'd likely feel the same, but the tender way he stroked her hair, the soft, approving sounds he made, made her feel connected to him on another level.

The petting stopped, and his movements came a little faster, losing rhythm. He let out a muffled shout and his cum hit her tongue.

He pulled out, stroking her cheek as she swallowed, then licked him clean. "Beautiful. You make me very happy. Do you know that, my sunshine?"

Tipping her head back, she smiled. "I hope so, Sir. I've never been happier than I am with you."

He was quiet for a moment. His hand wrapped around her wrist and he drew her up to her feet. "One day, the answer will be yes. Without hesitation. But hope is a good start." He guided her into the living room. "I'm going to read the paper and watch the sports news. You may sit at my feet and relax until I'm ready for our next scene."

"Yes, Sir."

Once she'd settled on the floor, her back against the sofa and her head on his knee, he continued. "We haven't spoken about Ladd's little brother and sister. It was nice of you to stay with them last night. You know they'll be living with me?"

The subject surprised her, as did his tone. He sounded like they were having a regular conversation over dinner.

A click and she heard the TV. She could smell the newspaper even before the rustle of the pages. She cocked her head, thinking over the discussion they'd had that morning. If they explored a 24/7 relationship, a lot of their days when he was home would be exactly like this.

Peaceful, with them still talking as they always did. Enjoying each other's company while continuing with the power dynamics that fit them so well.

She grinned. "Kimber told me she thought you'd change your mind as soon as you met her. That she'd try to be good, but everyone says she's a handful."

"Is she?"

Hmm...how can I put this? "She's spirited. And a little defensive until she gets to know you. But she's amazing with her little brother, and she talks about Heath like he's a superhero. I think you'll love her."

"I don't doubt it. I just wanted to be prepared." He smoothed his hand over her hair. "I'd appreciate you coming around when you can to help them settle. The transition might be easier since they know you a little."

"I'd love to, Sir."

"I won't order you to move in with me, though the idea's not really a stretch since we've already touched on the subject of marriage and children."

She could picture him grinning and shaking his head with amusement. She let out a happy sigh. "I won't move in, but I may stay so often, it won't make a difference."

"That sounds like a plan."

"As for children, I think the three we've got are enough for now." She rubbed her cheek against his thigh, so content she could remain here all day, without complaint. If not for the promise of another scene. She wasn't in a rush though.

Dominik barked out a laugh. "Not sure you want to claim Heath as your son, pet. You could end up a grandmother before you're thirty."

"All right, now you're going too far, mister."

"Excuse me?"

Oops. She bit her lip. There was no need to ask what she'd gone wrong. They might be having a casual conversation, but he'd been very clear about her showing respect. And there was never an appropriate time to call your Dom "mister."

"I'm sorry, Sir."

"You will be," he said pleasantly. "You just earned your first real punishment."

Chapter Twenty

"**R**eal punishment" could mean so many things. As Dominik hauled her up to her feet, Sahara went over all the ones she'd seen dished out at the club. She'd only experienced a "real" one once herself.

From Dominik, actually. She'd been mouthy to several club Masters because she was feeling lost and frustrated, and as the Dungeon Monitor, Dominik had taken her in hand. He'd proved spankings were good for more than foreplay, and there had been no playfulness involved like when Pischlar had smacked her ass.

Sahara wasn't afraid of Dominik, but his creativity made her a little nervous. He'd been known to make subs kneel on rice. Or count it. Holding up books or boots with arms outstretched was another of his signature penalties. If a sub got spanked, she was getting off easy.

The spanking he'd given her in the shower had been more funishment than anything. She knew the difference. And, while Dominik didn't seem angry with her, she had a feeling he wasn't playing games.

He brought her to the armchair, the one closest to the window by the feel of the sun on her back. After she sat down, he moved away from her. She heard water being poured. A glass set on the coffee table. Plastic being ripped.

"Open your mouth, pet. Good girl." She heard the smile in his tone when her lips immediately parted. "Now, stick out your tongue. This may be unpleasant."

A few drops and the nasty taste of hot sauce spread over her taste buds, setting them on fire. Her eyes teared as she swallowed and tried scraping her tongue with her teeth to lessen the burn. She sucked in air with her mouth open, but nothing helped.

You evil bastard! She panted, reaching around to find the glass. "Water, please, Sir!"

He chuckled and took her hand, pressing the glass against her palm. "Are you sure?"

"Yes!" She gulped down the water. It only made the burning worse. "*Ugh!*"

Using a tissue, he dried the spill under her lips. "Tell me what you did wrong, and I'll give you something that'll help. This will be a mild punishment, but hopefully one you won't soon forget."

"I shouldn't have called you 'mister.'" She sniffled as her nose started to run. "I'm sorry! I was joking, but I went too far!"

A tiny rip, of paper this time, and Dominik pressed his thumb against her bottom lip. "Open wide."

She whimpered, not sure she wanted to after what had happened last time. Only, she wanted to prove to him that she could take whatever he dished out. He wouldn't push her past what he thought she could take. Just saying she trusted him meant nothing if she balked the second he tested her.

Opening her mouth, she braced for something nasty, but instead, tasted the sweetness of strawberry candy. She chewed on the little gummy treats and the flames from the hot sauce retreated.

"More?"

"Yes, please, Sir." Sahara chewed on the candy he fed her, relief filling her as the lingering nasty taste disappeared. But, more importantly, Dominik was cupping her cheek, and she could sense his approval in his relaxed touch.

"My good girl. I'm impressed." He shifted closer, sliding an arm under her legs and the other behind her shoulder, lifting her. "I expected you to balk. Maybe tell me to go fuck myself."

Her eyes widened behind the blindfold. She quickly shook her head. "I wouldn't do that. You asked for respect, Sir."

"I did. And you slipped up, but you weren't trying to be rude, so we'll keep the punishment small this time."

"*Small?*" She probably shouldn't have said that out loud, but Dominik only laughed.

He carried her into the bedroom, dropping her lightly onto the bed. "Yes. Small. I picked up some cinnamon gum to go with the hot sauce in case you came up with any more creative things to call me."

Bracing her hands behind her, Sahara cocked her head, doing her best to bite back a smile. Dominik anticipating bad behavior wasn't *that* funny. Just sorta kinda. She giggled. "You know me pretty well, Sir. I was tempted to tell you *exactly* what I thought of you."

"So why didn't you?"

"Well, first of all, I love your mother, so I won't insult her."

"Very wise."

No kidding? His dry amusement didn't fool her. Anyone, sub or not, would suffer for calling him a "son of a bitch" or slighting his mother in any way. She'd be an idiot to cross that line.

"Second...well, I asked for this. I don't mean the punishment—that too, but I mean what we're exploring today. I needed real from you." She smiled, resting back on the pillows. "I don't want it to end."

"Neither do I." His hands slid up her thighs and his fingers hooked to the edge of her panties. "If we continue this, there will be some discipline, but I'm more interested in the power exchange. And the pleasure."

"Mmm, I think we're on the same page." She sucked in a breath as he rubbed his bearded cheek against her inner thigh. "May I touch you, Sir?"

"Not now, pet. Hands up over your head. You may hold on to the pillow." He pressed a kiss to the top of her bare mound. Buzzing sounded from somewhere near her knee. "And try not to scream."

The buzzing became the vibration of something round gliding down her leg. She moaned as he settled the heavy vibrator right on top of her pussy before pressing her thighs together.

"Shh. Hold it right there. Good girl." Dominik rose over her, lifted her breasts out of her bra and above the neckline of her dress. "Your gorgeous breasts have been sadly neglected. Let's fix that, shall we?"

His big hands massaged her breasts. He lowered his mouth to one, using his tongue and his teeth and his lips. As her nipples were stimulated, over and over, the pulse beating in her clit threaded up to the sensitive nerve endings until it felt like the vibrations and the sucking and the pressure were everywhere at once.

A small climax hit her without warning, never letting her come down, but instead intensifying until she was gasping and bucking, riding the sensations to another peak. The pleasure spiraled around her core, tightening like a rubber band wound around and around until it snapped. Her second orgasm reverberated through her very bones, tensing all her muscles and stealing the air from her lungs.

She trembled with the force of the spasms deep inside her, her pussy so tender the vibrations became almost painful. When Dominik turned it off, the relief brought another shudder of ecstasy. She pressed her thighs together and rolled to her side, basking in the afterglow.

The darkness behind the blindfold glowed red, spinning and swaying. The bed didn't seem quite solid beneath her. She reached around for a way to steady herself and found Dominik's thick bicep as he laid down beside her. He held her close, grounding her even though she still felt a little floaty.

This was nice. She was suddenly exhausted, but in the satisfying way she got after a good workout. Fulfilling, like the energy had been well spent.

"You look worn out." Dominik kissed her temple. "Ready for a nap, my sunny girl?"

"Mmhmm." Sahara snuggled up close to him, but she couldn't let herself fall asleep just yet. "You probably have stuff to do, but I wish you could stay."

"I can grant that wish." He ran his hand over her hair, soft and steady, his petting sinking into the peaceful darkness. "I'm not going anywhere."

* * * *

The hours passed too fast, but Dominik made sure not a moment was wasted. After resting for about forty minutes, he'd gently woken Sahara for a lunch of finger foods he had sent up by room service.

He fed her every bite as she knelt by his side, her expression so dreamy, he was positive she was still half asleep.

But as he put earphones over her ears and danced with her around the room, she didn't miss a step. He could faintly hear Jason Mraz singing "I Won't Give Up." One of the few songs he had on his playlist simply because it was a beautiful song. But he could see a change in Sahara as she absorbed the powerful words.

She lifted her hand to push the earphones back.

He reached into his pocket to press pause.

"I'm sorry, Sir. I love this song, but…it's making me all emotional." She lowered her head, and if she hadn't been wearing the blindfold, she'd likely be staring at the floor. "I just need a minute."

This wasn't a scene, so she didn't have to say yellow to express the need to stop to talk things over, but he reacted in the same way he would if she had. He took the earphones from her and laid them on the bed with his iPod. Then he moved close to her again to remove the blindfold.

Her hands came up the second he untied the ribbon. Her eyes were wide as she stared up at him.

"We will continue, pet. But I need you to share what's going on in your head with me." He thought over the lyrics, wondering if any had hit a trigger, but came up blank.

She put her hand on his arm. Tugged her bottom lip between her teeth. Exhaled noisily. "The words just feel so true. Like something you'd say to me."

He smiled. She was right about that. "Which frightens you?"

"No." Her throat worked as she swallowed. "I love you. And that scares the hell out of me."

The words had an impact, but not one of shock or fear. He wasn't afraid to love her. If he really looked back, he'd probably reached that point months ago. Her father had been wrong about playing games, but he'd been right that this wasn't a new thing between them. Neither of them had been in a place to accept what they could have.

But they were now.

His only regret was that he hadn't said it first. He slid a hand over her cheek and into her hair, holding her gaze. "I don't blame you for being a little scared. The last time you gave someone your heart, you got hurt. There's nothing more important to me than keeping you from harm. I love you too, Sahara."

"You do?" She didn't sound surprised. Exactly. More like she hadn't dared hope he felt the same.

"I do." He tipped her chin up, kissing her softly, pleased when she pressed against him, wrapping her hands around the back of his neck. The scenes they did all required trust, but she could submit to him and still hold on to the most fragile part of herself. He wouldn't have asked for more until she let him in.

But she had given herself to him in every way. And from the moment she'd first put her head on his chest and accepted his comfort, he'd been headed in the same direction. Slowly under the weight of his own uncertainty, but all that mattered was that he was here.

He took her hand. "Dance with me."

She grinned, lacing her fingers with his. "Isn't that what we were doing?"

"Yes, but not with the blindfold. Not as part of a playful scene. Just me and you." He leaned down and brushed his lips over hers. "To our song."

Nodding, she drew away from him. She picked up his iPod and hooked it up to the speaker alarm on the nightstand. Then she pressed play.

The song started from the beginning. She slipped into his arms and he held her close. Swaying to the music, he smiled, leaning down to press his cheek to hers. And he sang to her so she knew, without a doubt, that he meant every word.

Chapter Twenty One

Late that night, after having dinner with Heath and his siblings, and then helping Heath put his little brother and sister to bed, Sahara followed Dominik back to the room, not sure she'd ever been happier in her life. Granted, they'd planned a day of complete submission, but what they'd explored between them encompassed so much more than her accepting him as her Master.

He loved her.

She wanted to shout the words out loud—had ever since she'd truly accepted that she loved him—but fear of being alone in feeling that way had kept her silent. Until she'd looked into his eyes and seen he was with her. Even if she hadn't said the words out loud, his every touch, every smile, told her she wouldn't regret giving him her love.

If they went into the room and climbed right into the bed to sleep, today would still be perfect. This amazing, gentle, powerful man was hers. He kept all those he cared for, which was part of what made him so wonderful, but he still made her feel special. Like he'd guarded a part of himself that was a little more battered and bruised, but he'd let her past those shields because he needed her to stand there with him.

Nothing in the world meant more to her than proving she was worthy. That she was strong enough to protect the part of him that couldn't take losing more than he already had.

In the bedroom closet, she grabbed a nightgown from her suitcase and brought it to the bed. She reached back to unzip her dress. "I don't know anything about the high schools in Dartmouth, but Becky or Silver might know a good day care for Bran. He's such a sweet little boy, but I think he needs to be around other kids his age. He whispers when he speaks. He should be—"

"He talks to you?" Dominik rose from where he'd been riffling through the black bag that had fallen on the other side of the bed during their nap. "I agree, he's adorable. And very well-behaved. But he makes Ladd seem outspoken."

Sahara had hardly noticed how little the Ladd brothers had spoken, considering how well Kimber filled the silence. She thought back on the few times Bran had said anything. He'd been shy with Dominik at first, but then he'd let Dominik put him in the high chair—he was so tiny, there was no way he could reach the table without one—and he'd nodded or shaken his head when Dominik filled his plate.

But it was either Sahara or Kimber he'd asked for anything from. Twice he'd touched Sahara's arm and asked to go to the bathroom. Heath had gotten up and offered to bring him, but the poor toddler seemed almost as intimidated by his brother as he was by Dominik.

Kimber had cleared that up when they'd brought Bran to the woman's bathroom.

"Our foster parents were nice, but they were really strict. I'm old enough that I did my own thing, but Bran just wanted to make them happy. Greg—our foster dad—was a big guy. When he yelled, all the kids would hide. Except for Bran. He'd sit there, all quiet, and color. People forgot he was there."

Sahara's heart broke for the little boy. At his age, he should be making noise, asking questions, making a mess. Instead, he was constantly watching the adults around him, afraid to draw attention to himself.

She tried to keep her tone level. "Did they ever hit him?"

"No! You think I would let that happen?" Kimber folded her arms over her chest. "There were six of us. Bran wasn't even the youngest. Our foster mom had two babies to take care of. When I wasn't at school, I took care of Bran."

"But when you weren't there...?"

"She kept him clean. Fed him." Kimber hunched her shoulders. "She knew he wouldn't be there forever, so she didn't let him get attached to her. And the dad worked a lot. I don't know...I think things would have been better if our real mom hadn't died. She was nice. She used to brush my hair and tell me Daddy

loved me. I think she believed it. He wasn't around much, so I don't think he loved any of us. He wasn't at her funeral."

Damn it, these kids had been through so much. Sahara wanted to hug Kimber, but the girl held herself stiff and proud, glaring in a way that made it clear she'd see any affection as pity.

"I miss her. She was sick all the time, but she tried. Dad didn't. I'm happy he's in jail. I hope he stays there."

Nodding slowly, not sure how to respond, Sahara went to the door when she heard Bran trying to open it. The little boy might not talk much, but he was very independent. She held out her hand and he smiled up at her as he took it.

"Do you miss your nanny? There's been a lot of big changes, huh?" She bit back a grin when Bran shrugged. The kid was just like his big brother.

Kimber snorted. "She was nice enough, but Bran never got close to her. He never really got close to anyone 'cept me."

Bran smiled. "Kimber's my mommy."

"Kimber's your sister, sweetie." Sahara lowered to pick Bran up, hating how confused he looked. "But you have lots and lots of people who care about you. And her."

"He's not wrong. I'm kinda like his mom." Kimber stuck close to Sahara's side, speaking low. "I named him, you know. I taught him everything. So it's my fault if he's messed up."

"He's not messed up. Trust me, sweetie. Things are going to get better." She had to lighten the mood before they got back to the table. She braced Bran on her hip and put her arm over Kimber's shoulders. "Bran is a good name. Is it Australian?"

The girl laughed. "No, it's from Game of Thrones! I've read all the books. My foster parents wouldn't let me watch it, but I caught a few episodes online."

Bran's little hand pressed against Sahara's cheek. "I like the wolves."

"That's wonderful!" Sahara arched a brow at Kimber, who ducked her head abashedly. She might not realize the show wasn't appropriate for a girl her age, but she was well aware that her little brother shouldn't be watching it. "We'll find you some wolves. Are you ready for dessert?"

They'd gotten close to the table, so Bran had shrugged and hidden his face in the crook of her neck. He never did say what he wanted for dessert, so Dominik had gotten him small servings of several different things Kimber said he liked.

He'd taken tiny bites while sitting on Sahara's lap. Maybe he had been extremely quiet, but she hadn't been overly concerned about it at the time. He hadn't shut down completely; he was just slow about letting people in.

The more secure he felt, the better he'd adapt. And she'd damn well make sure that the little boy, that both kids, knew they were safe and cared for.

"Sahara, are you all right?"

Glancing over at Dominik, Sahara smiled. "Yeah, I was just thinking about Bran. He'll be fine."

"Yes, he will be. But you look somewhere between angry and determined. Is there something I need to know?" Dominik abandoned the straps he'd been securing to the bathroom door—she wasn't sure she wanted to know what those were for—and stepped up to her, wrapping an arm around her waist. "If either of them was abused, we'll need to look into therapy."

"More neglect than abuse I think, but it would be good for them to see someone... What are you doing?"

Dominik flashed her one of his particularly evil smiles. "Preparing to torture my sweet little pet. I figured you'd want to get out of that dress first since you've got chocolate stains on the front...and the shoulder from the looks of it."

She looked down and groaned as she saw the smears of melted chocolate ice cream. "Why didn't you tell me? I look like a slob!"

"You looked like you were carrying a three-year-old. And he was holding on to you so tight, no one saw a thing until we left their room. Which means only Ladd and me." He held out his hand, drawing her to him and bending down to lay an openmouthed kiss on her shoulder. "This flavor is delicious."

She shivered, her thoughts shifting from the worries for tomorrow to all the possibilities for tonight. When Dominik peeled off her dress and let it fall to the floor, her pulse sped up. He picked up the wrist cuffs he'd removed earlier and left on the nightstand, then crooked his finger.

Inching closer to him, she offered up her wrists.

"Very soon, we will find a collar to match these." Dominik secured the cuffs around her wrists. "You will be fully restrained tonight, but with a hard enough tug, these will give."

Nodding, she took a moment to admire the way the cuffs looked on her wrists. They were snug enough that she could only slip a single finger under them, made of quality leather that was downy soft on the inside. The color of red wine with an intricate tooled pattern. But beautiful as they were, it was the weight of them on her wrists that she loved the most.

Dominik led her over to the closed door with the black straps. He clipped her wrist cuffs to a metal clip above her head on the thin ones, then lengthened the thicker ones and secured the padded loops around her upper thighs.

"Feet parted. Very pretty." His soothing tone was deep with approval. "I will put the blindfold on you. And a small gag. It may be uncomfortable at first, but I need silence so I won't miss any of the instructions."

Instructions? She frowned at him as he grabbed a small black ball gag from the bag and returned to her.

He grinned. "I won't take your ability to hear just yet, so you'll understand soon enough."

The gag tasted awful, but the worst thing was not being able to ask him what the little pink rubber starfish he had was for. She really should have taken a look at what he had in that bag. He might have gotten rid of most of his sex toys when he'd questioned his desire to be in the lifestyle, but he'd certainly have no trouble restocking his collection.

He grabbed his tape from his sports bag. "This squeaks, so it will be taped to your hand. We wouldn't want you to drop it. One squeak for yellow. Multiple for red—unless I'm asking you a direct question. Then one for yes and two for no. Understood?"

All right, that sounded good. She still had a way to communicate with him. She squeezed the starfish once.

"Perfect." He brought the blindfold up to cover her eyes. A knock sounded at the door. "And excellent timing."

Who the hell is that? She swallowed hard, recalling his question about adding another Dom. Since she couldn't see, she'd have no idea who it was. Unless they spoke.

Of course, they would speak, wouldn't they? Dominik hadn't done anything to stop her from hearing. And he'd want to make sure she was comfortable with whomever...

No, he'd expect her to trust him. To submit to whomever *he* trusted enough to bring into their bedroom.

She didn't really like the idea of anyone else touching her, but this wasn't about what she wanted. Maybe Dominik needed to bring another Master in to experience a threesome without the loss he'd experienced in the past. He didn't share, but Doms had so many different reasons for sceneing with others.

Accepting his felt natural. She forced herself to steady her breaths and calm her racing pulse. She heard the footsteps coming closer. More than two sets.

At least she wasn't naked. Yet.

"*Mon Dieu*, doesn't she look pretty like that." The voice was familiar, but she couldn't place it as her heart started pounding, despite all her efforts to relax. "We need to pick up some of those straps. They're perfect for traveling."

Sahara's brain finally caught up with what was happening.

The Dom was Landon Bower. Silver's fiancé.

No. Hell no!

Shaking her head, she squeezed the starfish over and over and over.

* * * *

Dominik knew exactly why Sahara was squeaking "red," but he still immediately removed the gag, making a hushing sound when he saw she was panting. He hadn't expected her to have such a strong reaction—maybe he should have. She was nothing if not loyal, and she had a terrible habit of expecting the worst.

"Deep breaths, pet. Talk to me."

"I'm sorry, Sir, but I can't. If you need to have a threesome, I'll let it happen, but please, not with him. Silver will hate me." She took a deep breath, automatically following his orders even though she still sounded panicked. "There's no way she's okay with this."

True, Silver wasn't the type to accept her Doms playing with anyone else. He'd even overheard a few rumors about her initial insecurities with Bower and Richter exploring their sexual attraction to one another.

But what he found interesting was the way Sahara said she would "let it happen" if he wanted a threesome. She would submit to whomever he chose to add to their scenes—barring a man in a relationship—but sex with two men wasn't something she wanted or needed.

He wouldn't lie. That pleased him.

"Bower's here to show me a few tricks, pet. He won't touch you at all." He grinned when she let out a sigh of relief. Behind him, both Bower and Richter chuckled.

"Oh. Then I'm sorry. I didn't mean to—"

"No need to be sorry. I should have anticipated your reaction." He kissed her cheek. "If it helps, Dean is here as well. I doubt he'd be comfortable watching you and me play with his man."

She giggled, completely at ease now. "You never know. Max would enjoy it."

Cheeky. He grinned, happy to see the unpleasant surprise hadn't ruined their scene.

Richter cleared his throat. "I'm here *because* neither Dominik nor Silver are comfortable with Landon touching you. If you're going to be cheeky, we might discuss how a flogger doesn't count."

Sahara pressed her teeth into her bottom lip. "I'm sorry, Sir."

Many Doms weren't comfortable with other Masters disciplining their subs, but considering how often Dominik had dealt with Silver at the club as Dungeon Monitor, it seemed only fair. Besides, if he was going to bring Sahara to the club, she'd have to learn how to interact with the Masters there.

Thankfully, Richter seemed satisfied, so Dominik wouldn't have to put his plans on hold to watch Sahara being flogged.

Instead, she could spend a few moments wondering what the hell he and the other two Doms were up to.

"Feeling better now, pet? I can put the gag back in and we can continue, or I can release you and—"

"No, Sir. I'm good, Sir. We can continue." The edges of her lips were twitching, like she was trying very hard not to smile. "Please."

Replacing the gag, Dominik ran his knuckles down her cheek to comfort her, then turned to Richter and Bower. They were speaking low and Bower laughed at something Richter said. He reached for Richter's tie.

"If you think I'm sitting here half naked while you're fully dressed, you've gotten too many pucks to the head, Landon." Richter shoved Bower's hands away and stood. "Lose the T-shirt."

This should be interesting. Dominik folded his arms over his chest and watched the big goalie peel off his black T-shirt. There was nothing submissive about the gesture, or the expectant look he gave Richter after tossing his shirt on the bed.

"Come on, Dean." Bower hooked his thumbs into the pockets of his jeans. "Don't be shy."

"Fuck off." Dean shook his head and sighed, loosening his tie. He muttered something to himself, then pulled it off and removed his black suit jacket. "I've never been on the receiving end of a demonstration. Do not rush me."

"I've never asked you to be on the receiving end of anything other than a blow job. Play nice and maybe we can negotiate one for later."

Both Richter and Sahara inhaled sharply. Dominik inspected the carpet near the foot of the bed. Sahara had missed a few spots when she vacuumed.

"We've got Mason blushing. Let's get this over with. I can show him plenty with just your shirt off." Bower set the large metal case he'd brought with him on the bed beside Richter as the other man removed his white dress shirt. "I have a fresh set of electrodes you can use, and there's two different kinds of gel. We'll stick with simple stimulation this time, but if you enjoy it, I'm doing a demo at the club this summer."

Dominik nodded, relieved that they were getting to the actual instructions. He didn't have issues with man-on-man action, but Richter was his boss, and he tried not to think too much about what he and the team's star goalie did in the bedroom. Their interactions were making it difficult not to get a very clear mental picture.

"I won't suck his dick in front of you, Mason. Don't worry." Bower slapped Dominik's shoulder and grinned. "Now, see how hard his nipples are?"

Richter snorted and braced his hands behind him on the bed. "Landon, stop toying with the poor man. You're edging on sadistic pleasure at his discomfort."

"I am, aren't I?" Bower picked up the gel and squirted it right on Richter's chest. His lips slanted in a crooked smile when Richter cursed. "Putting the gel directly on the electrodes is less messy, but the reaction from the cold can be enjoyable."

The lesson continued, first with nipple stimulation, which had Richter breathing hard and fisting his hands in the duvet. Bower explained all the safety rules as he raised the voltage. Once he'd reached a certain level, Richter's back bowed and he yanked the electrodes off his chest and punched Bower in the stomach.

Not hard enough to do any damage, but enough to show his displeasure. He glared at the younger man. "You're going to fucking pay for that. He doesn't need a demonstration of how the TENS can be used for punishment."

"Sorry, man. I got carried away." Bower smirked, then shoved Richter onto his back on the bed. "I'll be gentler."

Dominik wasn't sure if the two men would fight, or fuck, when they returned to their room, but he was damn eager to try the electric stimulation on Sahara. He checked on her as Bower unzipped Richter's pants—despite the GM's protests—and was pleased to see she was enjoying the auditory stimulus. Her cheeks were bright pink and she appeared to be paying very close attention to the two other men's exchange.

Bower glanced over at Dominik, drawing his attention back to the demo. He had four electrodes set in a wide square on Richter's pelvis. "Normally, with a man, I would suggest this formation on his ass, but I won't push it. I like my balls where they are." He chuckled when Richter grunted at him. "But if you remember what I said about how the electricity pulses in the muscles, you'll find sensitive spots all over the body can be toyed with."

This time, Bower kept the setting reasonably low, but it was still enough to make Richter's muscles contract and release. Richter's erection strained against his pants. He slammed his fist on the bed.

"Enough." Richter inhaled roughly when Bower removed all the electrodes. "I hope this has been helpful, but I'm done. Come to the club demo. Silver will be the victim on display and she rather enjoys it. I don't."

Once Richter had his shirt back on and buttoned up, Dominik held out his hand. "I appreciate both your help. Thank you. And I'll see you before the game tomorrow."

Richter inclined his head as he shook Dominik's hand. "Enjoy your night."

The GM left without another word while Bower was still cleaning up his equipment. Dominik frowned when the other man handed him a pack of fresh electrodes.

"Hey, don't worry. We're good. He probably wishes I was a sub so he could beat my ass." Bower stretched his arms over his head and cracked his knuckles. "But he'll forgive me by the end of the night."

"That's good to hear." Dominik latched on to Bower's hand and pulled him in for a quick hug. "Thanks again. From both of us."

After seeing Bower out, Dominik grabbed a chair from beside the small table and brought it to the bedroom. Placing it beside Sahara, he watched her from the corner of his eye, assessing whether or not she was prepared for the actual scene.

Her breathing was steady, her muscles were relaxed, and there was a peaceful expression on her face. She knew what was going to happen since she'd heard all of Bower's instructions.

And she wasn't worried.

Bower's demonstration on how the TENS could be used for punishment was interesting, but Dominik wanted it to be a tool of pleasure with Sahara. He might spank her for discipline, but on the whole, he'd avoid pain as a penalty. Pain could add a nice edge to pleasure, and he hoped they could explore that at some point. But he'd have to be careful with his approach.

He attached the fresh electrodes and covered them with gel, one at a time. Once he'd laid them all on the chair, he placed his hands on Sahara's sides, stroking her warm flesh as he kissed her shoulder.

"We're alone, sunshine. I'm going to take off your bra, then put the electrodes on you. They shouldn't be too cold since the gel is already on them."

She smiled and nodded.

"I will increase the voltage very, very slowly. Just for this, we'll change what the squeaks mean. One tells me the bite of electricity is reaching your limit. Several means I've gone too far. Which shouldn't happen." He reached behind her to remove her bra. Then decided he was an idiot. He'd left it on to give her a sense of modesty in front of Bower and Richter, but stripping a cuffed sub wasn't very practical.

Cutting the straps wasn't an option, since she'd mentioned she only had two bras. He could simply lift her breasts out of the cups, but would that be comfortable?

He'd ask, but she was settled nicely into a passive headspace. He felt along the straps, then found a spot where the hook of the strap could be removed.

There we go. Not so difficult if you use your brain, Mason.

Fine, he felt like an idiot, but at least his fumbling hadn't been noticed. Sahara wiggled as her bra came off, sticking out her chest as though aching to be touched.

He stroked both her breasts, eager to get started. But one thing still worried him.

The TENS would be a good tool to experiment with, but he had no idea of the sensation. He'd experienced the lick of the flogger and the whip. He'd been struck with a paddle and a cane. But he'd never had electricity used on him. Even for an injury. He'd been lucky.

"A few more minutes and we'll begin, my sunny girl." He picked up two of the pads, recalling Bower's instructions, and placed them on his forearm. The gel had warmed to room temperature and the thumb-sized pads looked harmless.

He turned the knob on the TENS. Felt nothing.

A little more and there was a slight buzz. He watched the numbers as he increased the pulse. Then the voltage.

Finally, the pulse was high enough that his muscles tensed on their own. A bit more and his whole hand closed. More.

Too much. He ground his teeth and quickly lowered the voltage. The pain was different, like a sharp jolt which had made his muscles jerk. He left the electrodes on at a bearable level and checked the numbers on the display. Sahara might not be able to take even this much, but at least he had an idea of the sensation.

He put a fresh dab of gel on the pads and carefully placed them on either side of her nipples. Then he did the same with the other two pads.

Sahara twitched, even though the pulse wasn't even turned on. His girl was a little nervous.

Grinning, he kissed her cheek. *This is going to be fun.*

Chapter Twenty Two

The tingles in Sahara's nipples continued, long after the electrodes were moved. In the darkness behind the blindfold, she imagined she could see the sparks, even though the part of her mind that wasn't lost in sensation told her that was impossible.

Several of the things she felt were impossible though. Still bound, she drifted in and out of the restraints. Not quite floating, but like she wasn't quite solid. Only Dominik's touch seemed to make her real. The slightest brush of his fingers and all her nerves flared to life.

"Where are we at, Sahara?" Dominik's tone reached deep into the darkness, like the sun shining into the clear sea. "Open and close your empty hand if you're ready to continue."

Sahara took a minute to become aware of her body again. Her arms were a little sore from being up for so long, but not too bad yet. The gag wasn't pleasant, and she couldn't wait for it to come out—still, not worth stopping for.

She opened and closed the hand without the squeaky starfish.

"I can tell you considered your answer. Good girl." Dominik brushed his knuckles down her cheek. "You'll feel cold metal against you. Don't be afraid."

The metal touched her hip. A snip and the fabric of her panties parted. The same on the other side and they were pulled away.

Dominik slid two fingers down her belly, then over her slick pussy. He made a soft sound of pleasure as he circled her clit with his fingertips. "So wet. I won't wait much longer to take you, pet."

Tipping her head back, Sahara focused all her attention on his fingers as they dipped into her, teasing her until her knees trembled and she gasped around the gag. Between Dominik's words and the nipple stimulation and now his fingers, she needed a release more than she needed air.

His fingers left her. The straps on her thighs tugged upward, lifting her off her feet, baring her to him completely.

He moved away from her. Returned and cool liquid spilled down over her exposed back hole. The blunt head of something smooth pressed against her. She pushed to let it in, swallowing back whimpers of discomfort as the form thickened, stretching her more and more before finally settling inside at the narrowed base.

"Almost done. Don't forget to let me know if the charge is too high," Dominik reminded her before placing small, sticky...electrodes. Four of them, two on each butt cheek. "Here we go."

Rhythmic pulsing, reaching deep, flowing through her muscles and making them clench. The butt plug seemed to grow as her insides tightened around it. Her body swayed when she writhed with the sensation.

"Perfect." Dominik moved between her thighs and slid the thick head of his dick up and down between her folds. He positioned himself at her center and sank in, an inch at a time. "Fuck, you feel good."

Good didn't begin to describe the feeling. She was so full, so desperate for movement. For him. She needed him closer, riding the never-ending pleasure with her, taking her over and over until he was completely sated. He'd spent so much time giving her pleasure, she had to return the favor.

But she was powerless to do anything but let him take whatever he wanted from her. Which was exactly as he'd planned it.

Holding her hips, he used the straps to swing her toward him. He leaned in, kissing her neck, his hot skin moistening with sweat as he moved her onto him faster and faster.

His dick drove into her and dragged out with each movement of the swing. The electrodes had fallen away at some point, but her muscles still clenched around the plug. Her cunt squeezed him as he drove into her, and the ache for release intensified until she teetered on the ledge.

A deep, powerful thrust tossed her over into a pool of pure fucking ecstasy. Dominik found his release deep within while she undulated around him. He pressed his cheek to hers, his breath rough as he held her. With his arms wrapped around her in a firm embrace, she rode the current of bliss until it receded to a gentle, lapping wave.

Completely spent, Sahara tried to lift her head as Dominik reached behind her to remove the gag, but her body refused to cooperate. The butt plug came out next and her whole body bowed. Fuck, she was tender down there. And even though she'd been held up by the straps the entire time, she felt like she'd run a marathon. Staying on her feet when he lowered her thighs was a challenge, but when he released her cuffs from the straps, she realized all her bones and muscles had gone liquid.

She struggled to stand on her own, but Dominik took one look at her and chuckled. He scooped her into his arms. "You're a little unsteady, my sunshine. Let me take care of you."

He carried her to the bed and laid her down. The unexpected brightness made her squint; she'd been wearing the blindfold so long she'd completely forgotten about it. But having the thick cloth gone was a relief.

Dominik's golden eyes, his gentle smile, comforted her as her eyes adjusted. She smiled and let out a quiet sigh of pleasure as he bent down to give her a slow, undemanding kiss. He was just as naked as she was, but she was blissfully worn out and just really wanted to fall asleep in his arms.

"Are you coming to bed, Sir?" Sahara rolled to her side, deciding she absolutely loved this bed. Nice, cool sheets. A heavy duvet. The only thing that would make it better would be if Dominik would come cuddle. "You need your rest—you've got a game tomorrow."

"I'll be with you in a minute." Dominik disappeared into the bathroom and she heard the water running. He returned with a washcloth and used it to clean her. Everywhere.

Finally, Dominik stretched out beside her and pulled her to nestle against his side with her head on his shoulder. He idly trailed his fingers up and down her arm, and she tipped her head up to see him gazing down at her.

"Is something wrong, Sir?" He didn't look upset, but it would probably be good to talk over their day before they both fell asleep.

"Wrong? No. But I'd like to hear how you feel about your 'prize.'" He shifted over, leaving one arm under her head, making it a bit easier for her to meet his eyes. "Was there anything you absolutely hated? Something you hope to do again?"

"Nothing I hated...I wasn't crazy about how I reacted when I heard Landon though. I should have known you'd never put me in a position to betray my friends."

"True, but it was a very honest reaction. For all you knew, Silver had been involved in the decision and both of her Doms were free to play with whomever they chose. You've seen those dynamics at the club, but you didn't even consider the possibility." He didn't look like he minded in the least. "You weren't comfortable, and you didn't hesitate to let me know."

So...a good thing? She'd learned not to guess with him, so she considered her question carefully. "But if we're in a full-time BDSM relationship, shouldn't I find a way to be comfortable with what you ask of me?"

"Once we've been at this long enough for me to know what limits I can push, maybe. There's a ways to go before we reach that point."

"But other Doms won't touch me."

"Not if it's a hard limit. Unless you're being punished." He slid his hand up to the hair that had slipped over her shoulder and gave it a little tug. "I enjoy being part of the community, and I intend to continue as a Dungeon Monitor at the club. I'm often involved in disciplining naughty subs, as are the other monitors. But if you're on your best behavior, you'll have nothing to worry about."

She would definitely try, but she wouldn't make promises she couldn't keep. "I'll do my best to make you proud, but if I mess up, I'll accept whatever punishment I've earned."

"Yes, you will." He bent down to kiss her. "I don't expect perfection, but nothing irritates me more than a badly behaved sub who acts out, then bitches about the consequences. I don't see that being a problem for you though. You've had your bratty episodes, but you accepted your punishment gracefully."

"Crying like a baby after isn't exactly graceful."

"I disagree. Tears can be a release you need. And I have absolutely no problem fulfilling that need." His lips slanted when she rolled her eyes at him. "You're not surprised?"

"Nope. I know a few mean ol' Doms."

"Who are you calling old?" Dominik attacked her ribs with his fingers. She squealed helplessly, trying to wiggle free. He put his hand over her mouth. "Shh. It's late. People are sleeping."

"That was not nice." Sahara stuck her tongue out at him as he relaxed onto the pillows with his eyes closed.

"Sticking out your tongue at your Dom is not smart."

Nibbling at her bottom lip to keep from giggling, Sahara lowered her head back to his shoulder. She loved playing with him, but he really did need his sleep. If the Cobras won tomorrow night, they'd be one game away from eliminating the Islanders.

She didn't hate the team, but she was eager to get a break from anything connected to Grant or New York. As much as she loved the city, she needed some distance from her parents. Maybe then she'd figure out what kind of relationship she'd have with each of them. Separately.

Her father had seemed weak last night, but considering how much her mother's biting remarks and her careless attitude had hurt after just a short time with her, how damaging would dealing with that every day be? When her father had been constantly on the road with his team, he'd spent so little time with his wife, he'd likely only seen her perfect, practiced mask. The one that had smiled so brightly for the camera.

Once the divorce was finalized, her father would have a chance at real love. And her mother... Well, Sahara wouldn't hold her breath. She'd wait a bit to call her and take it from there.

You have your own life to live. Sahara rested her hand on Dominik's bare chest to feel his heartbeat against her palm. She still couldn't believe how lucky she was.

Falling in love was easy. But finding someone who cared about what made you smile or frown? Whose touch was always tender and always wanted you near? Who listened to your dreams and your fears? Or just really *listened* to what you had to say…?

She'd only ever dreamed of a man like him. And now, her dreams were a reality.

Chapter Twenty Three

The bakery was small, with the glass display taking up more of the space than the few tables scattered along the floor-to-ceiling windows, but Dominik found himself and Sahara a seat in the corner that had just been vacated. While she went to the counter to talk to the elderly couple that ran the place, he quickly tossed out the napkins left on the table and picked up the empty coffee mugs.

"Oh, you don't need to do that, sir." The tiny Italian woman hurried over, fussing at him, a rag clenched in her small, age-spotted hands. "I'll give it a quick wipe. Give me those and sit!"

"Gina, don't yell at the customers!" her husband called out, laughing.

Gina took the mugs in one hand, scrubbing the table with the other. "He's not a customer; this is Sahara's young man." She looked him over, then gave a sharp nod. "I approve. You're a good-looking boy and you have kind eyes."

"Thank you, ma'am." Dominik caught Sahara whispering "Sorry" and shook his head. From what she'd told him, these people cared about her very much. He might not have impressed her mother, but maybe he'd get an actual chance to make a good impression here. "Sahara's told me all about your bakery. Everything looks and smells delicious."

The old woman preened. "Doesn't it? I make the pastries, but my husband bakes the bread, the cookies, and the muffins Sahara loves so much. What are you in the mood for, Mr. Mason?"

"Please, call me Dominik." The aroma of freshly baked bread made his mouth water, but he was too old to start indulging in empty calories. "With the game tonight, I need protein. The breakfast sandwich Sahara brought me the other day was amazing." He grinned at Sahara as she joined them.

"From the looks of you, one is not enough. I'll fix you two. With my special home fries." She patted his shoulder as he pulled out Sahara's chair. "Would you like some coffee? I know Sahara enjoys hers, but I haven't fed many hockey players. My son used to play rugby, and he would only drink orange juice or those disgusting blue drinks. Sometimes raw eggs, but I refuse to serve that here."

"Coffee is fine. I'll take mine black." He turned to Sahara once Gina headed back behind the counter. She was watching him, her brow furrowed slightly. "What is it?"

"You usually take two creams in your coffee."

She'd been paying attention. He grinned. "Yes, but not typically on a game day. I try to avoid any kind of dairy. A little cheese in the sandwich will be fine, but for some reason, my stomach does not appreciate certain foods if I'm going to be pushing my body to the limit."

"That's good to know. I won't forget." She inhaled slowly and lowered her voice. "I'm a little surprised Gina brought up her son. He died a few years back—he was part of a recovery unit in the Marines."

Dominik swallowed hard, thinking about Josh. His brother had just finished his fourth tour and he'd likely be heading back any day now. Hoping Josh might take a break or retire was pointless. After the third tour, even their mother had stopped begging him to give it up and just let her pride take over. Josh had avoided any serious relationships because his focus was entirely on the next mission, and he'd felt guilty enough leaving home when Cam was still young. If Josh ever had kids...?

Cam had once told Dominik their older brother had mentioned getting a vasectomy when he'd been drunk. Which wasn't all that surprising.

Their mother would be crushed if she found out, but so long as their sisters never found out, it would be Josh's secret.

Sahara touched the back of Dominik's hand. "I'm sorry, I shouldn't have brought that up. You're worried about Josh, aren't you?"

He shook his head and turned his hand to hold hers. "No, actually, I was thinking about kids."

"Is you biological clock ticking?" She grinned when he arched a brow at her. "We already have three—wait, I take that back. Two. Heath isn't a kid."

"He is, but we'll do just fine with them. I'm relieved that my mother has enough grandchildren to keep her happy."

He almost wanted to take the words back, considering too late that Sahara might think he never wanted children of his own. Whether or not it was early in the relationship for family planning, some women may consider that a deal-breaker.

Instead, Sahara cocked her head, nodding slowly. "She's proud of all her kids. I can see her wanting more little ones to cuddle, but seeing all her children living good lives seems to be the most important thing."

"Did she say anything about Cam?"

"Just that she thinks he's doing well working for the team. She didn't seem worried, but you could tell she had been."

"I still am." Dominik chuckled when Sahara frowned at the table like she was racking her brain for some way to make him feel better. "Hey, it's fine. Josh and I always worry about Cam. It's our job."

Conversation halted as breakfast was served, then continued on to more pleasant topics. Sahara told him about the Ice Girls' routine for the next game and how she and Akira had been working with the choreographer on a new song. He discussed his concerns about his manager and his thoughts on finding a replacement over the summer.

They were halfway through their meal before Sahara's phone went off. She blushed as she pulled it out. "Sorry, I didn't bother turning it off because not many people have my new number. Do you mind if I check if it's important?"

"Not at all." Dominik took out his own phone, which he hadn't turned off either. Despite their jokes about leaving their phones at home, it wasn't really practical. Neither of them was the type to have their phones constantly in their faces, so the issue was more about being understanding when a call or text did come in.

But by the expression on Sahara's face as she read the text, he was going to wish he'd told her to wait.

"It's Pischlar. He said it's important, and he wants to know if he can come meet us."

The "*us*" told Dominik this could be serious. Pischlar and Sahara were still friends; the man had a good reputation of keeping boundaries with his past lovers, but he had a carefree attitude that sometimes rubbed their teammates the wrong way. If given the choice, Pischlar would likely give Sahara some space to avoid causing friction between her and Dominik.

Dominik needed to hear what Pischlar had to say. He nodded at Sahara. "Tell him to come here. If he hasn't eaten yet, we'll make sure he does."

She let out a breath of relief and texted a reply.

No more than five minutes later, Pischlar came into the bakery. He glanced around, then came right to their table.

"I won't stay long." He reached into the stylish jean jacket he was wearing. Over nothing but jeans. He pulled out a thick envelope. "I'm so fucking sorry for—"

"Please sit." Gina dragged over a chair and smiled at Pischlar. "Oh, those holes in your ears must have hurt. Are you hungry? If you're Sahara's friend, I'll feed you well." She tilted her head to one side as Pischlar blinked at her. "You're one of those hockey players, aren't you? I'll feed you like I did Sahara's man."

Pischlar's cheeks reddened. He looked at Dominik. "I don't want to intrude."

"You're not. Sit. I'll feel better if I see you eat. You're a wreck lately, man." Dominik leaned back in his chair as Pischlar sat and laid the envelope on the table. "How are things going? Have you apologized to Richter?"

"Yeah." Pischlar rubbed a fresh bruise on his cheek with a wry smile. "Bower was there and he flipped out. I think that helped with negotiations. Richter said being punched more than once means there's no need to put me on the market. If the shit I pulled gets out, they won't get a fucking cent for me. My agent is happy. He about lost his mind when I said I might need to explore my options. Coming out the way I did hasn't made me very popular."

"I'll bet." Damn it, Pisch was a mess. And Dominik wasn't sure how to help him. Sahara had been one of many women the man had played with at the club, but there was only one person who could make Pischlar straighten up his act. But unless White returned Pischlar's feelings, there was no point in hoping he'd be of any use.

Sahara leaned across the table, hesitating to touch his hands until Dominik nodded to let her know it was okay. "What happened? Is White okay?"

"I wouldn't have bothered you about White." Pischlar stared down at his hands, then turned one to hold Sahara's. "The envelope will tell you everything. I think you should let Dominik look at it first."

Sahara drew away from Pischlar and hugged herself.

Dominik frowned. "Just tell us, Pisch."

Fisting his hands on the table, Pischlar sighed. "The woman who posted those death threats to Sahara on Facebook? Well, she was let out on bail the other day. And she sent me this." He put his hand over the envelope on the table. "It's a love letter. And a piece of Sahara's window seat. The woman confessed to breaking in to Sahara's house and chopping it up with an ax. She writes fan fiction about me and Demyan and got a little obsessed."

"A little?" Sahara rubbed her hand over her mouth as she went pale. "She was the one who commented on your picture, wasn't she? She used a different name for the threats, but unless there's more than one fan going nuts for you..."

"Hey, I'm not claiming the really crazy ones. Those are all Higgins's."

"They're not breaking in to Sahara's house," Dominik said dryly. "Where is this woman now?"

Pischlar's brow furrowed as he stared at the envelope. "She's been admitted for psychiatric care. Her father called my manager, who called me. The man said his daughter's always had issues, but they've been contained until now. Jail time won't help her. So I hired a lawyer to speak on her behalf. He's going to ask that she be committed. My manager found a great facility where she'll get the help she needs."

"That's nice of you, but why do all this for a woman who could have hurt Sahara?" Dominik reached out and took Sahara's hand. "There are other charitable causes you could focus on if you're feeling giving."

"Her father's a huge fan of the team, and he's been looking after her ever since she lost her husband and her baby in a car crash." Pischlar scowled at Dominik. "You're right, she deserved to rot in jail."

Nice going, Mason. Dominik shook his head. "Shit, I'm sorry, man. I didn't—"

"Don't worry about it." Pischlar sat back as his breakfast was served. "She's not the problem anyway. Higgins's lawyers got wind of this and they're pushing for his case to be thrown out, claiming that Sahara lied about him breaking in and now they have proof. It's all over the news, but I hoped you'd hear it from me first."

"Thank you, Pisch." Rising from his chair, Dominik held out his hand for Sahara. "We should get you back to the hotel where you'll be safe."

Sahara stood but hesitated. "Am I allowed to argue with you, Sir?"

Interesting question. If she'd been joking, he'd have said no, but she sounded very serious. "You're allowed to disagree with me. Why?"

With a bit of mischief in her eyes, she took his hands and pulled him back to his chair. "How did Gina put it?" She gave his hands a little tug. "Sit!"

"Sahara—"

"The danger hasn't changed and you need to eat. A sub's job is to take care of her Dom." She speared a potato with his fork and brought it up to his mouth. "I'm also aware I've probably earned a spanking."

Pischlar chuckled. "If you're lucky."

She stuck out her tongue. "You eat too."

"Careful, pet." Dominik grabbed her by the hips and sat her on his knee. "But you're right."

"So we can stay?" She fed him another potato before he could speak and giggled when he frowned at her. "Sorry."

"You're being a brat, but I appreciate the concern. And I suppose this news doesn't affect us right now." He hated how stressful things would be when they got back to Dartmouth. Sahara would have to speak to the police again. And the lawyers. She'd have to make sure they had enough evidence to try Higgins on domestic battery and assault. Relive the worst parts of her past again and again.

But there was no point in dwelling on what they'd face together when they got home.

So he wrapped his arms around Sahara's waist and rested his chin on her shoulder. "You're very lucky though."

She glanced back at him, confused.

He grinned, clearing things right up. "You're definitely getting spanked."

Chapter Twenty Four

The Cobras' win over the Islanders had been brutal but, most importantly, the game was coming back to home ice. Hopefully to eliminate New York and carry on to the second round.

In the three-day break from the last game, Sahara had enjoyed helping Dominik settle Heath and his siblings into their new home. New furniture had been delivered for Kimber, and several of the Cobras had spent the day painting the office Dominik had given up for her bedroom. Sahara could tell Dominik wasn't a fan of the dark red shade Kimber had chosen, but he was damn good at assuring the teen felt comfortable making the room into her own little sanctuary.

For the moment, Heath was sharing a room with his little brother, but when Dominik wasn't training or spending time with the kids, he was busy house shopping. Both nights since they'd gotten back to Dartmouth, he'd tucked the little ones in with Sahara, then sat up with her in his bed, asking her opinion of houses he'd found online.

He'd made his intentions very clear.

"I'm thinking we'll move in August. That gives the kids time to settle in before school starts. And you and I won't seem like we're rushing into living together."

"But you want me to help choose the house, so you're assuming we will *be living together?"* She couldn't help but tease him a little. He'd been very serious lately and she needed to see him smile. *"Have my cleaning skills met your standards then, Sir?"*

Dominik snorted, closing his laptop and setting it aside before pulling her on top of him. "Not yet, but you're getting there. Thankfully, your other talents make up for the odd sock I find under our bed."

"Our bed?"

"Yes. I've decided you belong here." *Dominik ran his hands up her bare thighs as she straddled him. "Do you object?"*

"No, Sir." *Her eyes drifted shut as he lifted her nightgown up over her head. "I feel like I belong here too."*

Life wasn't perfect, but it was pretty damn close considering everything else going on. The first day back, Sahara had spent hours with the district attorney, going over her statement and giving even more details about her past abuse. Grant's lawyers were pushing for a deal, and the DA had explained to Sahara exactly what that would mean.

If Grant pled guilty, he would be deported and serve six months in jail in New York. He'd have to go through anger management courses for thirty-six months after and wouldn't be eligible to request permission to return to Canada for five years.

His career would be over.

Sahara couldn't help feeling responsible, even though most people would think she was being stupid for taking any blame.

Thankfully, talking to Dominik helped her put everything in perspective.

"He fucked up his career, sunshine. You let him get away with what he did to you once—gave him two more years to play the game and get fucking therapy." *Dominik cupped her cheek in his hand and forced her to meet his steady gaze. "I'm grateful that you don't have the guilt of his other victims on your head. If he's let off the hook again, you will."*

In Dominik's bedroom, ironing her Ice Girls uniform for the game tonight, Sahara squared her shoulders, finding strength in the confidence Dominik gave her. This wouldn't be easy, but she wouldn't back down.

Hearing Kimber's bright laughter coming through the partially closed door, Sahara smiled. If Dominik's encouragement hadn't been enough, seeing Kimber's trusting gaze every day certainly was. The girl looked up to Sahara, which was scary and empowering all at once. Scary because she wasn't sure she could be the hero Kimber seemed to expect her to be. Empowering because there was no fucking way she'd let that sweet child down.

The noisy play from the other room quieted. Sahara put down the iron as she heard Bran's quiet sobs.

"Hey, buddy, don't cry." Dominik's tone was soft and soothing. "We were having so much fun with the cars, you didn't realize how badly you needed to go. We'll get you cleaned up and keep playing, okay?" Silence. Bran had likely nodded, because Dominik continued. "Can you get him a change of clothes, Ladd? I'll go run him a bath."

No worries. My man's got this covered. Sahara grinned as she continued ironing out every crease in her skirt. She used to send her uniform to the dry cleaners, but Dominik had decided to add laundry to her list of chores. He'd also told her, in no uncertain terms, that using the dry cleaners for anything that she could throw in the washing machine was cheating.

She didn't mind. Even though this was taking forever, she found the mindless task relaxing. And his warm approval when she completed each task was worth the extra effort.

The water stopped running. She could hear Bran giggling and splashing. That would please Dominik—he was always trying to make the boy smile. He'd also gotten the kid an excessive amount of toys, so Bran was probably in the water, up to his ears in bubbles, soaking Dominik and having a blast.

Ding! Ding! Ding!

"I'll get it!" Kimber called out.

The doorbell. Sahara stopped ironing, trying to think of who would be visiting right before they headed to the Forum for tonight's game. She heard the door open hard. Kimber let out a muffled scream.

"Where the fuck is she? Don't fucking move, Mason. I don't want to hurt the kid."

Grant. Sahara set down the iron and slipped quietly toward the door. She could see Dominik halfway across the room, facing Grant with his hands up. A few feet behind him, Heath stood in the doorway of the bathroom, looking back and forth between his little brother, who hadn't seemed to notice the shouting, and Kimber.

"You don't want to do this, Higgins." Dominik spoke calmly, but Sahara could see the rage in his eyes. If Kimber weren't in danger, Dominik would kill the other man.

"I want to talk to that fucking cunt."

Sahara pushed the door open all the way and cleared her throat. "I'm right here, Grant."

"You ruined me! I loved you, and you fucking ruined me!" Grant shoved Kimber toward Dominik and came at Sahara too fast for her to react. He spun her around with his hand on her throat, keeping her between himself and Dominik. "Move, and I'll snap her goddamn neck. I have nothing to lose, man."

The stench of alcohol came to Sahara with Grant's every heavy breath. He'd probably met with his lawyers, gotten plastered, and come straight here. She wasn't sure how he'd found Dominik's place, but she had to get him out.

"Grant, you're scaring the kids." She struggled to inhale past the pressure on her windpipe. "Please let me go. We can talk about this."

Grant let out a cold laugh. "Talk? What's the point? You're not going to drop the charges, and even if you did, my reputation is shit."

All right, getting him out wasn't going to be good enough. He'd beaten her unconscious when he was still at the beginning of a promising career. If he got her alone now, there was no telling what he'd do.

He loosened his grip on her throat a little though, so she took a deep breath, struggling to keep herself calm. "What do you want, Grant?"

The muscles of his chest tensed as he pulled her tight against him. He panted into her hair. "Just you. I lost everything because of you, and I'm not letting you go again."

Don't fucking bet on it, asshole. Sahara met Dominik's eyes. His jaw ticked.

She slammed her head back as hard as she could. Grant cursed and she dropped her weight to free herself, then drove forward into his knees.

He hit the wall hard, latching on to her hair before she could duck out of reach. She tried to knee him in the balls, but he blocked her, dragging her close as Dominik reached them.

Her eyes teared as she struggled to twist free. Her scalp stung with each sharp tug.

Self-defense had taught her to preserve her energy, but she couldn't help panicking with Grant's hands on her. Dominik couldn't reach her with Grant using her to shield himself. Maybe easily snapping necks was only in the movies, but if Grant kept jerking her head back, he'd do some serious damage.

He'd almost let her go when she'd struck him with the back of her head. Maybe she'd broken his nose. One more hit and he might let her go.

Squirming, she shoved her hand up into his face. Slick, warm blood covered her fingers as the heel of her palm reached his nose. Which had probably been broken so many times on the ice he wasn't feeling it as much as he should.

So she pressed up farther, jabbing her fingers into his eyes.

Wrenching back, Grant released her and brought his hands to his face. She crab-crawled out of reach.

Dominik pinned Grant to the floor. "Motherfucker, I should end you for this."

Before his fist came down, Heath grabbed his arm. "Just hold him there, man. The cops are on the way."

If Heath is here... Sahara pushed to her feet, wiping her bloody hands on her jeans. Was Bran alone in the bath? Where was Kimber? Had she seen—

"Sahara, they're fine," Heath said softly. "I got her into the bathroom with Bran as soon as the bastard was focused on you and Mason. Kimber took my phone and called 911."

Swallowing hard as her stomach twisted with nausea, Sahara stumbled into the kitchen. She still needed to see if the kids were all right. But not covered in blood. Shit, there was so much blood.

On her clothes too. She had to get changed. Her eyes teared.

Big hands settled on her shoulders. She jumped.

"It's me, my sunny girl." Dominik turned her in his arms and tipped her chin up. "Grant's been taken in. The nice detective has a few questions. Here, let me." He grabbed a paper towel and wet the edge under the running water. Then he gently wiped her cheek. "What did I say? My girl is tough."

"I don't feel tough." A shaky laugh bubbled up, but the sound was weak. She was breathing too fast and her heart was pounding out of her chest. "I feel like I want to curl up in a little ball and hide."

Dominik nodded slowly. "Yes, but when it counted, you didn't freeze up. You didn't hide. You were strong." He tossed the bloodstained paper towel in the sink and gathered her close. "Next time his face haunts you, remember that."

Resting her head on Dominik's chest, Sahara took a deep breath and nodded. She hadn't seen Grant's face, but she'd never forget the moment she'd managed to fight back.

And break free.

* * * *

Dominik packed his sports bag, dropping his gloves three times before he forced himself to stop and calm the fuck down. The cops had taken off over an hour ago, but he hadn't let himself lose it in front of Sahara or the kids.

Sahara was in the bedroom, getting ready for her performance on the ice. She had bruises on her neck, but the paramedic who had come along with the police had checked her out and said she was fine. So Sahara had simply showered—with him hovering close—then gone through the routine that seemed all too familiar. She had a palette of makeup she'd expertly applied until the marks almost disappeared.

He couldn't watch anymore. He longed for the fucking day she could throw all that extra makeup in the trash. For when the only bruises she'd have would be from knocking her shin on the coffee table or maybe landing hard on the ice after a spin.

He was so damn proud of Sahara, but he wasn't sure he'd ever get the image of her struggling in Higgins's hold while Dominik stood there, completely helpless, out of his head. If Ladd hadn't stopped him, he would have beaten Higgins to a bloody pulp minutes before the cops walked in.

If he had a fucking key to the man's cell, he'd go take him out now. He'd never craved another man's death this badly. The extent of his own rage kinda freaked him out.

Heavy footsteps came up behind him. Stopped by his side. "Was I wrong?"

Dominik scowled up at Ladd. "You're going to have to learn to use complete sentences, kid. Wrong about what?"

"Wrong to stop you. Kimber's got a swollen lip. She's being all brave, but she's still shaky." Ladd bent down and handed Dominik his glove. "I'm her brother. I'm supposed to keep her safe, but I've done a shitty job."

"You're still a kid yourself, Ladd. I'm surprised you still want to stay with me." Dominik rubbed a hand over his face. "I just fucking stood there."

Ladd inclined his head. "Yes. I saw. You stood there and didn't risk my sister's life."

"She shouldn't have been in danger! How the fuck did he even find my house?"

Staring at the floor, Ladd clenched his jaw. "Everyone knows I live with you. The press takes photos of me every time I bloody leave."

"Shit." All right, they were moving much sooner than August. And getting a fucking security system. And having a chat with the little ones about not answering the door. *Ever.*

With a *Whoop!* Bran came running out of the bedroom he shared with his brother. He threw himself at Dominik, then perched on his thigh, smacking his chest. "Cobras!"

"Yep." Dominik smiled, looking the little boy over. Thankfully, he hadn't seen or heard anything to traumatize him. He'd seemed impressed by the police, but not really sure what was going on. Dominik wrapped an arm around Bran as the little boy rubbed the team logo. "Are you excited for the game?"

"Yes! I'm you!" Bran hopped up and turned around. He was wearing #6, with MASON across the top.

Why...? Dominik looked at Ladd, who grinned and shrugged.

"The guys who painted my room brought us a few jerseys." Kimber came over to sit cross-legged in front of them. "I'm wearing Heath's #4. Bran wanted to wear your jersey, Dominik. He said he wants to be just like you when he's big."

"He said all that?" Dominik was happy with the few words the little boy had spoken up to now, but he'd love to hear a full conversation.

"I want to be this big!" Bran opened his arms the width of Dominik's shoulders. "Heath isn't big."

Ladd snorted. "You're one to speak, squirt."

Bran stuck out his tongue.

Dominik hugged the tiny child and laughed. Damn, it was hard to stay mad with his house full of youth and innocence and life. He might not have been able to spare Sahara from facing down Higgins one last time, but he'd meant it when he'd told her to remember how strong she'd been.

Speaking of Sahara, he could sense her presence as she stepped into the room. She was wearing jeans and a Cobra hoodie, her uniform in her hand on a hanger in a clothing bag. Her hair was straight, spilling over her shoulders with a soft golden glow.

His beautiful, loving, fucking tough woman looked like an angel as she smiled at him. He stood, lifting Bran when the little boy put his arms up, and strode up to her to claim her lips. A quick kiss since the kids were watching, but it was all he needed to assure himself she was really all right.

"I heard him talking to you." Sahara tapped Bran under the chin. "And he's letting you hold him."

"I think he figures, if you trust me, I must be worthy."

"Hmm." Sahara rose up on her tiptoes to steal another kiss. "He's a smart kid."

Chapter Twenty Five

Today had to end. Dominik had assumed the worst was over but, while he couldn't compare the mess the team was in to what had gone down with Higgins, it wasn't fucking pretty.

Bower couldn't play. He'd come, determined to get out on the ice, but the man's skin was green and he couldn't stand for more than a minute without rushing off to puke. Richter wasn't sick, but when the doctor had asked what he and Bower had eaten, he'd mentioned being in the office all day. Since neither Silver nor Bower could cook worth a damn, they'd probably gone out to eat somewhere.

Hunt was the one looking sick now though. The young backup goalie sat alone on the other side of the players' lounge, dressed in only his goalie pants and huge black and gold pads, taping his stick and talking to himself. A few of the guys had tried talking to him, Dominik included, but Hunt said he wanted to get "in the zone."

Fair enough, so long as he didn't psych himself out.

A tense quiet filled the room, followed by murmurs as the door to the players' lounge opened. Vanek came in first, followed by Zovko and Chicklet. For some reason, Vanek was eyeing all his teammates with a challenging gaze, hovering close to Zovko, who was holding Chicklet's arm.

The big Croatian moved gingerly, which wasn't unexpected considering his injury, but as he spoke softly to Chicklet, she guided him around a table, leading him over to Hunt.

Dominik set aside his skates which he'd been relacing and strode across the room, ignoring the whispered remarks from all the guys who seemed too uncomfortable to even welcome Zovko back. There was clearly something wrong, but as captain of the team, Dominik had to make sure the team understood Zovko wasn't to be treated any differently.

"Zovko, good to see you, man." Dominik smiled and shook Zovko's hand before pulling him in for a hug. "What's the damage?"

Vanek let out a rough sound in the back of his throat. His eyes glistened as he glared at Dominik. "Fuck, Mason. I wasn't expecting you to be the one asking stupid questions."

"Cool it, boy." Chicklet put her hand on the back of Vanek's neck in a gesture that was both restraining and comforting. "Raif's got this."

Drawing away slightly, Zovko put his hand on Dominik's shoulder. He lifted his head and appeared to be staring at something in the distance. He gave Dominik a grim smile. "I'm glad you brought me in on the hotel investment—I'll need a new project to keep me distracted. Which is actually why I came. I went over all the information you left me, and I believe, between myself and Hunt, this will be a successful venture." He looked over in Hunt's general direction. "If he's willing to work with me."

Hunt swallowed hard, staring at Zovko as though he'd just come to a terrible realization. "You're not coming back, are you?"

"No." Zovko squared his shoulders, his jaw clenched. "But your only concern tonight will be winning this series for us. I've heard that the mess with the hotel distracted you. There's no reason for you to worry about it any longer. I'll be up in the press box, cheering you on." He shifted his unseeing gaze to the rest of the room. "All of you."

There was no avoiding the brutal fact. Zovko was blind. Dominik rubbed his lips with his fist, trying to think of the right thing to say. Sorry wouldn't fucking cut it. Besides, Zovko had come here tonight to show his support, and he wouldn't appreciate anyone's pity.

His career was over, but he would find success, regardless of the obstacles. Even if he wasn't out there on the ice with them, he was a fucking Cobra. And Cobras were the best at beating the damn odds.

"If there's space for another partner, I'd like to be involved with the hotel as well." Dominik had several strong investments of his own, but facing how quickly life could change made him more determined to make sure he had more than his hockey career to fall back on. "I'm probably not too far away from retirement myself."

"Ha! Not so fast, Mason. I expect you to keep my boy out of trouble." Zovko reached out and put his arm around Vanek as the young man shifted closer. Vanek looked sad but determined as he stood by his Dom's side. "But he's promised to be on his best behavior."

Dominik grinned as Vanek's face reddened. "I've dealt with him at his worst. I'm not worried."

Conversation had resumed around them, and Chicklet dragged a seat over for Zovko and herself as he told Dominik the details of his vision loss. His optic nerve had been damaged, but there were several treatments that might help him regain at least part of his vision.

Not enough to get him back on the ice, but Dominik couldn't imagine that being a priority at the moment.

About half an hour before warm-up, Richter came in with his daughter, Amia, and his niece, Casey. The way he greeted Zovko made it obvious he'd already been aware of the man's condition. They made small talk while Casey went over to sit beside Hunt.

She smiled up at the goalie shyly, holding up a small plastic container. "Mommy said you're playing tonight because Uncle Landon ate bad food. So I brought you good food."

"Thanks." Hunt took the container and opened it. His brow furrowed, but he kept smiling. "Cookies?"

"They're not fucking donuts, Hunt," Demyan shouted from the other side of the room, looking ready to come over and either snatch his daughter away or punch the goalie. He grunted when his partner, Pearce, elbowed him in the ribs. "Language. Sorry. But if he doesn't eat those cookies, I'm gonna—"

Pearce elbowed him again.

Casey sighed and shook her head. "Don't mind my daddies. They're peanut butter, and Uncle Landon eats them all the time. He says they make him stronger, and I make them for him a lot."

Dominik bit back a laugh as Hunt picked up a cookie and took a big bite. The baby goalie was blushing all the way up to his ears, and he didn't seem to know what to say to the little girl who was watching him expectantly.

Swallowing, Hunt nodded. "They're really good."

"Do you want some milk?" Casey clasped her hands behind her back, bouncing on the toes of her tiny Chucks. "They're better with milk. I could get you some."

"No, that's okay. I like 'em just like this." Hunt shoved the rest of the cookie in his mouth.

Richter chuckled and stood, holding Amia on his hip. "All right, time to go, sweetie. You want to wish your fathers luck before we go?"

"Yes, Uncle Dean." Casey hesitated. Then she shot forward, planting a kiss on Hunt's cheek. "I think you're more handsome than Prince Eric."

Giggling, Casey skipped across the room, hugging both Pearce and Demyan before running back to take Dean's hand.

Hunt finished the rest of the cookies, looking like someone had hit him in the head with a shovel. After Chicklet and Zovko left and the rest of the team headed to the locker room, Hunt just sat there, a confused expression on his face.

"Come on, kid." Dominik had to fight not to laugh. He held the door open as Hunt ambled over, that same dumb struck expression still present. "I'm surprised you're not used to girls falling in love with you by now."

"She's, like, *five*."

Demyan threw his sports bag into his stall, practically growling. "She's almost eight, Hunt. Still too young, but you better be fucking nice to her until she decides she's in love with Justin Bieber or something."

Pearce's eyes went wide. "Hey, that's not funny, Scott."

"You know what I mean."

Slumping onto the ledge in front of his stall, Hunt shook his head. "It's cute and I'll be nice. I just…"

Dominik waited. Then sighed when it became clear Hunt wasn't going to complete the sentence. "What?"

"Who the hell is Prince Eric?"

Every man in the locker room burst out laughing.

Vanek tossed a roll of tape at Hunt. "Are you serious? You've never seen *The Little Mermaid*?"

That only had the men laughing harder. Dominik grinned as he pulled on his equipment. He was feeling good about this game. The atmosphere in the locker room was positive. Even Pischlar and White seemed to have made up. Pischlar was holding a comic book he'd pulled out of his stall. He gave White a crooked smile, then went over to sit by his best friend, holding the comic book like it was the most precious thing in the world.

The rest of the guys were joking and laughing, eager to get on the ice. More than once, he heard a player mention winning "this one" for Zovko.

You're damn right, we will. Dominik stood by the door, holding up his fist to bump with each player as they passed. Ladd and Hunt were the last two, and tension radiated from both men as they stared one another down.

"You're teammates. Hate on each other after the game." Dominik sighed when Hunt's eyes narrowed.

"Seriously, man." Hunt folded his arms over his chest. "What the fuck are you staring at me for?"

The edge of Ladd's lip twitched up with amusement. He reached out and brushed something off Hunt's chin. "You've got cookie crumbs everywhere. Just thought you should know."

As Ladd took off, Hunt shook his head. "That guy is fucking weird."

"Maybe, but he spoke to you. That's some fucking progress."

"I guess." Hunt took a deep breath and dropped his gaze. "Zovko though...that fucking sucks. He's a great guy."

"He is." Dominik shifted his gaze as he saw the younger man tear up. The last thing they needed was for the kid to be an emotional wreck before stepping between the pipes. "He's gonna be okay, kid. He didn't come here to upset you."

Hunt shook his head and tucked his glove under his arm, pulling his hand out to dry his eyes. "He didn't upset me. He made me see that all the shit I'm dealing with is nothing. I want to prove to him I've got this."

Good man. Dominik slapped Hunt's shoulder. "Damn right, you do."

* * * *

Sahara jumped to her feet as she watched Dominik snatch the puck from an Islander forward. He led the charge, whipping a pass to Heath on the breakaway. Heath sped across the ice, faking a shot, then lifting the puck high stick side.

The goal light went off and the crowd cheered. By her side, Bran hopped up and down. Kimber let out a deafening scream of excitement. Sahara gave both a high five as their brother's first goal in the league was announced.

On the ice, Dominik retrieved the puck, then joined the throng of players hugging and congratulating Heath. Heath was smiling from ear to ear as he skated by the Cobra bench, knocking fists with the rest of his teammates.

"We win! We win!" Bran climbed up on his seat, arms up in the air.

Laughing, Sahara picked him up and hugged him tightly. "Not yet, buddy. But we're leading two-nothing."

The second period was almost over and the Forum was buzzing with energy. Sahara had been around the game too long to count the Islanders out just yet, but she had a good feeling with how well the Cobras were playing.

Five minutes later, and the high of Heath's goal had faded. The Islanders had finally gotten one past Hunt. He still looked solid, but the comfort of a two-goal lead was gone. The Cobras had to score a few more goals to guarantee a win. Facing the backup goalie might have given the Islanders a false confidence at first, but they wouldn't make that mistake again in the third period. Not when they were fighting for their life in the playoffs.

During the break, Sahara brought Kimber and Bran to the wives' room for snacks. She smiled when she saw Akira and Jami, but her smile faded when she saw the blotchy redness of Jami's cheeks.

A woman touched her shoulder. She glanced over to see Becky.

Becky motioned her forward. "Go talk to her. I'll watch your little ones."

"Thank you." Sahara crouched down in front of Bran. "I'm going to talk to my friends. Can you stay with Becky?"

Bran frowned and handed Kimber his plate. "I come."

"Have you met my daughter, Casey?" Becky held out her hand. "She brought all kinds of toys. I bet she'll let you play with them."

Bran's lip quivered, but he took Becky's hand. And stuck his thumb in his mouth as she led him to the group of children playing at the other side of the room.

Sahara bit her lip, hating how upset Bran was about her leaving him. Fine, she wasn't going far, but he'd been with her for the past few days. It would take much longer than that for him to stop worrying that she wouldn't come back.

Kimber came over and hugged her. "He'll be all right. I'll stay with him. Go on, you're allowed to have a life."

"Which you're part of." Sahara sighed and kissed Kimber's hair. "I'll be right over there. Come get me if there's anything."

"I will."

Crossing the room, Sahara pulled up a chair and sat in front of Jami, taking both her friends' hands in hers. "Hey, what's going on?"

Jami closed her eyes, tears trailing down her cheeks. "Sam's moving out. Things are really bad with her and Luke, so I get it, but..." She swallowed hard. "She's moving in with Oriana. She's letting her adopt the baby."

Damn, that's... Sahara shook her head. What could she say? That was actually pretty smart of Sam. The girl was young and in no position to care for a baby. Jami had been looking forward to helping raise Luke's nephew, but the tension between Sam and her brother wouldn't have been good for any of them. Least of all the baby.

The facts wouldn't make Jami feel any better though. Sahara considered her words carefully. "What does Sebastian have to say about everything?"

Rolling her eyes, Jami hugged herself. "He thinks it's the right choice. He went with Sam to talk to Oriana and Sloan and Max. They've set up a room for her, and they're going to take care of her until she has the baby. After too. Their lawyers are drafting all the paperwork for an open adoption."

"Sam has a lawyer?"

"Yes. Sebastian hired one for her. And I kind of hate him for it." Jami dropped her head to her hands. "Ugh, not like I really hate him. I love him. But I'm so mad. We could have given Sam's baby a good life. She could do everything she's doing with Oriana with us!"

Pulling Jami into her arms, Sahara made a soft shushing sound while Akira rubbed Jami's back. "I'm so sorry, babe. This isn't your fault. It's not really anyone's."

"I know, but...this isn't over. Will you come with me?" Jami sat up, her teary eyes wide. "Sam's with Oriana right now. Maybe if I talk to her, she'll change her mind."

Bad idea. Very bad idea. "Jami—"

"Please! It's not too late, and she should know she has options." Jami pushed to her feet, pulling away from both Sahara and Akira. "Oriana can have someone else's baby."

Akira met Sahara's eyes as Jami headed out the door. "This will go ten times worse if we're not with her."

True. Sahara nodded, stopping by the door to look over at Bran and Kimber. Both seemed to be having fun. Becky was sitting on the floor beside Bran, exclaiming over the colorful lumps he'd formed with Play-Doh. The kids were in good hands.

She slipped out the door and ran to catch up with Jami and Akira.

They reached the press box and Jami strode in, not even looking at her father when he called out to her.

Walking straight up to Oriana and Sam, Jami touched Sam's arm. "Sweetie, we need to talk."

"Jami, please don't be mad at me. This is the first time that I feel like I'm doing something good for my baby." Sam pulled away, shifting closer to Oriana. "You'll still get to see him. So will Luke and Seb."

The third period had started. Sahara split her attention between what was happening on the ice and the drama unfolding in front of her.

"You need to think about what you're doing, Sam."

"I have! Jami, you and Luke and Seb are trying to have your own baby. As much as he pisses me off, Luke is right. I want to go to school and get a good job. I'm not ready to raise a kid." Sam pushed her red-streaked blond hair away from her face irritably. "I'm a fucking mess. Tell me you don't know that?"

"You're confused."

"Not about this."

The argument continued, both Sam and Jami getting more and more irate. Oriana tried to speak up, but Jami rudely cut her off.

On the ice, the Islanders crashed the net. The ref called the goal. It was sent for review.

Good goal. The game was tied.

"Are you sure this is what you want, Sam?" Jami's voice broke. "I know Luke's not the easiest person to live with sometimes, but he does love you. You can't do this because you're giving up on him."

Sam shook her head, reaching out to pull Jami in for a hug. "I'm not giving up on him. This feels right. You know Oriana. You know Max and Sloan. They'll give my son a great life."

Holding Sam tightly, Jami nodded. "I know. And I'm sorry. I guess I pictured everything differently, you know?"

"So did I. I wasn't planning to get knocked up so young." Sam let out a teary laugh. "But my kid won't pay for it."

All right, this was good. Jami and Sam had worked things out. Maybe the discussion hadn't been pleasant, but better now than after the baby was born.

Sahara went over to hug both girls and excused herself so she could check on Bran and Kimber. When she got to the wives' private box, Becky was holding Bran, and Kimber and Casey were staring down at the ice with their hands over their mouths.

Heath was down on his hands and knees, spitting blood. Dominik was beating the hell out of an Islander forward, and every player on the ice was fighting. Including the goalies.

"Sahara!" Bran held out his arms, squirming in Becky's hold. "Heath's hurt!"

Taking Bran into her arms, Sahara whispered thanks to Becky and stroked the little boy's hair. "He'll be all right, buddy. Look, the trainer's with him. He's skating all on his own."

"Is that good?" Kimber whispered.

Nodding, Sahara watched the teams being separated. She bit her lip as the refs handed out the penalties. Dominik would be in the penalty box until the game ended.

Luckily, the game ended with a tie.

Her phone went off in her pocket. She pulled it out and checked the text.

Jami: Sam just went in to labor. This is all my fault.

Sahara: It's not your fault. She's almost nine months along, isn't she? Maybe it was just her time.

Jami: We're bringing her to the hospital now. Can you come meet us there?

Another text came in. It was Dominik.

Dominik: Can you come down for a minute?

This was crazy. Sahara stared at her phone, torn between wanting to be there for Jami and needing to be there for Dominik. Jami had Akira. Dominik had his teammates.

"Do you need me to watch them again, honey?" Becky asked.

Sahara nodded, happy to see neither Bran nor Kimber seemed upset that she'd have to leave them again. She quickly sent a text and hurried out to the hall to jump on the elevator.

* * * *

Dominik had gotten an earful from both Sloan and Coach Shero for his penalty, but he wasn't hearing much of anything. After coming to the locker room, he'd picked up his phone to text Sahara and seen the message from his brother.

Joshua had been called for another mission. He wished Dominik luck. Couldn't say where he was going. He'd be in touch.

Barely managing not to put his fist through the wall, Dominik sank to the bench in front of his stall and blocked out the entire world. He couldn't fucking do this anymore.

But he had to.

"Dominik?" Sahara approached him, sinking to her knees and placing her hands on his thighs. "Talk to me."

Fuck, just seeing her face calmed his racing pulse. He slid his hands over her cheeks and into her hair. Pressed his eyes shut as he leaned in to kiss her.

"How are Bran and Kimber? They know Ladd's okay, right?" He opened his eyes and looked over at Ladd, who was getting checked on by the trainers. The kid had lost a tooth from the slash and had gotten a few stitches on his lip. No big deal.

The kids might not see it that way though.

"They're good. You're not. What happened?"

He sighed, feeling stupid for asking her to come down. Seeing her was amazing, but he was a professional. He needed to pull his shit together. "I'm good. I kinda flipped when that guy took a swing at Ladd. Stupid fucking penalty, but Hunt kept us in the game."

"From where I was standing, it looked like a good penalty. They need to know not to fuck with our players," Sahara said, all bloodthirsty and sexy as hell. She gave him a wry smile and cleared her throat. "There's more though, isn't there?"

"Josh was called up for another mission." Dominik rubbed his hand over his eyes. "He's doing his job. I need to do mine."

Lacing her fingers behind his neck, Sahara met his eyes. "Yes, you do. But you get to be worried about him."

Maybe, but Dominik was supposed to be leading his team to a fucking victory. They were so damn close. His head had to be in the game.

"What about you? You were awesome in the pregame show. Sucks that they took out your performance between periods."

"Naw, people are too riled up to enjoy it anyway." Sahara dropped her gaze. "But I have to go."

What? "Go?"

"Sam just went into labor. Jami freaked out because she tore into her about letting Oriana adopt the baby. It's a mess." Sahara stroked his thick beard with her thumb. "If you ask me to, I'll stay, but I've been trying to be a better friend. Jami needs to be there when Sam has her baby. And she asked me to be with her."

"You should be." *I want you here, but I won't be that kind of man.* Grant had come between Sahara and her friends. He'd isolated her to the point that she'd lost many friends. She had to see how different life would be now.

She pressed her forehead to his. "I'll still be watching the game. And Becky's with Bran and Kimber."

"Good. Becky will be fine with them."

"Yes, but you need to listen to me." Sahara took a deep breath. "Do you remember when I asked you to score a goal for me?"

"Yeah."

"Now I need more. Win the game. For me, for the team, for your mother and your brothers, because you know they're watching. Take this round for all of us."

Dominik nodded. He could do that. And she was right.

She didn't need to be in the stands to support him. He'd taught her how to feel him with her even when he couldn't be. And after he kissed her, after he walked her to the locker room door, he still felt her presence.

Even more so when he stepped back onto the ice.

* * * *

Climbing into the back of the cab she'd called since she'd come here with Dominik and couldn't take his truck, Sahara gave the cabbie directions and pulled the game up on her phone. The puck was dropped. The play was fierce, rushing from one side of the ice to the other. Hunt made a spectacular save.

She'd worried that she'd made the wrong choice in leaving, but Dominik looked amazing out there. With powerful hits, moving faster than the younger players, he was on his fucking game. His passes were crisp, and soon, she had no reason to doubt the choice she'd made.

The excitement in the announcer's voice mounted as he called out every play.

"Mason snaps up the puck on a pinch. Whips the puck over to Perron. Perron passes it back. Mason dodges a check and tucks the puck back to Ladd... Ladd scores! The Cobras win!"

THE END

Visit the Dartmouth Cobras
www.TheDartmouthCobras.com

Game Misconduct
THE DARTMOUTH COBRAS #1

The game has always cast a shadow over Oriana Delgado's life. She should hate the game. But she doesn't. The passion and the energy of the sport are part of her. But so is the urge to drop the role of the Dartmouth Cobra owner's 'good daughter' and find a less...conventional one.

Playmaker Max Perron never expected a woman to accept him and his twisted desires. Oriana came close, but he wasn't surprised when she walked away. A girl like her needs normal. Which he can't give her. He's too much of a team player, and not just on the ice.

But then Oriana's father goes too far in trying to control her and she decides to use exposure as blackmail. Just the implication of her spending the night with the Cobras' finest should get her father to back off.

Turns out a team player is exactly what she needs.

"Ms Sommerland takes us on an extremely incredible journey as we watch Oriana's master her own sexuality. She comes to realize that there is more out there that she craves and desires, than she has ever realized." Rhayne —Guilty Pleasures

"With a delicious storyline and kinky characters outside of the norm, Game Misconduct pushes you outside of your comfort zone and rewards your submission with phenomenally erotic sex. If you're a fan of hardcore BDSM, then this book is going to top your list of must reads!" Silla Beaumont —Just Erotic Romance

Defensive Zone
THE DARTMOUTH COBRAS

Silver Delgado has gained control of the Dartmouth Cobras—and lost control of her life.

Hockey might be the family business, but it's never interested Silver. Until her father's health decline thrusts responsibility for the team he owns straight into her hands. Now she has to find a way to get the team more fans and establish herself as the new owner. Which means standing up to Dean Richter, the general manager and the advisor her father has forced on her. The fact that their "business relationship" started with her over his lap at his BDSM club shouldn't be too much of a problem. Their hot one-night stand meant nothing! But how can she earn his respect when he sees her as submissive? Can they separate work and the lifestyle she's curious to explore?

Balancing her new life away from Hollywood, living among people who see her as the selfish Delgado princess, has her feeling lost and alone until Landon Bower, the Cobras new goalie slips into her life and becomes her best—and only—friend. The time they spend together makes everything else bearable, but before long his eyes meet hers with more than friendship, reflecting what she feels. Which could ruin everything.

Two Dominant men who see past her pretty mask and the shallow image she portrayed to the flashing cameras. A gentle attack from both sides that she can't hope to block unless she learns how to play.

But she's getting the hang of the game.

Breakaway
THE DARTMOUTH COBRAS

Against some attacks, the only hope is to come out and meet the play.

Last year, Jami Richter had no plans, no goals, no future. But that's all changed. First step, make up for putting her father through hell by supporting the hockey team he manages and becoming an Ice Girl. But a photo shoot puts her right in the arms of Sebastian Ramos, a Dartmouth Cobra defenseman with a reputation for getting any woman—or, as the rumors imply, man—he desires. And the powerful dominant wants her...and Luke. Getting involved in Seb's lifestyle gives her a new understanding of the game and the bonds between players. But can she handle being caught between two men who want her, while struggling with their attraction to one another?

Luke Carter's life is about as messed up as his scarred face. His mother is sick. His girlfriend dumps him. When he goes to his favorite BDSM club to blow off some steam, his Dom status is turned upside down when a therapeutic beating puts him in a good place. He flatly denies being submissive—or, even worse, being attracted to another man. He wants Jami but can't have her without getting involved with Sebastian. Can he overcome his own prejudices long enough to admit he wants them both?

Caught between Luke and Jami, Sebastian Ramos does everything in his power to fulfill their needs. His two new submissives willingly share their bodies, but not their secrets. When his own past comes back to haunt him, the fragile foundation of their relationship is ripped apart. As he works to salvage the damage done by doubt and insecurity, he discovers that Jami is hiding something dangerous. But it may already be too late.

Offside
THE DARTMOUTH COBRAS

A pace ahead of the play can send you back to the start. And put everything you've worked for at risk.

Single mother and submissive Rebecca Bower abandoned her career as a sports reporter to become a media consultant with her brother's hockey team. A failed marriage to a selfish man makes her wary of getting involved with another. Unfortunately, chemistry is hard to deny, and all her hormones are dancing when she gets close to the Cobra's sniper, Scott Demyan.

Zachary Pearce 'came out' to the world last season to shift attention away from a teammate. And his one night with Scott Demyan had been unsettling. There could be more there, if only Scott was a different person. Instead, a night of sensual BDSM play with Becky leaves him wanting more, but she thinks he's gay and questions his interest. It's been a long time since a woman has attracted him both as a man and a Dom, and he'll do everything in his power to prove she's the only one he needs. Or wants. His one time with Scott was a mistake.

Scott might have forgotten what happened in his childhood, but the effects linger, and he specializes in drunken one-night stands…until he meets Zach and Becky and sees what he's missing. But neither one believes Scott can be faithful. Although he's trying hard to clean up his act to avoid getting kicked off the team, they want more from him. He's willing to make changes, but the most important one—putting their happiness before his own—means he'll probably end up alone.

Delayed Penalty
THE DARTMOUTH COBRAS

All choices have consequences, only sometimes they're . . . delayed.

Cortland Nash fled Dartmouth to avoid being arrested for murder, but his best friend, Ford Delgado, is in danger. Cort returns, prepared to keep his head down, and do whatever it takes to keep Ford breathing, but when he finds a beautiful young woman out in the snow, frozen in fear, his plans change. He needs to make sure she's safe—even if the greatest danger is him.

Akira Hayashi never thought she'd overcome her fear of men, but the care of an experienced Dom helped her achieve so much more. She's embraced her submissive side, and found her strength as the captain of the Dartmouth Cobras' Ice Girls. There's nothing she can't do—except function when she's mugged in a parking lot. The intimidating stranger who rescues her makes her feel things she never thought possible. The only problem is his connection with Ford, a man she'll hate forever because she refuses to feel anything else.

With the constant threats from the crime lord he once called "Dad," Ford Delgado has no room in his life for love. Unfortunately, Akira already has his heart—which is split in two when he discovers Cort is dating her. The betrayal has him lashing out, trying to move on, to grow as a Dom, and free himself from Kingsley's criminal empire. He tries to forget what Akira means to him, but one look into her eyes shows him the last thing she needs is for him to let her go.

Iron Cross

Too many penalties may leave the goal vulnerable without the IRON CROSS.

After overcoming a potentially career-ending concussion, Tyler Vanek, Dartmouth Cobras first line forward, couldn't be happier with his life. Until his boyhood hero-worship for Raif Zovko, a newly acquired player, develops into more. His mistress, 'Chicklet' encourages him to explore his feelings, and with her enjoyment of toying with the powerful Dom, Tyler figures it might be fun.

Laura Tallent, a dedicated officer with the Halifax PD, and Chicklet's first sub, is tired of Tyler's fun disrupting the structure of her world. Devotion to her mistress kept her silent for two years, but a horrible case and more proof that Tyler is the worst sub in existence has her wondering how much better life would be if he was someone else's problem. Someone like Raif.

Raif won't deny the lust he feels for Tyler, but he refuses to play games with a young man who's questioning his sexuality--he won't be an experimental phase for an unruly submissive. But when Laura draws him into a plan to remove Tyler from her poly relationship with Chicklet, his protective instincts take over. He partners with Chicklet to protect Tyler and dig deeper into the reasons behind Laura's scheming. Chicklet clearly loves her boy, she won't let him go. And before long, Raif realizes neither can he.

Blindsided by the discord in her household, Chicklet struggles to fulfill her subs' needs as their careers throw challenges at them all. Control is slipping from her hands, but with Raif by her side, she prays her relationships can be saved. Salvaging the future means rebuilding with a new foundation. But the only way to make the base solid is for them all to work together. And with all the secrecy and lies, she has no idea where to start.

About the Author

Tell you about me? Hmm, well, there's not much to say. I love hockey and cars and my kids…not in that order of course! Lol! When I'm not writing—which isn't often—I'm usually watching a game or a car show while networking. Going out with my kids is my only downtime. I get to clear my head and forget everything.

As for when and why I first started writing, I guess I thought I'd get extra cookies if I was quiet for a while—that's how young I was. I used to bring my grandmother barely legible pages filled with tales of evil unicorns. She told me then that I would be a famous author.

I hope one day to prove her right.

For more of my work, please visit: www.Im-No-Angel.com

You can also find me on Facebook, and Twitter

Also by Bianca Sommerland

The Dartmouth Cobras

Blind Pass (The Dartmouth Cobras #0.5)
Game Misconduct (The Dartmouth Cobras #1)
Defensive Zone (The Dartmouth Cobras #2)
Breakaway (The Dartmouth Cobras #3)
Offside (The Dartmouth Cobras #4)
Delayed Penalty (The Dartmouth Cobras #5)
Iron Cross (The Dartmouth Cobras #6)

Also

Deadly Captive
Collateral Damage
The End

Rosemary Entwined

The Trip

Made in the USA
San Bernardino, CA
03 November 2017